Kathryn Kelly

Misconduct

A Death Dwellers MC Novel

By Kathryn Kelly

ISBN 13:978-1517157562

ISBN 10: 1517157560

Formatting by Swish Design & Editing

Editing by Swish Design & Editing

Cover design by Crystal Cuffley

DeLonn Donovan, you're awesome. ☺ Thank you for being my friend. I look forward to working with you in the future.

To Survivors everywhere—Never give up and always believe.

I'd like to start off by thanking my mother and my daughters. Without their support and understanding, I couldn't seclude myself to bring my characters to life. Creating the world of the Death Dwellers is so much fun, but it is also time-consuming. Thank you for never complaining.

After Misled's release, I decided to continue with the series because of the overwhelming response. Over the months, lines have been drawn, especially between Christopher and Kendall. Your passionate loyalty on both sides continue to inspire me, even as the series comes to a close.

Without a solid team behind me, producing each book wouldn't be so seamless. Thank you Kaylene Osborn and Kimberly Osborn of Swish Design and Editing for top-notch editing and gorgeous graphics, Crystal Cuffley of Rockin' Red Promotions for my beautiful covers, and Claire Richards, the best assistant in the world.

August 5, 2015 changed my life forever with the breast cancer diagnosis. To everyone who has sent me words of encouragement and advice, I can't thank you enough. When you contact me just to say hi or to check on me, my spirits are lifted.

It feels like old times because that's what you always did. I may be slower to respond, but I'm no less appreciative.

Jordan Marie, you took matters into your own hands and did what you do best—handled it. You took the time out of your busy and hectic life to help me. I love you, lady.

Kaz Blonde and Kaylene Osborn, thank you for my beautiful bouquets and for reminding me to stay strong! Kim Beale and AC Bextor, I always look forward to your text messages.

Danni List Werner, Melanie Cooper, Crystal Cuffley, Claire Richards, Angie Stanton, and Kristin Inselman, you're the bestest friends a girl could ask for. I love you all! Once I kick cancer's ass and send up a lot of prayers in thanks, we need to celebrate Magic Mike style. I vote for Dallas or Miami. ;-)

Zoey Megahey, the rocking pixie cut you gave me made it easier when it came time to shave my head.

DeLonn Donovan, Travis Lee Ferguson, and Daniel Sobieray, it continues to be a pleasure to work with you.

Neal and Robbie Gibson, thank you.

If I've forgotten anyone, please forgive me.

Much appreciation and love to you always.

Dear Reader,

Originally, I intended to have Peyton Cooper as Digger's love interest. As Ellen's sister, there was a built-in backstory and point of conflict. If you've followed the series, you may remember Ellen was one of Outlaw's women from Misled, book number one. However, Peyton ended up being a rather reprehensible and unredeemable character. Her lack of repentance for her actions made me not like her. Therefore, I couldn't defend her as I do Kendall during lively discussions about Johnnie's heroine on my Facebook page.

Before I realized I utterly detested Peyton, I'd written about her and her motivations, even looking into her past with Ellen. Because Sharper is mixed into this, I've kept their POVs in, as if Peyton remains the heroine.

Therefore, Digger is the only Death Dweller who starts off with two heroines.

I hope you enjoy this tale of betrayal, revenge, and redemption. And, of course, Outlaw.

Love, Kat

MISCONDUCT
A Death Dwellers MC Novel

PART ONE
A Past Comes To Haunt

Three Christmases Ago

All the hustle and bustle prior to Christmas Day, purchasing gifts, planning menus, attending parties, wishing good cheer to everyone, always came to *this.* An anticlimactic disappointment that sank like stone in the pit of Peyton Cooper's belly. Like everything else in her life, the holidays divided her feelings. Each year, she anticipated the season, just as much as she loathed it.

Her mother often discussed the old days when Christmas hadn't become so commercialized. Audra always pinned the avariciousness of retailers on the declining importance to the actual reason for the season.

Peyton scoffed, sick to death of seeing that annoying little phrase plastered on too many church signs to count.

She filled the gin to the brim of her glass, drowning out her mother's slurred disapproval. For the past couple hours, she'd been drowning out everything Audra had been muttering. The same old sorry crap added to Peyton's unsettled feelings.

Ad nauseum, Audra moaned about missing Peyton's father. The man left for another woman, then lured Audra back for reconciliation before leaving again for a different woman. Her mother blamed herself for the dick-loving, pussy-eating slut Peyton's sister, Ellen, had become. She also regularly reminded Peyton of all the blood on their hands.

Draining half her glass, she glared at her mother. Or, more aptly, Dr. Audra Cooper. Only, *Dr. Cooper* passed off her Hypocritical Oath as Hippocratic. Audra had been running scams since Peyton's and Ellen's father left the first time. In the last five years, however, she'd outdone herself, somehow becoming a doctor when she'd barely finished high school because she'd been pregnant with Ellen.

Peyton understood Audra's actions. Their family needed to survive, and she meant for them to do it in style. Continuing the high life her mother had given them was the reason Peyton had fucked her way through medical school. College. Hell, high school.

So many demons she'd had to fight. This latest, the one she assisted her mother with, would cling to her for the rest of her life.

Fitting, when her mother offered assisted suicide to the terminally ill.

Peyton finished her drink and laid her glass against her overheated forehead. How the hell had her mother gotten clients *anyway*? Audra certainly hadn't been able to advertise her services: Death for Dollars.

However she succeeded at her murder-for-hire schemes should be book-worthy. Or Lifetime Channel movie worthy. Unfortunately, anyone who saw Audra now wouldn't believe her capable of murder.

She looked so frail, her light brown hair interspersed with gray. Age spots dotted her arms and her face was haggard with wrinkles.

Audra sobbed, the words incoherent. Not that Peyton really cared. As soon as Ellen arrived and Peyton gave her sister her gift, she'd get away from both her and their mother.

She had a hot date with her co-worker's husband.

Footsteps pounded down the hallway. So lost in her thoughts, she hadn't even heard the door opening. A moment later, Ellen appeared and trudged into the small dining room, a step up from the days they'd lived in a motel.

Peyton sniffed at her older sister's appearance and turned her head. Unlike Peyton's dark hair, Ellen's strawberry blonde hair added to her sister's hardened features. Ellen had their father's blue eyes, while Peyton had their mother's brown ones.

For long moments neither of them spoke, each assessing the other. Whereas Peyton wore an elegant, rust-colored pantsuit, Ellen's short leather skirt and black chiffon blouse underscored their difference. In Peyton's eyes, she was class and Ellen was trash.

"You eat yet, babe?" Ellen asked, always the first to cave in their staring contests.

Whore she might be, but the sadness in her sister's voice compelled Peyton to narrow her eyes. The utter defeat in Ellen's features shocked Peyton. What was wrong with her sister? She was a Cooper woman and Cooper women had all sorts of shade.

They'd never met anyone who could best them and who they couldn't exploit in some form or fashion. So why did dark circles ring Ellen's blue eyes? Eyes that always snapped with arrogance and belligerence were now dull and filled with pain.

"Ellie?" Audra called.

"I'm here, Mama," Ellen said quietly.

Audra stood and rushed to Ellen, enveloping her in an embrace. Peyton choked when Ellen tightened her arms around Audra's neck and burst into tears.

Real worry and concern hit Peyton and she bit her lip. Things must be really horrendous in Ellen's life for her to be so broken up. Audra guided her to one of the dining room chairs and helped her into a seat. Swaying, she clutched the edge of the table and swallowed.

Peyton sighed. "Mama, go wash your face off with cold water. It'll help clear your head." Unlikely after all the crying she'd done and alcohol she'd consumed. Peyton wasn't even sure why they'd bothered with glasses. They both had fifths of gin at their place settings. "I'll talk to Ellen until you freshen up."

Audra wiped her nose on her gold, sparkly sleeve. "Are you sure?"

"Yes." The days of Ellen and Peyton getting into physical fights had long passed. Peyton tolerated both Audra and Ellen, but she was so much better than they were. She lived in an expensive apartment with fine furniture. Wore designer clothes. Drove a sports car. Was in her first year of residency.

And assisted Audra in doling out death.

Peyton scowled. "Go!" She hadn't meant the word to come out so harsh, but she really wanted to be in her new lover's bed, rewarding him for gifting her with the diamond earrings she wore.

Audra scampered away and Peyton leaned back in her chair. She grabbed the gin and tipped the bottle back. "What's the matter?"

Ellen lifted woeful eyes to her and palmed her tears away. Her mouth twisted in a bitter smile. "I was supposed to get married," she croaked, hoarse with tears.

Wait. *What?* Ellen married? At the ridiculous idea, she almost burst out laughing. Instead, she lifted a brow. "Uh-huh."

No biting remark. Just a sniffle. A sinking sensation fluttered in Peyton and she straightened in her seat. Ellen wasn't kidding.

She was getting married. No. She was *supposed* to get married. "What happened?"

Peyton wanted to know. Not only what had happened that turned the sure thing into…whatever Ellen was facing, but *how* she'd come on the verge of a wedding in the first place.

"Outlaw…he…we—" Another sob.

The sound went through Peyton because not much upset her big sister. But she knew the name, Outlaw. Ellen had mentioned him on and off for years. For the last few months, Ellen had been the MC president's old lady.

"He'd proposed to me and we were gonna announce it at the spring social. And…and…this little bitch came and stole him from me." Ellen drew in a shuddering breath. She leaned her head on the table and cried so hard her body shook. "Boss Foy's little blonde whore of a daughter. She took my man from me. He…he even threatened me. Forced me to take her shopping."

"That bastard!" Yes, he was an outlaw biker, a man who lived and breathed death. And, yes, Ellen knew he went from woman-to-woman. But *he'd* promised to marry her sister, so Peyton held him responsible for Ellen's current state.

No way was Ellen lying about this. She was too distraught. It had to have been the truth.

"It isn't him." She sniffled and sobbed. "It's *her*. Megan Foy," she spat. "He thinks she's so innocent when she's fucking Rack and John-Boy, Outlaw's cousin."

Peyton paused in the midst of bringing the bottle to her lips and frowned. "Haven't you fucked Rack and John Boy?" She'd never met these men, but she'd heard enough about them to know where they stood in Ellen's life. "And Val, Mortician, Digger, Snake, K-P, Boss—"

"How can you bring that up now, Pey? Who I fucked never mattered to Outlaw. Now, he even put his hands on me in a violent manner and threatened to bury me," she said in a small voice. "I was so terrified at his unprovoked attack."

Peyton felt like crying. For herself and the memory of one of her relationships that had been abusive. For her sister and her lost dreams. For another Christmas gone by with the emptiness inside of her.

She took a deep draught from the bottle and set it aside. "I-I'm sorry, Ellen," she whispered. And, for the first time in a long time, she meant it.

"Outlaw didn't hold none of that against me. Then *she* came. And she's with him now, at his mother's house. I was supposed to be there this year. He was going to introduce me to Pat. His mother," she clarified at Peyton's confusion. "But he took Megan and invited Digger, Val, and Mortician."

"Ellen," Peyton crooned, wanting to offer her sister comfort. But gentleness had been lacking from their lives for so long, she felt rusty. Even sex was sex or fucking. Her one weakness was kissing. She loved a man's mouth on her lips. It gave her a type of power, a veil of intimacy that she controlled. If her lover displeased her, she withheld her kisses, turned sex into base fucking. But her men knew her kisses meant they were in her favor and worked hard to stay that way.

"I love him so much, and he loves me," she wailed. "He told me so. He didn't look at no other bitch until that little slut arrived."

They were Coopers and no one bested Coopers, especially a little whore who dropped out of nowhere.

"Is there any way to get rid of her?"

The thought seemed to brighten Ellen's face. Then, it fell again. "She throws a tantrum if he leaves her side for ten minutes. I couldn't get close enough to her to do her anything."

Peyton swallowed more gin and contemplated Ellen. "She sounds like a coward."

Ellen nodded. “She jumps at her own fucking shadow. She’d betray her own mother to keep herself safe. And my man just can’t see that. He can’t see if worse comes to worse, she’d sacrifice his life for her own. *All* of our lives.”

Unable to remain seated across from Ellen a moment longer, Peyton jumped to her feet and rushed around to her sister. She kneeled and pulled Ellen into her embrace, stroking her hair. It was coarse and frizzy, and Peyton decided she’d take her sister for a day at the spa in a couple weeks.

“I want revenge.”

“And you’ll get it. I promise. Call me tonight.” She rattled off her telephone number just as their mother staggered back into the room.

Ellen Cooper rubbed her chin against the thin strip of hair covering Kiera's pussy. Her tongue darted out and licked Kiera's sopping slit. Using her long, red-polished nails to hold her pussy lips open, Kiera raised her hips, her clit Ellen's special treat. Lifting herself up, she climbed onto Kiera's body and kissed her in a long, open-mouthed kiss, grinding her own sated cunt against Kiera, who'd licked her for hours. They'd needed release after suffering through the New Year's Eve party at the MC. Though they'd attended the celebration for years, Outlaw had always been available to them. This year…*this year*…

That's why Ellen had called Sharper Banks and told him everything. *Everything*. From the way Digger said Outlaw popped Big Joe—which Sharper already knew—to Big Joe's daughter showing up out of the blue. Helping Rack to get Snake on club property hadn't worked. Stupid fuck had shot Outlaw, instead of Meggie.

What did you expect, cunt?

Snake's voice blared in her head from the day she'd confronted him about almost killing Outlaw. He was right. She should've known better, given how much they hated each other.

It's just that she hated Megan more. Sharper swore he was going to take care of everything. That it would take time, but she just had to have patience. It was hilarious to her that a great minister had co-founded the Death Dwellers with Logan Donovan, an even bigger asshole.

She didn't know the entire story, but she'd gleaned enough from her years of after-fuck talks to understand *something* had prevented Sharper from wielding the considerable power he had in the club. Power that she knew about, thanks of Snake and Rack.

Whatever that something was that kept Sharper in line had wrecked Big Joe, and would soon be the death of anyone who wouldn't swear allegiance to Sharper once he got control.

Ellen hadn't expected the man to make any moves against the club. She'd called for help with Megan. But he didn't like the fact that Outlaw seemed to be regaining his equilibrium with that girl's presence. She was changing him, giving him back the passion he'd lost for the club in the wake of Big Joe's death.

"Ellen, please," Kiera whined, bringing Ellen's attention back to their fucking.

Ellen bit down on Kiera's tender bottom lip and she moaned. Rising up, she positioned herself so that she and Kiera were clit-to-clit and began to pound their juicy flesh. She nailed their pussies, their moans and juices mingling together. Kiera's head thrashed from side-to-side, her body trembling with Ellen's onslaught, her pussy gushing wetness. Ellen didn't care. She hadn't come yet this time and wouldn't stop until she did, despite how sensitive she knew Kiera's cunt would be.

Kiera deserved it, anyway. She deserved the tears sliding from her eyes at the discomfort Ellen's hammering caused. She deserved the way Ellen paused to bite her nipple and draw blood. And she deserved Ellen pulling away from her pussy and forcing herself onto her mouth, grinding all her sloppy wetness against her face.

Because, whether Kiera knew it or not, Ellen was aware that Outlaw felt a little more tenderness for Kiera than he did for Ellen. And she hated Kiera for it.

Squeezing her eyes shut, she imagined wrapping a scarf around Kiera's lovely neck, yanking it tight, and pulling it until she stopped breathing. The thought made Ellen come hard. She kept her pussy covered over Kiera's mouth and nose, milking her release, the fleeting idea to smother her with her pussy floating away when Kiera shoved her roughly away.

Kiera sat up and swiped her hand across her mouth. "You bitch!" she snarled.

Next time, she'd tie the cunt up, cover her mouth with her pussy and pinch her nose until she suffocated. For now, she needed her. She wanted revenge against Megan Foy.

The thought of the girl marched across Ellen's head and she scowled. Megan with her big, blue eyes and golden hair was a rival she couldn't win against. The girl was young, gorgeous, and disgustingly sweet. Until provoked. Then, she turned into a flaming bitch, who'd had the gall to push Ellen on her ass and confront her during an argument.

Worse, Ellen wanted to fuck Megan so badly. She wanted to corrupt her before she killed her. She hadn't been so innocent in years and she'd never had someone as pure and guileless as Megan Foy in her life. Usually, Outlaw would've laughed at her suggestion and got the bitch into their bed. That's what they did. To those bikers, all women were fair game and the women understood the rules. Now, if Ellen even suggested such a thing, she believed he'd choke the shit out of her.

To him, Megan was some untouchable little goddess. He couldn't see she was changing him, taking his edge away.

Kiera's movement reminded Ellen that she needed to soothe the woman's pique.

"I'm sorry, babe. I'm just on edge after the party."

"At least Outlaw lets us in," Kiera responded grouchily. "I got to meet his momma and everything. Never thought I'd see that day."

Bitter fury churned in Ellen's belly. Despite the lies she'd fed to Peyton, Outlaw had never considered them good enough to bring home to Momma. She considered herself as good as he was. And *he* was a cold-blooded killer. How dare he place himself above them!

"It isn't us," Kiera protested.

Ellen frowned, realizing she'd spoken the last part aloud. "It's his mother. He don't want us tainting her."

"He taints her," she snapped.

"Ellen, come on, babe. Ease up. Outlaw love his momma. I don't blame him for trying to protect her."

She restrained herself from jumping on the beautiful, olive-skinned woman next to her. Her dark hair spread over the pillows and the anger at Ellen's forceful oral sex had eased from her dark eyes. They'd been friends at one time. Real, true friends. But Ellen wanted Outlaw for herself, and she wouldn't allow anyone to stand in her way.

"And what about Megan?"

Eyes clouding, Kiera's lower lip trembled, as much in love with Outlaw as Ellen. "She's a real good girl. I can see why he fell for her," she said quietly. "Meggie makes him think about shit that none of the rest of us can. When was the last time Outlaw barred somebody from the club then changed his mind? If it wasn't for Meggie, you would've been banned until March."

"You're okay that that little cunt came and stole our man?" Ellen almost choked on those last words. *Our guy.* It wasn't that Outlaw had ever claimed he'd be faithful to them. He'd told them if they didn't fuck him together, they wouldn't fuck him at all. But Ellen wanted it all. She wanted to be Outlaw's property. She adored him. But if she went all batshit crazy, she'd never win him.

"She didn't come and steal shit, Ellen," Kiera pointed out. She placed an arm behind her head and her breasts jutted out, watering Ellen's mouth. "Outlaw wasn't ours in the first place."

"He could've been." Petulant, she leaned back and opened her legs, stroking her slit, her mind wandering. An idea came to her. "What about if we can get her out the picture?"

"You want Outlaw to bury us?"

"*We* wouldn't do it, you stupid bitch."

Ellen thought of her little sister. She'd planted the seeds in Peyton's head and all she needed was to get Megan in Peyton's company. But that plan had all kinds of flaws. Outlaw didn't let the reckless little bitch out of his sight. And, worse, he might discover Peyton's connection to Ellen and then he *would* bury her. Bury them both. Peyton deserved better than a gruesome death at Outlaw's hands. Because he might not hurt women, but he wouldn't give a damn when it came to Megan. Her pussy held that much power over him.

"C'mon, El. Let it alone. Meggie's a good girl."

"And you okay with him fucking her and throwing us aside?" She shot to a sitting position and narrowed her eyes. "Or have you been fucking him behind my back?"

"I'm not exactly happy that we're not in his bed no more. But I care about him enough to want him happy, and she makes him happy." Her face crumpled. "No, by the way. I haven't been fucking him. When he left her in Long Beach, I offered just to see, and he turned me down."

Ellen considered Kiera's explanation and accepted it for what it was. "He don't cover his dick with her."

Kiera sucked in a breath. "How do you know—?"

"Because," she began impatiently, "Megan told me. When we went shopping and stopped at the drugstore, she was looking at condoms. She said he didn't use none with her."

Satisfaction surged through her at the hurt blossoming in Kiera's eyes. Ellen already knew Kiera wanted Outlaw's kid.

"He's trying to get her pregnant?" she whispered.

"Yes," Ellen said with a definitive nod, although she wasn't sure. That might have been a one-time thing just to feel his dick in Megan's young pussy with nothing between them.

Kiera's throat worked, then she nodded. "What do you have in mind?"

"Rack been wanting to know when they get back to town. He's planning on doing some sick shit to her, but at least she'll be out our way."

"You're okay with that? Letting him put her on that rack thing he has?"

Okay with it? She'd love to watch. "Of course not, babe," she soothed. "But I was talking about sexually. He'll probably just strangle her afterward."

"Then we'd have Outlaw back to ourselves?"

Ellen nodded, pleased that Kiera seemed clueless she'd meet the same fate, as soon as she could arrange it.

"What we have to do?"

"Just call Rack. Let him know where Megan is. She's been staying with Outlaw's mother in the woman's old house. Patricia's leaving in two days, so if we don't act now, we'll lose our chance."

"His momma might get caught in the crossfire."

"Nah," Ellen assured her. "Rack promised he just wanted Megan, and no one else would be hurt."

Kiera studied her for a moment. "Okay. Do it."

Once Ellen made the call, she and Kiera sixty-nined before falling asleep in each other's arms. A rude yank jerked her awake and she opened her eyes, blinking at the bright overhead lights, the taste of Kiera still in her mouth.

Intense blue eyes stared at her, and her heart banged in rapid beats. She started at Kiera's scream and turned her head just in time to see the woman dragged from the bed by her hair.

"Sn-snake?" Ellen choked out, noticing six other men ringing the bed.

Joseph Foy II AKA Snake stared at her, his blond hair scraped back, his ponytail swinging as he leaned toward her. Beside her, one of Snake's boys was restraining Kiera, turning her onto her back, and thrusting into her ass, slamming his fist into her jaw.

Snake reached out his hand, his battered face looming too close to her. She shrank away, the menace in his eyes intimidating. Kiera's brutal sodomizing and agonized screams sent waves of fear into Ellen. Anytime they were so merciless to Ki—the sweet one—they'd do God only knew what to Ellen.

"What are you doing here?"

Trembles traveled along her spine as he shoved his pants down, freeing his erection. She covered her ears to drown out Kiera's begging sobs.

"I can't take fucking hypocritical cunts like you, bitch," Snake snarled, slamming her down onto the bed and filling her. He pressed his thick, muscled arm against her neck and Ellen struggled for air. With each slam into her body, he increased the pressure until her lungs burned and her vision blurred. My God! My God! The sick asshole was enjoying depriving her of air as he fucked her. He was—

The thought sobered her and she realized she'd been thinking about doing the same thing to Kiera. How had the roles been reversed? She stared up at him, struggling to hold onto consciousness, hoping her gaze conveyed the mercy she was requesting.

He jerked inside her as spots danced at the edges of her vision. Shuddering, he collapsed on top of her, relaxing the compression on her neck. A moment later, he lifted himself on his elbows and glared at her.

"No, please, please," Kiera cried, the fear in her voice affecting Ellen so much that her eyes watered and she sniffled.

Sucking back her tears so they wouldn't escape, Ellen cringed when the man who'd so harshly used her dragged her out of bed. Her nails scraped along the sheets. Somehow, Kiera managed to break free and spring next to Ellen, despite Snake's presence.

Ellen grabbed Kiera's hand, protective instincts surfacing.

"Snake, please." Kiera grabbed Snake's arms as tears streamed down her face. "Please don't let them hurt us anymore."

Us.

The word got to Ellen. Because she wouldn't have begged for mercy for anyone but herself. For some reason, Megan and the girl's entreaty to Outlaw on Ellen's and Kiera's behalf came to her. Despite everything, Megan requested that he allow them to come to the club after he'd banned them *because* of her.

Ellen couldn't fathom how these women would help a rival.

"You're terrified, aren't you, Ki?" Snake's feigned sympathy broke into Ellen's thoughts. He moved away from her and went to Kiera, guiding her back and kissing her. "You always liked kissing. Sinking into her, he turned to Ellen. "Rub your cunt while I fuck Ki."

At Snake's command, some of her fear abated. Ellen massaged her swollen clit, spreading Snake's cum around her pussy lips as he powered in and out of Kiera.

"I'm going to make you come hard," he swore, kissing Kiera's hairline, "then I have a surprise for you."

Each time he drove into Kiera and his ass cheeks flexed, Ellen arched her back, pleasure gripping her deeper at Kiera's moan. Snake bent and licked Kiera's nipples, still driving into her. Since he'd come in Ellen, it took longer for him to get off this time, even after Kiera screamed out an orgasm and Ellen joined her. Finally, he grunted and shook, before sagging against Kiera.

Noticing Snake's boys leering at them and awaiting their turn to fuck, Ellen searched her mind for a way out of whatever had set Snake off. Since it could be anything—

"You come all over Outlaw's cock like that?" Snake asked suddenly and Ellen's heart sank. This was so bad. He hated Outlaw. Mentioning him now meant something real bad would happen. He got to his feet and dragged Kiera up with him. "Do you, slut?"

"Snake—" Kiera began, stopped by Snake's fist slamming against the side of her face.

The hit propelled them right back into a nightmare.

Kiera wrapped her arms around Snake's neck. "Whatever I've done, forgive me. Please, give us a chance to make it up to you."

Unmoved, Snake pried Kiera's fingers from around his neck and pushed her to the guy who'd attacked her. He shoved a pillowcase over her head, subduing her struggles with the help of two others.

"Why are you here?" Ellen asked after they'd dragged Kiera out. The words hurt her throat. She blinked to subdue her tears of fear and anger, helplessness overwhelming her. With Snake, she *was* helpless. He was evil, conscienceless, her worst nightmare.

He knuckled her mouth and stared at her a moment before slapping her across her cheek. She cried out.

"I'm here, you stupid bitch, because you called Rack and told him where Meggie was."

"I-I was helping Rack," she protested.

"No, you were fucking being a conniving cunt. You forget, Ellen, *I know you.*"

She shivered at his ominous tone. He did know her, and he wasn't a man who took kindly to betrayal. That's why he hated Outlaw so much. "I didn't connive against you," she wheedled.

He slapped her again. "Not me. Megan. My sister."

Ellen blinked, sure she'd misheard. Snake despised Meggie, too, for being in bed with Outlaw. He felt she was betraying their father by sleeping with Boss's murderer.

"Oh, don't worry. I'm going to let her watch her lover die before I put a bullet in her head. But you delivered the innocent little lamb right into Rack's greedy hands." He slid a long finger along her cheek. "Tsk. Tsk. Not to help him out but to get rid of your competition. Knowing you, Kiera would've been next."

"Please. I'm sorry," she sobbed. "I'm so sorry." Then the rest of his words penetrated and she stared at him in horror. "Outlaw?" she asked with a strangled gasp. "You have Outlaw?"

A malicious gleam brightened his eyes. Nodding, he climbed onto the bed and rose above her, shoving his soft dick into her mouth. She trembled.

"Be careful what you ask for," he breathed, holding her head and gagging her with his cock. "Backstabbing has a way of catching up with you."

All of a sudden, Ellen knew. *She knew*. In her quest to get Megan out of Outlaw's life, she'd signed their death warrants, including her own.

Peyton stared at nothing in particular, impatiently tapping her foot as she awaited Ellen's arrival. Today, they were going to the spa and having a late lunch to plot out their plan to get to Megan Foy. But Ellen was up to her usual tricks, not arriving on time as promised. This wasn't some family dinner they could hold up because Ellen was too involved with whatever to arrive on time.

They had set appointments, and the spa she'd booked them into was very exclusive. If Ellen screwed up Peyton's reputation with them, she'd never forgive her sister. As it was, she should be happy Peyton would even bring Ellen with her to the high-class place instead denying even knowing her.

But Ellen was at an emotional low point. Peyton had talked to her every evening since Christmas, listening to her sister's heartache. Now, it was several days into the New Year, and she hadn't talked to her sister in two days. Maybe, Ellen had worked shit out for herself with Outlaw. The very least she could've done was called Peyton. Drawing in breaths, Peyton decided to give Ellen a chance. She didn't want it to start with an argument between them.

Audra wobbled in, and Peyton sighed. Averaging one death a month must be working on Audra's conscience. Her mother sat on the sofa, her posture ramrod straight, her hands on her lap, but the ringing of the doorbell prevented Peyton from asking any questions.

Ellen had a key to the house, so she knew the impatient person incessantly ringing the doorbell wasn't her sister.

Her irritation grew when she looked through the peephole and noticed two men standing there, wearing leather cuts, proclaiming them members of the Death Dwellers MC. Outlaw's MC. Unlocking the door but keeping the screened door secured, Peyton noted their solemn expressions.

Unease kindled inside of her. "M-may I help you?"

"We looking for Mrs. Audra Cooper." The short, muscular speaker sported a crew cut, greenish-blue eyes, and a strong jaw.

"I'm her daughter," Peyton announced sharply.

"She here?" the other one asked. He had a shock of white-blond hair and pale eyes that gave him a creepy look. He reminded her of death, and she backed up a little. "Audra Cooper here or not?"

Peyton nodded.

The short one drew his brows together in a fierce scowl. "Can we see her?"

"Is this about Ellen?"

The two men exchanged glances before the normal looking one sighed. "Yeah."

Figured. That was the only reason anyone associated with the MC would come to this house. Huffing, Peyton unlatched the screen door and allowed them entrance. "Follow me," she ordered, marching down the short hallway to where her mother still sat, in her zombie-like state, in the living room.

Peyton struggled to hold onto her patience. "We have visitors, Mama."

She couldn't imagine what Ellen had done to send these men here. Probably for money. What other reason would losers like them had reason to seek a woman like Peyton out? She frowned and sized them up. They seemed so innocuous. Weird, yes. The dangerous criminals Ellen painted them to be, no.

"What can we do for you?" Peyton bit out when Audra only narrowed her bloodshot eyes at the duo.

"I'm Traveler," the short one said and pointed to the other man. "This is Bin."

Peyton responded by folding her arms and lifting her brow, showing them with actions rather than words she had no time for idiots like them. They were both staring at her chest, revealed in the V-neck shirt she wore and meant to draw attention to her small tits.

"Outlaw sent us here," Traveler explained and shifted his weight. "Ellen's been killed."

"What?" The word blared in her head but came out in a strangled gasp. "No."

"It's true," Bin insisted and shrugged.

For a moment, the ground shifted beneath Peyton's feet and her stomach lurched at how sincere he seemed.

No, no, no. They were lying! Who walked into a person's house and blurted such news with no warning? This *had* to be an elaborate joke. The thought helped helped her to brush off her shock and shook her head in denial. Ellen couldn't be dead. She'd spoken to her two days ago. "That's impossible. My sister is meeting me here for us to go to the spa."

The two men exchanged glances and nausea rose in Peyton at their sad expressions.

"Sorry, babe," Traveler said with sympathy. "It's true. Outlaw wouldn't have had us search Ellen apartment to find somebody to call if she wasn't dead."

Peyton stumbled back. "You're lying! This is some cruel prank. Ellen is—"

"Dead," Bin said flatly. "And Outlaw dealing with his own issues. Burying his Mama, for instance."

"Wh-what? His mother is dead, too?"

"Killed by Snake. Just like Ellen," Traveler explained as if Peyton shared a personal acquaintance with those people.

"Outlaw's old lady almost got killed, too," Bin went on.

Peyton focused her wavering gaze on him. She'd never fainted in her life, but she was on the verge of it now. Her sister was dead? That couldn't be. They were going to the salon. They had an appointment for massages, manicures, and pedicures. Ellen *wasn't* dead. The very idea was insane. Coopers didn't just get fucking killed. *They* killed.

She drew herself up. "I have to call my sister. She'll tell you—" She swallowed. "She'll say she's just pranking me. I'll get mad at her. Then, we'll go to the spa."

Hands held up, Traveler stepped closer to her. "Babe, I'm sorry. That's not happening. That's never going to happen. Ellen's dead."

Peyton laughed, a little hysterical. "No. You don't understand." She marched up to him and jabbed a finger in his chest. "Ellen is *not* dead." She hurried to the window and shoved open the curtains. "See? Outside? The sun is shining. My sister…the sun wouldn't be shining if Ellen was dead. Something would be different. The world wouldn't look the same."

The two men exchanged uncomfortable glances; then Bin cleared his throat. "Don't matter who dies. Sun still shines. Rain still falls. The world goes on."

No! No! No! Not for her. Not for Ellen. They were each other's world. Peyton, Ellen, and Audra comprised the fucked up Cooper world.

She yanked her phone out of her pocket and dialed Ellen's number. It went to voicemail. "Ellen, call me." Peyton's voice wobbled. "Call me now!"

She gripped the phone, her entire body shaking, belatedly realizing she needed to disconnect. Both men pulled out two stacks of cash from the leather jackets they wore and held it out to her.

"Outlaw sent this. To take care of the funeral," Traveler announced.

Peyton's eyes snapped to his, the truth of Ellen's death sinking in at the sight of money. Her sister was dead. Dead.

D-e-a-d.

DEAD.

Her entire body shook, and she backed away without touching the money. "The least Outlaw could've done was deliver the news himself."

Traveler threw the straps of cash onto a table then thinned his lips. "Didn't you hear what we said? His momma got popped. His old lady managed to save herself but couldn't do nothing for Ellen."

"His old lady?" Peyton echoed, the world spinning in slow motion.

"Yeah," Bin said. He followed Traveler's suit and threw the stacks of cash down. "Megan."

Megan. She'd saved herself and left her sister to fend for herself and die. She'd already destroyed Ellen by stealing her man from her. She had to make sure Ellen was no longer a threat.

"If you need anything from us…" Traveler let his voice trail off and started for the door. "No need to see us out, babe."

He and Bin left without another word. Peyton stood in shock, blinking through tears, dissecting all the two bikers had told her.

"Peyton?" Audra squeaked from behind her.

When she turned, she found her mother white with shock and tears shining in her eyes. She hurried to her, and they wrapped their arms around one another, sobbing together.

Peyton wasn't sure how many minutes passed before her mother finally quieted. She threaded her fingers through Audra's hair, hating to see her pain.

"Everything's going to be fine, Mom," she whispered gently.

"It's just you and me now, angel," Audra returned in broken tones.

Nodding, she urged her mother to her room, promising to bring her a drink to relax her. Alone, she sobbed all over again. Now that Ellen was gone, Audra would focus all her attention on Peyton, making even more demands on her. Audra would also live the rest of her days in grief and misery.

Not sure which thought compelled her next actions, Peyton hurried to the bathroom and her mother's medical bag where the poisons were kept. After pouring enough to kill two oversized men into Audra's glass and then topping it with gin, she brought the mixture to her mother.

Audra downed the contents in a few gulps and satisfaction rolled through Peyton. She couldn't watch the toll the poison would take, so she kissed Audra's forehead and hurried from the room. Once she cleaned up the evidence, the fact of Ellen's murder soaked in completely.

A burning desire for revenge that Peyton was determined to exact slid into her.

She wouldn't rest until Megan was dead and she'd align herself with anyone with the power to assist in her goal. Buoyed by her plan, Peyton checked on Audra and found her staring sightlessly at the ceiling, blood and foam leaking from her mouth.

Dialing '911', she allowed her grief to pour out of her to play the grief-stricken daughter.

PART TWO
Mistake Number Three

End of February
Present Day

Marcus "Digger" Banks sunk his neck further into his padded jacket, seeking warmth from his own body heat, though he doubted he'd ever thaw. Deep in the interior of British Columbia, it was fucking freezing. His breath puffed out in front of him and his footprints tracked in the snow as he walked across the grounds of his father's compound. Unfortunately, Digger shared a small cabin he occupied with his nephew, Tyler, and his girlfriend, Peyton.

True, he should've been more grateful that his father, the Reverend Sharper Banks, had allowed him refuge once he'd blown through his money in Europe. If not for Sharper's "generosity", Digger wasn't sure where he'd be. Of course, it wasn't *really* generosity on Shaper's part, but another form of control. But he had no one but himself to blame. Once before, he'd detached himself from Sharper's games. The only thing he'd needed to do was steer clear of Outlaw. He'd fucked up all around, so, no, he wasn't grateful.

Besides self-loathing, the only other fucking things he felt were disgust, regret, and fear. By now, Outlaw had probably gotten the fucking word that Digger was back with Sharper, which meant he was more than fucked. He was fucked painfully and gruesomely.

If only Digger knew how the fuck to leave the small town where he'd holed up with Sharper and his bodyguard, Osti, Digger's cousin, the meanest motherfucker…fuck, other than Outlaw.

At the thought, Digger shoved his hands into the coat pockets, aware of Osti dogging his steps as they approached the storage cabin. The motherfucker had demanded Digger come with him because of an unexpected summons from Sharper. Digger hadn't known they'd returned from wherever they'd gone.

Gritting his teeth, he stomped ahead, hating the barren surroundings. They lived on what he described as a fucking settlement in the middle of fucking nowhere, like they were Marco Polo motherfuckers, out to discover the world. But that wasn't their goal. Sharper intended to ruin lives. Kill. Overpower the weak and unwanted. Rule from the kingdom he'd created through blood, lies, and hypocrisy. To effectively continue his ruthless reign, Sharper had to disable the one motherfucker who could bring him down.

Christopher "Outlaw" Caldwell.

While Sharper was cut off from his mega-church and devoted followers, he still had power because he still had a lot of fucking money. As long as a motherfucker had money, they had fucking power. So, yes, Sharper had the power to have his little outpost with two cabins to use as living quarters, one for eating, another for laundry, and the final one for storage. Not a motherfucker questioned him when supplies were delivered each month.

Sighing, Digger opened the door and entered the cabin. His breath whooshing out of him, he halted so quickly Osti ran into him.

"Move the fuck out the way," Osti ordered, shoving Digger forward.

Too shocked to do anything but allow himself to stumble, Digger swallowed, his blood running as cold as the fucking snow outside. Sharper had gotten more girls. Six...no, seven, if he counted the dead one who had a knife protruding from her eye.

Another girl, shackled to the others, would soon join the dead girl. This almost-dead girl trembled hard enough to shake the girl chained next to her.

Blood oozed from her neck and the pain and plea in her eyes made Digger's nostrils flare in horror. It smelled of death and sounded like misery and insanity. Hysterical giggles and pleasurable grunts pounded through his head, but he couldn't drag his eyes away from the girls. More girls. All Sharper ever did was find girls to sell. Or kill.

If he ever got away from Sharper again, he'd become a beggar in the fucking street before he returned.

Resignation dimmed the girl's eyes. She knew her last breath would soon come. He wanted to end it for her then, put her out of her misery. But she...she was young.

This shouldn't be her end.

Unable to look at her anymore, he turned and surveyed the entire scene. To his left, Sharper sat in the corner, nude, his eyes alert and hawkish. This was some type of test, one he'd worry about in a minute. First, he needed to drag Tyler's naked ass back to the cabin. Peyton, he just wanted gone. High and wearing not a stitch of clothing, she was the bitch laughing like a hysterical hyena as she crawled around the shackled girls. The terror in their eyes reminded him of what a dumb motherfucker he was. At first, he'd been so fucked off with Mort for taking up with Bailey. Never mind the fact he felt as if he was always in his brother's shadow. Digger had felt betrayed. He'd tried to play it off but once Mort married Bailey, he'd turned into a stupid motherfucker. End of story. All along Mortician had been right about their old man, but Digger refused to listen.

Stubborn fuckheads made pansy asses. He'd had to find out the hard way that the motherfucker was a fucking devil. Not only because he stole girls to sell them on the black market, but because he was fucking corrupting a child, the boy supposedly his son. In actuality, Tyler was his grandson, fathered by Mortician. This had been Sharper's chance to correct the mistakes he'd made with his sons. He'd done the complete opposite.

His thoughts fueling his anger, Digger glared at his thirteen-year-old nephew. "Get the fuck up. Get fucking dressed," he snarled, noticing the kid's bloody hands and limp dick, glistening with pussy juices.

Giggling, Peyton staggered to her feet, her body still flushed from fucking. Her cheeks and thighs were coated with cum. Digger's jaw clenched. He didn't need details. He already had a good idea of whose DNA she wore so carelessly.

She was much smaller than her sister, Ellen, had been. If she hadn't produced proof of her relation to Ellen, Digger never would've believed it.

Licking her lips and glancing at him through her lashes, she tweaked her nipples. "I'm back from tagging along with Osti to pick up Tyler, Sharper, and our latest sales items," she announced as if she wasn't standing right the fuck in front of him.

He huffed at her reference to the brutalized girls as sales items.

"You missed me?"

"Didn't even know you were gone, girl." Truth. What in fuck did that say about their relationship?

"You're mean," she pouted.

Ignoring her, he focused on his father. "Where you went?"

"Nowhere to concern yourself with," Sharper answered.

Before Digger responded, Peyton stood on her tiptoes and placed her mouth on his. When he didn't bend so she could put her arms around his neck, she balanced her palms against his chest and ground her body against him. The dead girl didn't bother her. The other chicks and the sounds of their pitiful weeping and sniffling went over her head, too. The dying girl didn't faze Peyton, either.

She was one heartless fucking cunt. He almost hated her and cursed the day he'd found her in the bar. He'd seen her as a way out. She'd seen him as a way in. They'd each had their own agendas when they'd met.

Suffocating under the weight of regrets and self-recriminations, Digger pushed Peyton away and started for Mort's son, sliding in a pool of blood and scowling. "I said get dressed."

"No." Tyler's one word didn't change his calm expression. He, himself, was a cold little motherfucker. The sweet boy Digger took under his wing over a year ago had begun to change as the weeks wore on. Peyton had a lot to do with it. Tyler's genes didn't help matters, either. His mother had been one of the most vicious cunts around before she'd been killed and put out of her fucking evil misery.

Sometimes, Digger felt like putting Tyler out of his misery, too.

"Let my boy stay," Sharper ordered, puffing out his chest. His dick lay against his thigh. For all intents and purposes, his father was impotent. It took a lot to get his motherfucking cock to work, but from the stickiness on his thigh, he'd succeeded today. "Reward for that." He nodded to the dead girl.

He wasn't a bitch. He wasn't a bitch. He wasn't a bitch.

Over and over, Digger silently chanted the reminder. It didn't help. He still felt like one at his father's announcement. A fucking rough dude like him wanted to fucking boo-hoo down, hearing that Tyler had killed one of those girls. Granted, Digger was a killer, but he'd been a grown fucking man when he'd become one.

Scrubbing a hand over his face, he wasn't sure what to do with his helplessness. If Mort was there, he'd knock some sense into Tyler, the stupid little fuck. But, Mort wouldn't have ever found himself in this situation. Generally, Mortician was a laid-back motherfucker, at peace with himself and comfortable in his own skin. His happiness came from within. As fucking corny as that was, it was also true.

On the other hand, Digger needed things to make him happy. He needed approval. Until he'd veered from the path he'd been riding alongside his brother, he'd never realized the reason he'd thrived. In the back of his mind, he'd always known it was Mortician he wanted to impress and emulate. He'd also always resisted the slight resentment he felt toward his brother, even before Bailey. Simply because he'd idolized him so much. Kind of like Johnnie with Outlaw.

Rubbing the back of his neck, Digger sighed. Mort wasn't there to straighten up Tyler, so that left Digger to do it.

"We don't hurt chicks," he reiterated for what must've been the thousandth time. *Fuck.* He realized his mistake immediately. It should've been *they* didn't hurt girls because to be with *them* meant he was against Sharper. The rule of not hurting women was a Dweller code, not a Sharper dictate.

"Hear what this motherfucker said, Unk?" Osti chortled, circling Digger like a fucking shark on the scent of blood. "Sound to me like I was right and he's still loyal to Outlaw."

"Fuck you, you overgrown motherfucker," Digger said, his short fuse on the verge of igniting. It didn't matter that he wasn't armed and Osti was. "You not fucking questioning my loyalty and getting away with that fucking insult."

"There's no loyalty amongst thieves and madmen," Peyton called, twirling around, her dark hair swinging with her. It had grown out a lot since they'd met her. "Remember that saying?"

"The word should be honor, not loyalty," Digger corrected with impatience.

"Settle down, all three of you," Sharper cut in, stepping into his pants. He glanced at the clock on the wall. "Almost time for our daily Bible class."

Tyler sucked in a breath at the statement and scrambled to his feet, mimicking Sharper and pulling on jeans. It was almost time for the mad man to become the fucking crazy reverend. A motherfucker didn't suddenly shed insanity because he preached the gospel.

"What are these chicks doing here?" Digger asked, flipping Osti off when he gave Peyton an open-mouthed kiss that she returned. Like him, Osti wore his hair in dreads, but his cousins were uneven and unkempt. Kind of like his fucking brain. "If bitches start turning up missing in the area, don't you think motherfuckers might start a manhunt?"

Using his church as a front for his sex ring had been bad enough. But at the fucking outpost where they were hiding out?

Digger glanced at the girls again, wanting to get them away. The other girl was paling and Digger knew the wound on her neck was just deep enough to where she bled out slowly.

Yeah, fuck it. He was a bitch. Nausea roiled through him. He couldn't fucking figure out how to save these girls and undo the evil that had claimed Tyler.

"These girls are just like the others," Sharper explained calmly, shrugging into his shirt. "Throwaways."

And to Sharper, throwaways were trash. Disposable. He didn't take into account that they were human. Just like Big Joe hadn't when he'd started on his fatal, drug-addicted path.

"Throwaways. Throwaways. Throwaways," Peyton chanted, dancing around the girls, who sat in the middle of the floor. She paused and kicked the only blonde girl in the face.

Flinching, Digger turned, already knowing the blonde would die an even slower death than the girl whose light of life slowly faded away from her eyes. Knowing why, too. Which was part of the reason why he hadn't gone back to Prez and begged for his life. Begged to be patched back in. The sanctions against him wouldn't have mattered. Even the beating he would've received.

He'd once again underestimated his father's vileness. On the spur of the moment, he'd called Sharper. He wanted back in the States and he was afraid Outlaw would immediately be alerted. Motherfucker seemed to have eyes and ears everywhere.

If only he would've thought the shit out further. Then, he'd arrived, frustrated by the changes in Tyler and outraged by Peyton's behavior. The bitch was supposed to have fallen in love with him, just like Meggie, Kendall, Zoann, and Bailey had fallen in love with the others.

But, no, she'd been on a personal mission, not a quest for love. She wanted to kill Meggie and avenge her sister, Ellen's, death.

"We'll be leaving soon again," Sharper announced, looking shrewdly at Digger. "We're days away from getting on club grounds."

Only the death rattle of the girl and the weeping of the others broke the sudden silence.

"You moving against Outlaw?" Digger asked to be sure he understood.

Sharper nodded and Digger's skin crawled with unease.

Fear glinted across his father's face, then smoothed out into serenity again. He cleared his throat. "I'd prefer not to leave myself vulnerable to Outlaw."

Yeah, retaliation *was* due. No, apparently, that shit was imminent, after fourteen months of planning. Sharper wanted revenge for Outlaw blowing up his house, killing some of his bodyguards and ruining his reputation along with his church.

Digger understood it was a get-them-before-I'm-fucked-up-tortured-and-praying-for-death type of deal.

It said something about the sanity of Outlaw, if the man who saw himself as invincible, the mega-rich, crazier-than-crazy, Sharper Banks, was pissing himself in fear, scared to shit that Outlaw might find him first.

Was it because Sharper had sent Logan back to the club? Because of K-P's death? Did it have anything to do with the girls who were kidnapped and sold? Not really. That would be a dividend in Outlaw's rage for fucking with his girl.

"Then there's the hydro-grows on the compound," Sharper went on. "The money this shipment will bring in is supposed to be astronomical. I need to get the key and the letters from wherever they've been hidden at the clubhouse."

"Holy fuck," Digger exploded, the smug words tipping him off. "You got a fucking informant in the club, don't you?" That was the only explanation Digger had for Sharper's knowledge.

"Ye of little faith," Sharper retorted. "You don't believe in my abilities to discover information on my own? Perhaps, my long association with the club provides me with built-in knowledge."

"Outlaw too fucking criminal minded to let shit like this get out or to keep the same MO. He know how to cover his fucking tracks."

"He was until Megan got there," Sharper shot back.

Digger wouldn't comment on the truth of Sharper's words. He wouldn't say that he regretted that they hadn't killed her when she'd first arrived. Thinking it was one thing. Speaking it aloud seemed a betrayal. He certainly wouldn't express his thoughts on Meggie. She was a cool chick, even though she'd fucked up everything by coming into their lives.

"What do you say to that, Mark?" Sharper asked.

What the fuck was he supposed to say? Yippee-yi-yay? Hie-ho, hie-ho, off to the fucking club we go?

"I get to pop Mortician," Tyler called.

"No! No, the fuck you don't, little motherfucker," Digger snarled, reacting immediately and advancing toward his nephew.

Osti jerked him back, but before Digger punched him, Sharper spoke again.

"Lucas's with them and Tyler's with us. He's loyal. He deserves to take out your brother."

"What the fuck, man?" Digger yelled. "Do you see what you did to the kid? What you turning him into? Do you?" he repeated when Sharper blinked in surprise as if he really didn't know. "Tyler was good. He had a fucking future. Now—"

"Now, he still has a future," Sharper interrupted.

"*Now*, he's nothing but a motherfucking killer. You turned him into this on purpose. Your ultimate revenge."

Sharper chuckled softly, neither denying nor confirming Digger's accusations. "The attack on the club is close. Time for you to decide if you're with them or us."

"Fuck you!"

Osti drew out his gun and pressed it against Digger's temple, cocking the trigger.

"Brain him, Uncle Sharper, or what?" he asked casually.

Fuck it. Digger was tired of being on the run with these madmen and didn't care how he escaped his father. Death would be fucking better than what was about to go down.

Anticipation lit Osti's eyes. "I can let Tyler slit his throat."

Sharper buttoned his shirt and studied Digger as if they shared no blood at all. "That depends."

They were toying with him, treating him with the same disregard they did anybody outside their little group. Fury surged through Digger and he didn't give a fuck that he'd probably die in the next few minutes. He wanted to fuck Osti up.

"On?"

"Fuck all," Digger spat, interrupting Osti's amused question. He hated the hurt and disappointment he felt toward his father. It let him know he still expected better from the man.

But hadn't Mort warned him?

Hadn't Outlaw?

"Fucking fire," he bit out. Fuck, he *really* didn't fucking care anymore. Mort hated him. The *whole* fucking club hated him. "Just get it fucking over with."

"No!" Tyler said.

At first, Digger's heart sped up at his nephew's pleading tone. It hadn't changed its pace in fear, but now it did with regret. He wished he'd done better by Tyler, If only he'd known how. The thought of using his fists on him like Sharper once did to Digger wasn't appealing. But, maybe, there was a way to atone for how ruined Tyler was. Maybe, if Digger found a way to survive, he could somehow warn Mort about Sharper's intentions. The idea renewed his determination to make it out of the shed alive.

"We can test his loyalty, Father," Tyler explained.

Sharper's brows lifted. "How, son?"

Shifting his weight, Tyler thought for a moment, then nodded to the frightened girls. "Make him kill one."

No. He didn't fucking kill women. He just didn't. Since he'd been with his father, he wasn't proud of some of the things he'd overlooked, but it was survival of the fittest.

Besides, he'd tried to make up for his shortcomings by saving Bailey's life.

"How bad do you want to live, son?" Sharper transferred his gaze and his term of endearment to Digger.

Bile rose in his throat at the word son in reference to him. He'd been his mother's son. He wasn't his father's anything. Nor did he want to live bad enough to hurt...at that moment the girl with the cut throat gurgled, blood dripping from her mouth.

Osti waited, his eyes glinting with amusement and the same fucking craziness that infected Sharper. Either madness was ingrained in their fucking DNA and insanity bred fucking insanity or living so close to it had driven Osti to the other fucking side.

"There's only one fucking bullet in this gun," Osti taunted. "Either you get it or one of those cunts."

She was nearly dead, he reminded himself grimly. He needed to live long enough to find a way to get a message to Mort. Tell him they intended to hit the club soon.

Snatching the gun from Osti's hand and so fucking tempted to shoot that fucker, he raised it and fired at the girl with the slit throat. She might already be dead. He prayed that she was. While he was at it, he prayed for the souls of the girls left and the one who'd been dead when he walked in. He prayed for Tyler, too, even if he felt his nephew was long past the point of redemption.

Blood sprayed from the gaping hole in her head. Luckily, from his position, none of the other girls had been in his line. Otherwise, they would've gotten fucked up, too, instead of the bullet exiting the back of her head and embedding itself in the wall.

The other girls screamed while Digger's stomach churned.

Unable to resist, he raised the weapon and fired at Osti. *Click.*

"Told you," Osti said with a smirk. "One bullet."

Sharper laughed as Digger backed away. "He's just a little peeved that you intended to shoot him, Osti. No harm done."

Osti nodded his big ass head. "Of course, Unk.

Digger turned and walked back out into the frigid weather, bent over and vomited.

His father may have thrived on the throwaways. Digger had come to hate when they arrived.

Five days later, tension knotted Peyton's belly. Not because of all that had happened with the girls in the storage cabin since their arrival. She'd come to look forward to when Sharper brought in new merchandise. Months ago, she'd gotten used to the perks of knowing Sharper. He didn't judge her, but applauded her ingenuity, including the murder of her mother, an event not even Digger knew about. Sharper had a way about that convinced a woman to open up to him with promises of the good life. But his latest promise that she could kill Megan Caldwell fired her up. Peyton's anticipation ran deep. She intended to make that bitch's death slow and painful.

Standing in the middle of the small living area in the cabin she shared with Digger and Tyler, she thought of the woman responsible for her sister's death. Happy. Alive. Married to the man Ellen should've wed. Bearing the children Ellen should've had for him.

That night in the bar when the now-missing Sheriff Moncette had Peyton to get Johnnie alone for an ambush, she'd wasted her chance with Outlaw. Mistake number one had been her awe of those men, starting with Johnnie and his silver eyes and blond hair, like some immortal sun god. His looks and his voice immediately captured her. He'd been the perfect gentleman. Classy. Charming. Dangerous.

Yet, he'd refused her repeated attempts to lure him away. Moncette's bone-headed plan hadn't concerned Peyton. He wanted revenge and she wanted Megan Caldwell…no *not* Caldwell. She wouldn't give that cunt such respect. That should've been Ellen's last name. Megan *Foy.*

Then, *Outlaw* had sauntered in. Immediately, she saw why Ellen had fallen in love with him. His green eyes were like emeralds amidst fire. They *burned.* With confidence. With arrogance. With *life.* But they were also blind to anyone other than fucking Goldilocks.

Val, the road captain, had merely nodded at Peyton. Mortician had been too interested in Johnnie patching back in. That had left only Digger, who resembled Mortician in many ways. They both wore dreads, although Digger's was only shoulder-length. He was a fraction taller than his older brother and much leaner, but they were both panty-dropping handsome. Digger had been the only one available who could help her reach her goal. Not that he'd known her true intentions. At the time, he hadn't even known her connection to Ellen. They'd exchanged numbers and he'd promised to call her when they returned from whatever run they'd interrupted to find Johnnie.

Since she hadn't been able to lure Johnnie away, she'd hoped to get any information from Digger and bring to Moncette. But Digger hadn't caved. Moncette had been furious that she'd allowed Johnnie to slip away and only days of fucking him had soothed his anger.

Turnabout was fair play, she supposed. Meeting Moncette through Ellen had afforded her a casual acquaintance with the lawman. Once her sister had been killed, though, she'd gone to him and cried on his shoulder. She'd wanted Megan to suffer ASAP. But he'd calmed her and asked her to have patience. If she helped him, he'd help her. She hadn't told him about Audra. Sharper was the only person who knew she'd killed her own mother.

Moncette's grudge against Outlaw fit so perfectly with her plans toward Meggie. After everything Peyton had gone through, Fate was finally on her side.

It should've been so easy to seek vengeance, then reclaim her life. She'd actually left her residency to focus on this project.

Three years later, she still hadn't succeeded.

Then, Moncette had vanished, and she suspected Outlaw and his club had something to do with it since the stupid fuck had shot Outlaw's sister, Zoann.

Moncette's disappearance left Peyton on her own to get to Megan. Although Digger had been easier to reel in than expected, he *still* wouldn't put her in Megan's path. Maybe, he was suspicious like that. Or, maybe, they were all required to protect the little cunt.

Or, maybe, Megan was as much of a slut as Ellen and gave pussy away to all the brothers, earning their loyalty with her body.

Whore or not, she was also so much more. Later, Peyton had discovered *exactly* what Megan was. The key. *Sharper's* key, rather. The one he'd used to reveal all the missing links with such simple words to get Logan Donovan back in the States. *Joe's daughter is conspiring with Christopher.*

Piece one had been resurrecting Logan Donovan.

Peyton scrunched her nose. Really, *that* had been mistake number one. Logan was killed. According to Digger, Johnnie had done the deed.

Oh, well.

Killing K-P filled in piece two of the puzzle. The execution had been flawless.

Piece three, the reason K-P had to die, were the goddamn letters in his possession. The ones revealing too much. Not only the extent of the sex ring but Sharper's and Logan's love affair.

Ironic how the man purported a racist had actually enjoyed sucking black dick.

Taking Bailey, K-P's daughter, when she'd been pregnant with Mortician's child garnered the attention of Outlaw sooner than anyone had wanted and put Sharper on his immediate radar when they'd involved Megan.

Unfortunately, the event led to Peyton's second mistake. The day they'd gotten Bailey, Megan had been in the apartment. And Peyton had left her alive at Digger's urging, a decision she regretted so fucking much. Fearing Sharper's wrath, she'd complied with Digger's orders not to harm Megan. Then, he'd just left the girl with those men. Knowing they'd kill her when he'd stopped Peyton. Megan had been pregnant again. Killing her at that time would've also freed Outlaw from the two additional brats she'd spat out of her pussy.

Outlaw shouldn't have only *one* woman if it wasn't Ellen.

Distracted, Peyton walked to the darkened bedroom, hating the isolation of the tiny place. The only thing she had to amuse herself was dick and pussy. She couldn't even go shopping. Damn Digger and his stupidity. No matter how much she enjoyed all that Sharper had to offer, she could manipulate Digger a little easier, especially where money was concerned. He didn't think he had anything else to offer a woman except bank.

The beeping of her phone pulled her back to the present and she scowled. She'd forgotten all about the thing. Craning her neck in all directions to assure herself she was alone, she crept to the bureau and opened one of the drawers. Luck was on her side that she was alone. Her carelessness could've gotten her caught. Instead of hiding the burner phone, she'd just left it laying on top of the socks in the drawer. As soon as she read the text message, she'd hide it properly. She didn't need Digger to know about her access to the outside world when he wasn't allowed the same privileges. What use was a phone to a dead man walking?

> *Must move ASAP. Outlaw knows your location and will move in next week. Strike first. Best opportunity at Bailey's baby shower in ten days. Meggie is hosting. Will open gate as they walk from houses to club.*

Peyton read the message. Once. Twice. Again. She didn't misunderstand the words. They were quite clear. Somehow, Outlaw had discovered their location. Ellen always said the man had an uncanny ability to figure shit out. No doubt, if he'd tracked them.

Peyton read the message a fourth time and slid her finger over the screen in reverence. Relief settled into her, a breath of fresh air in her quest for vengeance. This message had to compel Sharper to act now rather than in a few weeks with a surprise attack. Under those circumstances, if they went in blasting, the Dwellers wouldn't stand a chance.

Neither would Megan. *Finally.*

Smiling, Peyton placed the small cell phone in a pair of rolled up socks, shoved them to the back of the drawer, then slammed it shut.

She had no idea how anyone could betray someone they called family as Megan was being betrayed. True, Peyton hated the girl, but if you couldn't trust those closest to you, then you couldn't have faith in anyone.

The door opened, the winter brightness momentarily blinding her.

"Hey." Tyler's voice cracked around the word.

He really was a beautiful boy. A little unsure about what was right and what was wrong, but he'd understand in time. She'd help him to understand.

"Hi, love."

Loping forward, he offered her a shy look. He still wasn't comfortable with his body or hers. When he stopped in front of her, she reached up and curled her fingers around his twists, running her finger along his scalp. He wanted dreads like Osti and Digger had.

"What have you been doing today?"

He shrugged. "I've been talking to the girl. Jerri."

Revulsion and hatred turned Peyton's stomach. Jerri. The blonde.

"I've been telling her to cooperate. She's the last one here."

She was the last one there because of Peyton, not because of lack of cooperation. Peyton wanted her to suffer. Each time she hurt Jerri, she imagined it was Megan.

Peyton touched his smooth jaw. He was perfect, his puberty fueled sex drive something to behold.

"She'll be leaving soon."

The bitch had to go, especially if they'd leave for a few days to take out Megan and get into the club.

"Osti is fucking her right now." His jaw clenched. "He won't let me take her pussy anymore."

Yes, because Tyler had *taken* it. The girl had fought like a little demon, but he was big and strong and had overpowered her.

Vaguely, she wondered what Mortician would think of the murderer and rapist his son was turning into.

"You like her, love?" she cooed, surprised that she'd wonder about Mortician's feelings. As if she cared.

Uncertainty flashed in Tyler's eyes and he straightened.

She stroked his chest. "Come on," she coaxed, her fingers gliding over his hard cock. "You can tell me."

"Father said not to get attached to any of them," he admitted. After all, he was still a boy, easily manipulated for the time being, no matter the little killing and sex machine he was turning into. Some of the best killers needed direction. "But she's so pretty."

"Is it her blue eyes?" she asked, nipping his chin. "You don't like my brown ones anymore?" She cocked her head to the side. "Or, maybe, all that golden hair?"

Just like that bitch.

When Peyton went to Jerri tonight, she'd humiliate her ten times worse than what she had since her arrival. The girls who'd been left alive had been sold off, which gave them the cash they needed to make a move.

"You're dumping me already?" she continued coyly.

Tyler smiled faintly. "No, of course not. You're pretty, too."

"Prettier than Jerri?"

His gaze slid away and she had her answer, even before he decided to lie and shake his head. "Yes. You're way prettier than she is."

"I think I might reward you for that," she breathed, then stepped back when Digger walked in and glared at her closeness to Tyler.

"Go the fuck to your room," he growled to the boy.

Peyton rolled her eyes and watched as Tyler threw Digger a mutinous look. Digger took a step toward Tyler.

"I'm going," he mumbled, stalking away. Despite Tyler testing his manhood, Digger was unpredictable. Whether he knew it or not, Tyler carried a certain fear of his uncle. He also respected him, but Digger wanted to be so unlike his father, he'd lost the authoritative edge he had on Tyler.

With Peyton's and Sharper's help.

"You really need to learn how to talk to him," she chastised.

"I don't have a pussy like you do," he retorted, going to the cabinet and pulling out a bottle of vodka. "Unless I use my fucking fists on him, *talking* is all I got."

She sashayed to the sofa and sat, wishing they were somewhere warmer so she could wear her short little skirts. At the moment, she was too covered up to effectively seduce Digger.

Patting the spot next to her, she said, "Join me?"

His nostrils flared and the inscrutability of his gaze made her a little nervous. He wasn't armed, but he'd acted as if he hated her ever since the scene in the cabin with the girls.

"Please?"

He swigged from the bottle. "Say what the fuck you gotta say, girl," he said irritably. "I can hear you perfectly fine from where I'm standing."

"You don't want me anymore?"

"I still fuck you, don't I?"

"Not in the last week."

"Why you worried about getting cock from me, when you get dick from the others?"

"Because you're a good fuck." And he was.

He smirked at her. "Ellen never complained."

"That was a low blow," she fired back, not wanting to think of Ellen going from a sexual being to a lifeless corpse. "According to her, Outlaw had a bigger cock and used it better than you."

"And? As if I give a fuck." If her retort angered him, he didn't show it. "Ellen still opened her pussy to me."

"You had his leftovers."

"No, baby. She wasn't fucking leftovers. She was all over. Outlaw didn't plan to marry that cunt and suddenly drop her, and then I picked her up. Ellen fucked everything she saw." Another swig. Another smirk. "Like you."

She threw him a dirty look. "You're such a fucking liar. You know as well as I do, Outlaw intended to marry Ellen." She'd never told him that part, but he'd pissed her off, so she might as well let him know that *she* knew how Outlaw had thrown her sister over.

Shock flared in Digger's eyes before he guffawed like she'd told some great joke, deepening her annoyance. "Whoohooo," he hooted, leaning against the table and clapping his hands.

"Asshole," she yelled, picking up the ashtray that sat on the lamp table and lobbing it in his direction.

Not only did he dodge it, he laughed harder.

"See how much you laugh when I blow Goldilocks's fucking head off." She intended to get her hands on a semi-automatic weapon. She wanted to obliterate Megan's face.

Her fervent words put the brakes on Digger's humor. "Don't be a stupid bitch, Peyton. No one hurts Megan and lives to tell about it."

"Megan," she spat. "I'm sick of *Megan*. She killed my sister. She ruined Ellen's engagement to Outlaw. Stole him away and sacrificed her to save her own life."

Digger sat his bottle aside and advanced upon her, yanking her to her feet and shaking her. "Shut the fuck up. Meggie never lifted a fucking finger to hurt nobody and Outlaw never been engaged to no other bitch."

"Liar!"

"I'm sick of your bullshit." He grabbed her by the throat. "You the stupidest bitch I ever met."

Her insides shook in anger and fear. For a moment, she believed Digger would kill her.

She grabbed at his wrist. "Please." Fear of dying was her weakness. She still had too much living to do.

The pressure of his fingers lessened, but he still crowded her in, his presence swallowing her, overwhelming her with his beauty and leashed power. His big hands moved from her neck to her shoulders and he stared into her eyes, his brown ones holding not a shred of warmth.

"I don't give a fuck if you have to avenge Moses," he barked and she wished he'd use the low baritone he had as he made love to her. "Spitting out lies about Outlaw's wife not ending well for you."

"She fucked over Ellen," she insisted because that's what Ellen had told her. That's what Ellen had been so heartbroken over. "And ruined her engagement to Outlaw."

He went quiet and studied her, his grip loosening ever so slightly. "Ellen fucking lied to you, girl," he told her gently, his temper calming as quickly as it had surged. Christ, the man was so blasted mercurial.

The way he regarded her almost made her believe he gave a damn about her. Not that it mattered. "Megan Foy had Ellen killed to save her own life!"

He shook her so hard her teeth rattled. His imagined tenderness and concern evaporated into blazing anger, his see-sawing emotions giving her whiplash. "That's a fucking lie."

"Please, help me," she said with urgency. Her reason for her vengeful quest was out in the open between them. She didn't want Digger's loyalty to *them*. She wanted to own him. As long as he held out on assisting her with Megan, his loyalties were split. "She fucked over Ellen and she fucked over Outlaw. You can get her to me and I can avenge all of you."

"I'm not hurting Meggie girl," he yelled. "Case closed. I don't know what the fuck Ellen told you about Megan but whatever it was, it was nothing but lies. Ellen—" He spat her sister's name and the tone cut through Peyton— "threw more pussy around than a whore on a holiday. Yes, Outlaw fucked her and took her as his—"

"So you admit it!"

"As part of a threesome," he gritted out, glaring at her. "Ellen knew fucking well she wasn't anything more to Outlaw than pussy."

"No! That's not true," she screeched. "Ellen said—"

"I don't give a goddamn what Ellen said. Ellen lied. The only thing Meggie ever did for your sister was try and get along with her. She might not have liked it, but as long as Ellen didn't give Meggie shit, Meggie tolerated her."

As always, Peyton shook her head in denial. Did he know what he was saying? He refused to listen to Peyton's words. Yes, her sister was hard and harsh, but she hadn't lied about her relationship with Outlaw.

Peyton sagged against Digger and sobbed. Instead of offering her the comfort of his arms, he tensed and straightened. But she wanted someone to understand her crazed grief. Her sister hadn't even had an open casket because most of her head had been shot away.

"Are you through?"

Peyton jerked away at Digger's cold voice. His look chilled her. She sniffled, surprising herself at how real her tears were. She nodded curtly.

Without another word, he grabbed his bottle and stalked away.

Cunts were the most beautiful creation known to humankind. Color, size or appearance didn't matter. Only the fucking perfect feeling they brought about. That fucking exquisiteness when cum blasted the fuck from Christopher "Outlaw" Caldwell's cock and into pussy. Like now.

After catching his breath, he nosed Megan's hair, still connected to her in the most basic way. She kissed his sweaty chest, her fingers skimming the bridge of his spine. Resting his weight on one elbow and threading his fingers through her damp hair, he smiled at her.

Right after he'd filled her pretty cunt with his cum was the best time to share his cuntal views. When she laughed, he joined her, mock-wincing at her shoulder thump. She thought him the funniest motherfucker alive. On the other hand, he was being a romantic motherfucker on their second "second" wedding anniversary. The first "second" came four months ago and celebrated their civil ceremony. He knew Megan secretly preferred this one because it celebrated their big ass church wedding. And this was the one day of the year Christopher always promised his girl he'd be a mushy motherfucker just for her.

He preferred their original anniversary, which would come in several months and celebrate their third year of marriage. These different fucking dates could confuse the fuck out of a motherfucker. It all resulted in the same fucking thing. Megan and her beautiful pussy legally belonged to him.

"All my ass fuckin' sayin', baby, is as beautiful as a woman cunt be, yours at the fuckin' top. The way you fuckin' keep all your golden pussy hairs so fuckin' neat and trim. Your cunt just perfection and I'm the luckiest motherfucker alive to call it mine."

Megan snuggled against him, her blue eyes so filled with adoration his chest hurt. "Thank you," she said hoarsely. He'd fucked her so hard she'd been fucking breathless one minute and screaming his name the next. "I think."

"What the fuck you mean? You think? I fuckin' promised you once a fuckin' year, I'd be fuckin' romantic."

"You *are* romantic, Christopher," she swore. Lifting herself from the crook of his arm, she kissed him, binding her words as the gospel truth. Her pussy cream and his dick juice flavored their lips. He grunted at her taste, his cock jumping. The motherfucker *never* tired of getting into Megan. She spoiled him by giving him pussy almost anytime he wanted. He was a lucky motherfucker that she liked fucking so much.

Seeing his rising cock, she wrapped her little fingers around his base and he flexed his hips, surging into her pumps.

"Your hand feeling fuckin' good, but your fuckin' mouth would be better, dontcha think, baby?"

"Yes," she breathed, sliding down his body, slanting light kisses along the way, branding his skin as only she could. His nerve endings prickled with the anticipation of her mouth on him. The silken fall of her hair and the softness of her small body tormented him, combining to make him one happy motherfucker.

His hips jerked when her breath finally fanned his cockhead a moment before she sucked him into her mouth. Closing his eyes, he groaned, fisting her hair and pumping into the up and down motion of her head.

"You suck my cock so fuckin' good, baby."

He wanted to watch as she used his cock for her personal fucking lollipop, but seeing her sucking him off undid him every-fucking-time, especially when it happened after he'd fucked her. That meant she was licking her own pussy juice.

She swirled her tongue around his sensitive cock crown. His breath sawing in and out of him, he trembled. To stop her and take control, he held her head in place, propelling his cock along her tongue in fast motions, while she fondled his balls.

"Oo—oo—oo fuck, Megan." Cum roared up his dick and Christopher lifted halfway. When she raised her sweet gaze to his, he tightened his hold on her, shuddering as his jizz fountained into her mouth. She sucked him one last time to make sure she swallowed every drop. "Fuck, baby. Fuck, fuck, fuck," he snarled through gritted teeth.

Releasing her, he relaxed his body, his heart about to fucking pound out of his chest. Fuck, yeah, because of the exertions but mainly because of Megan. She put her body and soul into fucking him—fuck, romantic motherfucker day—he backtracked. She put her body and soul into making love to him.

She nuzzled against him and he took her into his arms, kissing the top of her head. Rising up on his elbow, he smiled down at her, enjoying the sight of her red face and swollen mouth. As he began to run his hand over her hair, she returned his smile with one of her own. For a moment, they needed nothing more. Their silent communication spoke more than words ever could. Friends. Lovers. Parents. Spouses. Soulmates.

One motherfucking look said it fucking all.

Kissing her again, he slid his tongue into the warmth of her mouth and leaned into her fingers, caressing the hair at his nape.

Slowly, he moved down, sucking the tender skin at her neck, and farther, swirling his tongue around her pebble-hard nipple, licking his way down to her cunt. He tongued her slit, using his shoulders to widen her thighs.

Nosing her, he inhaled. Her pussy smelled divine, musky and *fucked.*

As he moved up again, he put his tongue into action and tasted her. Her thighs trembled against him. Pausing, he kissed each thigh, brushing his lips over the long-healed cuts she'd once inflicted upon herself.

He hated the thought of her in pain, but she'd had her fair share of heartbreak in her twenty-one years, some of it due to her association with him and his to the club. As long as Sharper roamed free, selling girls and planning the club's downfall, Megan was in danger.

Brooding now, he rested his cheek on her mound.

"Christopher?" she whispered, sensing his change, her voice bringing him back.

Megan's voice could bring him from the depths of hell. He'd die for her. He'd kill for her.

He lived for her.

Shoving away the fucking gloom and doom that had no place in a romantic motherfucker's life, he licked her again, sniffing her as if her scent provided his oxygen.

Gentle tugs on his hair halted his tongue and he lifted his gaze.

"Yeah, baby?"

"I don't want you to do that to me right now. I want you inside of me."

He smirked at her. "*That* huh, baby?" he asked, snickering. If she withheld her pussy the way she fucking resisted using filthy language, he'd be one cunt-deprived assfuck.

Rising above her, he sank into her and stilled, resting his forehead on hers.

She thumbed his lips. "It's okay, Christopher," she said softly, knowing him so well. "Sharper will never get to me, our children, or you. He'll get to no one in the club. We're safe because you make us safe."

"You fuckin' know how to humble a motherfucker," he said gruffly. She had an unshakeable faith in him.

Instead of responding, she lifted her hips, twisting her pussy against his cock.

"Wicked little bitch."

Just as they fell into rhythm, his phone rang, stilling Christopher's dick stabs.

Based on the ringtone blasting, John Boy called him. Motherfucker knew this was Christopher and Megan's anniversary. If not for that cunt he was married to, Christopher would think assfuck was inter-fucking-rupting on purpose.

Megan knew the call was important, too, because she halted her hooker moves and nodded, without him even telling her to stop her cock grinding.

With a growl, he leaned over and snatched his phone from the nightstand, his dick still buried in Megan. "What the fuck you want, motherfucker? Cuz, lemme tell you, John Boy, if this shit ain't fuckin' dire, I'm fuckin' breakin' your fuckin' hands. Interruptin' me and my girl—"

"Fuck, Christopher, would you just shut the fuck up?" Johnnie snapped. "We're having issues."

Fuck. "What kinda issues?" he asked slowly. It could be anything.

Their hydro-grow operation had expanded. With the legalization of recreational marijuana use in the state, demand had increased, although they'd still get thrown the fuck in jail with the volume they were doing. They supplied far and wide, however, with their support clubs doing most of the distribution.

Street value alone was way up in the tens of millions. In the event of his death, Megan and their children and their children's children would be set the fuck up for fucking life.

"Christopher?"

"What fuckin' issues?" he repeated, growling again because he had to pull out of Megan. He got to his feet, his swollen cock looking as angry as Christopher felt at the interruption.

Johnnie sighed.

Christopher tensed, not liking that fucking sigh. It meant some fucked-up shit he would fucking hate. "Fucking spill, John Boy."

"Digger is no longer abroad. Riley believes he's joined up with Sharper."

"Find the fuck out where," he barked. "Cuz if that motherfucker know that then he should fuckin' know where the fuck them motherfuckers at. I ain't fuckin' payin' Riley to only know half the fuckin' shit. Tell him…no, you ain't gotta tell him a fuckin' thing. My ass comin' and gettin' that motherfucker straight. Round the brothers the fuck up. Church goin' on in sixty."

"Minutes, right?"

"No, fuckhead. Hours. What the fuck you think? Yeah, minutes, motherfucker. One hour. That fuckin' clearer to your ass?"

"Yes."

"Lemme talk to Megan," he said and then hung up. Before he faced her again, he pulled on his jeans and carefully tucked away his disappointed cock, still with a raging hard-on. Motherfucker couldn't be more disappointed than Christopher.

When he turned, he found her sitting up with her knees drawn against her and the covers hiding her pretty tits from his eyes, her golden hair tangled about her head.

"Baby—"

"I heard, Christopher," she said gently. "Go. I'll be here. The kids are with Roxy and Bunny at Trader's place, and will be until tomorrow, so we have time to finish without interruption."

If she was disappointed, she hid it well, which made him feel fucking lower. This fucking day was so fucking important to her. This was the day they'd had their marriage blessed. If he thought about it, that made it more special to him too. She'd thought him worthy to stand before God and pledge herself to him.

"Maybe, I'll call Zoann and tell her I'm on the clock today," she continued. "I'll have something to do. Don't worry that I'll be bored or alone."

Although Megan and Zoann both owned the home-healthcare business, they were fucking respectful of each other's opinions and times, and they each had admirable work ethics. Johnnie's cunt, Kendall, was a very small partner, too, on the insistence of both Megan and Zoann. Kendall was also the company's attorney.

What-the-fuck ever. As long as Kendall acted like she was John Boy wife and Megan's friend—though Christopher would never fucking believe that shit—whatever the girls did was bitch shit. As long as Megan wasn't fucked with, he was the fuck out of it.

"Wait here. I ain't gonna be long. Go wash my cum outta you so it can be nice and fuckin' fresh when I put some fuckin' more in you."

She frowned and he winked at her, enjoying the fuck out of her blush.

Just to fuck with her a little more, he added, "The condition of your cunt don't fuckin' matter to me. I'll lick it and fuck it any shape it in."

Wrinkling her nose deepened her frown. "You're soooo bad, Christopher."

"Yeah, baby, I am," he agreed with pride, crossing their bedroom to one of the chairs where his shirt and cut lay.

The house was big, with more space than they'd ever need. Their bedroom and separate sitting room alone was huge, with walk-in closets and a huge ass bathroom. Megan hadn't even wanted this giant motherfucker. But this place was fit for a fucking queen. Fit for his girl. Because she was *his* queen.

He stopped fucking short at that thought. "Megan, baby," he started, straightening his clothes and shoving his nine in his waistband, hidden by his cut. Before he headed to the club, he'd stop in his man cave that Megan designed for him and grab his hollows. He needed bullets to wreck motherfuckers on the simple principle of interrupting his day with his wife. "You the best fuckin' thing that ever happened to me. You my every-fuckin-thing," he told her. This mushy romance was what the fuck she preferred. If he had to leave her for a little while, the least he could fucking do was o-fucking-blige her. "I love the fuck outta you. Ain't nothin' more important than you, baby."

That's why he hadn't gone after Digger as hard as he should have. Well, because of her and Mortician, but it was *mainly* due to Megan. Without her, he never would've fucking considered how Mort fucking felt about having to fuck up his kid brother. Even though the motherfucker had left his girl to die at the hands of his father's fuckheads, Christopher had backed off an active search because of Megan. That wasn't to fucking say if the motherfucker happened to run across Christopher, he wouldn't make him suffer a slow and fucking gruesome death. It just meant, finding him wasn't a fucking priority. At the time, it helped that he'd also parted ways with Sharper.

Then, too, Digger had fucking saved Bailey's life. He'd never fucking know what the fuck led to his former SAA's desertion. But Christopher believed part of the fucking reason was because Digger was just a stupid motherfucker and had gotten mixed up in Sharper's fucking games. Maybe, the motherfucker had felt left the fuck out with all of them falling in fucking love, especially Mort, who Digger fucking idolized.

"I love you, too, Christopher." Megan's sweet voice interrupted his thoughts. Her eyes twinkled and she smirked. "*Outlaw.*"

He hated when she called him Outlaw. Although that side of him was a big part of who he was, he never fucking wanted her to see him like that. For her, he was Christopher, her husband, and the father of her children.

"Yeah, baby, that's me. Rude and crude."

"And brilliant," she added.

Megan always saw the best in him.

He shrugged. What the fuck ever he was, was..."Ain't nothin' but a thing."

Right before he departed to make the walk through the woods to the club, he kissed her again. He wouldn't ruin their day any further by telling her *Outlaw's* intentions.

If Digger was back with his old man, then Outlaw intended to not only kill Sharper but Digger too.

And, this time, nothing she'd fucking say would stop him.

They were weak because *she* made them weak. Although he hated the fact Ellen lied on Meggie, her betrayal exposed the club's weakness clearly.

Ever since Outlaw had met Megan, he hadn't been the same. The Death Dwellers had suffered as a result. The trip part? From the beginning, Digger really liked Meggie. More than he could say for any of the rest of them, who'd all wanted to put her to ground, being Big Joe's girl.

Unfortunately, their world didn't have room for a romance-softened heart. After Outlaw fell for Meggie, the unthinkable happened. John Boy found love. Then Val. And, even fucking worse, Mortician followed suit and got a woman of his own.

From this point on, shit got realer than real.

Once Mort met Bailey, Digger felt left the fuck out. After Char and her bullshit, he never thought his big brother would fall for another bitch again.

But Mort had. And not just any random bitch, either, but the chick who happened to be the daughter of their father's mortal enemy.

Fate was just a motherfucker like that and threw more what-the-fuckery at motherfuckers than even the most twisted mind conjured.

Digger had nothing against love. He didn't believe or disbelieve in it. Mortician, on the other hand, had always craved a woman to fill up the missing piece of his heart. He'd gone on the fucking Yellow Brick Road and instead of little people, witches, flying fucking monkeys, and crazy motherfuckers behind a curtain pretending to be some dream-weaving fuckhead, Mort had found Bailey.

Bailey.

Mort falling for Bailey served as much of a bad omen as Outlaw falling for Meggie. Digger hadn't seen it at the time. If he'd had known the fallout, he would've killed both those chicks and gotten it over with. Outlaw with Meggie had pissed off Sharper, but Mort with Bailey just fucked everything right up the dickhole.

Now, Digger had the impossible task of protecting Mort and Outlaw, when Outlaw wanted Digger's body chopped up into little pieces for leaving Meggie to die. Digger didn't believe he could save all of them like some magician motherfucker. Loving his brother and admiring Outlaw, he'd made the choice.

What didn't they understand about that? When had pussy become more important than brotherhood?

When Meggie showed up.

Heaving in a breath, Digger pulled on his joint, wishing his head didn't run rampant with these thoughts whenever he smoked.

Maybe, if he didn't inhale?

Snickering, he took another draw and held the smoke in, letting it curl into his brain, only exhaling when a burn sizzled through his lungs and along the back of his throat.

This was some grade-A ass shit, too fucking good to allow even a smidgeon of smoke to evaporate.

At the opening and closing of the door, Digger tensed, not in the mood to see Osti or his father. Not even Peyton. Or Tyler. When he wanted to be alone, the cabin shrank and became small enough to hear an ant piss, so the whispers carrying to him from the room just beyond his door didn't surprise him. His ears perked.

"Pants down," Peyton demanded.

"Marcus might come in," Tyler whispered back, apparently unaware of his presence.

Frowning, Digger inhaled, held the smoke, and released, listening as Peyton, the fucking cunt, came on to his nephew. He needed to stop that conscienceless woman from fucking a child, even though the child in question had lost his virginity months ago.

"Peyton!" Tyler's voice cracked around her name and he groaned.

Digger staggered to his feet, stumbling toward the door, more fucked up than he'd thought.

"Get his dick out of your mouth," Sharper snarled before Digger opened his mouth.

Flesh connected with flesh and Peyton cried out. Digger stepped back into the shadows. The past few days he had been avoiding his father again. If the man looked into his eyes, he'd see Digger's dislike and regret. If only he'd listened to Mort, but what began as a jealous quest to defy his big brother had turned into...*this*.

"Father!" Tyler cried. "No, don't hurt Peyton."

"Cover your dick and go outside," Sharper instructed. "Find Osti. It's time for your bible study."

Tyler blinked in confusion. Sharper, the dirty, violent motherfucker, happened to be a religious zealot. At almost thirty-one years old, the two sides of his father baffled Digger. How could he expect a thirteen-year-old boy to comprehend it?

"Go, son."

"Yes, sir," Tyler mumbled, loping his tall, lanky frame toward the door, his eyes still slightly glazed with sexual frustration.

The moment the door closed, Sharper turned to Peyton. Her nose already bled from the hit he'd given her a moment ago. Remaining on her knees left her vulnerable to Sharper, but Digger barely cared.

"Mark doesn't work your cunt enough, slut?"

Never one to back down, Peyton glared at Sharper. "I'm sorry I ever met Digger," she spat. "He stands in the way all the time."

Peyton's statement concerned Digger. If she felt as if he blocked her from achieving her goal, one day she might fuck him up.

"What bothers you is he's lost his freedom being here with me, so you've lost yours."

"It's all because of *her*. Megan Foy. My sister's dead because of her and Digger got out bad because of her."

"Ellen's dead because she was a stupid cunt. Snake intended to strike back at Outlaw whether Megan had arrived or not. Retaliation for Big Joe."

"He would've left Ellen alone! Outlaw sent Ellen and Kiera with that girl—"

"Then you should blame Outlaw—"

"I'll re-evaluate who I blame once Goldilocks is dead." She huffed in agitation. "When I met Johnnie, I never thought it would take so long to get to her."

Once upon a time, Digger had liked her cold-streak, but he hadn't expected it to be used against his club brothers and their old ladies. By the time he'd gotten the real story, he cared about Peyton and owed his father a mountain of fucking money.

Too late, he'd realized only Mort bailed him out each and every time without any expectations of repayment.

"Where's Marcus?" Sharper continued, drawing Digger's attention again.

Peyton sniffled. "Asleep. Or gone. I haven't heard any movement from our room."

"Good. Good. What do you need to discuss with me?"

"You took long enough to respond."

"And?"

"Nothing, of course. But I heard through the grapevine, Outlaw's closing in," Peyton announced casually, deftly changing the subject.

"How soon?"

"Bailey's baby shower will take place in nine days."

Sharper scrubbed a shaking hand over his face. "We already know the contact's reliable, so we'll have to change our plans. Move in the next twenty-four hours."

"We're leaving tomorrow?" Peyton breathed.

"We have no choice, do we? Me, you, Osti, and a few reliable…*friends* have to leave to get there for this shower so we can strike. Make sure our contact will let us in, in the early morning. As the women and children are arriving, we cut them all down. That'll draw Outlaw and the others out in the open."

Fuck. They were going from sex trafficking girl killers to goddamn would-be baby killers. None of the children had reached their third birthdays yet, and his father wanted them shot to death?

Her lovely ivory-colored skin flushed, Peyton's eyes glittered with bloodlust. "I still get to shoot Megan and her children, right?" she asked, still on her knees, in perfect position for Sharper to stuff her mouth with his cock.

Sharper caressed her cheek. "Is that what you want, pet?" he asked, unzipping his trousers.

Nodding, Peyton pulled out Sharper's flaccid dick and wrapped her lips around it. At first, Digger had enjoyed sharing her with Osti and whoever else wanted her. Though he wanted a woman to call his own like the others had, he wanted his own emotions in check. Now, he only wanted Peyton gone. First things were first. He had to stop the intended massacre.

He yawned loudly, making a production of stretching and walking noisily into the room.

Sharper pulled his soft dick out of Peyton's mouth while she got to her feet. Pretending he didn't know what happened, he lifted his brow and offered a pointed look at the trail of dried blood that led from her nose to her cheek.

"Having fun?"

Peyton bit her lip at his question and his father cleared his throat.

"Where's Tyler?"

"Bible study," Sharper answered, turning toward the lone window and stuffing his hands in his pockets.

"Fuck, he study the bible more than some priests. What's up with that shit?" He didn't wait for an answer and went to the cabinets filled with cereal and non-perishable food. "I need a fucking juicy burger. I can't take this shit. I'm going to have to borrow the car and find a fast food joint."

Sharper sighed. "Best do it today."

"Oh?"

Without any more prompt, his father explained why.

With studied nonchalance, Digger shrugged. "About time. We can start fucking living again."

Sharper's eyes widened. "Would you like to join us?" he asked, both caution and curiosity crossing his face.

Digger didn't like the gleam in his father's eyes. Though he couldn't place the sentiment, he wouldn't ignore the look.

"Where we leaving Tyler?"

"He'll be with us. It'll be good experience for him."

Yeah, turning a kid into a fucking raving lunatic killer was fucking wonderful.

"You in?"

Pulling down a box of sugar pops and opening it, Digger dug in then shoveled some into his mouth. He couldn't appear too anxious. After a few chews, he said, "Yeah."

"Peyton wants to do Megan Caldwell and her three children. Who will you target?"

Fuck, he had to answer that. If not, his ass would be left behind. "I'll save Bailey for you," he said with a forced snicker, nodding to his father. "I'll take out Outlaw cunt of a sister."

"Then let's call Osti and Tyler in and finalize our plans," Sharper said. "We'll get your burger and fries on the way, Mark."

Fine with Digger. Once all was said and done, he hoped like fuck his father would be dead. Too bad he was stuck in the middle of nowhere with no gun, no ammo, no money, and no backup.

Otherwise, Digger would've gotten the job done before the club got into their sights.

Bunny Hamilton plastered a smile on her face as she stared at her long-time boyfriend, Trader. Since he lived and breathed the Death Dwellers MC, he refused to acknowledge he'd ever had a given name. Instead, he insisted on going by his road name.

It had been that way since he'd been one of her customers at the strip club.

Now, she stared at the tell-tale bite on his neck, fed up with his bad temper and his cheating.

"Walk out that fucking door anytime you want to, cunt," he told her when she relayed the thought to him. 'Cunt' had become her new nickname.

Clenching her jaw, she focused on the kitchen counter in the apartment she shared with him. Tonight, she'd spend the night at Meggie's house, since Bailey's baby shower would happen bright and early tomorrow. Bunny wanted everything cleaned up before she left so Trader wouldn't have a reason to complain.

If only she could be so lucky. Last week, when the kids and Roxy had spent the night because of Meggie and Outlaw's anniversary, Trader hadn't been happy.

He crowded her in, pressing his hard cock against her butt, the scent of perfume floating to her and turning her stomach.

Not because of the betrayal the smell represented. She believed her suspected pregnancy caused the reaction. Being unsure of what Trader might do if he discovered their impending parenthood, she kept delaying the test.

"You think you'll be able to prance around my fucking club like some uppity whore if you walk out on me?"

She leaned as far away as possible, but since his body caged her in, she really had nowhere to go. "I can't continue to live like this. You screw everything you see."

"I only fuck a few bitches. I have everything I see suck my cock since you won't do it anymore." He gripped her arms and she tensed, never sure when he'd hit her. "I take you off the fucking strip pole and this is how you repay me?" He laughed, the ugly sound going through Bunny. "I've been thinking about telling the brothers what a slut you are. I'll bet Outlaw doesn't know you sucked cock for money. Think he'd let you be around his precious Megan if he did? I could get me a lot of favors if I let some of the brothers fuck you."

Fed up, she elbowed him, satisfied at the sound of his grunt. He loosened his hold on her and she made her escape, running toward the bedroom. Hot on her heels, he caught her halfway to her destination and spun her around.

Grabbing her neck, he slammed her against the wall and yanked down her shirt. He shoved her bra aside and punched her breast.

The pain of a second hit sent tears to her eyes. Still, she attempted to knee him in the groin. He tightened his hold on her neck.

"You better hope you don't bruise. I don't need that black bitch in my business," he said, referring to Roxy, as Bunny attempted to pry his fingers away. "I'll just fucking kill you and dump your body somewhere if your neck's bruised."

Bending, he tugged her nipple into his mouth and bit, laughing when Bunny gasped in agony. He shoved her to the floor and she landed on her hands and knees.

"If you want to go, get the fuck up and walk out and *keep* fucking walking. You're welcome in that club because of me," he screamed. "Me! You leave me, you leave it."

Surely, Meggie would understand why, and wouldn't shut Bunny out. An image of Outlaw rose in her head. Meggie would understand, but her husband might not.

"Then what'll become of you? You can't get a teaching job. Remember? That's what happens to sluts and whores."

She hung her head and sobbed. How could she forget the day her life had been ruined? If not for that day when she'd lost her teaching position at a private elementary school because of her second job as a stripper, she never would've left Arizona.

"I guess you go back to the pole and sucking cock for more money." Looming above her, he slid his zipper down. "I think I'll give you a dick licking refresher."

Scrambling to her feet, Bunny stumbled backward, swiping at her wet cheeks and hating the sound of Trader's mocking laughter.

"That got you moving." He walked closer to her and rubbed her cheek. "Why you have to be so pretty?" As if the thought angered him, he slapped her across her face. "You like being a pretty bitch? You liked grinding your cunt in other men's faces?" Gripping her arms, he shook her. "You're fucking nothing without me."

"I'm nothing *with* you, you piece of shit," she spat. "I'm sorry I was stupid enough to believe you loved me. I'm sorry I ever left Phoenix."

"You didn't leave for me, Bunny," he said, sounding hurt, instead of angry. She never knew which way his mood swings went. When he decided to fight, he beat her up, whether she cowered or stood up to him. Just as he went with his mood, she went with hers. "You left because your fucking mother and father was ashamed of you. They couldn't hold their heads up because of the scandal."

"I left with you because I thought I loved you." Sometimes, in his sweet moments, she still believed she'd love him again, one day. Although he hadn't regretted his cheating since it started months ago, he always regretted hitting her. "I left with you so we could have a future together."

"A future?" he sneered. "Like kids and marriage?"

She nodded.

"Why the fuck would I want a whore to bear my children or my name?"

"I'm not a whore," she said vehemently, hating her second nickname as much as she hated the first. "I'm not proud of my past, but I've tried to make up for those times."

"You're only good for one thing, *Albany*." He sneered her given name. "Fucking. Being a servant to Outlaw's bitch. You're a slut and society doesn't forgive sluts. They'll forgive a murdering bitch before they overlook one who fucked and sucked as many men as you have."

She wanted to refute that, but she couldn't. While Meggie knew a lot of her past, even she didn't know she'd supplemented stripping with prostitution. And, for no other reason than being stupidly arrogant and willful, determined to show her parents they couldn't control her.

As Trader's old lady, she'd started hanging out at the MC a few weeks after he'd finally convinced her to leave Arizona. By then, they'd had an on and off relationship for almost four years.

With a new beginning, Bunny had felt free from all her mistakes for the first time. Gypsy had been her first friend not connected to her old life, the one where she'd crashed and burned after trying to balance a stripper lifestyle with her elementary teaching dreams.

Besides Trader and Gypsy, she hadn't trusted many people, fearing someone turning against her if they discovered the 'old' her. Then, she'd tagged along with Gypsy on an outing with Meggie. Once Meggie befriended her, she felt truly accepted. Meggie made everyone feel welcomed.

When Outlaw sought her out to assist his wife during her pregnancy with the twins, Trader had grown meaner. As she and Meggie grew closer, he'd reminded her every step of the way that if she walked away from him, she'd walk away from Meggie, leaving her with only her brother. She couldn't impose on Gabe like that. His life was wrapped around his tattooing. She knew that, so she'd kept his apartment cleaned. He'd never been the neatest person and she wanted to repay him after he'd followed her from Arizona to watch over her when she'd turned her back on him and their parents. She sighed. Once again, she'd deserted Gabe. It had been months since she'd last cleaned up for him or laundered his clothes. Though he'd taken it upon himself to move closer to Bunny, it wouldn't be fair of her to expect her little brother to fill the void she'd have if she left Trader.

Sagging against the sofa, she sobbed into her hands, overcome with shame and humiliation.

An opening door made her lift her head.

"You wanna leave, cunt?" Trader nodded to the deserted hallway. "Go. I'll have a new bitch by nightfall and I'll make sure every brother know your pussy's theirs to do with what they want if they run across you. I'll broadcast it to everyone that you're not fit company for respectable women and children. You want that?"

She shook her head.

He slammed the door shut. "I didn't think so. Now, I need to ask you something and if you fucking lie to me, I'll make you fucking regret it."

"Okay," she said hoarsely, just wanting to get to Meggie's house. There, she could pretend her past had never happened. She could forget her worry that everyone would think differently of her if they knew the truth.

Trader tipped her chin up and she flinched. For several days after these run-ins with him, she jumped at everything. "When was your last period?"

"Um..."

He gripped her jaw tighter. "Remember what I said. I'll hurt you bad if you lie to me. Let me give you some background to save yourself the temptation of not telling me the truth. I haven't noticed you with any female products in two or three months. I haven't even seen unopened boxes of anything around here. Only reason that can be is if you let me knock you up." He squeezed harder. "You let me do that to you after I told you I don't want your fucking babies?"

"N-no...I-I mean I...Trader..."

"Trader," he mocked, in a horrible imitation of her voice.

"I don't know," she admitted, seeing no choice. "I might be pregnant."

"If you are, you either get rid of it or leave."

She clamped her jaw. "I'll leave," she said tightly. "I'll not sacrifice my baby for you."

He started in surprise, then narrowed his eyes. "Let's see," he said, laying a finger on his jaw. "You leave me, you won't have *me* or your "friends"—he made air quotations—"at the club. Maybe, you'll have Gabe, but he needs you to keep his house and clothes clean. Otherwise, he's just a filthy little bastard who only wants to focus on his shop. So how the fuck you intend to raise my kid alone? A kid I don't want you to have, by the way."

"I'll find a way," she cried. "Just like every other woman who get involved with good-for-nothing assholes. If you don't want to know your child, that's fine. I'll pack up tonight and leave tomorrow, straight from the baby shower. You'll never have to see me again."

The idea seemed to appease him.

Smiling, he nodded. "Let's go buy a pregnancy test. Before me or you jump to conclusions and make unnecessary decisions."

"Do you really want to know?"

He shrugged. "It's my right, don't you think? It would be my dick swimmers that made it."

"I need to get to Meggie's in an hour. We have to finish cooking for tomorrow."

"Who's we?"

"Me. Meggie. Roxy. Bailey. Zoann. Kendall. Even Gypsy."

"Derby's bitch?"

"Yeah," she answered.

"She the cunt who introduced you to Megan?"

"Yes."

He grinned, a thoughtful gleam in his eyes. "Come on, babe. Let's see if you have a bun in the oven, then I'll decide."

"What's there to decide?"

"Don't worry. You'll see," he said, winking at her.

A chill traveled through Bunny, and she hesitated.

"Trust me, sweetness."

Deciding her foreboding was a residual effect from the intensity of their fight, she hurried and grabbed her purse, hoping she was pregnant.

And praying she was not.

A couple hours later, Trader's pacing increased Bunny's nerves and unease. She wished he'd leave her alone, but they were in their bedroom, awaiting of the outcome of the pregnancy tests on the dresser.

Two pregnancy tests. One for her and one for him.

"To see if this shit works," he'd said.

"Do you know if a man takes a pregnancy test and it comes out positive, that's an indicator of testicular cancer?"

Glaring at her, he'd thrust his face into hers and shoved her. "I don't need your fucking hoity-toity, think-you-know-it-all bullshit. You're nothing, Bunny. You're a stupid bitch who's lucky to have me."

Their earlier encounter had already taken an emotional toll on her, so she'd shut up and not spoken again until they'd returned to the apartment.

Now, Trader paced, paused at the tests, turned once he reached the window and started the entire process again.

This time, when he halted at the tests, he lifted hers and dangled it beneath her nose. "Well, look what we got here. You're pregnant."

The tiny thrill she felt at the prospect evaporated at Trader's sweep of her.

Swallowing, she got to her feet. "I'll be out of here within the hour."

Surprised, he lifted his eyebrows. Bunny scooted around and went to the utility closet, where she'd stored her empty luggage. Although she had more clothes now than when she'd first moved to Hortensia, she'd pack only the bare necessities tonight. Tomorrow, when Trader was wherever he went to, she'd get the rest. She wanted to clear out as quickly as possible.

Back in the bedroom, she found Trader leaning against the dresser, blocking the access to her drawers, arms folded.

"Well?"

Well what? She cleared her throat. "We're having a baby," she said softly, not knowing what else to say. A small, silly part of her hoped he'd take her into his arms and hug her. Say the words most women longed to hear at such an announcement. Encouragement. Comfort. Hope. Reassurance everything would be fine. A promise he'd be right at her side through her pregnancy.

"I'm waiting," he said in a cool tone.

Flushing, she looked at her toes, feeling like an errant child at the note in his voice.

"Answer me!"

She jumped at his shout. "You already know!" she fired back. "But since you're talking in riddles, *I* need to know what you're thinking."

"You really don't know?" he sneered.

"The only thing I can think of is you're going to throw me out. I'm saving you the trouble because I'm leaving."

Bitter laughter escaped him. "You let me knock you up. Now, you're expecting to just walk the fuck away with no explanations. No nothing. You can't even give me the goddamn courtesy of listening to what I have to say. Just running the fuck away because that's what you fucking do."

"That isn't true!"

"The fuck it isn't. You ran away from that bitch who gave birth to you, instead of fucking facing her like a grown ass woman."

She swiped at her tears, hating to admit that Trader was right. "I hurt my mother terribly, but that wasn't the only reason I left. I wanted to be with you."

"Lucky me."

She held onto her tears. "I'm not doing this right now, Bryce," she said, his given name slipping out before she caught herself.

He didn't give her a chance to apologize, before he backhanded her. She landed on the bed and clutched her jaw, scrambling away when he lunged for her again. "I'm leaving." By sheer will, she kept her tears at bay. Still, her voice trembled. "I won't ask you for anything. I'll leave it up to you the extent you want to be in your baby's life."

Once she arrived at Meggie's, she'd announce her pregnancy and they'd all congratulate her. They'd give her the support Trader was refusing to offer. Holding on to that thought, she got to her feet, uneasy with Trader so close, just staring in her direction, following her every move.

"I'm sorry for using your name." He had quite the hang up about that. Why, she wasn't sure. At this point, she wasn't interested in finding out.

He didn't respond, so she inched past him. She didn't need her belongings right now.

"Don't walk away from me."

"We can talk when you calm down," she answered as she headed out of the room, not wanting to inflame his temper by giving him the silent treatment.

"Think you're bringing your ass to Megan Caldwell?"

Pausing at the door, she glanced over her shoulder. "Yes."

"Not if you walk away before I allow you to go."

She huffed. "Trader—"

He smirked at her. "Remembered my name rule, huh, cunt?"

Her lips tightened into a straight line. If she walked away, he'd pursue her and *really* hit her hard. Besides, he was right. She owed it to him to listen to what he had to say. He'd fathered the baby she carried, so he should get his feelings out in the open. She raised her chin, preparing herself for any cruel words he might throw at her. "I'm listening to whatever you have to say, then, please, let me go to Meggie's. They need my help."

"You think?"

Shifting her weight, she glanced away. She wouldn't let Trader's meanness affect what she knew were genuine friendships on Roxy and Meggie's parts.

"Come here."

Already knowing what he had to say, she leaned against the door. "I never meant to get pregnant. I must've forgotten my pill at some point." His look darkened. Any other words she might've said died on her lips. "I'm sorry," she finished, cutting her conversation short.

"It's done now."

If not for his coldness and the fury lighting his eyes, his statement might've given her hope.

"I'm having you barred from the club."

"What? You can't—"

"Why not?" He laid his finger against his jaw, one of his favorite gestures when he was being a full-blown asshole. "Oh, I know! You're good friends with Outlaw's cunt."

Oh, she wished she was recording this, so she could let Outlaw hear Trader calling Meggie a cunt. She frowned. On second thought…did she really want nothing left of him? Outlaw would obliterate Trader.

"You're at my fucking club because of me, not her. You're not her equal. Outlaw married that bitch. I'm never marrying you. You're not good enough to have my name." He stalked closer and thrust his face into hers, his favorite intimidation tactic. "You work for that little bitch. Otherwise, you're nothing."

She opened her mouth to defend herself and Meggie.

"You know I'm telling the truth," he cut in. "Outlaw protects her to the point of obsession. If we're over, you're out."

"You'd do that to me? Make Outlaw bar me and cut me off from the only income I have?"

Could he do that? In this case, who'd have more weight? Outlaw didn't allow his boys to abuse women, but there was also a no-interference policy in place for all other matters between the brothers and their women.

She gave Trader an imploring look. "I don't care if you're with other women." He fucked around, whether she cared or not. "You can even drop me, but, please...Please, keep our breakup between us. Meggie's my friend and—"

"Meggie's your employer."

Technically, she was, although Outlaw signed her pay checks. But Meggie had never treated Bunny as only an employee. They were friends. Not that Trader wanted to hear that. At the moment, he didn't want to hear anything she had to say. She'd never get Trader to listen to her reasoning while he was in his current frame of mind. "We'll discuss this tomorrow. I know the pregnancy is a shock. We'll work this out. I don't want our baby to live in a hostile environment." *She* didn't want to live in such an environment any longer.

Wrapping his hand around her hair, he jerked her head back and stared into her eyes. In his gaze, nothing reflected back. Not love, hate, or compassion.

The first blow to her stomach trapped her breath in her lungs and she gasped, too shocked to feel initial pain. The second punch caved her body in. Trader released her hair and she crumpled to the ground. He kicked her and a scream finally escaped her. She attempted to curl into a ball but he dropped to his knees and gripped her thighs.

Instinctively, she fought through her agony, attempting to protect her stomach and the fragile new life inside her. But it was too late. Already, wetness seeped between her legs and cramps assailed her.

Trader yanked her to her feet and punched her stomach again, administering three additional blows in quick succession. Silent tears streaked her face and the pain immobilized her. She was losing her baby. She should've left when she'd had the chance. If she'd gone by what a sonofabitch Trader was, she wouldn't have stopped.

"Now, sweetness," he huffed out, "clean yourself up. If I haven't taken care of the problem, I will when I get back. Everything will be back to normal between us, so you're welcome to stay with me. Oh, yeah," he added, "if you have the ability to walk after your well-deserved ass beating, head on over to Outlaw's house." He snickered. "Personally, I don't think you'll be going anywhere, anytime soon."

Through her haze of tears, Bunny watcher Trader saunter out of the room, whistling a cheerful ditty. As if he hadn't just taken from her the one thing she'd wanted most.

Christopher swigged from his bottle of tequila, waiting for his shot at the pool table. So far John Boy was pocketing those motherfucking balls without fail. Glaring at Johnnie's increasing smugness, Mort wrapped his hands around his cue stick and rested his chin, until Bailey stood on the other side of the man cave, a recreation of the main room at the club. The girls were there after finishing last-minute shit for Bailey's baby shower tomorrow morning.

Suddenly, Mort didn't look so fucking outraged at Johnnie's luck. He straightened, leering at Bailey's exposed skin. Taking another swig and looking over his shoulder, Christopher snickered and thumped Mort's shoulder.

"Hey, pervert," Val called. "The action over here."

"No, the action with Bailey and all her pretty skin she showing off."

"She's showing off her belly, not her skin," Johnnie came back, indicating the pocket he was aiming for. He had one fucking more to go before the eight ball.

Kendall threw a kiss at Johnnie and he pretended to catch it. Winking at her, he placed a hand over his heart. She blushed.

An idea formed in Christopher's head. Something to stop Johnnie's winning streak. Motherfucker was decent at pool, but this shit was ridiculous. Out of all of them, Val and Arrow were the best players, hands fucking down. Arrow and Cash seeing to the Bobs left Val to shine at pool. Motherfucker hadn't even gotten a shot since Johnnie broke the goddamn balls.

"Watch this, Val," Christopher said under his breath. He cleared his throat, as Johnnie positioned himself. "Fuck, I think Kendall ain't happy. Just look at that bitch all sad and frowny."

As expected, Johnnie turned as he pushed his cue stick. Distracted, he didn't take such care aligning himself. The shot went wide. Unfazed, he set the stick aside and headed for Kendall.

Mort clapped Christopher's hand with his. "That's some low-down ass shit, Prez."

"Who gives a fuck?" Val crowed, while Christopher powdered the cue's tip. "It fucking worked."

Keeping a watch on Megan out of the corner of his eye, Christopher indicated the far right pocket. Megan laughed at something Johnnie told her and it took all his concentration to make the shot. Payback was a motherfucker.

"I'm over here, Johnnie," Kendall called.

Val groaned. He leaned against the banister that separated the pool table from the rest of the room. "We shouldn't have invited the girls, Outlaw."

"You been noticing a change in Red?" Mort asked, swiveling his head between the women and the pool table. "She been reverting back to the pre-separation days."

"Don't make me any more fuckin' sorry I ain't finished chokin' the fuck outta her when I had the fuckin' chance," Christopher grumbled, setting up his eight-ball shot.

"Puff told me Kendall stopped her meds."

Mort's mouth dropped open. "Why the fuck Red did that?"

"That's what I say," Val responded. "But Puff didn't know. She believe Kendall got a reason, though. She been working on some big case with Brooks and she said the anti-depressants take the edge off *everything.* She not as aggressive in the courtroom either and that's fucking with her."

"Prez, uh, you okay with that?" Mort asked. "I mean I hear where Red coming from. If it calm her down, it's reasonable to say it affects all areas of her life."

Christopher pocketed the eight ball. "As long as it don't affect Megan, I'm leavin' that bitch alone."

Megan went behind the bar to the refrigerator. When she returned to the tables where the girls sat, she placed a bottle of sparkling cider and wine on the table, then headed to them, holding Mort's pint of Skittles-infused vodka.

"Thanks, Meggie girl. Nobody blend it as perfectly as you do."

She rolled her eyes and giggled. "Whatever." Turning to Christopher, she braced her hands on his chest to balance herself, then stood on tiptoe. "Hey, you," she whispered.

"Hey baby," he told her, bending and kissing her. "Soon as Ghost and Arrow get the fuck here and we have our meetin', I'm gonna fuck you."

"I can't wait for you to come." She gave him a saucy wink at her play on words.

"Wicked brat."

"Bad biker."

She spun away, giggling as he slapped her ass.

"Thanks for getting the glasses, Bailey," she said, her voice floating to Christopher after she returned to the tables.

"Damn my woman fine," Mort commented, guzzling from his vodka.

Johnnie returned with a glass of Scotch. "Not finer than my woman."

The door opened and CJ stepped in, dragging a red-faced Rebel behind him. Never letting CJ too far out of her sight, Harley toddled in their wake, as fast as her little legs could carry her.

"MegAnn!" CJ yelled. "Ant Woxy say bwing Webel. Her falled."

"Hey, boy," Christopher called before Megan spoke. She was already out of her chair and heading for CJ and Rebel. "Get the fuck over here, CJ."

Megan lifted their girl into her arms. Christopher marveled at how much the two of them resembled each other. Same golden hair and bright, blue eyes. It was fucking scary. He had images of Rebel growing up and falling for some old motherfucker who Christopher had already decided to kill.

Now that Megan had Rebel, their girl began to cry. CJ still hadn't moved, so Megan interrupted whatever she told Rebel to talk to CJ.

Stepping beside him, Mort studied Harley, who'd taken CJ's hand now that he didn't hold his little sister's.

"Prez, you think we gonna be in-laws in the future?"

CJ giggled at whatever Megan said, and Harley imitated him, laughing around the binky in her mouth.

"Fuck, Mort, I ain't sure."

"You two do realize they're children? Babies?" Lifting his glass to drain it, Johnnie joined Christopher and Mort. "Thirty-one months and sixteen months, respectively. Their attachment doesn't mean shit."

"You no fun, John Boy," Val complained, his eyes lighting up when Ryan crawled in. He paused in the doorway and didn't continue forward until his twelve-month-old brother, Devon, caught up to him. Ryan had taken it upon himself to teach the kid that crawling trumped walking any day. Since Devon had just started walking, Christopher understood that crawling, to Ryan, was a faster mode of getting from point A to point B.

"Um'mon, Dev. Like this," he instructed, darting toward Zoann.

Behind Devon, Christopher's other son and Rebel's twin, Rule, toddled in, with Rory tottering behind him.

Kendall clapped. "The king has arrived!" she cried. Rory threw her a gummy grin, obviously enjoying those words.

Instead of taking offense, Christopher decided it was some type of game they played.

"Yo, Megan, you ever lettin' my boy get his ass here? He fuckin' know better than to call you MegAnn."

"MegAnn *my* mommie, 'Law."

He shared an amused, knowing look with Megan. "That's *my* wife, boy."

Just like Kendall calling Rory a fucking king, this conversation between him and CJ was their thing.

Adjusting his mini cut, CJ rushed to Christopher, climbing onto his boots and lifting his arms. He hadn't encouraged the boot climbing to pick his boy up. Initially, it had been so CJ could reach the handle on the clubhouse door. Standing on Christopher's boot gave him the extra height to reach it.

"Up, 'Law," he whined, wiggling his fingers. He looked tired. It was past CJ's bedtime, but Megan had allowed the kids to stay up since their cousins were visiting, although the seven kids acted more like siblings.

Obliging his boy, Christopher grinned at the feel of his son's little arms around his neck.

"MegAnn mine," he said, leaning back to stare into Christopher's eyes.

"She mine first," he countered. "She my beautiful angel."

"MegAnn 'Law angel?"

He nodded.

"MegAnn *my* mommie and 'Law angel."

"How fuckin' generous."

Carrying Rebel, Megan guided Rule by the hand to where Christopher and CJ stood. On her tiptoes, she kissed CJ's shoulder. "I'm your mommie and Daddy's wife. Remember?"

"Uh-huh," his boy answered, nodding his head with exaggeration.

She raised her hand. "High-five."

"High-five," CJ echoed happily, slapping his hand against Megan's.

Turning her attention to Christopher, she frowned, worry creasing her brow. "I still can't reach Bunny."

"Maybe, she got fuckin' tied up with Trader, baby."

"She would've called."

"Want Bun-Bun," CJ blurted.

Sighing, Christopher set his boy down. CJ promptly went to Mort, who now held Harley and was making a fucking ass out of himself for her laughs. Binky still in her mouth, she gripped his dreads and concentrated on him with adoration.

Megan handed Rebel to Christopher, then lifted Rule, the quietest of all the kids. He was an observer and a thinker. CJ was a doer.

Christopher kissed Rebel's forehead. She was a cross between both of her brothers, and Christopher hadn't decided if that was good or bad. Once she touched his cheeks and chin, she laid her head on his chest, content to be with her daddy.

Meanwhile, Christopher didn't like Megan's worry. "Listen up, baby. If she not here or you ain't talk to her by the time these motherfuckers leave, I'll send Arrow or Cash to their fuckin' place."

"I'm so worried. A few weeks ago, her arms were all bruised. I think Trader's mean to her."

Weeks ago, Megan had said something similar and Christopher had pulled Trader aside, warning the motherfucker to leave Bunny the fuck alone if he was doing her something.

Even fucking with her head by flaunting other bitches to her. A couple days later, Megan mentioned she'd found Bunny in tears in the guest room she sometimes used. Exercising more fucking patience than he was used to, Christopher had gone back to Trader and told the motherfucker how much Megan cared about Bunny. Unless Trader was a completely moronic motherfucker, he should've taken Christopher's *second* conversation as a warning. This bullshit was upsetting Megan, so it upset Christopher. But it was also working on his fucking ass.

Grabbing her jaw, he pulled her to him and kissed her. He never got enough of her kisses. "I know how much Bunny mean to you. Ima check into shit."

"Okay."

He bent closer to her ear, intending to fuck with her, but he couldn't resist licking the shell and biting her lobe. She shivered and gasped. "Gimme a hour then I'm tearin' your pussy up."

Her eyes brightened and she flushed. "Can I suck you off first?" she breathed.

"Megan, c'mon, baby. You really gotta ask to suck my cock?"

Shaking her head, she kissed his chest.

"Harway!" CJ whined as Bailey took Harley, although Mort didn't look pleased.

"We have a big day tomorrow, sweetheart," Bailey explained to CJ. She released Harley and crouched to eye-level with his boy.

"Fuck, Bailey, stand up."

Ignoring Mort, Bailey smiled at CJ. "We're having a party for the new baby. Help Mommie with your brother and sister, then sleep so you can be nice and fresh to watch over Harley for me tomorrow."

"Okay, Ant Bail." CJ threw his arms around Harley, who hugged him back. "Night-night, Harway."

She babbled to him.

"Omigod, we so have to get photos of them together tomorrow," Megan said happily as Bailey got to her feet.

"We do," she agreed, turning to Mort and plastering her mouth to his before saying, "We'll be at the house, Lucas."

"We just got some business to finish here, pretty girl."

"Let's see if Momma has any King Cake stashed away."

"I'm all for that," Zoann called.

"You greedy, Puff."

Bitsy flipped Val off, and Val snickered.

"Don't call a woman greedy, Val," Megan chastised. Although she tried to be playful, to Christopher, every move and word around Val sounded and looked forced.

Christopher still couldn't figure out the lingering tension in Megan whenever she talked to Val that started when Bitsy was shot. He couldn't get anything out of her. She swore it was all in Christopher's imagination and even if something had happened, Christopher had taken care of it when he shot Val based on an assumption.

Except her body language screamed differently.

"Come on, buddy," Megan said to CJ, lifting Rule and Rebel into each arm.

"I stay 'Law, MegAnn," CJ said, folding his arms and glaring like Christopher sometimes did.

"No, you're coming with me," Megan countered firmly. "Daddy has business."

"I stay," CJ insisted. "You go."

Rule squirmed in Megan's arms and Rebel started to whine. Anarchy was imminent.

"Take the twins. CJ can stay, baby."

She eyed him suspiciously. "He's tired, so think about that before you discipline him."

Ignoring her, he nodded to the door. "Go, Megan."

Although she wanted to argue, the twins left her no choice but to follow Christopher's orders. When the door closed, CJ grinned at him, then yawned. He climbed on Christopher's boot and reached for him.

"You ain't playin' with Harley tomorrow, boy," he said. "You shoulda went with your Ma when she asked you. And you stop callin' her by her goddamn name. You either fuckin' listen or you suffer the consequences."

Water filled CJ's eyes, a moment before he laid his cheek against Christopher's thigh and sobbed.

Hearing his boy's tears made Christopher want to take his words back, but he didn't know how to get his point across to CJ about talking to Megan as he did. Before he flipped to CJ's side, Christopher guided his son off his boot. As CJ threw himself to the floor in a tantrum, Christopher headed to the bar, gritting his teeth to stay firm. He grabbed beers from the refrigerator, then went to the tables the girls had been sitting at. He put the cold beers down, grabbing the bottles that hadn't been moved before Megan and the others departed. Once he finished clearing the table except for beers, an ashtray, a grinder, rillos, and a baggie, he sat.

"Want Mommie," CJ wailed, bracing his hands on the floor to cry better. "Mommie, 'Law."

Sliding Mort, Johnnie, and Val their beers as they sat and charging Val with the weed-rolling, Christopher returned to his sleepy son and lifted him into his arms.

"Stop, cryin', boy," he said gruffly.

Immediately, CJ attempted to halt his tears. They continued to fall silently while he drew in such big sniffs his chest shook.

"Listen up, son. Stop callin' your ma by her name. As much as I wanna tell you you can play with Harley all day tomorrow, I don't know what the fuck else to do to make you fuckin' listen. Hear me? You just gonna have to be with me tomorrow."

"Want Mommie," CJ repeated pitifully.

"If I let you go to her, you gonna listen?"

"Uh-huh."

"You gonna help with your brother and sister?"

He sniffled. "Yeah."

"And you ain't callin' her MegAnn?"

"No."

"You gotta respect her. Protect her. Not only your ma but your sister and cousins and aunts. All girls. Okay, boy?"

"Okay, 'Law."

The door opened and Megan peeped in, holding her hand out to their son. "Come on, my sweet potato."

Christopher set CJ on the ground and he ran to her, grabbing her legs. "'Law say I not pway with Harway."

Megan nodded and stroked his hair. "It's okay," she soothed. "Daddy wants you to listen. I do, too."

Truth. But she wouldn't gainsay him in front of CJ. It had been her idea that they always put up a united front with the kids. If they disagreed over the way one of them handled a situation—and he suspected she did now—they'd do it in private. Not knowing anything about being a father, Christopher agreed. So far, it worked well.

"Aunt Roxy has Rule and Rebel, so you get Mommie to yourself."

He lifted his head, excited at that. "Okay, Mommie."

Megan devoted one day a month to each of their kids, where they had her exclusive attention. On the fourth week, she took all the kids. More often than not, though, she had to take the twins together. They hated to be separated, although Rebel was quicker to leave Rule than the reverse.

"Once I get you ready for bed, we'll call Bunny again."

CJ nodded, staring at her with devotion.

Satisfied that she'd appeased their son, Megan came to Christopher, gifting him with another sweet kiss.

"Can you two keep your lips off each other?" Johnnie said, sounding disgusted. "This has to be the tenth fucking time you two have found a reason to kiss, and the third just in the last hour."

Megan poked her tongue at Johnnie. "I'll send Kendall in here so you can have a little attention if you'd like."

"Funny, Megan," Johnnie said.

"Not trying to be, Johnnie," she returned with a sniff.

"It's not a big deal that CJ calls Megan by her name," Johnnie said once Megan and CJ left.

Val lifted a brow. "No shit?"

"It teaches children that no one's better than they are."

Mort snorted, leaned back, and folded his arms. "That's fucking bullshit, Johnnie. It teaches kids how to fucking ignore authority. A parent not a child's peer."

"Not true," Johnnie denied, guzzling his beer. "We have a life beyond parenthood. It's important for Rory to remember we aren't *only* Mom and Dad. Saying Johnnie and Kendall reminds him of this. It doesn't diminish our roles or alienate us. Kids either respect their parents or they don't. Tacking on 'Mom' and 'Dad' won't make much of a fucking difference."

Christopher lit up a smoke and dragged on it. "What the fuck you on, John Boy? Mom and Dad let a motherfucker know immediately what the fuck comin'. Hell or salvation. CJ hear Mommie, he think of sweetness. He hear Outlaw or Daddy and he know I ain't fuckin' around. My boy lookin' me in the eye and say *Christopher* do make him equal in his eyes."

"But calling you 'Law doesn't?" Johnnie countered.

"Yo, Val. When you call my ass fuckin' Outlaw, tell me what you think?"

"Not fucking equality," Val said with a snigger, nearly done with the joint. "I mean, we equal in some ways. But we know you a fucking law unto yourself and if we fuck up, we get fucked up."

Mort adjusted in his seat and sipped his beer. "Little Man calling his father Outlaw, to me, adds another layer of respect. Different than saying Daddy, but not as disrespectful as *Christopher.*"

"Me and Kendall feel differently."

The argument boring him, Christopher shrugged.

Val got to his feet. "Where the fuck Cash and Arrow at?"

"Probably fucking the new Bobs," Mort said with a sigh.

Puffing on his cigarette and releasing the smoke, Christopher snickered. "Doin' the final fuckin' consultation. Makin' sure them bitches live up to their fuckin' title."

After lighting the joint, Val inhaled, then handed it to Christopher. He set his cigarette in the ashtray, then hit the joint.

"You ever tempted to do the *'final consultations,'* Christopher?" Johnnie asked once he'd taken his puff. "We're still men. Still human."

Johnnie and that fucking human shit. "How 'bout I fuck you up and turn you into a fuckin' ghost? Cuz, you know, this human bullshit work the fuck on my ass." Mainly because it *always* involved Megan.

"Fuck off, motherfucker," Johnnie growled. "You know exactly what I'm saying. You have to miss being with other women sometimes."

Mort settled his elbows on the table, hit the joint, then gave it back to Val. "Do you?"

"Yeah, John Boy," Val began in a choked voice, talking on an inhale. "You can't have it both ways. You can't have Kendall and other bitches, too."

"I don't want any other woman," Johnnie insisted. "But Kendall—"

"But Kendall nothin'," Christopher snapped. "You either cryin' cuz she gone or cryin' cuz she here. What the fuck you want? I don't miss other bitches. If I ain't ever met Megan, I woulda still been fuckin' everything I see and I wouldna known what me and Megan got. Not knowin' it, I wouldna missed it. Although Megan disagree. She think I woulda ended up with Kiera."

Finishing his beer, Christopher went for more, considering Megan's belief. He had cared for Kiera and Ellen, but he'd picked them to be his women at random. They'd been at the bar one night and he'd fucked them the night before. He'd enjoyed their company and he'd been lonely, so he'd made the offer, with the stipulation that they had to be with him together or not at all. Although Megan didn't like either of them, she'd tolerated Kiera better and thought Christopher felt a little more for the dark-haired beauty than he had for Ellen.

Johnnie frowned upon Christopher's return to the table. "Megan really said that about Kiera?"

"Why the fuck shouldn't she? Ki was a good girl and she ain't deserved how she went out. Neither Ellen. But, fuck, I took them two for me, so, yeah, I cared 'bout them in a way. Don't mean I agree with Megan that me and Kiera woulda ended up together."

Curious, Johnnie turned to Mort. "Do you talk to Bailey about Char?"

"We don't make it a daily fucking discussion, but, yeah. Once I told Bailey about Charlemagne, I stopped hiding shit from her. She wanted to know about her. My feelings. All of that. Women curious, brother."

Next, Johnnie focused on Val. "You talk to anybody about Zoann?"

"Nope, cuz she the only bitch I ever loved."

Christopher wasn't sure what Johnnie was getting at, but he decided to open the closet so another fucking skeleton could drop out. "You ever go into detail with Kendall 'bout Megan?"

"She's much better, so I don't want to poke the lion."

"You ever want to?" Mort asked.

"Sometimes," Johnnie admitted, then slid his gaze to Christopher. "Something will remind me of those days I spent with her. I can't listen to ICP without thinking of Megan singing *Santa's a Fat Bitch* to me."

A scene Christopher had walked upon and ended up punching the fuck out of Johnnie over. "Don't mean nothin'. I hear *Voodoo Child* and I think of Ki and Ellen. They had some good pussy and I fuckin' swore they used their cunts to put on fuckin' spell on my ass." That wasn't the only reason. "That's also what the fuck was playin' right before I met Megan."

"Everything always goes back to Megan," Johnnie said with slight resentment. "You can't even reminiscence about another woman's pussy without bringing her up."

"And you still hate knowin' I got her and you didn't."

"That insinuates disloyalty to Kendall and that's a misplaced thought. I love my wife. She's just been difficult the past week and I don't know why."

So, apparently, Kendall hadn't told Johnnie about not taking her medicine. It fucking figured. "When the fuck that bitch not difficult?"

Johnnie scowled.

"Listen up, Johnnie. Ain't nothin' better than havin' a woman who know you inside and fuckin' out. Or knowin' her the same way. I don't know what the fuck goin' through your fuckin' head, but you love Kendall. I know that. That cunt love you, too, so don't fuck up with her. Kendall work my last fuckin' nerve. If I never got to look in her bitchy face again, I'd fuckin' dance naked in the fuckin' rain. Do that fuckin' dance I saw Megan and Bailey doin'. The Nae-Nae, I think?"

Mort guffawed. "Fuck, Prez, I wanna see that shit."

Johnnie wasn't as amused. "That's my wife, motherfucker," he snarled, and Mort stopped his loud fucking laughing.

Christopher thought for a moment, trying to find fucking words that would snap Johnnie back. "Your woman might be a fuckin' psycho bitch, but shit wouldna been the same without her fuckin' ass 'round this motherfucker. Each of them girls bring something fuckin' special. Your bitch do, too."

"That's why you almost fucking strangled her."

"I ain't said *I* fuckin' liked what the fuck she brought. But Kendall add her own flavor to the shit." Flipping Mort and Val off at their shocked expressions at what sounded like a defense of Kendall, Christopher continued. "That shit for you to think, Johnnie. Not my ass."

"I love Kendall so much, but she says she has to talk to me later. With the way she's been acting, suppose she decides to leave me?"

Mort rolled his eyes. "Stop being a little bitch. Red not leaving your dumb ass."

"Yeah," Val agreed. "Zoann tells me shit like that about needing to talk. It makes me nervous, but I don't ever think she's leaving me. Last serious conversation was about some expensive-as-fuck school that she wants to send Ryan to."

Megan had had that same fucking conversation with him. "That must be the same school Megan sending CJ to."

"It is, Outlaw," Val told him.

"The school Kendall and I have chosen for Rory has a waiting list. Kendall said not just anyone can get in. Charlotte Redding sits on the board, so Rory should have no problem getting in."

Not with their attorney's fucking snob of a wife pushing shit.

Christopher sighed. “Once a snob, always a snob, huh, Johnnie?”

He shrugged. “I’ve always been in favor of education.”

“Your ass just spoiling for a fight,” Mort said to Johnnie, tapping his fingers on the table.

“Ima ignore the dig, Mort, so don’t fuckin’ sweat it.”

“It wasn’t a dig, Christopher,” Johnnie barked. “Not unless you’re self-conscious about it. My words wouldn’t get to you if you didn’t give a fuck about not finishing school.”

“Nice,” Val said sarcastically.

“Fuck you, assfuck,” Christopher growled. “Think ‘bout what the fuck you sayin’, cuz the same go with you and your bitch. Ain’t no reason for you to fuckin’ worry over her wantin’ to talk to you unless there’s something there not quite fuckin’ right. Otherwise, you wouldn’t be so fuckin’ sensitive. If there ain’t no smoke, there ain’t no fire. Judgin’ from your fuckin’ words, it’s smoky like a motherfucker, which mean a blaze roarin’ all ‘round your ass.”

That shut the shit down immediately.

After a few minutes of silence in which Mortician returned to his roots and played bartender, Johnnie changed the subject.

“We got any motherfuckers to kill? I need the edge taken off. I may need to start something just to have someone to fuck up.”

Mort sat back in his seat, happily drinking his last pint of his special vodka. “Fuck, that’s a new one.”

“What, Mort?” Christopher asked.

“An elitist sociopath.”

Johnnie glared at Mort but didn’t comment.

Val smacked Johnnie’s back. “I think he got you pegged.”

“Fuck off. I’m being fucking serious and you assholes are making fun of me.”

"We not making fun of you any more than you doing with us," Mort pointed out, trying to deflect the fact that most of the digs had been at Christopher.

Tired of the conversation, Christopher glanced at the time and scowled. "I know them motherfuckers better come soon. I want in Megan's pussy, sooner rather than later. I prefer her awake all the way when I fuck her."

Johnnie threw Christopher a dirty look.

Mort took a casual sip of vodka. "Why Meggie girl such a fucking touchy subject with you?"

"She isn't. I'm just sick of hearing about Christopher fucking her every day. You don't hear me talking about Kendall like that. Val doesn't talk about Zoann. Mort—"

"Say how much he fuck Bailey all the fuckin' time," Christopher interrupted, "so shut the fuck up."

"I do. You just don't pay as much attention to that because it doesn't involve Red or Meggie," Mort agreed. "I think part of your problem is Red forced you to get over Meggie, instead of letting it come natural."

"No. No one can force me to do shit. I got over Megan because I wanted to."

"No, motherfucker, you got over Megan cuz I woulda fucked you up if you ain't." Worse than he was considering at the moment.

"Psycho stalker Wildman has entered the building," Val chortled.

Christopher flipped Val off. "You got over Megan cuz she told your ass to in that fuckin' cave you took her to when you wanted to know if Kendall would like it. The same fuckin' evenin' you told my girl to help you tell me we was half-brothers."

Johnnie's mouth fell open. "She told you about that?"

"Yeah, she told me everything. How she let you touch her mouth and give her a small fuckin' kiss. Her words was *I let*

Johnnie go and told him to let me go too." Remembering her anguish, Christopher sighed. Because for all her perfection, she had one major fucking flaw and he was looking at the motherfucker. "I fuckin' left her with you." No one would ever know his regret. The chain of events afterward was his fault. "She got attached to your fuckin' ass. If I ain't come back when I did, I might've lost her. To you."

Johnnie lifted a brow.

Playing off his resentment, Christopher downed some tequila, then shrugged. "On the other fuckin' hand, you think she wasn't likin' the fact that both of us motherfuckers wanted her? She did. Most girls would." The situation was so complicated, it was sometimes hard for Christopher to work out in his head. The way Megan loved, idolized, and worshipped Christopher didn't change a certain fact. "I fuckin' accepted Megan loved you a long fuckin' time ago. Megan fuckin' adore me the way I adore her. If she loved you a little at one time, I ain't begrudgin' her that."

"Why are you telling me this?"

"Cuz. It goes back to your favorite fucking word. We *human.* Love, marriage, relationships, and commitment hard as fuck, cuz we complicate shit. We pretend shit one way and not another. We don't listen to what the other motherfucker sayin'. Or we think how we feel more important than how they feel. You cryin' in here, thinkin' Kendall leavin'. Instead of learnin' from what the fuck you and her been through and knowin' she stayin'. Cuz, Johnnie, your woman ain't leavin'. If I know that, why can't you? Why the fuck you doubt that bitch so much?"

"Think about this, Christopher. Iona left me for another man. Megan claimed she had feelings for me, but she refused to act on them because of you. And Kendall? She left me. Granted, I never loved Iona. I liked her and cared about her, but I *did* love Megan and everything I decided for Kendall was because I love her. But I've been on edge. We all have because of Digger."

A sore spot with Mortician, he immediately stiffened upon hearing his brother's name. Any mention of Digger made Mort tense. Christopher understood. As angry as he was with the assfuck, Mort loved his brother.

"We need to do something about him. Any headway, Mort?"

Mortician looked to Christopher at Johnnie's question.

"Most I fuckin' know is the motherfucker somewhere in Canada with Sharper and Osti," Christopher answered without much inflection as the door opened and Arrow and Cash walked in.

Johnnie barely paused to greet them. "Why? Riley can put all his resources together and find their exact location. Riley's ex-military. Ex-law enforcement. He has a lot of contacts, so why aren't you making him utilize them?"

"What he said," Arrow greeted, heading to the bar and finding a bottle of gin. "Breaking in new bitches might be pleasurable, but not for the fucking reason we had to do it. Six fucking girls deserting us thanks to all the rumors going around."

"Shut up, Arrow," Cash demanded. "We said we weren't bringing any of this up."

Christopher frowned. "What fuckin' rumors?" The interruption on his anniversary had been about fucking rumors. "I already addressed that. The club ain't closin'. We still makin' money and sendin' out the brothers' portions. Next payment due in a week. I ain't ever stopped them from comin' and pickin' up their dollars." That was the last rumor. That things had gotten so bad, Christopher wouldn't allow anyone on premises at any time if they didn't live somewhere on the property. "What I wanna fuckin' know is where the motherfuckin' rumors comin' from."

"The brothers," Arrow snapped. "What are they supposed to think? It's been months since we had a social or a barbeque. Since we had any fucking event with the Bobs."

"Club members can come on premises any time they fuckin' want," Christopher countered. "Ain't been enough around to call on them bitches."

"Club's on lockdown, Outlaw," Arrow gritted out. "That severely limits shit. Why? Because of goddamn Digger."

"No, because of Sharper," Mortician growled, coming to his feet.

Christopher stood, too, and situated himself between Arrow and Mort, silently warning both of them not to fight.

"Any specifics about where in Canada he's at?"

"Arrow, I swear you need to shut the fuck up sometimes."

He wouldn't back down. "Well, is there?"

"Nope, none. When we find the motherfuckers, your ass gonna know."

"You looking?" Arrow pressed sharply

Not enough. Instead of confessing to the slack, Christopher glared at him. "I'll let you fuckin' know if we fuckin' find exactly where the fuck they at."

"Arrow, back the fuck off," Johnnie warned, standing next to Christopher. "Enjoy being alive for a while longer."

Stiffening, Arrow narrowed his eyes and clenched his fists, his hand settling at his side. "What the fuck's that supposed to mean?"

Coldness dropped into Johnnie's gaze. "That once we re-engage Sharper, lives will be lost. I support Christopher's decision to leave things as they are."

Publicly, yeah. Privately or around Mort and Val, Johnnie gave him hell about it.

"We're preparing for the battle," Johnnie continued. "Reinforced gates and doors. More complicated codes. We're even trying to secure a location for any girls Sharper might have in his possession. But all of this takes time and we have more than just Digger and Sharper to think about. We have the church. Once Sharper re-emerges, his loyal members will want him back."

Yeah, an article appeared here and there about the congregation's need for their esteemed leader's return. They waited for that day like they waited for the Second Coming.

Another mistake of Christopher's was he should've blown that church the fuck up when he'd gotten rid of the motherfucker's house.

"You say all this shit now, Johnnie," Arrow shouted, "but that's not what the fuck I heard when Cash and me walked in."

Unlike when Mort and Arrow were about to go at it, Christopher stepped out of the way for Johnnie. Arrow needed to keep his fucking mouth shut. If he wanted to fuck with Johnnie, all the better. Johnnie was having fucking withdrawals because he hadn't killed anyone. If Arrow was stupid enough to provoke Johnnie, then he needed fucking up.

"Say that shit again, motherfucker," Johnnie said coolly. "I dare you. I'm a grown fucking man and I don't have to answer to you about what I talk to Christopher about. You have a fucking problem with that? Step up to me and tell me about it."

Red suffused Arrow's face, but he raised his hands and backed away.

"Yeah, I thought fucking not," Johnnie sneered.

Arrow stiffened but remained silent.

"Okay, this the fuckin' cue for me to tell motherfuckers to get the fuck out."

"My ass know where I'm not wanted," Mort quipped, stretching. He didn't look as happy and relaxed as he had before Arrow started with his bullshit.

The alarm beeped right before a voice said *front door open*.

Christopher yanked open the door to his man cave, colliding with Bunny, who was running toward the staircase, with her head down.

He grabbed her arms to steady her. When she lifted her head, tears glistened in her eyes and her throat worked, as if she wanted to talk but couldn't.

"Megan been lookin' for you."

Her chin wobbled and her nose reddened a little more, but she faked a smile. "Tr-Trader needed me," she said hoarsely.

Christopher narrowed his eyes as he released her. Something wasn't fucking right.

Cash stepped out of the man cave and searched Bunny from head-to-toe. "You look like somebody killed your best friend," he said, blowing smoke in the air from the cigarette he'd lit.

Wrapping her arms around her waist, she shook her head.

Johnnie stood on the other side of her. "You sure you're okay, sweetheart?"

She nodded and attempted another smile. "F-fine."

They stood silent, waiting for a moment, watching her closely, attempting to figure out just what was wrong. She was a tall, busty girl with a pretty face and a warm personality. Christopher knew a lot about her past, more than even she realized and not only from what Megan had confided in him.

"I know what's up, girl," Mort began on a teasing note. "You didn't want to do all that fucking cooking and decorating for the shower tomorrow, so you stayed away."

She forced a laugh. "Yeah, that's it, Mort," she agreed, fear and pain in her voice.

Fuck, if Megan saw Bunny so hurt and scared, she'd fucking flip. Seeing the girl now, Christopher suspected Trader *was* abusing Bunny in some way.

"You look kinda fucked up, babe." More than kinda. Completely. "Go upstairs to the room you use and rest. I'll tell Megan you here all safe and sound."

Still holding her stomach, Bunny nodded, then stumbled away.

"What's up with that?" Johnnie asked, watching as she reached the staircase at the end of the hall and started up.

"Trader," Christopher, Cash, Val, and Mort chorused.

"Don't see how," Arrow offered. "Trader was with me and Cash this evening."

"Getting his cock sucked by those bitches?" Christopher asked.

"Yup," Arrow chortled. "Each bitch took a turn at our dicks and a go at each other's pussies."

Christopher knew exactly how it worked.

"Well, fuck, maybe Trader went and told Bunny," Mort said. "Something have her looking like that."

"I don't know, Mort," Christopher returned. "She look like she in physical pain."

"It's not our fucking place to interfere," Arrow reminded them sharply. "If he's fucking over her and beating her ass, that's between them."

"Fuckin' over her? Yeah," Christopher agreed. "Hittin' her? No. The only reason I tolerate that motherfucker is because of Bunny. He's a fuckin' asshole."

"I agree," Johnnie said viciously. "Every time he sees Kendall, he comes on to her."

"So you see, Arrow," Cash began politely, "there's more than enough cause to fuck him up if he's hurting Bunny."

"We'll just talk to the motherfucker first," Christopher said, shutting Arrow the fuck up before he started in with his bullshit of staying out of Trader and Bunny's business. "Feel him the fuck out."

"Fine," Arrow said resentfully. The motherfucker loved to stir shit up. "I'm on my way to Dinah."

"Y'all fucking?" Mort asked, picking up on Arrow's insinuating tone just as Christopher had.

Arrow shrugged.

"Fuck me. If you stickin' your cock in her, you better not fuckin' hurt her," Christopher warned.

"Since I'm her fucking babysitter, I need something to do with her."

"That's kind of criminal, if you ask me," Val said, rejoining the conversation. He'd been silent, texting Zoann. Although he hadn't said who he was texting, he didn't have to. When they were apart, those two texted like school kids.

"I didn't fucking ask you," Arrow snarled.

"Just saying, brother," Val went on, not bothered by Arrow's hostility. "I mean the bitch just got some sense back when Roxy knocked it into her. I don't know how long you been getting in her pussy, but if it was while she was a fucking basket case, that's fucking criminal."

Christopher folded his arms. Val had taken the words right out of his mouth.

"Wasn't like that, Outlaw," Arrow swore, scratching behind his ear and looking at the floor. "She just had things I fucking needed and I didn't know it until I started really listening to her."

"What the fuck that mean?" And why did Christopher feel as if Arrow meant something entirely different?

Arrow heaved in a breath. "A connection to K-P," he said. "She talked about him so much. I miss that motherfucker every day. Being with her makes me feel closer to him."

"I understand," Christopher said quietly, still not liking the gut feeling there was an underlying motivation to Arrow's statement. Maybe, it was just his guilt that he hadn't done as much as he should have to get to Sharper, even before Digger rejoined his father. He put his hand on Arrow's shoulder. "We movin' against Sharper in a few weeks. We gonna take him down once and for all."

"I think Sharper had my brother killed because of the letters."

The letters Bailey had been kidnapped over. The ones she'd found in K-P's closet.

The ones now missing.

"You still have them, don't you?" Arrow asked as if he'd read Christopher's mind.

"I do." And he did. He just didn't fucking know where. Other than being the reason for Sharper taking Bailey, Christopher saw no real value in the motherfuckers. Yeah, it exposed the fact that 1.) Logan was a crazy fucking racist who hated him and almost everyone; 2.) Logan and Sharper had been lovers until shit went bad; 3.) Sharper was the boss of a very extensive sex ring.

While Christopher would tip off the badges after they got Sharper in the meatshack, the rest of the shit was of little importance. Sharper was a dead fucking man walking, anyway, so why worry about the fucking letters? They were somewhere on premises. Probably still in some of the boxes of shit in the storage shed of the house, waiting to be unpacked. He could always tip off the badges about the sex ring *now*, but they might get to Sharper first and Christopher wanted his hands on that motherfucker for what his men had subjected Megan to.

"I'm heading out," Johnnie said, already walking toward the door.

"I'll walk with you," Mort called.

"Yeah, me, too," Val added.

"Hey, Curly, Larry, and Moe!" Cash taunted, laughing like an ass.

"Fuck off, son," Mortician called, stomping ahead and opening the door.

Johnnie smirked at Cash. "I prefer Athos, Porthos, and Aramis."

"Three Stooges or Three Musketeers don't mean shit," Christopher said, shaking his head. "It all amount to three motherfuckers walkin' home together."

"Kendall and I took Rory to a play of the Three Musketeers. We want him cultured and well-read."

"What the fuck ever," Christopher said with a snort while Mort just rolled his eyes again.

"Give me fucking strength," Val groaned. "What the fuck's happened to you, John Boy? Wanting your son to call you by your name? Going to fucking plays? I walked in your house the other day and Opera was playing. *Fucking Opera*."

"Shut the fuck up," Johnnie spat. "Kendall wants our son exposed to the best life has to offer. It doesn't mean *I'm* changing."

The fuck it didn't, but whatever. He was still solid in the club so Johnnie could grow a fucking pussy to make Kendall happy and Christopher wouldn't care. "You motherfuckers finished?"

"We're leaving, Outlaw," Cash said soothingly. "Hold on to your dick."

"That's the fuckin' problem. I want Megan holdin' it."

"Good night!" Johnnie called, starting off a chorus of goodnights from the others.

"Good night, motherfuckers," Christopher said cheerfully, slamming the door behind them. "Fucking finally."

He walked the first floor, checking the locks on the doors and either turning off lights that shouldn't be on or turning on nightlights. Usually, CJ was with him for the nightly routine and Christopher missed his boy's help. In the kitchen, he uncovered some of the pans Roxy had left on the stove. She had a shitload of food here, so Christopher could only imagine how many bitches would invade the club tomorrow. A couple of Probates were arriving early to search cars and use metal detection wands.

He couldn't be too careful where Megan's life was concerned.

Finding a spoon, he dipped it into the spiced up rice. Jambalaya, he remembered Roxy calling it. The shit was good and peppery, with shrimp and smoked sausage in it. Next, he moved to the red beans. She used some kind of fucked up meat to season the beans with. Pickled pig tails or rib tips. The beans alone were delicious, thick and creamy, with a shitload of butter. Although he wanted a taste, he'd wait until tomorrow. The shit made him fart up a storm.

Sneaking a praline, he stuffed it partially in his mouth and then carefully recovered the food he'd peeked at. Roxy would have his ass if he didn't. She'd probably counted her pralines, to know if he stole one or not, but fuck it. It was in *his* house. Fair fucking game.

By the time he reached the second floor to do his nightly sweep, he'd finished the candy. As he passed Bunny's door, he heard sobs.

Pausing, he stopped to listen. Raised his hand to knock, then decided against it. He really didn't know what to say to her or what to ask her. It was obvious she was hiding something. Perhaps, it was only Trader telling her about having the Bobs suck him off. Or, maybe, it was something more. Whatever the case, it was fucking time to get to the bottom of exactly what the motherfucker was doing to Bunny.

Tomorrow would be soon enough. Trader was hanging with him, Johnnie, Mort, Val, Cash, and Stretch, so Christopher would have a lot of opportunity.

On the third floor, he checked on the twins and noticed CJ's empty bed. Knowing exactly where he'd find his boy, he tucked the covers around Rule and Rebel. In his room, Megan and CJ were curled together in bed, asleep. He took his boy into his arms and carried him to the nursery, laying him carefully in bed.

"Night-night, Daddy," CJ murmured, opening his eyes for just a second then closing them again.

Christopher stroked his boy's head and nodded. "Night-night, boy," he whispered gruffly before returning to Megan and undressing.

Cock already hard, he climbed into bed, pulling her into his arms. She shifted against him, laying her cheek against his chest.

"Christopher?" she mumbled sleepily.

He answered by rolling onto her. Automatically, she opened her legs and cradled him between her thighs.

Groaning, he sank into her hot pussy, feeling like the luckiest motherfucker in the entire world.

Bunny stared at herself in the bathroom mirror, located in the private guestroom she used whenever she slept at Meggie's and Outlaw's house or didn't care to see Trader. And she definitely didn't want to look at that asshole any time soon. Logically, she knew her reprieve had only been overnight. At some point today, she'd see him and she'd have to pretend all was well between them. If she wanted to continue to have access to her friends in the club.

Studying her reflection closer, she swallowed, happy the makeup covered her bruises. Yesterday, she'd been looking forward to Bailey's baby shower. Normally, she enjoyed club events. Today, she wished to stay in bed and lick her wounds from Trader's latest beating.

This time, at the expense of her baby.

Tears pricked her eyes at her deep sense of loss. She thought of calling her mother, but to say what? That Virginia had been right about Trader, and Bunny hadn't?

She'd put her parents through so much, she didn't deserve their forgiveness.

"Yo', Bunny, where the fuck you at?"

Wincing at the sound of Outlaw's voice, Bunny opened the bathroom door, startled to find him in her room. He never entered, respecting her privacy. But she'd stumbled in late, last night, hours after she'd been due.

Her arrival interrupted Johnnie, Mortician, Cash, Stretch, Arrow, and Val's departure. She'd been in so much pain she could barely speak. Somehow, she'd managed a smile.

Somehow.

Just like she did now. "Is Little Man looking for me?"

Trader's words kept replaying in her head and she knew he was right about Outlaw. No way in hell would the man allow anyone not connected with the club near his wife, under the circumstances. And how could Bunny continue to be associated with the club if she and Trader split? Once he got another old lady that would leave her as little more than a hang around chick. In other words, Club Ass.

"What the fuck wrong?" She jumped at Outlaw's bark. "You fuckin' heard me?"

"No, sorry." Attempting a smile hurt her face. "Can you repeat what you said?"

She flushed at his intense stare. His green eyes narrowed, his gaze touching on every angle of her face.

The insanely gorgeous man intimidated her sometimes, although he didn't do it on purpose. Like now.

"Roxy missed the breakfast Megan cooked cuz her ass just got here. She asked if you fuckin' ate. Since we ain't fuckin' reachin' you, I came the fuck to check on you." He opened his mouth to say something else, then snapped it shut, scrutinizing her again. "Roxy!" he yelled suddenly, startling her again.

Trader was turning her into a nervous wreck.

"You don't have to call her." Bunny started past Outlaw. The fast movements intensified her pain and she staggered. Her stomach hurt so bad. Unable to go forward, she paused and clutched her belly, breathing heavily. "I'm going check on Meggie and the kids, then I'll find Roxy," she panted, after the ache eased.

"You look kinda fucked up, babe."

She laughed nervously. "I drank too much last night."

"Get the fuck in here, Roxy!" he called again.

Roxy glided into the room, annoyance creasing her brow. Hands on hips, she scolded Outlaw. "Your ass really need to learn fucking manners, Outlaw."

In response, he folded his arms and nodded to Bunny.

Roxy focused on Bunny and straightened, her brown eyes veering between exasperation and anger.

Shame burned into Bunny at Roxy's look. In the months she'd known Bailey's mom, Bunny hadn't been able to hide much from the discerning woman whenever she visited. With Bailey pregnant again and still in school, those visits had increased.

"What the fuck you doing in Bunny's room, anyway, Outlaw?"

"She ain't been answerin' her fuckin' phone. Ain't been fuckin' answerin' my callin. Megan callin'. CJ kickin' the fuck outta her door. I thought her fuckin' ass was in here fuckin' dead." He made a slow circuit around her. "Ain't knowin' she was in here fuckin' fucked up."

Tears filled Bunny's eyes at Outlaw's casual statement. Of course, it didn't surprise her that he only had sympathy for Meggie. He made her pain sound like no big deal, though she hadn't confirmed his suspicions. "I'm fine." She waved, so far away from fine she cringed as she uttered the words and then pushed out another laugh. But Gabe, Meggie, Roxy, CJ, Rebel, and Rule were her only family. She didn't want to lose them like she'd lost her mom and dad. "Really. I just got into an argument last night with this bitch coming on to Trader."

Outlaw stared at her for another moment, before he nodded, buying into her story. "Motherfucker downstairs, babe."

She flinched. God, she didn't want to see Trader today. She needed to regain her strength and what little self-worth she had left. She needed to overcome her physical pain and her emotional wound, both because of her lost baby.

"He fuckin' workin' with us while Bailey shower goin' the fuck on," Outlaw went on.

At least she'd be surrounded by everyone so Trader wouldn't brutalize her. He'd treat her with a casual disregard.

Roxy cleared her throat, her jeans and white sweater, along with her ponytail, making her appear almost as young as her daughter. "Can I talk to you?"

"Later," Bunny promised. "After I set up everything."

"Yeah, let's get down-fuckin-stairs now."

She swallowed again, steeling herself to deal with Trader after he'd killed the baby she wanted so badly.

Outlaw nodded to Bunny. "I gotta talk to you and Trader 'bout something."

"Okay."

Not sure she wanted to know what Outlaw needed to talk to them about, Bunny hung her head and followed him, quite aware of Roxy behind her. At the bottom of the staircase, she heard the laughter of John Boy, Arrow, Cash, Stretch, Val, and Mortician, having been around them long enough to distinguish how they each sounded.

They were in the breakfast room, empty plates from the breakfast Meggie cooked still on the table. Val was just finishing a beer. Cash and Stretch drank coffee, while Trader and Arrow shared a bottle of whiskey. Outlaw, Johnnie, and Mortician had half empty juice glasses at their places at the table. Whether it was alcohol free or not, Bunny didn't know.

"'Bout ready to head out, fuckheads?" Outlaw's question halted conversation. "Megan should be bringin' CJ down to me in ten fuckin' minutes of so. He helpin' her with Rule. You motherfuckers help Roxanne and Bunny get shit to the clubhouse."

No one responded as they all focused on Bunny.

"You okay, sweetheart?" Johnnie asked slowly, getting to his feet. He wore a suit today, looking like the CEO of a Fortune 500 company, instead of the vice president of an MC. Not a light blond hair stood out of place on his head and his silver-gray eyes held nothing but concern. "Bunny?"

She squirmed under his scrutiny, very aware of Trader's presence and his amusement. "Fine, John Boy," she answered, wishing her voice sounded stronger.

She lifted her gaze to Trader and a little tremble shuddered through her. His eyes were gray, too, but darker, still perfect for his handsome face. Cruelness twisted his full mouth. Or, maybe, only she felt that way because none of the others even blinked an eye at his look.

Her hand went to her belly, her fingers pressing where her baby should be.

The realization she fucking hated Trader now struck her and she closed her eyes. She couldn't hang onto him. It didn't matter what walking away from the asshole cost her. If he hadn't wanted their baby, fine. *She* had, and he'd brutally taken it away from her.

"Bunny, you not looking too good, girl," Mortician told her, studying her just like the rest of them were. He lit a cigarette and his wedding band glistened in the sunlight coming in from the window.

Her glance flitted from Mortician's wedding band to Val's, then Johnnie's, and, finally, Outlaw's. They wore the symbols of the unions so proudly. She flexed her hand and blinked at her bare fingers.

Maybe, if she'd listened to her parents, she'd be married, too. Maybe, she'd be a mom. Now, she mightn't ever be. How could she trust another man again? More than that, how could she trust her own judgment about men?

Arms wrapped around her. Soft, motherly arms and she turned to Roxy, accepting her comfort when she'd rejected her mother's. She hadn't wanted to hear the truth.

"It's okay, sugar," Roxy swore. "Later, I promise I'm going to cut that motherfucker for you," she whispered. "I don't know what the fuck he done, but I know he did it and I'm not letting him get away with it."

She smiled at Roxy's vehemence, but straightened, determined to pull herself together. Stretch limped to her and thumbed away a tear. Until then, she hadn't realized she cried.

"You're sure nothing's wrong?" he asked, still handsome, though the slight crookedness of his nose made it obvious it had been broken. A long scar ran along the side of his face. The severe beating he'd gotten last year had left permanent marks on him. One of his legs had been broken in so many places, he'd never again bare a perfect gait.

Outlaw lit a cigarette and released the smoke. She wished he'd let up studying her. Even when she looked away, she felt his unnerving contemplation. "Bunny, Trader, we gotta get the fuck outside. Talk a fuckin' minute," he ordered.

Not wanting to ruin Bailey's shower, Bunny cooperated. Outlaw led the way with Trader right behind him. At least she didn't have to look at his awful smirk as he followed Outlaw's dictates.

Head bowed, Bunny trooped in the wake of the two men, the others following her. If Outlaw wanted her and Trader to participate in some activity, then…then she'd have to decline.

Stepping outside, she inhaled. Winter still hung heavily in the air. They stopped not far from the entry door of the house. In the distance, the dogs barking ferociously, and Outlaw frowned in the direction of the animals' fenced in area. They were still penned in because Megan and the rest of them hadn't left the property yet.

"Stretch, Cash, see what the fuck up with them barking motherfuckers," Outlaw instructed, puffing his smoke.

Trader settled his arms around Bunny's shoulders, scowling at her when she pushed him away. His gaze held a dire warning before he smiled at Outlaw. "Soooo, brother, what can we do for you?" he asked, as if he were Outlaw's equal.

Trader being in Outlaw's inner circle had gone to his head. That's when he'd become a violent pig as if he could do anything he chose and wouldn't face consequences. One day, she'd make him pay for what he stole from her.

"Ain't what the fuck you can do for me, motherfucker," Outlaw responded, tossing his cigarette.

The uncertainty creeping onto Trader's face satisfied Bunny.

"What's up, Prez?" Trader asked, a little humbler.

Outlaw smiled, a mere baring of his teeth that raised the hairs on Bunny's arms. "This 'bout your woman."

"Me?" Bunny squeaked nervously. Not only would she have to leave the club, she'd have to leave the state if Trader got in trouble because of her. He'd kill her.

"Her?" Trader spat, glaring at her. "This cunt is just a cunt, Outlaw. What can I s—"

Before he finished, gunfire interrupted and blood sprayed everywhere. A scream caught in the back of Bunny's throat as Trader's head seemed to explode right in front of her a moment before his body dropped to the ground.

"What the fuck, Christopher?" Johnnie snarled, glaring at his brother and swiping at the bits of brain and bone on his cheeks.

"This motherfucker been fuckin' her up," Outlaw snapped, indicating Bunny with his nine. "I told dead assfuck Megan like Bunny and to leave her the fuck alone. Ain't my fault motherfucker ain't listened."

"You and your head shots, Prez," Mort grumbled, scrubbing at the gore on his chin.

At Mort's annoyed statement, the scream she'd been holding in finally tumbled out.

"Babe, ain't mean for you to see this shit and I definitely ain't wanted to do this shit in front my girl's house," Outlaw said apologetically as Roxy hugged Bunny. "I was just wantin' confirmation that he was doin' you shit. But I fuckin' couldn't take hearin' that motherfucker another fuckin' minute."

"We need to make a public service announcement," Mortician said, as they circled Trader's body and frowned.

"What the fuck you talkin' 'bout, Mort?" Outlaw asked, torn between irritation and amusement.

"Let's see *Traveler* and *Trader*. Two for fucking two. Public service announcement should go something like 'attention, motherfuckers, if your road name start with tr, chances running high you'll be fucked up. Continue at your own risk'."

Outlaw snickered. "You might be right, Mort," he said, before calling, "Roxanne? Bring Bunny in-fuckin-side and figure out what the fuck Trader did to her then get her the fuck in bed."

"Outlaw's right," Roxy soothed. "Don't worry about anything today. We got every-fuckin-thing covered. You need to fuckin' recover."

"Trader—" she started a little hysterically, knowing he lay feet away from her, dead.

"Don't you feel guilty about his dead ass," Roxanne ordered.

She felt guilt and relief and guiltier *because* of her relief. Trader couldn't ever hurt her again and that relieved her. "He killed my baby!" Bunny finally sobbed, although she hadn't wanted him to die. At least, she didn't think she had.

Before anyone responded, more bullets began flying.

John Boy, Arrow, Val, and Stretch.

Digger watched as they grabbed their guns and fired in all directions, unsure where the threat came from. Bullets careened into each of them and they fell where they stood. Always ready to kill, Outlaw dove, bringing Roxy and Bunny down with him. He pulled his nine and fired, not even hesitating.

Digger didn't know any of the seven men whom his father had enlisted, but he watched two of them die before they knew what hit them. Judging from the damage, Digger suspected Outlaw had hollows in his chamber. His crack shot paid off right now.

Cash and Mortician scrambled for cover, bloodied but not too badly wounded. A small, frozen moat ringed the mansion that Outlaw had turned into a mini-fortress. If not for the snitch who'd given them the code to get into the gate, the shootings would've taken place as they all walked to the clubhouse. But Peyton and Sharper had been thorough in obtaining necessary information. An attack on the other side of Outlaw's property would've given them a chance at pursuit, without being as contained as one within the confines of the fence.

When Outlaw had walked outside earlier, Sharper hadn't given the immediate signal to attack. One, they'd been on their way to shut the fucking dogs up, but had taken cover when Cash and Stretch appeared. More importantly, they'd thought the old ladies and the children would shortly join them.

Digger had been positioned the farthest away from the house, so he knew they still didn't trust his loyalties. But then the dogs had been released and they'd had to act. It also gave Digger the excuse he needed to move closer to the house. Closer to Mort and Outlaw. It seemed as if he were escaping the dogs and finding safety.

Only minutes had passed. Minutes that seemed like a fucking eternity when he hadn't known if Mort had been hit or not. Sharper might tell his flock Mort's and Outlaw's stroke of luck was Divine Intervention. Digger saw it differently. This was his chance to get to one of them, warn them before it was too late.

Heart in throat, Digger went on the move again, darting from tree-to-tree.

Chaos scrambled the entire scene with the Rottweilers barking and growling, too close to Digger for him not to be in imminent danger.

Bunny held her head and turned in a circle where a couple of bodies lay on the frozen moat, screaming. At first, he thought she'd been shot. But, no, she was just hysterical, close to Digger with his latest movement.

After taking cover wherever possible, Mort, Outlaw, and Cash continued firing their guns. Soon, they'd run out of ammo and wouldn't have time to reload.

Meanwhile, on the ground…

On the ground, Johnnie, Arrow, Val, and Stretch lay unmoving and bleeding.

Out of the corner of his eyes, Digger saw one of his father's mercenaries aim at Mortician. Horrified, Digger didn't hesitate or second-guess. He fired, dropping the man but also giving away his position.

The moment Outlaw stopped firing, another one of the men rushed him. The stupid motherfucker didn't understand Outlaw's lethalness. Yeah, Sharper wanted him taken alive. That didn't mean they couldn't challenge Outlaw in an attempt to best him and show him who was boss.

And that cost him. Outlaw got him in a headlock and twisted. The man fell to the ground, twitching, his neck at a precarious position.

The gunfire died down, the sudden lull broken by eerie moans that the wind carried on the breeze, a harbinger of the death already come and the killing yet to be done. Outlaw turned in a three-hundred and sixty degree circle, squinting in every direction.

"Psstt," Digger called.

Switching clips, Outlaw snapped his head toward Digger's location just as Meggie rushed outside.

"Get the fuck inside, Megan! Now!"

Gritting his teeth, Digger prayed she complied. This was the day she was supposed to die and if Sharper didn't want Outlaw to witness her death, he'd already be cut down.

"Christopher!" Meggie screamed.

"Go, Megan," Outlaw yelled again. "This shit ain't contained."

As she thought it was since she'd come outside once the gunfire ceased.

"Leave, Meggie girl," Digger whispered. From her expression, she was torn between complying with Outlaw's demands and rushing to his side.

"Johnnie!" Kendall cried.

"Oh my God!"

That might be Zoann. Digger knew she and Val had worked out their shit, but he hadn't been around her enough to know her voice. Besides, the women were coming from all directions, sitting ducks, their kids right behind them, crying and screaming.

Outlaw yanked the gun from the hand of the man he'd killed. "Get the fuck inside Megan," he commanded a third time.

Movement caught Digger's eye and he turned. Peyton zigzagged through the trees, raising her own weapon, aiming it at Meggie's head.

"Get down!" Gunfire drowned out Digger's words.

As Peyton fired, Little Man grabbed Meggie around her legs. Instead of her head, the bullet hit her chest and she stumbled back, her eyes widening. Blood bloomed on her cream-colored shirt. She stared at herself then at Outlaw before crumpling to the ground.

*"**MEGAN!!!!**"*

Outlaw's inhuman roar, as he rushed to his wife, curdled Digger's blood. He'd never heard a sound so filled with rage and anguish. The quick-moving events made it a hard scene for Digger to process.

Meggie. Kendall. Bailey. Zoann. Another chick who'd come outside with Bunny.

They were all down. Shot. Bleeding and not moving. Except Bunny, whom he couldn't find. Where was she? Digger scanned the bodies, not identifying one as her.

"Mommie!" Little Man screamed, walking amongst the dead and wounded. Outlaw didn't seem to notice him, too busy cradling Meggie's limp body.

The kid's cries and his calls for 'MegAnn' and 'Law' mingled with the groans of the injured and voices of the survivors.

Needing to find Mort, Digger inched into the open, just as a bloodied girl with long brown hair stumbled into his line of vision.

"Little Man," Bunny cried, intermittent gunfire beginning again.

Unable to pinpoint anyone's locations anymore, Digger regretted losing sight of his father and the mercenaries. Knowing the positions of the club members would help, too.

They could all be moving forward to meet up in the middle and create one, big bloodbath.

Outlaw's son wandered closer to Digger, paying Bunny no attention. Tears streaked her cheeks as she dropped to the ground and crawled behind the kid.

"Kill the boy." Sharper's voice blared into Digger's earpiece. "You do it or I will."

Glancing around, Digger noted Sharper's position—nine o'clock and five feet away behind another tree.

He met his father's gaze. Sharper nodded to Digger, warning him without words to commence now. Digger's moment had arrived to show where his loyalties lay and redeem himself in Mort's and Outlaw's eyes, even if Digger had to sacrifice himself in the process. Unless a miracle happened, he had no chance of survival. Either Outlaw would kill him or Sharper. Maybe, even Peyton, Osti, or Tyler. First, he needed to save Little Man.

Digger nodded to his father and raised his gun, firing, his target on the mark enough where he missed both Bunny and Little Man but made it seem as if he'd done it by accident.

Bunny lunged for the kid, covering him with her body, as rapid gunfire started once more from all directions. Mort appeared from behind a tree, blowing his cover to protect Outlaw, who hadn't moved away from Meggie.

"Mark!" Tyler stopped Digger's forward motion to get Outlaw's son out of danger. "I'm going to kill him!" Bloodlust hardened his voice.

Digger followed Tyler's gaze and his heart sank, his worse fears coming to life. Fuck. The *him* Tyler wanted to kill was Mortician.

"Tyler, no!" Digger shouted, just as he and Cash caught sight of one another.

A bullet whizzed past him, aiming for Little Man, but too high. Another bullet, this time from Cash, brushed too close to Digger's head and sent bark flying.

The distraction gave Tyler time to slip away, weapon poised.

"Fuck!" Gun in hand, Digger scooped up Little Man, surprised when Bunny grabbed his legs and toppled him, fucking up his intentions to move the child out of the crossfire. Gunfire from behind him halted Cash's advance and he dove for cover.

"You sonofabitch!" Bunny screamed through her tears, digging her nails into Digger's jaws and scratching. "You're not hurting him."

The shock of her attack almost made him lose his grip on the struggling kid.

"Die, Lucas!" Tyler yelled, squeezing the trigger once before he dropped to the ground and disappeared in a cloud of blood.

"Tyler!" Digger hollered, still unable to release Outlaw's son, knowing, if he did, the kid was dead.

His nephew's groan floated to him and Digger sagged in relief, prioritizing the situation in his head. He'd find a safe haven for Little Man, then see to his nephew. If he could get to him…get him back to Mortician…the kid could be redeemed. He couldn't die out here.

But, fuck, Digger couldn't move. Between Bunny's hold and Little Man's kicking, he had no chance to go to Tyler and stop the blood flowing from his head.

Sharper paused over Tyler. Instead of bending to help him, he fired more rounds into his body, extinguishing all hope that Tyler might survive.

A bullet knocked Sharper back, but not completely. Shock marched across his face as blood spread along his arm. Ducking for cover, he turned to where Digger stood, narrowing his eyes at Outlaw's son. He aimed the gun at the child's head.

Shaking off the images, the horror, the hurt, Digger made a snap decision and shoved the boy to the ground. Another round of bullets fired and he prayed his father went down in the hail. Bunny grabbed Little Man in her arms and rolled backward. Not taking any chances, Digger followed Bunny, reaching her quickly. He jammed the gun her head, determined to escape before Sharper found a way to kill Bunny and Little Man.

"Get the kid," Digger snarled, low, his insides shaking but his hand steady. "Come with me or I'm blowing you the fuck away."

Peyton missed hitting Goldilocks in the head. At the last moment, the bitch moved. Or, maybe, Peyton had just been a bad shot, underestimating the girl's height.

Drowning out the shouts, the gunfire, the screaming women and kids, and the growling dogs, Peyton crept closer to where Outlaw cradled Megan. He didn't give a fuck that he was a sitting duck.

Where was Sharper? His goal had been achieved. Outlaw was suffering, falling to pieces, watching his wife die. Or…? Did Sharper want Outlaw to see his children die, too? Peyton couldn't remember.

Perhaps, that explained why none of the others had taken a shot at Outlaw.

But what about the kids? Why hadn't *they* been cut down yet? Six children mingled amongst the dead and dying, their snotty little noses glistening even in the gray day. She didn't know all the kids, but she recognized some of them. Harley with her head of black hair, cried over her mother, shaking her arm. The blonde-headed Rebel and her black-haired twin clung to Outlaw's legs.

Peyton doubted he knew he laid Megan on the ground and lifted his twins into his arms, hugging them tightly to him. His shoulders were shaking as he turned and ran with them inside the house, reappearing mere moments later, still in an absolute fog. The children stood in the doorway, screaming for him and their mother.

"Stay!" he ordered, calling out, "CJ, where you at?"

Yes, where was CJ? A quick glance revealed nothing.

Outlaw rounded up the other children and got them into the house, continuing to yell for his son.

As if he was so concerned for him. Once he got the children inside—minus CJ—he headed back toward Megan.

With more time, Peyton would sit back and confirm Goldilocks no longer breathed. But Peyton needed to escape. She felt as if she were the only one inside the gate of Outlaw's property. The others had probably retreated to raid the clubhouse and find those fucking letters and that key.

Determined to shoot Megan up close and personal, Peyton closed the distance between where she stood and where the girl lay. Nothing but the warmth of her blood against Peyton's skin would be acceptable. Then, maybe, she'd kill Outlaw...or take him hostage, fuck him, and make him beg for mercy before she shot him to death for abandoning Ellen.

So lost in her bloody vision, she didn't realize he'd spotted her, didn't know he'd reached her until her wrist snapped and her gun clattered to the ground. Her gaze flew to Outlaw's as his big hand grabbed her throat.

She stared into his green eyes, blazing with madness and fury, the wrath of hell shining in his depths. Fear slid into her and she whimpered.

She didn't want to die!

She didn't. All she'd wanted...What she wanted no longer mattered.

After two big errors in her quest to avenge Ellen, this third would be her greatest.

Mistake number three would cost her life.

"Mark!" Peyton's scream stopped Digger.

"You fuckin' cunt."

Digger blinked at Outlaw's yell, his hand trembling, caught between forcing Bunny and Little Man to the nearest car or remaining still to watch Outlaw. One good thing about the prospects parking the cars were the keys remained in them in the event they needed to be moved to make room for bikes.

"C'mon, baby boy," Bunny whimpered, pulling Little Man against her body.

Digger did a quick look around, searching for Peyton and Outlaw. When he found them, he saw no sign of Meggie. Only...

Peyton, who'd shot Outlaw's wife. And corrupted Tyler. Peyton, who'd once made Digger laugh and smile and not feel so alone.

Although the man had a gun to her head, he wrapped his hand around her neck, strangling her. Bodies littered the grounds, including one the dogs had brought down. His stomach turned, and he knew the exact moment Peyton's life ended.

She went limp. Still, Outlaw held onto her throat, gun pressed to her temple. His eyes were wild and tears streaked his face. There would be no getting through to him now. Meggie might've been the catalyst for all the bad the club experienced, but she was the only one who could rein Outlaw in, remind him he had some humanity left in him. But she wasn't able to talk him through his madness, so Outlaw pulled the trigger and let Peyton's body drop to the ground.

Pushing the scene out of his head, Digger refocused on Bunny. "One move and I shoot."

She tightened her hold on Outlaw's son.

Not wasting time, Digger pushed them into the car and peeled out. Sirens blared in the distance, but he knew at least two people who were beyond saving. Perhaps, they all were.

PART THREE
The Key

The moment that cunt's faceless body fell in a heap to the ground, Christopher turned back to his wife and gathered her into his arms, blocking out the screams of the kids, the barking of the dogs, and the blaring of the sirens. Megan's blood warmed his arms and dampened his T-shirt. All before when she'd been hurt he'd gotten to her *after*. This time, he'd seen her get shot with his own two fucking eyes. His whole life had stopped. He couldn't think or talk or *do*.

He wasn't the MC President or psycho stalker wildman. He was just an ordinary motherfucker whose life meant nothing if he lost his girl.

"Prez!" Mortician called, his voice frantic and his eyes wild, as he ran to Christopher. "Bailey and Roxanne shot."

Nosing Megan's hair, Christopher squeezed his eyes shut, the tracks of his tears burning down his cheeks. From the close sounds, ambulances were already on club property and heading toward the private access road that led to their houses. Built so the girls could park their cars on their own properties. Right now, Christopher was grateful for the easy access.

Two ambulances and several police cruisers stopped in front of his house. He frowned as they barreled through his gate, remembering the dogs. By now, they should've been bounding toward unfamiliar motherfuckers.

Either they were dead or someone had taken care of them. Watching as the badges and the EMTs swarmed the place struck Christopher as odd. It was as if they'd been expecting this emergency. Or somebody had called and directed them here while the gun battle was happening. Concerned motherfuckers could've done so, but...it didn't fucking sit right with Christopher. Fuck, what the fuck was he thinking? It didn't fucking matter who'd called. Megan needed help, so he ran with her to the closest emergency vehicle. Two techs were already rolling out a gurney.

"Save her," he ordered, clearing his throat so he wouldn't sound so fucking distraught. He laid her down and rested his head in the crook of her neck for a moment. He wanted to pray for her to live, but he didn't know how. He'd never known how because he and God had fallen out years ago. Straightening, he glared at the emergency workers, who hadn't touched her after he set her down. "This my Megan. Save her fucking life."

"Prez!" Mortician called again as police officers headed in Christopher's direction.

He ignored everyone. Megan needed to be loaded into the ambulance, *now*. She needed a hospital. He grabbed the fuckhead closest to him and shoved him toward Megan. "Get my wife to the motherfuckin' ER," he snarled.

The EMT snatched himself out of Christopher's grasp. "Excuse me, sir!"

"Please, just do it." Mortician sounded desperate.

"Work on her," Mutt ordered. He was one of the cops in the club's back pocket. There were others but Mutt and Jeff, as Johnnie called them, were in deep.

A second technician settled an oxygen mask over her mouth and nose.

"Fuckin' do that in there!" Christopher ordered, indicating the ambulance with a thrust of his chin. "She need to be on the way to the fuckin' hospital."

"Prez!" Mortician called. "They got to stabilize her."

"What happened here, Outlaw?" Mutt asked.

"What the fuck you mean?" Christopher barked. "What the fuck it look like? Some motherfucker got onto my grounds and shot up every-fuckin-thing. Shot Megan." He knew he was losing his shit. As long as Megan.... "FUCK," he screamed, thrusting his hands through his hair.

"Outlaw, get things in order here," Mutt ordered, pity in his eyes. "They'll do everything possible to save her."

Before Christopher could tell him to go fuck himself, Mortician spoke again.

"They all down!" he yelled. "John Boy, Val, Arrow, Stretch, Red, Chester, my woman, my momma-in-law. *EVERYBODY.*"

"Not Slipper and his boys. Get them the fuck here." His voice cracked around the order.

"Fuck!" The groan captured Christopher's attention and he turned to find Johnnie swaying behind him, his side bloodied and his eyes glazed. He bent, in obvious pain, searching in all directions, despite his weakness.

"Kendall? Where's my wife?" Cold fury threaded through the fear in Johnnie's voice. "Where's my woman and my son, Christopher?"

Shit was happening too fucking fast, yet creeping by in motherfucking slow motion. Christopher didn't know a goddamn, fucking thing except his Megan...

The contents of his stomach churned within him and he turned, hurling every-fucking-thing he'd eaten no more than ninety minutes ago. Breakfast Megan had cooked. She'd been so fucking excited about Bailey's baby shower.

"Christy!" Zoann hollered, and the sound made him dizzy.

Didn't these motherfuckers understand Megan's grave injuries? She'd been shot in her fucking chest. Chest wounds were usually fucking fatal.

"Where's Kendall?" Johnnie.

"Christy, please help me. Val's shot. PLEASE!" Zoann.

"Prez, they getting Bailey on a stretcher. I need to go with my woman to the hospital." Mortician.

"Outlaw, pull your head out of your ass." Cash stepped in front of Christopher. "If you want your son back."

Christopher stilled. It felt as if the little air left in his lungs flew out. He realized he was on his fucking knees and he didn't care, not having the energy to move. *Until now.* He stared at Cash. "What the fuck you talkin' 'bout?"

"Digger took Little Man and Bunny, motherfucker. Get up. Help us—"

"Digger?" The horrified question belonged to Mort. "No, my brother wouldn't—"

"I saw the motherfucker," Cash snarled, breaking into Mortician's denial. "None of you can go to the fucking hospital. Most of us are down. We have to get shit cleaned up here."

"Sir, we're transporting your wife in a few minutes," the EMT he'd shoved told him. "You're welcome to come and ride in the front."

As if he walked into a nightmare, Christopher turned toward the vehicle.

"Prez, we need you here!"

"Outlaw, where are you going?"

"Christopher, where's Kendall?"

"Christy! Val isn't…come please!"

The voices buzzed in his head and blended together. He couldn't make sense of who screamed what to him, of what any of them meant.

"You need to find your son, Outlaw."

"Sir? We're about to move Mrs. Caldwell."

"You can't leave, Prez!"

"Christopher, fuck! Let Megan go. Where's Rory? Where's *my* wife? You know where yours is. I need to find mine."

"Go and look for Red, John Boy. That's logic, motherfucker. My woman down, too."

"*Please!* Val won't open his eyes. Please!" Christopher blinked, all the words coming to him through a tunnel, where sound surrounded him but bounced off his eardrums. He shook his head to clear it, the crackling of radios and the flashing lights of the vehicles slipping past the white noise.

One thing became clear—he couldn't be Megan's husband because he had duties at the club. He couldn't let someone else take over. The MC had been hit hard, leaving it to him to bring some order.

"Take her," he managed, swallowing hard, tears hot on his cheeks. He couldn't look at her again. If he did, he'd never let them leave without him.

Once they loaded her up and closed the doors, he focused on the ambulance, pressing his hand against the cold exterior. When the siren wailed, he backed away, allowing the vehicle containing his Megan to pull away. Without him. He stood, frozen, in agony, as if someone ripped his heart the fuck out.

By now, Bailey and Roxy laid on stretchers, oxygen masks covering their faces, the attendants running like hellhounds chased them. Another wail echoed through the dismal day.

"Christy."

Christopher turned. Zoann clung to Val, blood staining her shoulder while his road captain lay motionless.

A snarl. A howl. He couldn't describe the fucking sound coming from Johnnie when he saw Kendall, face down and unmoving. He'd located her because of the EMTs heading to her.

Christopher noted the first responders had checked two bodies and shook their heads, indicating the unidentified people were beyond help.

"Cash, take over. I can't fuckin' do this right now. My wife probably dead and my boy gone."

He started to walk off as two more ambulances pulled away. Bailey and Roxy, he supposed.

At the clubhouse door, Mortician caught up with him. "Prez—"

"Get the fuck away from me," he thundered, hating himself and Mortician. They'd both failed the club and their wives for a fuckhead who'd betrayed them *again*. He shouldn't have listened to Megan or thought about how Mortician felt.

Megan's soft-heart had most likely gotten her killed.

"Prez, listen to me. I know this hitting you hard. It's fucking killing me right now, too."

"Shut the fuck up." Shoving aside all safety and the possibility of more motherfuckers on the property waiting to take him out, Christopher rounded on his friend. Unless he imagined shit, he'd clearly heard Digger call out to him. "All the fuck I know is them motherfuckers were *inside* my property, beyond club gates. Some fucker let 'em in. Every-fuckin-time you had the fuckin' chance to fuck that motherfucker up, you let him walk the fuck away."

Anger blanketed Mort's features and he balled his fists. "You think I permitted that motherfucker in so he could cut my fucking wife down? My mother-in-law? You fucking out your goddamn mind, Prez."

If he'd had bullets left, he would've shot Mortician then and there. Instead, he turned again and walked into his club house. Decorations for the baby shower hung everywhere. A large sign with *Congratulations, Bailey* hung in the center of the room. Presents that Megan had everyone stack in the corner in preparation for the day. The enormity of the shootings smacked him in the face.

Their women had been shot. He'd been right the fuck out in the open, but unless motherfuckers were terrible fucking shots, they'd purposely missed him while aiming for the girls. Megan, Bailey, Kendall, Zoann. Even Roxy.

He glanced at the monitors, surprised to see the words '*No* signal' on each of the screens.

Suddenly, a chair went flying and Christopher spun to see Mortician staring at the banner through teary eyes.

"Prez, yeah, I protected Digger cuz I didn't think he was so low, but I'd fucking lay down my life before I betrayed you. I know how you felt that day when you had to pretend you didn't know what happened to Big Joe and step up as president. I know that fucking hurt you. But our women strong, brother. They're gonna fight like motherfuckers to pull through. We gotta fight too."

"Fight for what, Mortician? Club gone to shit. Brothers droppin' the fuck out left and fuckin' right cuz we just about shut the fuck down. We ain't hardly got a fuckin' club no more. I shoulda walked the fuck away when I decided I wanted Megan. Fallin' the fuck apart ain't a sign of a strong fuckin' leader. But, Mort, I could take any-fuckin-thing..." His voice trailed off and he rubbed the back of his neck, recalling the first time he'd ever seen Megan in this very room as a scared eighteen-year-old in need of her '*Daddy*' as she called Big Joe. "I could take any-fuckin-thing but losin' Megan. Life don't fuckin' matter without her. It ain't worth livin'. She my everything."

"And she adore your children, Prez. When she open her eyes and find out the first child she ever gave you missing, it's gonna fucking kill her."

Mortician spoke the truth. Christopher needed to get his boy back.

What the fuck wrong with you, motherfucker? He needed his boy back. Nobody called him '*Law*' like CJ did.

The door opened and Cash walked in, assisting Johnnie through the door.

"Who we lost?" Christopher demanded.

Eyes red-rimmed as if he'd been crying, Johnnie sat at one of the tables, pale and in obvious pain.

"Three," Cash answered grimly, sidling Christopher a glance then transferring it to Mortician. He scrubbed a hand over his face. "I found Meggie's phone and called Ophelia to come and look after the kids. Right now, they're at your house, Outlaw, with Mutt's partner."

"Who the fuck dead?"

Johnnie rested the elbow on his uninjured side on the table and cradled his head in his hand.

Knowing it was bad, Christopher waited to be told who'd been killed.

Pale from the blood loss and fucking furious, Johnnie plowed his fingers through his hair and grunted.

"We lost Arrow," he said finally.

"Arrow?" Christopher echoed in disbelief. "K-P kid brother?"

"Yeah, Christopher," Johnnie confirmed, the news numbing Christopher. "You know another Arrow?"

Not responding to Johnnie's sarcasm, Christopher sagged in his seat, devastation cutting into him as sharp as a knife. Arrow had been one confrontational motherfucker, but he'd been loyal to the club. He looked after Dinah…*Fuck!*

"Where Dinah?" Jumping to his feet, he hurried in the direction of the hallway, pausing when Johnnie swayed. "Fuck, get to the fuckin' hospital, Johnnie."

"Before you search for Dinah, I need to tell you about casualty number two," Johnnie called weakly, palms flat on the table top.

"I thought Cash said three," Mortician put in.

Cash avoided Mortician's eyes. "Number three was a probate."

A sick feeling sank in Christopher's stomach and he turned his full attention to Johnnie at the sympathy in his eyes as he focused on Mortician.

"Tyler's number two, Mortician."

Mortician blinked and then stared, as if he couldn't understand Johnnie's words. "Tyler?" he said finally. "What do you mean? *Tyler*? I know you not fucking talking about *my* Tyler, so who the fuck you mean, John Boy?"

Christopher glanced at Johnnie, who gave him the smallest of nods.

"He only a boy, Johnnie," Mortician continued. "Barely in his teens. No fucking way he'd be out there."

"He was, Mort," Cash said, quiet but firm. "With a gun in his hand."

"No!" Mortician roared, the sound filled with pain and rage. "My kid wouldn't fucking be out there doing what the fuck Sharper did. He was my boy! My *son*. He was my son, and he never knew it." Leaning on the bar, he drew in great gulps of air. "One of us shot him." He covered his face. "Man, fuck, maybe I shot my own son."

"Mort—" Christopher usually had something to say in every situation. A piece of advice. Some shit he'd learned over the years and could impart. A smart fucking comment. But, right now, words fucking failed him. He couldn't offer anything to his friend because he had nothing in him to give. It all went with Megan. Unfamiliar with such uncertainty, he stepped up to Mort and put a hand on his shoulder. "Mort, we all fuckin' fired our pieces. Any of us coulda..." His voice trailed off. The thought that he'd killed *any* child almost broke Christopher. That shit said a lot in a fucking day of nightmares. "It coulda been me."

"None of us killed your kid," Cash said sharply.

Mort rounded on Cash, grabbing a bottle on the bar and hurling it. Glass and liquid shattered everywhere. "If we didn't fucking kill my kid, who did, goddammit? He fired on us, so we fired back."

Cash walked up to Mort and grabbed his shoulders, not letting go when the man tried to knock him away. "Sharper stood over your kid and pumped him with bullets."

"My father?" Mort's shocked outrage matched Christopher's.

Why they were shocked *or* outraged over any of Sharper's actions, Christopher didn't know. That meant *they* were the stupid motherfuckers. After years of dealing with the assfuck, no evil fucking deed he committed should've surprised them.

"I saw him with my own eyes, Mortician. Tyler was already down. He was breathing before Sharper got to him because I saw him moving."

Mortician shoved him. "If you fucking saw my old man, motherfucker, why the fuck you didn't take him out?" He turned away. "Never fucking mind. I need to bury my son. Where is he? Still outside?"

"Yes, but Mutt and Jeff have their boys checking the grounds," Cash explained.

Johnnie swayed again.

"Cash, get this motherfucker to a hospital," Christopher ordered, going behind the bar to find a bottle of vodka. "Mort, hold tight, brother. We don't know who the fuck out there." Something he hadn't considered when he'd come barging in. "Fuck."

Cash withdrew his weapon. "On it," he said, as if he'd read Christopher's mind, already heading to the hallway.

Johnnie staggered behind him, but Christopher said, "No, you too weak, John Boy. Just sit and be ready to fire."

Following his own advice, he removed the small handgun he'd started strapping to his ankle for emergencies after Megan's near-kidnapping in Bailey's apartment.

"Prez, I got to get my kid. If I would've taken him in the first place, he'd still be alive."

"Mort, you did what the fuck you thought best. We all know you woulda took him, but he'd just lost his Ma. You didn't wanna up-fuckin-set his entire fuckin world and tell him you was his old man."

"I didn't have to tell him, Prez. I could've just insisted he come with me instead of allowing him to go with Digger."

Mort wasn't thinking clearly right now, but Christopher still attempted to reason with him. "How the fuck you coulda done that? As his fuckin' *brothers*, you and Digger had the same fuckin' authority. The only way you coulda made him come with you is by revealin' your identity to him."

Mortician snatched the bottle and drank half the fucking contents before handing it back to Christopher.

"Your office has been hit pretty bad, Outlaw," Cash announced before either Mort or Christopher said anything else. "It's a fucking mess."

"They took anything?"

"Not that I can see at a glance."

Any important shit was kept under lock and fucking key and the letters wasn't an issue since they were not around. Whatever they'd been searching for either wasn't there or was inaccessible.

"Anywhere else? My old room?"

Cash nodded, his eyes flaring in surprise.

Christopher shrugged. "If motherfuckers searched my fuckin' office, it seem logical to think they searchin' my fuckin' room, too."

"K-P's, as well."

"Unless they had a layout, how did they know which room belonged to who?"

"I don't fuckin' know, Cash." At the moment, Christopher really didn't give a fuck.

Johnnie slumped onto the table.

Cash headed to him and hefted him to his feet. Placing his arm around his neck, he dragged Johnnie toward the door and exited without another word. Christopher wanted to go to the hospital for Megan, but he still had details at the club that he needed to see to first, mainly Mortician and Dinah, one as important as the other. He didn't want to leave Mort right now to search for Megan's ma while Mort was in such a fucked up way. Besides, if Dinah was somewhere dead, it was already too late for her.

"We'll give your boy the send-off he deserve, Mort."

Mort only nodded, not raising his head from his hands.

"You get to Bailey. Ima stay behind. See to Arrow and Tyler. Get them to the funeral home. ID the probate and call his fuckin' family."

"Fuck, man, Arrow," Mort responded, as if he'd just remembered Arrow, Bailey's uncle, had also been killed.

"We gonna give that motherfucker the best fuckin' send-off," Christopher swore. "Just like we doin' for your boy. No expense gonna be spared. You got my fuckin' word."

Mort nodded.

"Go to Bailey."

Instead of moving, he shifted his weight. "Suppose her and our new baby dead?"

Suppose they were? What could Christopher say? He had the same fear about Megan. "I don't know, Mort. I just don't fuckin' know."

"Prez?"

"Yeah?"

"Sharper mine," Mort gritted, low and vicious. "That murdering motherfucker. I'm going to make him personally fucking pay for all the heartache he fucking caused me."

Christopher nodded. "Okay, Mort. He fuckin' yours to fuck-up however you fuckin' see fit."

A cough snapped Christopher's attention in the direction of the grim reaper mural.

Dinah stood in the entryway, wearing jeans along with a pajama top and sneakers. Her hair hung in snarls and tangles, but otherwise, she appeared unharmed.

"Fuck, Dinah," he said, jumping to his feet and rushing to her. In the entire time he'd known her, he'd never been so fucking happy to see her as he was just then. Just because he knew how much Megan loved her. He hugged Dinah, so fucking relieved he didn't care how stiffly she held herself. He guided her to a nearby table and urged her into a chair, crouching to better assess any injuries she might have. "You okay, babe?" he asked, contemplating her from head to toe and finding her unharmed.

Her body motionless and her nostrils flaring, she stared at him, unblinking. What the fuck went through her head, he didn't fucking know.

"Meggie," she murmured, her wide stare fucking with him. If he was a bitch, he might freak the fuck out. Even owls blinked at some fucking point. Didn't they?

Christopher took Dinah's cold hand into his own. "Megan got hurt real bad, Dinah," he told her, gritting his teeth when her eyes filled with water. It made him want to sob like a bitch, too. This time, he might not ever get Megan back. "She at the hospital. I'm gonna go as soon as I can. As soon as I..." *See to Tyler and Arrow.*

Although he doubted Dinah's fragile state could handle Arrow's death, Christopher had to break the news to her.

Otherwise, what would happen if she didn't see the man? He heaved in a breath.

"Ain't no easy way to say this, so Ima just give it to you fuckin' straight. Arrow didn't make it."

Instead of falling apart, Dinah stilled, a bunch of emotions playing on her haggard face. She stood, forcing Christopher to do the same. After another long look at him, she turned and ran in the direction of her room, leaving Christopher to wonder what the future held for her.

Especially if they lost Megan.

"'Law! Want 'Law and MegAnn," Little Man said around tears and sniffles. "MegAnn got all red and falled down." He leaned against Bunny and wailed. "I want my mommie!"

Out of everything else that happened in the past twenty-four hours, hearing Little Man sob for his mother threatened to unravel Bunny. He wore a pair of jeans, a plaid flannel shirt, and a little cut that he was adorably attached to. He went nowhere without it. Because he was his father's son, but his mother's baby. Meggie adored him just as much as he doted on her. Outlaw, he idolized.

But Meggie was hurt, gravely so. She might already be dead, a tragedy that Little Man had witnessed. The clothes he had on might be the last ones his mom ever chose for him.

Bunny drew in a deep breath, stubbornly holding her tears at bay as the car sped past emergency vehicles and motorcycles, all hurrying toward the club. At the intersection of the main street and the dead end leading to the MC, traffic mounted.

Traffic. When this small town never suffered traffic. It underscored the magnitude of the morning's calamitous events.

The chaotic confusion aided Digger's escape. He swerved left. To frustrated drivers and rushing law enforcement, his maneuver would appear as a way to beat the ever-increasing vehicles. No one seemed to care that the car sped away from the scene and not toward it. The only one to do so.

Little Man tugged her hair. She'd had it in a careless knot at her nape, but lost her pins somewhere along the way. "Bun-Bun, want MegAnn."

Bunny hugged him tightly, afraid if she spoke, emotion would overtake her voice and he'd pick up on her grief and fear when he was scared enough.

"MegAnn," he repeated in a trembling tone.

"Shut him the fuck up, Bunny," Digger yelled, his voice vibrating in the small confines of the car.

Veering off the road onto a private access road, he waved around the gun he held. In case he pulled the trigger, she wrapped her arms around Little Man's head. Digger's anger made the child cry harder, so before Digger, or Little Man, or both of them completely lost it, she responded.

"Lower your voice and your gun. He's just a child and he's scared." Just as she was. Worse, now that her adrenaline nose-dived, her stomach pain returned. The return of her agony brought back the memories of Trader's beating and she shivered, cold inside.

Trader, who Outlaw had shot dead. For her. Because Meggie liked her.

Bunny held Little Man tighter. She wanted to cry over Trader's death, but couldn't.

They'd been together for several years. At one time, she would've reacted upon hearing gunfire the same as Meggie had and run to check on Trader. But the pain he'd caused her numbed any grief she might've felt for him.

"Potty, Bun-Bun."

"Potty?" Digger echoed, eyeing her nastily. "Since your ass followed behind the little dude, you got diapers?"

"He's potty-trained," she answered, flinching when his unnerving gaze caught hers. The carefree, friendly Digger she'd met so many months ago was gone. This Digger was a cold and conscienceless man, on the run because of his betrayals. He'd chosen to take Outlaw's son instead of facing the man himself. "CJ needs to use it," she added quietly, hoping he had a measure of sympathy for a child.

Instead of softening him, Digger glared at the back of Little Man's head.

"In a minute, buddy," she promised, ignoring the look. She strove for normalcy, knowing it was best to answer him. She only wished she had access to a bathroom. If Little Man was comfortable, he wouldn't cause too many problems outside of the worry for his mother.

"Hold your piss, lil' dude," Digger finally ordered, pressing on the gas pedal.

At their high rate of speed, the car barrelled through the branches that touched each other from one side of the road to the next. Through the overgrowth, dirt, grass, and gravel kicked up, leaving a cloud of dust and debris in their wake. Wherever they headed looked deserted and spooky.

Her suspicions rose and a shiver traveled through her. Digger must've chosen the isolated spot to execute them.

Clenching her teeth to keep from crying, Bunny sidled a glance at him. His shoulder length dreads hid most of his profile from her, but his big hands gripped the steering wheel. He could easily snap her neck.

No, thoughts like this would send her into hysterics. She had to hold it together, she reminded herself, for a chance to save Little Man and get him back to his parents.

A house with thick weeds and tall grass loomed into view. Digger swerved to a stop, as close as possible to the rotten wooden steps that led to an equally rotten porch, where grass grew through the cracked boards. Bigger, sturdier boards covered the windows. The farmhouse hadn't been tended to in a very long time, as if it hadn't been lived in, in years.

Digger turned to her, anger burning in his eyes. "I didn't have no fucking intentions of taking you or the kid. I can handle *him*." He lifted his gun and aimed it at her. "You, though? You want to live?"

She nodded vigorously, fear drying her mouth.

"Then you listen to me and do whatever I tell you to do. Understand?"

"Yes," she croaked.

"Get the fuck out. If you try any shit, you dead. Feel me?"

"Potty," Little Man sniffed pitifully.

"This might be the first place they all look," Digger went on as if he didn't hear the toddler. "But I need to get off the fucking road and regroup. You coming inside and not doing any funny shit." Keeping his gun on her, he nodded to the door. "Now, move."

Little Man sniffled with heartbreaking intensity, so hard his chest shuddered. Holding onto him tightly and whispering reassurances to him, Bunny got out of the car, almost falling to her knees at the pain in her stomach. Overheated and nauseated, she stumbled.

Once Digger stepped out and slammed the door, he walked to her.

"There's an apple orchard on the property," he told her. "A lot of fucking bodies buried there. Don't make me add yours to it."

"I gotta potty," Little Man sobbed, his arms around her neck.

"Fuck, kid. Come on."

Despite her protests, Digger snatched Little Man out of Bunny's arms, unconcerned by the high grass that hid a well-worn dirt path. Not trusting Digger, she hurried behind, skidding to a halt when he stopped abruptly.

"Outlaw teach you how to take a leak or did Meggie?"

Little Man smiled and nodded. "'Law say take dick out an' aim an' MegAnn mad if pee not right." He scrunched his nose. "Nasty, then seat back down."

"Okay, I think I understood. Meggie think leaving the seat up nasty after Outlaw take a piss."

"Uh-huh," he agreed in a squeaky voice.

"Okay. Got it. Pissing in the grass easier. We don't have a seat to put down. Just aim our cock and piss."

Little Man nodded.

"Let's do this shit together."

"No poopie," Little Man said with a frown. "Just pess."

For the first time since this started, Digger laughed. "You mean *piss*?"

Busily opening his jeans and going through the steps his father had shown him, Little Man's conversation had finished. Preoccupied with the little boy's task, she didn't realize Digger had also whipped out his cock.

Glaring at him, she turned her back. "Asshole," she mumbled under her breath.

"You not just a little impressed, girl?"

She didn't answer. He intended to kill her, so conversations about his dick didn't rank too high up there.

"'Law say shake like this."

She couldn't help but stifle a laugh, and flushed at the sound of Digger's chuckles. Warmth radiated in his laughter. Under other circumstances, she might've told him he had a nice laugh. Now, she recognized it for the deception that it was.

Trader's laugh had first caught her attention when he'd visited the strip club she worked at. She couldn't be duped by Digger's easy-going moments.

"Feel better?" Digger asked as he guided Little Man back to Bunny and smirked at her.

"Uh-huh," the child said and grabbed Bunny's hand. She cringed at the wetness on his fingers but refused to release him.

Digger headed to the porch, the wood creaking as he climbed the unstable steps. He tested the plank covering where the door should be. With his back to them, Bunny wondered if he'd left the keys in the ignition. He'd told her if she didn't cooperate he'd kill her. She knew that was his ultimate intention for her and Little Man. *The child could talk, too, couldn't he?*

She'd sprung after him to keep him safe. If he remained with Digger, he was in danger. Hoping for the best, she inched them back. Little Man lifted his gaze to her and she placed a finger over her mouth, indicating silence.

He cooperated.

Reaching the driver's side and opening the door, she threw Little Man in, spying the keys and—

Digger came out of nowhere, grabbing her hair and yanking her out of the car. She landed on her hands and knees, but Digger fisted her hair and pulled her to her feet, shaking her. Little Man screamed.

"I told you to fucking behave," Digger gritted, his eyes haunted and angry. And something else. Frightened. The clashing emotions panicked her. She had to calm him down before she lost her life.

Little Man squeezed between them. "Don't hurt Bun-Bun!"

"It's cool, lil' dude," he swore, not taking his eyes or his gun off Bunny.

"He's already seen his mom shot," she whispered, unable to stop her tears from slipping down her cheeks. "Don't shoot me. Especially in front of him."

"You not doing me no good. I can see now you'll be nothing but a fucking headache."

"I won't. I promise. I just want him safe."

Indecision danced across his face and Bunny prayed, hoping God heard her since she said her prayers every night as she'd been taught. Though she'd disobeyed her parents, even as a child, abandoned her given name, turned to the stripper pole for quick money and...she still said her prayers. That meant something, right?

"Get the kid and come with me," Digger said after a tense moment.

Not testing her luck, she took Little Man into her arms and hugged him. "I'm fine," she promised in a wobbly voice.

"Okay," he said, sucking back more tears.

"Start walking ahead."

Keeping Little Man as protected as possible from the brambles and overgrown foliage, Bunny trooped on, quite aware of the gun aimed at the back of her head. Between her legs felt wet and sticky, as if she were bleeding again.

"I scared, Bun-Bun. I want MegAnn."

"Scared?" Digger echoed, a forced lightness in his voice. "Don't be, kid. This just an adventure. You'll be back with Outlaw soon."

Although Bunny didn't believe Digger, the toddler did and he relaxed a fraction.

"A venture?" he repeated.

"Yeah," Digger responded with reassurance, a rusty shed rising into view, the grass around here so high she hadn't seen it. "Stop."

Doing as he ordered, she halted, keeping stock still when he stepped beside her. Tall and lean, he'd grown a beard during his extended absence. The fullness of his lips and the strength of his jawline and chin roughened his appearance but made him no less handsome.

"Anybody ever tell you that you a pretty chick?" he asked casually, aiming his gun toward the padlock on the shed.

"A lot of people," she said quietly, not explaining that drunken men murmured anything to their favorite strippers for an extra favor in the VIP room.

Digger fired, the blast hurting her ears and making Little Man jump. As soon as the lock pinged off and plopped to the ground, Digger returned his attention to her, studying her mouth.

"You like sucking dick?"

Flushing in embarrassment at Little Man's presence, she shook her head. Trader had constantly complained about her dislike of sucking him off. When the Bobs began coming to the club again, he made sure to announce he had his cock sucked on a regular basis. In the early days of their relationship, she'd given him blow jobs. But then he'd paid her to do it. In the club she'd worked in, almost anything, except actual penetration, had been permissible.

Gradually, Trader had staked a claim on her, luring her with promises of a normal future. He'd known she hadn't liked sucking cock and had sworn she'd never have to do it again in her life. Her love meant more.

She'd believed him.

"You like your cunt eaten?"

She frowned at Digger's question, sidling another glance between him and Little Man, hoping he got the message to stop being so explicit in front of the little boy.

He lifted a brow. "If you do, I'm willing to lick your pussy when we get time." He cocked his head to the side. "I even got my red wings, so that don't matter."

"You're a disgusting asshole. And if it was that time of the month, which it isn't, I wouldn't let you come near me."

"So you don't like your pussy licked?"

She did, but she didn't know how to tell him that. She frowned Why did she even *want* to? Having her pussy licked led to reciprocation and that she didn't like. "Can we not talk about this?"

"Suppose I told you I've found a way for you to be useful?"

Her insides froze at his insinuation and she clenched her jaw. Given a choice between living and submitting to him, she'd submit.

"I want your answer. Your honest answer. If I needed my cock sucked, would you do it?"

She shifted Little Man from one hip to the other. "If it meant surviving, yes."

Digger lifted a brow. "If you not attracted to me, then..."

"Then, what?" she snapped. "I'm *not* attracted to you. My long-term relationship abruptly ended this morning."

"Outlaw shot him."

"Nice to know you and your murderers were lying in wait, watching our every move."

He scowled. "Don't fucking worry about what we saw. Your man fucked up. What the fuck he did? How *you* feel about Outlaw shooting Trader?"

Confused. Relieved. Sad. Each emotion crammed into the other, leaving her exposed and raw.

"You pissed at Outlaw?"

"No," she admittedly hoarsely, ashamed of herself for being grateful to Outlaw for freeing her from Trader when she could've left. She *should've* left. Instead, she'd bought into the fear he'd instilled in her. "I don't know how to feel," she blurted. Digger was listening, even if it was with false concern. She needed to unburden herself, find some way to release her grief. "I think I should mourn him, but Trader was a real sonofabitch. I so wish I'd listened to my parents."

"You a grown fucking woman. What do they have to do with it?"

Nothing but the fact that she'd been out of control from the age of sixteen. Definitely not grown when she'd rebelled.

Agitated, she shifted her weight. "Even if you hadn't kidnapped me and keep threatening me, I couldn't be attracted to you out of respect to Trader."

His eyes twinkled. "I mention us being attracted to each other?"

Her face flushed.

"I asked if you would make yourself useful by being my personal cock sucker. I'm not fucking interested in nothing more than that."

He'd also asked if the sight of his cock had impressed her. Yes, he was referring to the size of it, but, to her, it also implied stirrings of attraction.

At her silence, he studied her, turning thoughtful. "Peyton's gone, too," he said finally. "But she brought it on herself with what she did to Meg..." He looked pointedly at Little Man, who had rested his head on Bunny's shoulder. "We were together for over a year, but I ended up hating her. I'm not going to fucking do hypocritical bullshit and pretend I'm sorry she gone. You...if Trader didn't treat you right..." He sighed and shrugged. "I used to admire how fucking cold Peyton was. Don't know why. I just thought I needed a chick like her for the life I led. I thought I'd find my own piece of happiness with her. Biggest fucking mistake of my life. One I'm never repeating."

She lowered her lashes, a twinge of sympathy for his sadness hitting her. He sounded so lost. And, maybe, he was. Maybe, he'd been caught between two violent men, and chose to go with the one he shared blood with. Bunny admired such family loyalty when she hadn't had any until it was too late. She still didn't know if what she felt for her family was loyalty or guilt.

"I completely understand why you think you'll never get into a relationship again."

"No thinking involved. I *know*."

"Don't you want a family of your own?"

"I thought I did, Bunny. I don't no more." He raised his eyebrows. "You do?"

Her devastation over the loss of her baby hit her again. Losing it, Trader's death, his abuse, was all too fresh for Bunny to honestly consider what she wanted for her future. The only thing she knew for certain was…"I never want to get involved with another biker again."

"I'm no longer a biker."

"Are you implying we get involved?"

"While we together, why the fuck not?"

"Are you always so impulsive?" she snapped. "Not five minutes ago, you said you'd never get in a relationship again."

"I'm not talking about a relationship with your ass. I'm talking about fucking you. I don't have to be in a goddamn relationship to stick my dick in you. Since I'm not a fucking biker no more, and I'm not proposing nothing more than some fucking, why do you say?"

"What do I say?" she hissed. "You're a kidnapper, a traitor, and impulsive. That makes you even worse than being a biker."

A hurt look crossed his face and Bunny regretted her outburst. Just because his words had gotten under her skin didn't give her the right to insult him.

Unexpectedly, Digger hugged her and threaded his fingers through her hair. They stared at each other, taking measure, searching for…*something.* But he didn't find whatever he searched for and neither did she. She held herself stiffly in his arms, until he took Little Man from her and kissed her forehead.

"You sure you okay?" he asked as he set the child on his feet. "You feel kind of warm."

"Let us go," she whispered, not responding to his question. Yes, she felt bad, but she didn't want him to know. He might see her as a liability. "Please. Let me get CJ back to Outlaw."

For a moment, she thought he'd relent. Regret passed across his features and coupled with his lingering sadness. He caressed her cheek, so tenderly. She moved her head away and he sighed. "You know anything about collateral damage?"

"Yes," she whispered, defeat bitter in her mouth even before he clarified his question.

"I never meant to take you, Bunny. I swear. I wasn't even intending to take the kid. I just wanted to warn Outlaw and Mort, but I couldn't get close enough. By the time I could..." He bowed his head.

Meggie had already been shot. She knew he'd been about to say that. Once Meggie went down, if Outlaw had seen Digger, he would've killed him on the spot. "Don't you think you deserve to have your life forfeited?" she flared. "You betrayed him. All of them."

"It seem that way, but I got extenuating circumstances. It don't matter right now. Staying alive does. Keeping the kid alive," he said, lower, although Little Man sat on the ground, at her bare feet. He was too quiet, a sure sign of the dire situation.

She frowned. Somewhere along the way, she'd lost her flats. As a matter of fact, neither she or Little Man had coats. At least he still wore his little motorcycle boots. On the other hand, Digger wore a black leather jacket, black shirt, and black pants, the perfect gear for a surprise attack.

"Our club about brotherhood. You, Bailey, Kendall, Meggie just collateral damage in the end."

"I dare you to call Outlaw, Mort, and John Boy's wives that to their faces."

"Fine," he relented immediately. "You got me. I wouldn't be that stupid. Just because I see them that way don't mean they do. And I like those chicks. I do. But they weaken the club."

"Meggie is the one who campaigned to Outlaw for your life!"

"It's complicated, Bunny. It's so fucking complicated. I don't love those chicks, but I love my brother and I respect Outlaw. For me, the decision easy."

"You could've gone to—"

"I couldn't. I was a stupid motherfucker at first, feeling resentment, like a fucking bitch ass. Then, I didn't want to. By the time I got my fucking head on straight, it was too late. I'd already left her in Bailey's apartment."

Meggie, he meant. "This long, pointless explanation is to tell me *I'm* collateral damage, right? That if I have to go, you'll take me out without flinching? Is that it?"

He slid a finger along her cheek and brushed away a tear. Not wanting him to touch her, she knocked his hand away.

"I'm sorry."

"Don't you fucking apologize to me, asshole," she growled, too overcome with what she'd gone through and what she faced to filter her words. "I don't want to hear it. Let us go and apologize then I might listen, otherwise shove it up your ass."

"I intend to let *him* go, if that makes you feel any better. When the time right. When Sharper…maybe before then. I took him at first to save his life, but as long as I have him, he's my leverage with Outlaw. I have to keep him until I can get a note to Prez."

"Then call him on the phone."

He shook his head. "I don't have a fucking phone."

Little Man sneezed and Digger frowned. "Don't get sick, okay, kid?"

"Okay."

Falling silent, Digger sauntered to the shed and wrestled the metal door open.

"March back the way we came," he directed the moment he came out with a tool box in one hand and his gun still in the other.

Holding out her hand for Meggie's son, Bunny started off as soon as the child placed his chubby fingers in hers. When they got back to the front of the house, Digger stopped long enough to get the car keys.

"Come with me, kid." Digger indicated the porch with the gun. "Help me get the door off."

"No! Wanna stay with Bun-Bun."

Digger's scowl didn't faze the little boy. If she knew nothing else about the child, she knew he was stubborn. Admittedly, she and Meggie's soft-hearted approach didn't help. The only person he ever snapped into line for was his father. One stern look from Outlaw achieved what ten timeouts from Meggie didn't. In this situation, either Digger would lose his patience or Little Man would throw a tantrum. Or both. One would lead to the other.

"I won't do anything if you leave him with me," she promised, meaning it. He had the car keys. Since her life was so expendable, if she took off on foot, he'd merely shoot her in the back.

"Fool me once, shame on you. I think you know how the fuck the saying finish."

"Digger, I swear."

His frown deepened.

"Please?"

"Fuck! Fine. You lying and I'm going to be pissed."

She nodded.

"I'm not leaving your ass here, so come on then."

Once they topped the porch, Digger had the plywood removed from the door in no time. The nails and rotten wood made the task easier than Bunny expected. Had it been nailed from the inside, a few hard kicks would've gotten them in.

After picking the lock on the door hidden behind the plank, Digger finally achieved entry. He leaned the board against the outer wall, then set the toolbox inside before motioning them forward.

Daylight angled through the opened door, revealing white sheets over furniture, and layers of dust and cobwebs. A musty, closed-in smell hung in the air.

Digger slammed the door shut and propelled them into darkness because of the boarded windows. Now, the awful smell condensed in the closed up house and turned her stomach and she heaved, bringing up only bile, since she hadn't eaten in hours.

"Fuck!" Digger snarled, throwing open the door again. Cold air blasted in, along with light. "I don't need a sick fucking bitch with me."

"Bun-Bun," Little Man whispered, touching her back.

"Come here, CJ," Digger ordered.

"I want 'Law and MegAnn," he countered on a cry, his calm disintegrating at Digger's sharpness. Maybe, even because Bunny had thrown up.

"Remember me? Uncle Digger."

The boy sneezed. "MegAnn falled!" he reminded them.

Bunny had the feeling that phrase wouldn't disappear from the child's vocabulary until he saw his mother healthy and happy again. If that would ever happen.

"You want to see Meggie and Outlaw again?"

"MegAnn got red and—"

"Listen to me, kid," Digger said softly, the tone reminding Bunny of the man she'd once known, however briefly. He shoved his gun in his waistband, his jacket shielding it from view. "We going on another adventure. Me and you. Bigger than this one."

A chill slithered down Bunny's spine at the noted absence of her name. Was her time up now? Later? The thought turned her stomach again.

"I'm gonna get you back to 'Law as soon as I can, but you have to listen to me."

Little Man sniffled. "I want MegAnn."

Digger huffed out a breath. "'Law might be the only one you get back."

A soft sob escaped Bunny. Outlaw might be the only one because Digger didn't think Meggie had survived.

"If you behave, I'll get you ice cream as soon as we safe," he said, not paying attention to Little Man's sniffles and cries for his mommie.

"MegAnn gone?" he asked with a sob.

"She might be."

"Mommie left me!"

"If she did, she's with angels and—"

"No! Mommie 'Law's angel. Him said it!"

"CJ," Bunny soothed, unable to allow this conversation a moment longer. She intended to offer as much comfort to Little Man as possible while she lived. Though it surprised her, Digger had begun to calm him down. Until he mentioned Meggie being with angels. She sat back on her haunches and pulled him into her arms. "Wherever Mommie is, she loves her sweet baby boy. You're her buddy, right?"

"Yes," he answered in a watery voice. "MegAnn say I'm her feet atato."

She kissed the top of his head. "Sweet potato."

He relaxed against her. "Yes," he sniffled.

"She needs you to cooperate. So does 'Law."

"You stay with me, Bun-Bun?"

"You'll be good if she's with you?" Digger interrupted before Bunny responded.

"Y-yes," he answered in a pitiful voice.

"Then, we'll keep her."

She snorted at his easy lie, but he lifted a brow, his inscrutable gaze sweeping over her.

"You sick or something?"

She felt flushed and overheated. Somehow, she ignored all her aches and pains. It was easy to do with so much going on. She *was* sick, though, a fact that Digger didn't need to know.

"Only a little hungry," she responded. Even if she were one hundred percent healthy, he had serious issues if he didn't expect her to be affected by what was happening.

"Stay here. I need to find candles so we can close the door."

She didn't respond or move until he returned a few minutes later, carrying a lit candle in each hand. He handed both to her while he uncovered a table. That done, he took one of the candles and set it down, then closed the door.

A chill still hung in the air and she shivered, not protesting as he took the second candle from her. Standing, she dusted off her jeans, the wooden floor quite cold beneath her feet. Little Man sneezed again and he rubbed an arm across his runny nose.

"Blankets should be in one of the bedrooms. Who knows? Maybe, even tissues for your nose. A lot of shit just remained in place."

Bunny raised her candle higher, not picking up a clue about who the house belonged to, but still seeing nothing but outlines of the furniture. "Where are we?"

Inspecting her throw-up, Digger sidled a distracted glance to her. "The Donovan farm," he said offhandedly. "Belong to the club now, although none of them have set foot here in years. Not even Logan when he rose from the fucking dead." He cocked his head to the side. "You know he has hiding spaces in the wall in his bedroom?"

She knew all about Logan Donovan and the thought of hiding spaces in the walls in association with him was scary. She imagined *real* skeletons cramming the spaces if Digger spoke the truth.

He grinned. "It once hid the money and the drugs from the club. Before our time. Prez never told you that?"

As if Outlaw sat around and told her tales from the club. "You're pulling my leg, right?"

"Nope. Maybe, Prez never knew. Who knows? So many fucking secrets. But Big Joe brought me here in the middle of the night after Logan disappeared. You should've seen the fucking money. Blood money, he called it. Made from innocence. His words. Didn't know what the fuck that meant. Now, I wonder if it was about the girls..." He swallowed. "Don't fucking matter. Big Joe burned the money."

"*Burned* the money?" she squeaked. "That's illegal!"

The candlelight didn't afford a very clear view of him, but his teeth flashed white. "As opposed to what, girl? Big Joe called it dirty fucking money."

She lifted her brows.

"Dirtier fucking money then. He wanted no part of it. Meggie's old man was something else. Good and bad all rolled up in one. He used the good in him, not to get too bad until no good lingered. He always loved Meggie, though. Always."

"Do you think he'd appreciate—"

"The way I feel about her making Prez weak?"

"Yes."

"Probably not. But as long as Meggie alive, Big Joe is, too. Everybody from that time gone, except her, with her daddy's blood running in her. And Outlaw," he added, then nodded to Little Man, who quietly picked at the threads on his cut that spelled out his name. "And their kids."

"Do you want her gone because she's making Outlaw weak as you say? Or because she's in danger?"

"I don't know right now," he admitted. "I just wish she'd never come."

"You want her to die, don't you?"

"I don't know," he said again. "It's probably too late anyway. Things have gone too far and it won't stop until one side is completely annihilated." He dropped his gaze to Little Man again. "Couldn't think of nowhere else to come once I scooped Outlaw's son. I can't fail this kid like I failed Mort's son."

Before she could ask what he meant, he halted. At first, Bunny didn't know why, until she heard the creak of the outside steps.

"I think that's the car he stole, Unk."

Digger set his candle aside, swept Little Man into his arms and dragged her to her feet, jerking her behind him. "Sharper and Osti found us."

Doubling her steps to keep up, Bunny hoped an escape route existed in the back of the house.

Otherwise, they were all dead.

Christopher still hadn't gotten to Megan, hours after she'd been taken away. Cash called with updates, so Christopher knew Johnnie would be released in the morning while the others were being seen to. Still, Johnnie would be in the same hospital as his woman. Mort awaited word on Bailey and Roxy *at the goddamn hospital.*

But MC duties kept Christopher from Megan, including calls to his chapter presidents, and ordering club wide lockdowns, stateside, in Canada, and in England. Sharper's reach extended as far as Christopher's.

He had to see that the codes on all the entry points were changed and wait for Ophelia to arrive to look after the kids. Call after call blew up his cell phone and he issued directions as best he could. Since most of his focus was on Megan, he could've been ordering motherfuckers to fly to the fucking moon.

Sweeping up the last of the glass from the mirror Mort shattered, Christopher dumped the shards into the overflowing trash container. Red stained his hands. His own dried blood from inconsequential injuries he'd received in the last few hours. And Megan's blood.

Her blood remained on his skin and his clothes. Her blood. Wanting a connection to her, he purposely hadn't washed it away.

The sight turned his stomach and he slammed the broom and dust pan aside, running to the kitchen. Opening the faucet to the hot water, he shoved his hands beneath the flow, not moving when the temperature spiked and scalded him.

"Why the fuck you didn't listen, baby? Huh?" His arms trembled at the pain flowing through him, but he didn't care. Nothing compared to his devastation over his wife.

Not a fucking thing.

"Christopher?"

His sister's voice rose from behind him. He straightened, still not bothering to move his hand from the water.

"Christopher?" Ophelia repeated, closer to him. A moment passed before she reached around him and turned off the faucet, taking his hand into her own. "Oh my God," she said in a wobbly voice. "Look at your hands."

He stayed motionless, unable to comfort his youngest sibling or to comment on her longer hair, in its natural color nowadays. She grabbed a dish towel from a nearby counter and began to dry off one of his hands, clucking when he flinched.

"What if I lose my Megan, Fee?" he whispered.

Standing on her tiptoes, she hugged him, running her fingers through his hair and kissing his cheek. "You're not going to lose her, Christopher."

"She was shot in the fuckin' chest. Got a collapsed lung. A lotta blood loss. Ain't even outta surgery yet."

Using the dish towel, she swiped away his tears. "Go to the hospital and I'll see to the kids."

"I ain't able to yet. I gotta…I still got shit to do here."

"Is there anything I can help you with? Do you need me to call Avery, Nia, and Bev?"

He jerked away, yanking out his cell phone and shoving it at Ophelia. "Fuck, Fee. Call them. They need to get the fuck here. I ain't trustin' that motherfucker not to go after them."

Ophelia quickly dialed. Until he heard Avery's voice, he hadn't known which of their sisters she'd called.

"Absolutely not," Avery said, once Christopher gave his version of events over speakerphone, offering facts not being reported in newscasts. "You didn't protect Mama. You didn't protect Zoann. And you didn't protect your wife. How the hell do you think we'll be safer with you? Your so-called protection leaves a lot to be desired."

Bleakness filled Christopher, and he nodded, although Avery couldn't see him.

"Really, Avery?" Ophelia said with incredulity. "You're not doing this to him right now. He doesn't need us to shit on him. He needs us to stand behind him."

"I ain't even needin' that, Fee," he said hoarsely. "All I fuckin' want is their fuckin' safety." He dropped his gaze to his phone. "Hear me, Avery? I ain't askin' us to kiss and make the fuck up. Just come to the fuckin' club 'til the threat passed. I can't stand your fuckin' ass like you hatin' on me, but we family and I wanna protect you."

"No."

"Avery!" Ophelia cried, desperation creeping into her voice. "Call Nia and Bev. They may feel differently. Think about the children. Your daughter and Nia's two."

Yeah, Sasha. Christopher couldn't remember which of his sisters was that one's ma. He couldn't even remember the names of his other two nieces, but he knew Sasha, the youngest. She'd taken a liking to Megan.

"Not happening, Ophelia. We'll take our chances right where we are, thank you very much. As for Bev and Nia, I *am* speaking for them. We knew he'd call one of us. Christopher to the rescue, when he doesn't give two shits about us otherwise."

"That ain't true! Sasha visit sometime."

"Nia allows her to visit Meggie and your children. *Not you*. You're worthless. You've always been worthless. You'll always be—"

Ophelia disconnected the call, then threw his phone on the butcher block table. K-P had gotten this on special order. *Kitchen Patrol.* Motherfucker loved to fucking cook. Now, he was dead and his kid brother was, too.

Christopher hung his head.

"Don't you dare let her get that in your head again!" Ophelia screeched. "I can't wait until Meggie is better so she can kick her ass for pissing on you when you're down. Avery didn't have a right to say any of those things."

Megan defended him to everyone and dared anyone to say what they all knew he really was. She was his greatest champion and he'd allowed her to get hurt. "Avery had every fuckin' right. I got ma killed. That was her ma too. Avery ain't ever cared much for me, but that just sealed my fuckin' fate."

"Outlaw," Cash called, appearing a moment later and halting when he saw Ophelia.

"You must be the man who called me," Ophelia said in an attempt at cheer, holding her hand out. "I'm Ophelia. His sister."

Nodding to her, Cash contemplated her from head to toe. "If you give me a minute, I'll escort you to the house."

"That's fine."

"Can you go check on Dinah for me, Fee?" Christopher asked, suspecting Cash needed to discuss club business with him.

Ophelia headed for the door. "She's in the same room she's always been in?"

"Yeah." At least he thought she was.

"I can take over from here," Cash said when Ophelia walked out. "Get to the hospital."

"I gotta go to the funeral home first. Make sure Arrow and Tyler bodies in good hands."

"Outlaw, as soon as I get your sister to the kids, so Art and Surrat can leave, I'll check into it. Or I'll call the priest."

"Art and Surrat? Ain't they two probates?"

"We couldn't get anyone else to stay with the children."

Sighing, Christopher scrubbed a hand over his face. "I tried to fuckin' get my other sisters and their fuckin' girls here, but they ain't trustin' me to protect them, Ghost."

"You did your duty," Cash returned. "It was up to them to accept. Speaking of sisters, Georgie is frantic. Sloane isn't allowing her to come here and the band has a few more concerts before they have a couple of days off. I promised I'd keep her informed. She wanted me to tell you she sends her love."

"Thanks."

"Your work here is done. Go to Meggie."

He didn't need to hear those words twice. He went behind Ophelia to give her the updated plans. After kissing her on the cheek and ordering her to keep at Avery—one of them—until they came to the club, he hurried to his bike and rode out, finally able to be Megan's husband, instead of the MC President.

Cursing under his breath and calling himself a thousand fucking fools, Digger hurried Bunny and Little Man to Logan Donovan's bedroom and the back wall. A hidden panel lay somewhere there, but hearing the opening of the front door fucked with his memory.

The fucking dark didn't help, either. The small flicker of the candle Bunny held was fucking useless. It didn't matter he sometimes worked in darkness. Fear fucked him up. If he hadn't been familiar with the house, his nerves would've had him bumping into shit. His impulsiveness had struck again. The last thing he'd expected to have when they'd infiltrated Outlaw's property was to leave alive and with hostages. Once he took Bunny and Little Man, this farm had been the closest hideout he could think of. Police had been speeding toward the club, ambulances in hot pursuit. Even worse had been the bikers arriving in a sea of chrome and metal.

Some of the brothers knew Digger by sight. All would know him by name. If they didn't know him, they knew Outlaw's son, and not only thanks to the cut proclaiming him the son of Outlaw. Then there was Bunny. The brothers knew her, too. Besides being a beautiful chick, she was also Meggie's friend.

He'd had to get off the road until shit died down. Plus, Little Man's screaming in the car had worked on his fucking nerves. The kid had lungs.

Finally, he found the correct panel and pressed against it, sagging in relief when it opened just enough for him to push Bunny and Outlaw's son through and to slip inside himself after he set the candle aside. In the small space, Bunny and Little Man pressed against him and awareness of her seeped into his brain. Although the kid touched more of him than she did, he still felt her trembles and detected her fear. A desire to protect her rose up in him, but he shoved it away. He couldn't afford an entanglement with her. She didn't have a very fucking high opinion of him anyway. Whether she worshipped the fucking ground he walked on, he never wanted another permanent woman in his life. If they survived. Digger was well aware that they might die at any moment.

Fuck.

He supposed she had a right to be scared. He was, too. If not for the survival mode he'd gone into, he'd remember…today. Sharper standing over Tyler and riddling his body with bullets. Meggie dropping to the ground. Outlaw screaming. His father using an opportunity to kill Mortician's son.

Jesus Christ.

Mort had invited Tyler to live at the clubhouse, but the kid had declined, wanting to stay with Digger on their European adventure. Because that's what he was good at. Bullshit and adventures. The promise of a grand adventure had ended in disaster. He'd promised something similar to Little Man. But Digger was determined to have a different outcome. Since Sharper was supposedly Tyler's father, Mort had backed off, wanting the best for the son whom his ex had insisted wasn't his.

Maybe, Tyler had been doomed from the start. Maybe, the kid was better off wherever he'd gone. Digger had been raised in the church, so he believed in heaven and hell, right and wrong. Judgment Day.

Tyler had been just a child, though, guided by corrupt adults. His soul could be saved, so he'd find the redemption in death that he never would've found in life. Grief swept through him and he heaved in a breath. He'd failed Mort's son. He couldn't fail Outlaw's kid.

Footsteps resounded just beyond his hiding space. Little Man squirmed and Digger swore Sharper and Osti stood *right on the other side*. If he abandoned his position now to check his theory, he believed he'd come face-to-face with them.

"I can't find him," Sharper growled in frustration, confirming their close proximity.

Since Digger heard them, they'd hear Little Man if the kid whined.

"He's here. Car and candles give him away," Osti responded.

Digger's weapon pressed against his side. If he went out blazing, he might hit them, but he'd be firing blindly. Whether the candle remained lit or not didn't matter. The area not touched by the fire's glow was dark. And, if Sharper and Osti returned fire, Bunny and Little Man's life would be endangered.

The kid whined and wiggled.

"Shhh," Bunny whispered, still too loud to Digger's way of thinking. "Please, keep quiet, CJ."

"MegAnn," Little Man murmured.

"You heard that?" Osti asked.

"Quiet," Bunny pleaded again.

"*That*," Osti said sharply.

"Mark, if you're here, come out," Sharper ordered. "We need to get a move on. I need medical attention. I've been shot."

Not fucking bad enough. It seemed as if nothing could kill his father. Not that anyone had ever really tried.

"This is the first place Outlaw will look."

"Unk, maybe, they on the grounds somewhere."

"Or, maybe, they're in another part of the house," Sharper countered. "Perhaps, we overlooked their hiding space as we overlooked the key at the clubhouse."

Key? What fucking key?

They couldn't mean a physical key. Could they?

"Peyton got Megan Caldwell, Uncle Sharper," Osti said, backing Digger's theory that *she* was the key.

"Mark!" Sharper boomed out. "I'm giving you sixty seconds to come out and turn over the woman and that motherfucker Outlaw made. If you don't, you're as dead as they are when I find you. One..."

As Sharper counted, anticipation hung in the air. The panel shook as if they knew Digger hid in the wall, but couldn't find the entry point. Any moment he expected the wall to open.

"We're going to get Outlaw," Osti taunted, as Sharper reached twenty. "And you. Once we retrieve the information we want, we're going to kill him slowly. After he watches his twins and whoever else loyal to him, die. We have a bullet waiting for his oldest son. We're too impatient to let him watch us shoot the kid. Hear what I'm saying, Marcus?" he yelled, as Sharper got to sixty.

"You stay behind," Sharper instructed. "Find Mark, kill him, that cunt, and the kid, then meet me at the safe house tomorrow afternoon. We need to get out of the area."

Footsteps faded away, but Digger felt no relief. Osti lingered in the house, maybe in the room, awaiting him to reveal himself so he could murder all of them. Digger had tipped his hand by staying put, but he'd had no choice.

"He's sleeping," Bunny said so softly he couldn't pick up on any fear she might have over the conversation they'd overheard.

Digger wanted to warn her to hold him tight because he'd become dead weight as he slept and there was no room for Digger to turn and take him from her, but he couldn't risk it, so he nodded in acknowledgment and remained silent.

As the time passed, he lost track of time. The growling of his stomach came and went and returned with vigor. By sheer willpower, he ignored the need to piss. Judging by the wetness on his back, Little Man wasn't as disciplined. Bunny shifted her weight, but kept silent other than to whisper soothing words to Outlaw's son. The one time she leaned her head against Digger's shoulder, she felt overly warm to him. However, he didn't comment since she held her shit together and helped Little Man to remain calm.

Just as his lids began to droop, the smell of smoke hit him.

"Fuck, we gotta move, Bunny." Digger pressed against the panel, gauging the warmth. He found it hot, so he hesitated. When he opened it, he could be met with a wall of fire.

However, if he remained in the fucking space, they'd burn to death for sure. Easing the panel open, he found thick smoke clinging in the air.

Bunny gasped.

"Get down low," he said, not voicing the thought that Osti might be lying in wait to shoot them down as he smoked them out.

Halting at the bedroom door, Digger pulled Little Man from Bunny. As long as they were Osti-free, it would be easier for him to get the kid to safety. In the hallway, Digger started toward the front door, but fire consumed the living room, flames licking the walls and climbing up. It was so fucking hot, sweat popped off of him and the intensity of the temperature threatened to melt his clothes off.

Momentarily disoriented, Digger's coughing fit allowed the fire to close in on them. Little Man gripped Digger's shirt, coughing just as bad.

Hanging his head, Digger swayed, still on his knees, one hand clutching Outlaw's gasping son and the other on the floor. The crackles and pops hurt his ears and the acrid smoke burned his throat.

Determined to push on, he backtracked to the room filled with smoke, but not on fire yet. His hand felt along the wall. Instead of plaster, he encountered wood. He was in the kitchen.

The kitchen with no running water.

The kitchen with…a side door.

Energy burst through him and he crawled to the door, his heart sinking when he found it boarded. Fuck, the other plank had been pulled down easy enough. Certainly, this one would give away as quickly.

Knowing they were running out of time, Digger stood, covering his nose with his arm. Two vicious kicks and the plank fell away, allowing him to stumble into the night and gasp for air.

Little Man continued coughing, but Digger didn't care. They'd made it. Turning to look for Bunny, he found...*nothing*.

"Stay here," he ordered, not thinking, only acting. On his hands and knees, he crawled back in, determined to go as far as possible. He didn't have far to go. He found her in the middle of the kitchen, too overcome to continue. "I got you, Bunny." Dragging her to the door, he heaved her over his shoulder the moment they were outside. "Come on, kid."

Assured that Outlaw's son stumbled along with him, they hurried to the front of the house, where the car and another getaway awaited them.

However, when they turned the corner and reached the burning porch, the car Digger had stolen, the car belonging to the keys in his pocket, had somehow been taken from him.

“The fucking car gone!”

Digger’s frustrations seeped through Bunny’s sluggish brain. The scent of smoke filled the air and even from her odd position the glow of the fire lit the night. The world looked upside-down, moving by her in a fast blur, as her body jarred against something hard.

“We got to hoof it, kid. Just stay close to me.”

His words didn’t hold a menacing undertone. Or her fatigue diminished the threat to her life he continued to be. Or, maybe, after being pressed against him for hours, she’d felt warm and protected for the first time in what seemed like forever.

“I can’t believe motherfuckers stole the fucking car I took,” Digger grumbled, and the hoarse tone vibrated through Bunny. The more Bunny bounced along, the further the fiery glare receded. “We playing Grand Theft Auto around this motherfucker or something.”

Bunny groaned.

“Bun-Bun!”

“I have her, lil’ dude.” Something swung her, then tapped her ass. “See? She’s over my shoulder. Don’t worry about her. No time for that shit. We have to find a way to escape. My throat's hurting so I can't talk too much."

Little Man coughed. "Too dark!" he wheezed out.

"Because your mama wimped you the fuck out by letting you sleep with a goddamn light on. Darkness don't hurt nobody."

His sniffles broke Bunny's heart. "I want MegAnn."

"If you listen, I'll get you back to Meggie," Digger promised, his irritation clear.

"Okay."

Both Digger and Little Man fell silent, relieving Bunny, though the little boy continued coughing and sniffling. She couldn't do anything about it at the moment.

After an eternity, they halted, with nothing but the cold night and the scent of smoke surrounding them.

"Why stop, Dig?" Little Man asked.

Digger bounced Bunny up, adjusting her, and then grunted. "All her weight must be in her tits and ass, cuz this bitch kind of heavy to be so skinny."

"Val like Bun-Bun's teets. Mar say Ant Bail's teets pretty. 'Law hit Val and John-John say 'Law sick fucka mudner cuz she gots pretty teets 'Law just not true. He love Ant Kenda, but he think Bun-Bun's teets pretty."

The last bit sobered Digger's hysterical guffaws at Little Man ratting out the conversations he'd apparently overheard. "Outlaw love Kendall?"

"No, 'Law say Ant Kenda a cun. MegAnn hit 'Law cuz he say bad word and I hear."

"So you meant Johnnie like Bunny's tits?"

"Uh-huh."

Bunny squeaked, the heat of embarrassment rising in her. "I can walk," she croaked out.

"Yes, in-fucking-deed," Digger rasped to Little Man, ignoring Bunny. "What else does Outlaw say? Anything about me?"

She slapped his back and kicked her legs, finally gaining his attention. He set her on her feet and she swayed against him, but he caught her in an instant.

"Don't question him," she said under her breath.

"Bun!" Little Man yelled and barreled into her legs. She almost toppled over, but Digger grabbed her forearms again.

"You okay to walk?" he asked in a curiously gentle voice.

"Yes." She sounded like a frog, but she still feared Digger seeing her as too much of a handicap.

"Let's start off again. It won't be long before the flames are seen. If they haven't been already. I need to find another car."

Not responding, Bunny grabbed Little Man's hand, determined she'd endure, hold on as long as possible, and walk on her own.

She bit down on her lip and followed Digger toward the road. The feel of Little Man's hand kept Bunny on her feet and helped her to focus. Sweat popped from her skin, despite the frigid temperatures.

By the time they reached the main highway, Digger walked ahead of her, but she couldn't go anymore.

"Digger!" she called. He continued on. Either he hadn't heard her or he ignored her. Summoning all her strength, she tried again. *"Digger!"*

This time, he stopped.

"What?"

Dizziness almost toppled her. Too weak to raise her voice, she fell to her knees.

He backtracked to her. "Fuck, the smoke getting to you?"

"I-I can't. I can't go any further," she said weakly. "Just please don't hurt him. He's not even three yet." She drew in a deep breath and even her lungs hurt. "Please?"

Digger touched her cheek. "You got fever."

In response, she curled on the ground and shuddered, the thought she'd die without making up with her parents prevalent in her head. For so many months she'd been too stubborn to admit they'd been right about Trader and, now, she'd never get to eat her mom's nasty tofu cake that she flavored with flaxseed and whey. She'd never join her dad and her brother in razzing her mom for being a health food nut. "Call my brother," she whispered. Knowing Digger probably hadn't heard her, or would ignore her if he had, she closed her eyes, unable to retain consciousness any longer.

He should kill her. Allowing her to live would slow them down. But, for some reason, he noticed how fragile and helpless she looked all curled up, unconscious on the side of the road. She'd never done anything to him. Not to mention Outlaw had always drummed it into them that women were not to be hurt if at all possible.

She'd protected Outlaw's son as though the kid belonged to her, and Digger couldn't help but respect that. She was so different from Peyton. Despite Bunny's background, or what he understood of it, she had something Peyton lacked. A conscience.

Peyton had been educated, but she wouldn't have thought twice about sucking his dick. While Bunny would've given him a blow job, she didn't pretend she wanted to do it. Not even to get on his good side.

As if he didn't have enough to contend with, the sirens were finally screaming in the night. He'd gone in the opposite direction to escape notice, but they needed to shelter somewhere. Kidnapping wasn't as easy as he'd thought…fuck, therein lay the problem. He *hadn't* thought.

Little Man started his nerve-wracking whining again. Digger gritted his teeth. Understanding the boy's fright and exhaustion, he tried for as much patience as possible. When he'd been Little Man's age, he'd always had his mom to comfort him. And, if his mom hadn't been there, Mortician was. Although Digger was only two years younger than Mort, his brother had protected him from the time he'd been born.

If he'd have found a woman before Mort, no way in hell would Mortician have gone off half-cocked and jealous. He'd never tried to impress women with money either. Bitches took Mort as is or he told them to fuck off. He took care of his money, to the point of fucking stinginess.

Heaving in a breath, Digger set Little Man on his feet and crouched down. "We need to get Bunny out of the road. Stay close to me, okay?"

"Okay." His little voice was hoarse and sad, his cheeks smudged with dirt and soot. "Bun-Bun sleep?"

"Yeah, kid."

As he scooped her up into his arms, headlights shined on him and he jumped back. Near them, the car slowed down, until it stopped right next to him.

Fuck, with Bunny in his arms, he couldn't reach for his gun, so he'd have to play it cool. The window rolled down and the interior light flicked on. An older, white-haired man squinted at him.

"Everything okay, sir?"

Before Digger responded, Little Man said, "MegAnn falled."

Fuck him in the middle of the road, but why the fuck would the kid say that? At first, the driver's brows drew together, until he leaned over and saw Little Man standing there. His gaze went from Digger to Little Man and back again. Suspicion lit the man's face. Reeking of smoke, they must've looked pretty fucked up.

The door locks popped up. "Get in out the cold. I can bring you to the hospital."

Hadn't this dude heard about picking up strange motherfuckers?

"Mommie got red. Bun-Bun—"

"Told you we don't have fucking buns!" Digger snapped out.

The man narrowed his eyes. "Bun-Bun?"

Little Man nodded and glanced up at Digger. Just as he opened his mouth to blab a little more, the driver spoke again.

"How'd Mommie get red, little fella?"

"A big boom," he sniffled, "then MegAnn falled and 'Law gone."

Digger growled, stopping Little Man before he said anything more incriminating. "This chick heavy. If you not giving us a goddamn ride, get to fucking going. We through talking."

The older man contemplated Digger suspiciously, then he nodded once more. "Get in."

The offer answered Digger's question. Not only had he not heard about stopping for strange motherfuckers, he was fucking clueless about picking them up. Deciding to see how this played out, Digger accepted the invitation.

Once he situated Bunny on the back seat and secured Little Man next to her, Digger got into the passenger seat, thankful his hands were now free to draw his weapon if the need arose. "We don't need a fucking hospital. I need to get to my old lady's brother."

"Potty," Little Man said.

Digger didn't answer. While stuck in the fucking wall, the kid had been pissing on himself all day. If it took him pissing on himself to keep him quiet, Digger wouldn't interfere or lie and promise he'd have a "real" potty soon.

"Poopie potty."

"Strange happenings going on around these parts today," the driver said, ignoring the kid just like Digger.

No shit. Feigning surprise, Digger lifted a brow. "For real?"

"Shooting happened down at the MC."

Fuck, he didn't need this old motherfucker recognizing him and high-assing to the police. Those in the club's pocket would bring Digger right to Outlaw, instead of jail.

"About a dozen dead," the driver continued as Little Man wailed, "I gotta poopie!"

"Hold it, kid," Digger snapped, his stomach dipping at discovering the number of casualties. Tyler and Peyton were amongst them, but of the remaining ten, how many deaths were his father's hired guns and not anyone associated with the club? "Any names released?" he asked, thinking of Meggie and wondering if she might be one who didn't make it.

Another searching look, then the man shook his head. "This old brain can't remember all that." He glanced at Digger again and sniffed. "There's a big fire raging at the old Donovan place right now.

"Hmm." What the fuck else could he say?

The kid grunted. Suddenly, a horrendous smell enveloped the closed-in car.

No. This *wasn't* fucking happening.

Scowling, he flipped on the overhead light and turned, focusing on Outlaw's son. A glazed expression blanketed his face. He was having the shit of a lifetime.

Digger frowned and held his breath, attempting to trick his brain into accepting the stench because he expected it. He exhaled. Annoyance welled in him. The mind game hadn't worked. It still reeked to high fucking heaven.

"What the fuck your little ass ate?"

Little Man widened his eyes and thought for a moment.

"Hungry, Dig!" he yelled as if Digger's words reminded him that he hadn't eaten in hours. As if the foul odor he'd caused wouldn't fuck up their smell receptors for years to come.

Nasty little motherfucker.

The windows slid down and fresh air blew around the aroma of smoke and shit clinging to the three of them.

The driver cleared his throat and scowled at Digger. He glowered back. *He* was the nosy motherfucker who'd stopped.

"My tummy hurts! Hungry!"

He had to give it to the kid. He'd not once complained of hunger until Digger mentioned it. A lesson learned. Digger should've shut the fuck up about food and Little Man wouldn't have started his loud ass crying all over again. Folding his arms, he glowered into the dark, just wanting this fucking night over.

"Shut the fuck up!" he said in frustration. "I don't have nothing to feed you right now."

"Got a half-eaten bag of chips," the driver said, nodding to the glove compartment.

Digger grabbed the bag and shoved it at the kid. "Eat that and shut the fuck up."

The kid listened. *Thank you, Jesus.*

Nearing one in the morning, they arrived at Gabe's tattoo shop. Despite the late hour, lights shone from inside, a good sign to Digger. In silence, the man watched Digger take Bunny into his arms and order Little Man out of the car, right beneath the blaze of a street light. He frowned at the shit stain on his beige seat.

A tug on his jeans made Digger glance down and look into tear-filled green eyes, missing the driver's departure.

"Want home," Little Man said around sniffles.

"I'm gonna get you home," he promised, then turned to the tattoo shop. "Soon. For now, stay close to me and keep quiet, kid. Understand?"

"I unnerstand, Dig."

"Come on." Keeping a close watch on Outlaw's son and adjusting Bunny in his arms, Digger started across the street. At the shop entrance, he hesitated. If Gabe had company or wasn't in at all, Digger would be in trouble.

He had to do something, though. If he didn't keep moving, he risked discovery and not by some old motherfucker who seemed a Good Samaritan but was just fucking nosy.

Unable to maneuver the door and hold Bunny, he kicked on the glass, the thump not very loud. After of few minutes with no results, he repeated the move.

"Motherfucker," he said under his breath when no one answered.

Little Man tipped his head back to look at him.

"Can't open the fucking door," Digger explained.

After an exaggerated nod, the kid squeezed in front of him and stood on his tiptoes, trying to reach the handle. He wasn't tall enough to succeed. It fucking figured.

"'Law say on boot."

When Digger frowned, Little Man pointed down. Since Digger couldn't see the ground with Bunny in his arms, he said, "What?"

"On boot, Dig!" Little Man growled in frustration.

Scowling, Digger stepped back, to better glare at Outlaw's son. "What the fuck that mean?"

"Boot, ashfuck!" he ordered, pointing again, looking uncannily like his old man when he glared at him.

Not waiting for Digger to understand him, Little Man lifted himself onto Digger's boots, stood on his tiptoes and grunted as he attempted to pull open the heavy door. Understanding dawning on him, Digger turned and caught the door with his body weight before it fully closed. That left him facing away from the interior and unable to call out.

"Squeeze your lil' ass through the gap and go find some motherfucker to help us," Digger instructed around puffs of breaths.

"'Kay."

Digger managed to allow the kid just enough room to follow directions before he released his strained hold on the door. He turned as Little Man disappeared around the corner. He couldn't imagine a motherfucker in the shop not hearing the type of commotion that had just gone on, especially if the fucking door was unlocked.

A few minutes passed before Digger adjusted his position again. Just as he threw Bunny over his shoulder, Little Man led Gabe toward the door.

Through the glass, Digger saw the resemblance between Bunny and her brother. They both had the same brown hair and similar height. While Bunny was tall for a woman, Gabe was average sized for a dude.

Upon seeing them, Gabe also lost what little color left in his face. "What happened?" he asked, the moment he pushed open the door and allowed them to enter. "It has to be bad for Outlaw's son to be running alone in my shop in the middle of the night and smelling like shit and smoke."

Yeah, the little motherfucker had quite the aroma.

"Can I get in trouble with Outlaw?" Gabe continued. "Will he kill me?" Well, that might explain why he looked so sick.

Obviously, it hadn't dawned on him that Digger carried his sister since only her legs and ass were visible. "Your sister been hurt bad," he said, indicating Bunny with a nod.

"Jesus!" Without asking any more questions, Gabe turned the lock on the door. "Follow me."

As he left the reception area, Gabe flipped off the lights, then headed past the area where the outlines of two tattoo chairs loomed in the darkness. He paused long enough to close the door of the only private room in the shop. Afterward, he led Digger to another door. Cold, rancid air blasted in when he opened it, but, having no choice, he followed behind Outlaw's son, who stumbled behind Gabe.

"The alleyway is kind of dark," Gabe explained unnecessarily as he locked the shop door.

"No fucking shit," Digger grumbled. *Kind of* dark? What a fucking understatement. He barely saw in front of him, until Gabe raised up his cell phone, a flashlight shining from the screen.

They walked down the long alley and turned a corner, arriving at a small house.

Walking into the house, Gabe kicked aside pizza boxes and beer cans in the living room. He kicked shit out the way all the way to bedroom, where he moved crates off a bed. Only because his arms and shoulders were going fucking numb did Digger lay Bunny down.

"This not your room," he said, studying the crowded space and bare mattress.

"No, my room's across the hall."

"Either you find some sheets and covers for this bed or I'm bringing her in *your* room."

Little Man started to climb next to Bunny.

"No," Digger said firmly, and the kid halted immediately, uncertainty dropping into his face. "You got to clean up."

"I tired."

"I don't care, kid. You can't put your little shitty ass on this bed."

For a moment, Little Man looked at him, his eyes going wide before they filled with tears and he face-planted onto the mattress with a loud wail. Bunny jumped and groaned, but didn't open her eyes, while Little Man hung half on and half off the bed, sobbing.

"Fuck, kid. I got a fucking headache. Can you please shut the fuck up?"

Instead of quieting, Little Man cried harder.

"Um, why don't I see to him," Gabe suggested, not waiting for Digger to answer. "Come on, CJ." He lifted the bawling boy under one arm and hurried out of the room, leaving Digger alone with Bunny and the lingering stench.

Spying a window, he opened it, breathing in the brisk air and clearing his own lungs. He'd inhaled his fair share of smoke as well, but whatever Bunny had been suffering with at first hadn't helped her.

He turned to look at her, again noting her loveliness, her peaches and cream complexion currently marred by soot. Her long lashes fanned high cheekbones and pretty lips, while her hair reminded him of coffee beans, shiny and rich. Bone-straight, the ends reached her breasts.

She had such a soft, sweet look, with no hint of the lifestyle she'd once led. Maybe, some chicks didn't allow whatever trials they went through to make them mean and bitter.

Like Peyton had.

Brooding, he walked out of the room and shook his head at the mess in the apartment. The compact kitchen revealed dirty dishes and glasses strewn across the counter while pots and pans sat forgotten in the sink. Flies buzzed around the overflowing trashcan.

Gabe was a fucking slob. No doubt about it.

He needed to fill a pan with warm water to clean Bunny up. Maybe, he'd even discover the source of her injury. By then, he hoped she awakened. If she didn't, he wasn't sure what he'd do.

As he opened the cabinet doors, he realized all the kitchen shit Gabe owned was dirty.

"Filthy motherfucker."

Finding the biggest pan—which wasn't that fucking big—Digger moved all the other dirty cookware to a stove crusted with burned sauces. At least, Gabe had dish detergent. Scrubbing the pan as clean as possible, Digger then returned to the room where Bunny lay. He wouldn't fill the pan with water until he found clean towels and something for her to wear.

Bunny hadn't moved, and Digger scrubbed a hand over his face.

"I know what went down at the club," Gabe said, into the silence.

Digger whirled and glared at him. "You lucky I'm not fucking carrying no heat, fool. You scared me." He glanced in the hallway behind Gabe. "The kid?"

"In my room. I thought I'd let Bunny use it since I only have one sheet set."

Without responding, Digger lifted Bunny into his arms again. In Gabe's room, he halted. Not only because Little Man had climbed onto the bed with his hair still damp and no clothes on, but because the sheets were an odd grayish color.

"When the last time you washed this shit?"

Gabe flushed. "About six months ago. I've been busy," he said defensively when Digger glared at him. "Bunny used to clean up for me but ever since she started working for Meggie, she hasn't had the time."

"Let the record show if she get sicker from this nasty bed, I'm fucking you up."

Not responding to Digger's threat, Gabe stared at his sister with concern as Digger laid her down. "Wh-what's wrong with her?"

"A fucking lot," he said, explaining his version of events right up until they landed at the tattoo shop. "That's why I need your help. Bunny need medical attention."

"I'll bring her to a hospital."

"No! You not fucking hearing me. Outlaw looking for me. Sharper looking for me, Little Man, *and* Bunny."

"Yeah, but if I get Bunny and CJ back to Outlaw, they'll be safe."

"If I let them go, I'll be dead," he countered. "I have no means to get out of town or nothing. If we stay here and Outlaw find me with his kid, he might give me a chance to explain."

"Hell no!" Gabe flared. "I'm not allowing you to use my sister as your goddamn bargaining chip."

"You don't have a fucking choice," Digger snapped, advancing toward Gabe. "They stay with me until I figure out how to make Outlaw listen to my side."

Although Digger was several inches taller, Gabe straightened his shoulders, determined to hold his ground. "Fuck you."

Balling his fist, Digger punched Gabe in the jaw and sent him reeling back. The dude recovered quick and swung at Digger, clipping his chin. Losing his patience, Digger kicked Gabe's leg and grabbed him in a headlock before he fell to the ground.

"Listen, motherfucker, I don't want to have to break your fucking neck to shut you the fuck up." He put pressure on Gabe's neck to emphasize his point. "I'm not going to hurt her." Not anymore. Besides, she'd only been trying to save the kid. She shouldn't lose her life after doing something so brave. "I need help. I need a place to take her and Little Man so we can be safe. I need medical supplies. I don't need bullshit." He'd had enough to last a lifetime. "I think Bunny love you a lot, so I'm not fucking you up yet, but I promise I will if I have to."

Gabe's pulse pounded beneath Digger's fingertips. If he had to kill him, he'd be another innocent victim. Digger couldn't blame the dude for trying to protect his sister.

"We clear on where we stand, bro?"

Gabe nodded and Digger shoved him away, watching as Gabe doubled over and coughed.

"I need towels. *Clean* towels and something for her to wear. I also need your fucking cell phone."

"I'm not going to betray you," he said hoarsely, holding onto the wall.

"At the fucking moment. But when I leave your company to take care of Bunny, you might decide to call some motherfucker."

"While you're caring for her, I could leave if you have my phone."

"Not if I fucking tie you up. Even better, I can knock you the fuck out."

Gabe glanced toward the door and then the bedroom where Bunny and Little Man lay. "If I help you and Outlaw find out, I'm dead."

"All you have to do is make sure he don't find out."

"You kidnapped my sister."

"She had Outlaw's son. Now, I only want to save both of them."

"They're safe now, so—"

"So, fuck it," Digger snapped, tired of the wrangling. "Keep the bitch. I'll just get the kid and clear the fuck out." He'd tie Gabe up, so he'd get a head start to....*somewhere*. But Digger didn't intend to stand there for hours, negotiating with the motherfucker. "And if the kid get to be too fucking much for me without her, I'll just get rid of him." He allowed the insinuation to hang in the air. Instead of telling him if he had to, he'd leave the kid somewhere...outside a fire department or police station, or even the hospital, he allowed Gabe to believe that he meant to kill Outlaw's son.

Handing Digger his cell phone, Gabe quickly found two raggedy washcloths and a threadbare towel. "Motherfucker, you need a study in home economics. Basic fucking housekeeping might work, too."

"I told you I've been busy."

"You just got fucking busier. While I'm cleaning up Bunny, you start doing the kitchen. We haven't eaten in hours and I don't want to get food poisoning from dirty fucking dishes. Scrub them. Hard. And with lots of hot water."

"You're insulting," Gabe threw over his shoulder as he stomped in the direction of the kitchen.

While Digger still didn't trust the motherfucker not to pull a fucking trick, he had to see to Bunny, so he went to the bathroom, placed the pan under the bathtub faucet, and ran the hot water. Raising the toilet seat, Digger frowned. If he didn't have to piss so bad, he'd walk the fuck away. In case some airborne disease floated from the disgusting toilet, he held his dick as far away as possible, then raised his leg and used his foot to flush.

The clubhouse toilets were cleaner than this one would ever be again. What the fuck was wrong with Gabe?

Turning off the faucet, he lifted the filled pan and headed back to the room where Bunny lay. After using his arm to slide shit aside on the crowded dresser and sitting the pan down, Digger turned to her.

First, he wiped her face off, removing both soot and makeup, and frowning at the light bruise on her cheeks and the small cut near her eye. Fresh injuries.

Studying them a second longer and ignoring the ugly thought that Trader might've had something to do with them, Digger grabbed one of her feet, smiling at her polished toenails. A woman's feet were important. He couldn't be with a bitch who had ugly, unkempt nails. Cracked and chipped polish was fucking trifling. Straight-up. One nail? Fine. That could be overlooked until it was corrected. *All* the nails? It was a turn-off to Digger.

For some reason, he raised her hand, merely to check her nails. He found them unpolished but neatly trimmed. The bottom of her feet were dirty and bleeding, the result of not wearing shoes. At some point today, she'd lost them.

He sat next to Bunny and positioned her so he could pull her shirt up. Doing so revealed a serviceable blue cotton bra. Nothing to impress a motherfucker. The thought pleased him and he grinned in approval.

Seeing the black and purple bruises covering her arms and stomach melted his smile. He slid a finger over one and frowned at the raised skin. She'd rolled out of the way with Little Man during the gun battle, then she'd fallen earlier, but had either event been hard enough to cause the type of damage he saw? The marks just reaffirmed Digger's belief of what had happened. Or *who* had happened. *Trader*. He must've beaten her up. No wonder Outlaw shot the fuck out of him. If he'd still been alive, Digger would've wanted to fuck him up, too.

His blood beginning to boil, Digger left her bra on and cleaned the soot from her arms. He'd save wiping off her tits for last. The two, tempting mounds demanded every shred of decency in him to ignore.

Dropping the washcloth into the cooling water, Digger worked on her jeans. Once he'd gotten them completely off, he froze at the sight of her blue, blood soaked panties and all the discoloration on her thighs and lower stomach.

The blood had dried. He hesitated, clearly remembering her saying it wasn't her time of the month, so what the fuck was this?

Scratching his jaw, he tapped his foot on the floor. His mind searched through what could be wrong with her. If not her time of the month, then Trader must be responsible. If her injuries were internal, it would cause all types of problems. Seeing the extent of her cuts, bruising, and bleeding made unseen trauma a distinct possibility. No wonder she'd fainted. She'd lost a lot of fucking blood.

And hadn't once complained about pain or discomfort. He admired her strength.

"I'm going to get you to safety, girl," he promised, guilt hitting him for the first time, knowing he used her to make things easier for him. With her around, he'd be able to keep Little Man and bargain for his own life.

Quickly, he removed her panties, revealing her hairless pussy and ignoring the blood smeared on her thighs. Fuck, but she was pretty. With only her bra on, she was a fucking wet dream in the flesh, with endless legs, curvy hips, a small waist, and nice cleavage.

She was also incapacitated and he had absolutely no fucking business lusting after her. Wiping off her thighs and stomach, he refused to invade her privacy any more than he had and touch her cunt. As much as he wanted to. Not only because he *wanted* to but to check for any wounds.

He hurriedly removed her bra and licked his lips at the sight of her strawberry-tipped nipples and round tits. Also sporting bruises.

"What the fuck, man?" Gabe's angry voice broke into the silence. "What did you do to her?"

"Nothing," he snapped, yanking the covers over her, although Gabe had already turned his back. "I think Trader beat her up and that's the reason Outlaw popped the motherfucker this morning."

As Little Man started coughing in his sleep, Gabe turned and faced Digger, worry creasing his brow. "My sister's going to be okay, isn't she? I promise I'll help any way I can if it means saving her and keeping CJ alive.

Digger had already forgotten about his unspoken threat to kill the kid.

"I even have a place you can hide out at," Gabe continued. "I swear on Bunny's life, I won't tell anyone where you're at."

"Give me a T-shirt to dress her in, then, if you're serious about helping, I'll tell you exactly what I need."

Several hours later, a friend of Gabe's came to the house with medical supplies, prescription drugs, and IV paraphernalia, while Digger took Little Man and hid in the shop. After starting Bunny on an IV line, the guy left and Digger returned to Gabe's house, where he finished giving the dude instructions on what he needed to make his getaway and hopefully save all of their lives in the long run.

Christopher stood in his old room at the clubhouse, dressed in full leathers. Twenty-four hours had gone by since the shootings and he fucking felt nothing. Not one goddamn, motherfucking thing. Like he'd gone to a fucking dentist and had his entire body shot the fuck up with novocaine.

After surviving surgery, Megan lay in ICU, connected to too many tubes and wires. Critical but finally stable. This time yesterday he'd just been walking out of his door to talk to Trader. Maybe, punch the fuck out of him. But the motherfucker had pissed Christopher off, talking about Bunny as he had. If he didn't fucking want her, that was his fucking choice. But if he fucking disrespected her to Christopher like she was fucking trash, then Christopher could only imagine what the fuck Trader did to her in private.

Bunny had enough fucking shit to deal with. Christopher knew all the fuck about it. No fucking way would he let fucking Trader hold that over her head. Since he didn't have the patience to give motherfuckers more than a warning or two, he'd taken care of the problem. Bunny might fucking hate Christopher or she might thank him. He didn't know and he didn't give a fuck.

He'd done what was necessary to protect her. He hadn't expected to put him to ground right away as he had.

Not that any of it mattered at this point. Motherfucking Trader was the only one who was where he should be.

Ignoring his unmade bed and heading to the bathroom, Christopher faced the mirror and braced himself on the sink. He hardly recognized himself. Dark circles ringed his bloodshot eyes, and worry pinched his mouth. After returning to the club last night he'd barely slept. He'd wanted to stay with Megan, but Cash had called and said Mort wanted Tyler taken care of ASAP, so they'd decided to bury Arrow, too. Even if Arrow had survived, Christopher wanted to show Mortician the respect he deserved, as a man who'd lost his kid without ever really knowing him. And, simply, as his brother and best friend.

Christopher straightened, knowing he had to be the leader the club needed. He had to be strong on the outside, when he was so fucking wrecked inside. Back in the room, he walked to the photo of Megan pregnant with CJ. It was a reprint of the original that had once hung in the same spot, until they'd moved into their first house. The one that had been blown to bits and fucking pieces.

Swallowing, he reached out and touched the photo, laying his hand over her protruding belly, much like he had in the picture. He remembered that fucking day, feeling the baby move, thinking Megan was having a girl because him and Johnnie had been the only dicks born into the family since the birth of his doomed uncle. During the photo shoot, Christopher had decided to buy all that pink shit to surprise Megan with when the baby was born.

Now, that baby was missing and Megan was critical.

Was that why they'd been each other's soulmates, met when she was still so young? Why they'd been each other's everything almost from the moment they'd met? Because she was destined to die before her twenty-second birthday?

Dropping his hand to his side, he hung his head, reaching for his cell phone, stuffed in one of his pockets.

He dialed her number, because he'd fucking lost his mind. *One and Only* by Adele blasted through the room, the vibrations of her phone thumping on the desk.

"Hey, this is Meggie. Leave a message."

At the sound of her sweet little voice, he leaned his head against the photo and drew in a deep breath. "I miss you, baby," he told her quietly. "That bullet shoulda been for me. I'd give my fuckin' life just to know you safe and alive. Don't fuckin' leave me, Megan. Please," he added as if that could make a fucking difference.

A knock sounded on his door and he disconnected the call. He clenched his teeth, determined not to look at Megan's favorite brick wall, the one she'd always turned to when he'd hurt her or pissed her off. When he'd tried to sleep, he'd faced away from the wall, his grief and misery running deep. He hadn't been able to bear setting foot in the house. Everywhere he looked, he felt Megan. He'd thought it would be better in his old room, but she was here, too.

She was in his heart and soul. He could go to the fucking moon and he wouldn't escape her.

"Prez?"

Mort's tired voice carried through the door, and Christopher remembered hearing the knock.

"Come the fuck in."

The door opened and Mort stepped in, followed by Johnnie. The three of them stared at each other before Christopher cleared his throat.

"Mort, Tyler gonna be in a separate fuckin' parlor at the funeral home. Ain't wanted to have to fuck up a motherfucker if you shed some fuckin' tears over your kid. I'm gonna say what I gotta for Arrow, but I wantcha to hang tight at the funeral home. Talk to your boy, then even if just me and you there, Wilcunt gonna say Mass for Tyler."

"They're Baptist, Christopher."

"Don't give a fuck, John Boy. Ain't knowin' no Baptist minister. Wouldn't know a Catholic priest if it wasn't for my girl."

"Prez right, Johnnie," Mort said. "In the end, we all Christians."

Johnnie shrugged, one arm clutched to his side in a sling. After Cash called Christopher, he'd gone to check in on everybody before he left. Val had taken shots to the shoulder, arm, and thigh, but he'd had his fucking eyes opened by the time Christopher was ready to leave. Zoann had also gotten shot in the arm and upper back. She'd been resting comfortably. He'd had to search for Johnnie and found him limping from Kendall's room with the intention of returning to his own. Once Christopher had brought him up to speed, Johnnie hadn't been happy with having to stay in the hospital. So much so that he'd checked out, despite the doctor recommending an overnight stay. In the midst of Christopher, Mort, and Cash finalizing last minute plans for the funerals, Johnnie had walked in.

"We're Christians, Mort, but he isn't," Johnnie said, nodding to Christopher.

"Ain't made no secret 'bout that."

Lifting a brow, Johnnie searched Christopher's face as if he expected words. Since Christopher couldn't think of anything he should say, he kept his fucking mouth shut, pissing Johnnie the fuck off. He clenched his jaw, resentment dropping into his face. "How are the twins?"

What the fuck crawled up his ass, Christopher couldn't imagine. "Don't know, John Boy. Ain't seen 'em since yesterday mornin'."

"Why? They're your children. Now, more than ever, you should hold them tight. Do you want to end up like Mortician? Losing a child without ever knowing him."

"Johnnie, if this your idea of offering fucking advice, your ass need to take some fucking pointers," Mortician growled.

Under-fucking-statement, but Christopher wouldn't hold Johnnie's fucking hand. He'd have to fucking deal with everything, just as Christopher was.

However, in case the motherfucker forgot…"I already lost a fuckin' kid that I ain't ever know. Patrick. Remember him?"

Johnnie's scowl darkened. "How can I not when you made sure no one forgot your wife's pain? Or the fact that you stick your cock in her and she ends up pregnant every goddamn time. They all do. Our dicks have turned into fucking fertility sticks. Imagine if you hadn't had your dick snipped? She'd probably be close to death *and* pregnant."

What. The. Fuck? Had Johnnie lost his fucking mind? What the fuck did any of the bullshit he was talking about have to do with anything? "Listen up, John Boy. I under-fuckin-stand you ain't fuckin' likin' your tongue in your mouth right the fuck now. I fuckin' swear if you don't shut the fuck up, you gonna be missin' that motherfucker."

Megan not being pregnant had nothing to do with the vasectomy-that-wasn't. She was back on her fucking pills and had talked him out of the dick snip.

"You have something to say to me, Christopher?"

"You fuckin' deaf? I just fuckin' said what the fuck I had to say. Next fuckin' step is showin' you."

"We're past this." Johnnie sounded hurt. "At least I thought we were."

"What's your damn problem, son? On the real. We don't need this shit right now, Johnnie."

"Don't worry 'bout it, Mort," Christopher said. "Motherfucker got a right to be pissed at what went down. Ain't showed the best leadership." He rubbed the back of his neck. "I tried to get my sisters to come here with their girls, and Avery got pissed the fuck off pointin' that shit out to me. How I failed every-fuckin-body."

"Does any of that matter? Or is it only how you think you failed Megan?"

"Ain't no thinkin' in it, Johnnie," Christopher snarled. "She laid up in fuckin' ICU. Fuckin' fail right there. My ass back at the fuckin' club, instead of at her side. Another fuckin' fail."

"You're human, Christopher. You make mistakes. Am I fucking pissed about yesterday? Yes. It's worse because I have no one to fucking kill to release my frustrations. I resent the way you're rushing through everything at the club for personal reasons. The members need you here. Not at the fucking hospital."

"Where the fuck you goin' after Arrow's send-off? Back to the fuckin' hospital, right? Where the fuck Mort goin', John Boy? What the fuck wrong with my ass bein' with Megan?"

"Because you're torturing yourself," Johnnie yelled. "She's not fucking conscious. There's fuck-all you can do, except stare at her and wonder if she'll live or die. Here, though, you can start searching for meat shack motherfuckers. You can talk to the members arriving on our behalf."

"You right," Christopher agreed, his head pounding. "I can do all that fuckin' shit. But I ain't. Ima see to sendin' off Arrow and Ima stand with Mort. Ima come back to the club and toast K-P kid brother, then Ima go sit at Megan side and Ima try my fuckin' best not to fuckin' move 'til I know how I gotta bring my girl home. Dead. Or alive. If you don't like my fuckin' plan? Tough shit cuz I ain't fuckin' changin' it."

Johnnie threw him another long, searching look. "Anything else you have to say to me?"

"Not a fuckin' thing. Cuz I didn't have *that* to fuckin' say to you. My ass just told you what the fuck Ima do outta respect."

"There's nothing else? Nothing to ask me."

Christopher scrubbed a hand over his face. "Look, motherfucker, I ain't up to your preppy fuckin' games. If my ass forgettin' something, clue me the fuck in. If I ain't? Shut the fuck up and get the fuck outta my face."

Disgusted, Johnnie brushed passed Mortician and stalked off.

"Johnnie just stressed, Mort. Don't let what that motherfucker say get to you," Christopher explained, the moment they were alone, compelled to defend Johnnie, in spite of how much he felt like fucking him up.

Mort nodded. "I know, Prez, but he was wrong to lay that bullshit down to you. Only reason I'm here because of Tyler. If not for him, I wouldn't have left Bailey's side and I don't give a fuck who said what."

"Why the fuck Johnnie here?" Christopher asked, torn between anger at his attitude and understanding his reasons. Johnnie didn't do fear well and Christopher knew he was worried about his wife. "I ain't ordered him to leave Kendall to bring his ass here."

"Don't know why he showed up if he came with bullshit, Prez. Right now, I don't give a fuck. Only thing that would take the fucking edge off John Boy is if he fucked up a motherfucker."

Christopher smiled. "Ain't no motherfuckers to fuck up right now. Johnnie do good to hold that rage in 'til we get who the fuck did this to us."

Christopher remembered Johnnie's nervousness over Kendall needing to talk to him. Yesterday morning, he'd given no indication that he'd gotten bad fucking news from her. But Kendall was Kendall, so who knew? However, that might explain

Johnnie's present mood.

"You know he been kind of on edge lately."

"Look at the cunt he married to. My ass would be on edge too."

"Damn, Prez."

"I know, Mort. In the last twenty-four hours, I been tryin' to put all that shit behind us. Any-fuckin-thing for Megan to live. But Kendall hurt Megan, too, and that ain't shit I can forgive. I realize, though, I ain't wantin' the bitch dead unless she fuckin' make me fuck her up. I especially don't want Kendall fuckin' hurt cuz some motherfuckers invaded *our* fuckin' territory. Even if only that cunt had been fuckin' hurt if it came from the fuckin' outside, then the motherfuckers who hurt her gotta die. She belong to Johnnie. That make her part of the club and we protect our fuckin' own. That's fuckin' it. Other than that, I can't stand her. *And* she turnin' Johnnie into a whiny fuckin' cunt." Christopher frowned and rubbed the back of his neck.

"What?"

"A few days ago, I was tellin' Megan that cunts the best creation in the fuckin' world. But I meant the fuckable cunts, not annoyin', talkin' ones."

Mort snickered. "Meggie girl right. You fucking psycho." The moment the words left his mouth, his smile fell away. Bleakness filled his eyes, heightening Christopher's own emptiness.

An awkward silence passed between them.

Clearing his throat, Mort averted his gaze. "Guess we better go."

"Yeah."

Neither of them made a move. The longer they stayed in the room, the longer the inevitable could be put off. Unfortunately, time slid right the fuck on. Christopher knew hiding did no good. Life still caught up and fucked them in the ass.

"You ready, brother?"

"Yeah, Prez. As ready as I'll ever be."

Lucas "Mortician" Banks studied the body of his son, laid out in a white shirt and yellow silk tie. He wasn't sure why he'd gotten Tyler a yellow tie. The cheerful sunny color represented an illusion of joy, when happiness was such a fleeting emotion, here one minute and gone the next.

Like Tyler.

He'd grown since he'd last seen him the night Harley was born. In death, he looked older than thirteen, but he hadn't seen him alive and animated to know if that might've been the cosmetics they'd used for his lay out.

The parlor was silent, though right beyond the doors several dozen brothers mourned Arrow. Mort couldn't, though. That would remind him that he'd also lost K-P.

He'd remember seeing his wife on the ground, with two bullets in her.

He'd howl at the missed opportunity to take down his father. His father, who'd made eye contact with Mortician and then shot Bailey.

Blinking away his tears, he stared at Tyler again. He'd been a fine boy, handsome, a cross between Char and Mortician, taking the best they each had to offer.

"I loved your mama once upon a time, Tyler," he began, stroking his son's morbidly cold cheek. "Charlemagne had always been beautiful. I'm sure you knew that." He stared into the casket, wishing Tyler would open his eyes. The words Mortician spoke now should've been said months ago. But he'd put it off. It had been easier. He hadn't wanted Tyler's presence to interfere with his relationship with Bailey. Having him around would've always reminded Bailey of Char. The fact that Mortician had loved her first and had allowed what went on between them to affect his relationship with Bailey. The fact that Char had intended to kill Bailey. Allowing Tyler to go with Digger had been the easy, coward's way out.

Now, his son was gone.

"I'm sorry, Tyler. I'm so, so sorry. For taking Char from you and for not stepping in like I should've."

Until that moment, he'd never once regretted killing Charlemagne. If she'd been alive, Tyler would've been with her. He would've been safe, instead of being forced to go with Digger and Sharper to fight a war that wasn't his to begin with. Tyler had been innocent in this, collateral just like their women and other children.

Not only had he lost Tyler, but he was also on the verge of losing Bailey and the baby she carried.

"Mortician?"

Swallowing, Mortician straightened at the sound of Johnnie's voice, his guard going up. Johnnie was going off the fucking deep end. While Mort understood, he couldn't talk Johnnie through this shit. The motherfucker had to stop lashing out when emotions were so intense. He had to fucking realize that love wasn't all sunshine and roses. One moment, it blazed brightly and the next it unravelled at the seams, where only a strong, solid bond mended any tears. Johnnie gave Kendall her way because he loved her and wanted her happy. But also because it was easier. Red was a formidable force and Johnnie never stood a chance against her. Mort believed their relationship was solid, but Johnnie needed an outlet for his frustrations and targeted both Meggie and Prez with his bad moods. He knew they'd always forgive him. He knew they had his back, so he took fucking advantage of that.

Johnnie cleared his throat. Probably because Mortician had yet to face him. He couldn't, not while he was so torn up.

"I'm sorry for earlier," Johnnie said into the silence.

"I don't hold it against you," Mort responded, willing away the hoarseness and hurt. When one fell, the others were there to hold him up. Usually. But this time, they'd *all* gotten knocked down. How did they come back from this? Silently analyzing Johnnie was supposed to ease his heartache, not add to it. All that they'd had as husbands, fathers, brothers, might be gone for good. "After all these fucking years, if I can't cut you some fucking slack, I'm not much of a fucking friend."

Johnnie remained silent.

"Seen Prez?"

"Yes. They just rode out for the cemetery. Christopher's interring Arrow in Big Joe's tomb. That's where K-P is."

Mort flinched at the reminder. Both Bailey's father and uncle were gone, leaving her without anyone from K-P's family.

"How is he? Christopher, I mean."

Anger rising in him, Mort sidled a scowl at Johnnie. "How the fuck you think he is, motherfucker? What kind of bullshit was you throwing at him earlier?"

"He hasn't once asked about Kendall."

Mort turned back to his son. "And? He got other shit to do. According to you, he has a fucking club to run."

"He let Megan stop him from going after Digger, and that got Kendall shot."

"It also got Bailey shot." Mortician threw him a dirty look, not in the mood to discuss Digger with Johnnie. He wanted his brother's head on a fucking platter. Maybe, Mort did, too, but the stupid motherfucker was still his brother. Prez got his turmoil. Johnnie didn't. That spoke volumes, showing why Outlaw was a leader and Johnnie just a killer. "Not going after Digger got Arrow killed. *Meggie* shot. What the fuck wrong with you?"

"You think I don't know that? But what if she dies? Am I going to have to bury Christopher?"

"Yeah, Johnnie," Mortician responded without hesitation.

Fear darkened Johnnie's face and he gave a bitter laugh.

"If Meggie die, you will have to bury Prez."

Anger, resentment and grief slid across Johnnie's face, unable to cope with such a possibility. Johnnie was only cool under fire when it came to killing. Emotions like this left him stunted. But Mort also suspected Johnnie was pissed because Prez hadn't asked about Kendall.

Fuck, Prez hadn't asked about his own children. He was only able to run the club because he'd lived and breathed the club for so long. He could lead it in his fucking sleep.

"Under the circumstances, Prez holding up better than me. I would say fuck all these motherfuckers and stay with Bailey. That's what the fuck I intend to do the moment Tyler buried." He gave Johnnie a hard look. "Tell me you'd do shit different."

"I'd ask about *everyone*."

"If Meggie girl die, then you get the chance to do shit different. If Prez don't die of grief or fuck himself up, no way would he stay in the club."

"Bullshit. Christopher wouldn't let anyone come between him and the club. What else does he have? This is all he knows. Without the club, he'll be lost."

"This just your bitch-ass roundabout way of saying you can't run this club."

Balling his fist, Johnnie stiffened.

Mort backed away from Tyler's coffin and folded his arms, waiting.

"Fuck, fine," Johnnie huffed out. "I don't want to run the club."

"That'll do." The admission would be as close as Johnnie would come to acknowledging his inability to lead the Death Dwellers. "About Digger."

"What about him? Not that I'm really interested."

"I'm pissed with him, Johnnie, but that's still my brother. Meggie was the driving influence behind what Outlaw did, but I think he did it for me, too. He think about us more than we give him credit for."

"If that's the case, then he could've gotten both you and him killed. Digger betrayed the club and *he* betrayed it by not going after the man the way he should have."

Mortician wanted to fuck Digger up for all the shit he'd done. Right now, he also felt like slamming his fist into Johnnie's self-righteous mouth. "You disparage him all the fuck you want. He let my brother live—"

"And as a result, Digger betrayed us again. He took CJ."

Mortician shook his head. "I admit I didn't think about too much since Bailey got shot and Tyler was murdered." Beyond the fact that he'd seen Bailey go down and he'd run to her, instead of pursuing Sharper. "But Digger wouldn't take Little Man to harm him. I know my brother, man. I do."

Cold hostility radiated from Johnnie, but Mort wasn't intimidated. His gaze remained steady and unflinching. "Let's drop the conversation for now," he said tightly. "Your grief is clouding your thinking."

"And your assfuckery clouding yours," Mortician snapped.

"Fuck off." Johnnie turned on his heel and tension eased from Mortician. If they'd kept at it, they might've murdered each other. "I'm going to Kendall."

"For real, motherfucker? After all the shit you gave Prez your ass not going back to the club to toast Arrow?"

"I never intended to do that. Christopher just assumed I would. Kendall wants me with her, so I'm going."

"But Prez can't do the same?"

"Kendall's awake, Mortician. Megan's not. She may never wake up again." Devastation crossed his face so quickly Mort might've imagined it, but knew he didn't. "Why should he be there to watch her die?"

"Fuck, Johnnie, you hear what the fuck you saying? Where the fuck he supposed to be? If Meggie breathe her last and Prez not there, he'd fucking unhinge."

"Anyway it goes he'll unhinge," Johnnie snapped. "He already has."

Mortician held onto his temper by sheer will. But Johnnie running off at the mouth about Meggie forced Mortician to think of Bailey and her critical condition. He wanted to be at her side, hear all the monitors that indicated she was still alive. He had an obligation to Tyler, though, so he *couldn't* be at her side. But he was well aware his situation was similar to Prez's. "If Bailey di..." No, he wouldn't fucking speak those words, even if she'd been shot in the chest like Meggie. "My ass on the verge of unhinging. What about you? What would you do if you lost Red? Cry? Cuss? Kill? I doubt you'd be here if Red was so critical. You talk your bullshit but your woman not near death. Know why? Because Sharper want me and Prez destroyed. Not you. Not no other motherfucker. We all a little fucking lost right now. In fucking shock. Shit had been good for us, despite Sharper being on the loose. All of a sudden, everything fucked and we looking for solid fucking ground again. So until you in my shoes, until you in Prez's shoes, shut the fuck up about who the fuck should do what. I'm standing over my son's dead body, fucking pretending I'm not. I'm fucking analyzing you, dissecting your attitude, to keep from thinking about Bailey and how she hooked to all those machines. I'm trying not to remember my fucking father tried to murder my Bailey. Judge me and Prez, all the fuck you want. Or be the motherfucker you once was. The one who supported Prez."

"I still support him."

"Publicly."

"That's where it counts."

"Not with the bullshit you give him in private. Sometimes, the measure of a motherfucker not what the fuck he do in public, but how the fuck he act in private."

Johnnie's eyes flared wide, as if the statement had gotten through to him, before the coldness returned. "Kendall or Megan shouldn't have gotten shot. Christopher's lackadaisical attitude is at fault."

"Stop with the big words."

"You're a college graduate. You understand them."

That motherfucker. "You just full of fucking shade today, huh, bro?"

"I meant nothing by that. Both you and Christopher need to stop being so sensitive. What's wrong with using words with more than one syllable?"

"It complicates shit."

"This isn't the time to discuss my vocabulary. I want to point out something regarding our previous conversation."

"And that is?"

"I'd never go against Christopher in public. Never. But I'm so fucking furious with him, Mortician."

"Then you must be fucking furious with me, too." Mortician glanced at Johnnie and shook his head. "But, not really. You blame him because he's the president? Or his decision might lead to Meggie's death?"

"Fuck you."

"No, fuck you. And you just gave me my fucking answer, so get the fuck away from me."

Through with Johnnie, Mortician turned back to Tyler.

"I love Kendall."

"Never said you didn't," Mort responded without turning.

"I'm *in* love with Kendall."

"Figured that shit out as well."

"Then what the fuck did you mean?"

"Nothing, brother," Mort said on a tired sigh, emotionally drained. "I meant fuck-all." He glanced at Johnnie and saw his confusion. Instead of dropping the subject, Mort shook his head, deciding to open up to Johnnie a little. It might help the stupid motherfucker. "Charlemagne was special to me at one time," he confided. "I…sometimes when Bailey ask me something about Char, a good memory of what we once were to each other might break though. I might smile. Or feel a little wistful. Or…I don't know…I might just *remember* what it was like to be with Char. It don't mean I don't love Bailey with everything in me. It just mean I loved Char at one time, and the good and bad times I shared with her will always be a part of me. I killed her, but I regret it right now because if I hadn't, Tyler might be alive. Yet what choice did I have? She was going to hurt Bailey." He turned back to Tyler, the son he'd never know. "Life not cut-and-dry. No matter how much we say otherwise. You pissed with Prez cuz you think he got the first girl you ever loved hurt. You do everything in your fucking power to erase all the good memories between you and Meggie by being a raging motherfucker to her the majority of the time. That's not changing shit. It's just changing *you*. So before you let your fucking mouth get ahead of your fucking brain and you lay more bullshit on Prez, step the fuck back, cool the fuck off, and face the fucking facts."

Instead of responding, Johnnie stormed away.

"Motherfucker," Mortician mumbled. Stress was turning John Boy into an unfeeling lunatic…*more* of an unfeeling lunatic.

"You heard that, Tyler?" Mortician said, turning back to the casket. "John Boy don't have much empathy for anyone. Red. *Mostly*. Outlaw. *Sometimes*. Meggie girl. Well, fuck, not in a long time. Whenever shit go wrong, he liked to take it out on Meggie. Motherfucker is smart, though. He has a business degree.

Something you...if you'd lived." Moisture gathered in his eyes again and he almost wished Johnnie and his fuckedupness would return so Mortician's pain would go away. He heaved in a breath and focused on talking, instead of his grief and guilt. "You would've liked Val. Motherfucker can be dumber than a fucking dildo, but he have your back. Cash a hard motherfucker to know and Stretch not been the same since Hanson was killed and he was so badly beaten."

Mort drew his brows together and skimmed his hand over his son's hair. "The world a cold fucking place, son. I failed you. Char did, too. But, maybe, you better off, huh? I mean you don't ever again have to worry about all the hate floating around. Motherfuckers just thrive on hatred." He looked at Tyler's still face again and smiled through tears. "Yeah, son, maybe you better off."

And, maybe, he needed to say that to feel better.

Whatever the case, truth or a balm to his pain, Mort twisted off his skull ring and worked it onto Tyler's finger, the only offering he had for a boy gone too soon.

"Christopher?"

At the sound of Johnnie's voice, Christopher lifted his head from where he sat at Megan's feet. He blinked, silent as Johnnie walked to the window and opened the blinds, revealing the first glimmer of morning lightening the sky.

Just under seventy-two hours ago Megan had been shot. To Christopher, it felt like a lifetime. So much shit had happened, but he hadn't left her side in the two days since the funeral.

At some point in the night, he'd leaned over and settled his head on Megan's hospital bed, just as he had the night before last. At her feet. For an hour, he'd told her about Arrow's and Tyler's send-offs, willing her to open her eyes, wanting their connection to be deep enough that she somehow felt his pain and came back to him. She hadn't even twitched. If only this was a bad fucking dream, but this shit was real. Standing, he stared at Megan, once again waiting for her eyelids to lift. They didn't. She remained connected to IVs and oxygen and all types of machines. Each little noise one of them motherfuckers made reminded him of his wife's critical condition.

He couldn't even kiss her. To do so, he had to remove the oxygen tubes that had replaced the ventilator she'd been on until last night. Her lips would be still beneath his and that would tear him apart.

He gripped them the railings on her bed, so tight his fingers turned white.

"Christopher?" Johnnie called again, sounding exhausted. "Zoann went home last night. Stretch will be released later today. About ten minutes ago, Roxy signed herself out to take care of Harley since Bailey's not conscious yet. So far she hasn't lost the baby, but she seems to be threatening a miscarriage."

Christopher nodded, distracted by Megan not responding to his silent plea. He needed to say something to Johnnie's report. But what?

"Val's pissed," Johnnie continued, moving his arm in the sling and reminding Christopher that out of all of them, Bailey and Megan were still the gravest.

Of course, it had to be them. Sharper hated Christopher and Mortician the most.

"Val wants to go home, too. He wants to check himself out like Roxy. He was shot in the side, a little more serious than her injury."

Dropping back into the chair he'd slept in, Christopher scratched his jaw. He should take care of the stubble. Megan preferred him clean shaven. She'd want him groomed. He had his shaving kit here as well as his toothbrush. He brushed his teeth every day but fuck shaving.

Johnnie sighed and backed toward the opened door. "I'll keep you updated."

Relieved at Johnnie's imminent departure—he didn't have to fucking talk if the man left—Christopher started to nod. Then, it fucking hit him. Johnnie had left someone off. Frowning, he rubbed his eyes. "And Kendall?"

Tension flashed between them and Johnnie stiffened. "Do you really care how she is?"

"On your fuckin' behalf."

"Really? You couldn't leave Megan's side *on my behalf* to help me find Kendall the other day. Now, you're suddenly concerned about her *on my fucking behalf*? How long have we been here? Three days? In all that time, this is the first time you've asked about her. I wanted to see how fucking long it would take you to remember she existed."

Was this really the first time he'd asked about Kendall? Christopher couldn't fucking remember. He barely remembered his own goddamn name. If he'd eaten since Megan had gotten shot, he'd be one surprised motherfucker.

"You don't give two fucks about Kendall, so save your bullshit. Forget all of us while you worry about your wife."

Anger sparked in Christopher and he glowered at Johnnie, not quite believing the motherfucker's words. He'd allowed Megan to be transported to the hospital with fucking strangers so he could stay at the club and take care of shit. "You a bunch of grown motherfuckers, fuckhead. In case you fuckin' forgot, let me refresh your fuckin' memory. My ass stayed fuckin' put. I coulda fuckin' lost my Megan before I ever fuckin' saw her again. She went while I fuckin' stayed."

"Not for me and certainly not for Kendall."

What wasn't this motherfucker understanding? Exactly where was the mis-fucking-communication entering this conversation? Christopher wished he fucking knew before he fucked Johnnie up. "Look, assfuck, I wanna know how the fuck your bitch doin'. Otherwise, I wouldna fuckin' asked. You don't wanna tell me? Fuck it. I ain't losin' fuckin' sleep. But if that cunt die, it'll tear you the fuck apart. Since that bitch belong to you, motherfucker, she fuckin' part of the club, so, yeah, I was askin' how the fuck she doin'."

"Jesus, fuckhead, even now you can't give my woman a fucking break. She was shot just like the rest of them."

"And just fuckin' like the rest of them, I asked 'bout the fuckin' bitch, so shut the fuck up. I ain't gettin' into this bullshit now."

"Of course not. Because of Megan. You can't show Kendall any kindness, because of *your* goddamn wife. You're falling the fuck to pieces because she's shot," he spat.

Just as Avery's words stung, Johnnie's observation cut through Christopher. Not because he fucking felt as if Johnnie should have more fucking understanding. Especially toward a motherfucking girl he'd once professed to fucking love. Johnnie's words upset Christopher because he couldn't fucking deny the accusations. He fucking *was* falling to pieces. In his entire fucked-up life, he'd never had no-fucking-body who understood him the fucking way Megan did. Who had his fucking back like her. Who motherfucking loved him without fucking restraint and with almost no fucking conditions.

Her requirement was keeping his dick in his pants unless he intended to stick it in her. Easiest fucking order ever. Christopher had no desire for another bitch.

One fucking smile from Megan lit up his entire existence. If he lost her, his life had no meaning. He'd never be able to return to who he'd been before he met her. Fucked up or not, he wouldn't know how to live without her alive and happy. With him. Without him.

Just as long as she fucking *lived.*

He sucked in a painful breath.

"You don't even have it fucking in you to run our fucking club and guide us without her," Johnnie went on, using the opportunity of Christopher's lowest point to un-fucking-leash all his anger and resentment.

Christopher understood, although Johnnie's bullshit about that fucking cunt pissed him the fuck off.

"*She's* the fucking reason you didn't do anything about Digger sooner," he continued. "You let her interfere in club business and it got us all fucked up. It got your son fucking stolen and Bunny more than likely killed. Megan's fucking interference got my wife shot."

Jumping to his feet, Christopher growled and started for Johnnie. "Say what the fuck you want 'bout me, Johnnie, but I'll rip your fuckin' head off if you ever again blame Megan for your bitch gettin' shot."

"What's going on in here?"

Roxy's voice cut through Christopher's head and halted him. He glared at Johnnie's raised fists, then stalked back to the window.

Assfuck was right.

"None of your goddamn business," Johnnie barked to Roxy as she hobbled closer.

Free of makeup, she was still pretty, although she looked a little gray.

Limping forward, Roxy jabbed her finger against Johnnie's chest. "Look, motherfucker, you boys don't have time for this shit," she fired back. "Can't rest in a goddamn hospital, so I checked myself out to take the day and gather my strength. Then, in between watching the kids, I can hunt down the motherfucker who shot my baby *and* my ass. And I mean literally my fucking ass."

Grimacing, she turned and pointed to her uneven ass cheeks. One side must've been bandaged.

For some reason, with the production she made of showing her injury, Christopher believed she wanted to cheer him up and break the tension.

He drummed up a half-smile. "Ain't your fuckin' ass supposed to be in a fuckin' wheel-fuckin-chair, babe?"

"Bitch out there waiting for me with the wheelchair, Outlaw. I was coming to check on Meggie before I fly the coop and I heard you two arguing as I opened the door and walked in." She glared at Johnnie and planted her hands on her hips. "No, I heard this motherfucker arguing. You so fucking smart, genius motherfucker? Telling Outlaw what the fuck he should've done. You the fucking VP. Why didn't you bring your fucking ass out there and hunt down Digger yourself? Outlaw just a fucking man like the rest of you, so don't start hitting him with no bullshit that you could've taken care of yourself."

Christopher returned to his seat and leaned back, thrusting his fingers through his hair in agitation. "Leave the motherfucker alone, Roxanne. He right. Your fuckin' ass right too, but don't fuckin' take away the fuckin' truth behind what the fuck he said."

Johnnie's anger, his sister's hatred exploded inside of him and left behind a startling realization. He couldn't run his club anymore. He was no longer what the Dwellers needed. He couldn't be Megan's husband and the club's president. In the end, that was un-fucking-fair to everybody. His divided loyalties fucked everything up.

"Me and Megan been through fuckin' hell and back. When she lost our kid and I almost fuckin' lost her, I fucked up with her. When she open her fuckin' eyes a-fuckin-gain, I'm gonna kiss the fuckin' ground she walk on. Megan gonna come first 'til I breathe my last fuckin' breath, so I'm out, John Boy. I quit. You right. I ain't did fuckin' right by you motherfuckers. I ain't done right by my girl. I just fucked up all 'round, so I'm patchin' the fuck out."

Two gasps met his statement, the finality in his tone leaving no doubt to his sincerity.

Johnnie jerked as if he'd been shot. "Christopher—"

Not much shocked Johnnie, but judging by the way color dropped from his face, Christopher sure the fuck had. That hadn't been his fucking intentions at all. He'd thought Johnnie would welcome the news.

Roxy gaped at him before she managed to speak. "Outlaw, I didn't mean—"

Christopher raised his hand, tuning out whatever Roxy and Johnnie might've fucking said. "Ain't listenin' to fuck else. You both right. I ain't only let fuckin' Megan get in my head 'bout fuckin' Digger, but Mort, too. I thought the fuck 'bout how you and me would fuckin' protect each other's back, so that ain't makin' me the best Prez for the Death Dwellers." He stood up and removed his cut, holding it out to Johnnie, who'd turned a fucked-up shade of white.

Without his cut, he felt hollow and cold. Vulnerable. His patch, his rockers, defined him. Gave him focus. Meaning. Purpose. Different from the way Megan did. But walking away was the right thing to do after the fuckups of the past few months.

He shook the worn leather at Johnnie. "Take the motherfucker."

Johnnie inched back and swallowed. "This club's your life."

Funny how the motherfucker had lost his fucking anger and hostility.

"Yeah," he agreed, addressing Johnnie's statement. "But Megan my world."

"Who's going to run it—"

Laying the cut over the back over the chair and feeling naked without it, Christopher lifted a brow at Johnnie, surprised at the question. "Who the fuck you think, motherfucker? You."

Johnnie shook his head. "I was just venting."

"Tough shit. Ventin' or not, it's fuckin' true."

"Look, I'm sorry. Your disregard for Kendall grates."

"Don't give a fuck. Told you I can't stand her—"

"Her and Megan are truly friends. You're the only one who still treats her so bad."

Uninterested in rehashing old fucking news, he'd concede a few points to him and his psycho bitch. "John Boy, have that bitch got better? Yeah. I even under-fuckin-stand her ass. Don't mean I still ain't hatin' on her. I ignore her ass as much as possible. Let her say what the fuck she want and keep the fuck quiet my goddamn self. She just like the other girls. I'm fuckin' tired of tellin' your ass I do that shit for you and Megan."

To Christopher's shock, Johnnie looked lost, as if he had no fucking clue which way was up and which way was down. Wanting to ease him, he searched for the words Johnnie needed to hear. "You gonna take this fuckin' club to places I ain't ever been able to. You gonna be the best fuckin' Prez ever, John Boy," he said, believing wholeheartedly in the man's abilities. "You educated. This club can go fuckin' far with you."

"No," Johnnie denied, shaking his head. "Are you fucking kidding me? I'd never be able to do what you've done. I run the lab, but it was your idea. The club gets money no matter what the fuck's going on with other enterprises because of it. The hydro-grow operation—your idea. You made this club. You *saved* this club."

Swallowing, Christopher glanced at Megan and then stood. He walked to the window and stuffed his hands into his pockets, just to have something to do with them without doing what he really wished. Gather Megan into his arms and hold her close.

"Ain't done shit, John Boy," he said finally, not really focusing on anything beyond the glass. It was fucking daylight and brighter than it had been the day before. Beyond that, he didn't see, so why continue to look? "Big Joe had the gun-runnin' in place and other side businesses. I just came up with fuckin' ideas and got lucky."

Instead of responding, Johnnie made his way to the side of Megan's bed, the first time he'd looked at her since...since she'd been admitted. Reaching out, he touched her hair and brushed his fingers across her forehead. A muscle ticked in his jaw. "She's going to pull through," he said with soft vehemence.

Johnnie loved his bitch. Christopher knew that. He'd gone fucking crazy without her. But Christopher still got the sense that some-fucking-where, deep down, he still *felt* something for Megan. A part of him would always want her. Maybe, that's why he fucking hated her a little.

Roxy cleared her throat. "Can I talk to Outlaw alone?" Somehow, she'd become a mother figure to them, even Mort, who still pretended not to like her. She and Johnnie were always at odds, but Christopher knew he respected her as well.

Johnnie backed away from Megan's bedside and nodded to Roxy. "I'm going to Kendall's room," he said before walking out.

Touching his chest to hunt for a cigarette reminded Christopher he no longer wore his cut. Ignoring his sense of loss, he grabbed the cut and pulled out his smokes and the other shit he'd stuffed in the pockets. He threw his keys, wallet, and cell phone on the small table containing the landline and a pitcher of stale water. That done, he pulled his T-shirt from his waistband to cover his nine holstered at his side.

When he finished his tasks, he got a cigarette, but Roxy snatched it from his mouth before he lit up. He glared at her.

"I already got fucking shot, Outlaw. I'm not fucking looking to get blown up." She nodded to the oxygen.

He scowled at her but silently agreed he'd almost made a stupid motherfucker move.

She stuffed the cigarette in her pocket. "Any word on Little Man and Bunny?"

"No fuckin' trace."

She studied him, then limped to the other side of Megan's bed and smiled down at her, gripping her hand. Nothing. No response. No squeeze back. "I know you love your children, so shouldn't you be out trying to find your son?"

He flexed his hands, wishing he had a cigarette or a drink, fucking *something*. Maybe, he needed to leave, check on the twins. Take a shower. Once upon a time, he'd had to leave Megan in the hospital, not a man able to stand idly by and fucking grieve at her bedside. Now, he could do nothing else, *think* of nothing else. Not even his missing boy. "I ain't winnin' no fuckin' father of the year award."

Roxy threaded her fingers through Megan's hair and Christopher looked away. Other than resting his head near her feet, he hadn't touched her since she'd been wheeled from recovery after her surgery and into ICU. Not like Johnnie and Roxy had.

He'd feel even more helpless when he touched her and she wouldn't move.

A sheen of tears coated Roxy's eyes and she raised a pitiful gaze to him. "What if she dies? What happens to you then?"

He clenched his jaw to hold back his grief and anger. The bullet hitting Megan, the shock on her face, the blood spreading across her shirt and her drop to the ground, kept replaying in Christopher's mind, fucking with his head.

"Your children are going to need you. They won't know what to do without her."

He snorted. "And my fuckin' ass fuckin' will?"

"Me and Meggie have faith in you that you would if something ever happened to her. Now, you sitting your ass here, staring at her bed while your son is wherever. You should be looking for him and Bunny."

"Already fuckin' said that. But I ain't fuckin' movin' from this motherfucker 'til I know if Megan livin' or dyin'." His voice cracked. He couldn't believe he'd actually spoke those words aloud. Fucking actually talked about her in association with *death*. Fuck him. Elbows on knees, he hung his head and covered his face.

A moment later, he felt arms around his neck. "It's okay, Outlaw. Tell me what I need to do. Nobody ever got to know either. Mortician in about as bad a shape as you with his son being killed and the state my Bailey's in."

"How you keeping it together?"

"I won't do my daughter no good by falling apart." She smiled, despite the tears in her eyes. "I need to get my grandbaby and make sure she's okay."

"My lil' sister, Ophelia, lookin' after the kids. Megan two annoyin' as fuck friends helpin' out, too." They'd been at the house when Christopher had checked on Rule and Rebel after Tyler's funeral.

She nodded. "Johnnie is unhinging because Kendall was shot, although she's awake. He wants justice. Know what? All those boys looking to *you* to do it. He just trying to make you get up off your ass to do the shit none of them got the balls to do."

Christopher pulled away from her, surprised how he'd accepted her affection so easily since she'd come into their lives. That was because of Megan, too. Everything good in his life happened because of his girl.

"Any of them motherfuckers can do the shit I do."

"No and I'm not taking nothing from any of them, but you one mean motherfucker. Case in point. Kendall. When everybody else has forgiven her, your ass can't and never will. But that's just the man you are, sugar. You the kind of man who killed your daddy and Meggie daddy and didn't lose fucking sleep over it because you knew those motherfuckers had to go. That's some cold-ass shit."

"Ain't lost sleep over Cee Cee. Over Big Joe? Yeah."

Roxy shrugged. "Fine. Point is this club is going down in fucking flames if you walk away now when it's in such a crisis. If you want to leave, get the brothers through this and make sure the old members come back before you walk away. Otherwise, all the shit you did 'til now for the club will be fucking worthless."

He glanced at Megan again. "She coulda died before I got shit fuckin' straight at the club." He could voice this to Roxy. She'd understand. "I'm her fuckin' man. My ass shoulda rode with her here. I had to fuckin' do right by my brothers. That shit not happenin'. Ever a-fuckin-gain."

"Meggie wouldn't hold your duties against you. She know how you feel about her."

"Don't give a fuck. I fuckin' wanted to be with her but had to be at the fuckin' club. I don't even fuckin' know what the fuck I ordered motherfuckers to do."

"I bet you still got it done."

Had he? He didn't fucking know. He'd been living in a fucking fog.

"What the fuck could you have done here but worry the fuck out of yourself if you'd come with her to the hospital?"

"Fuck all, Roxanne," he gritted, losing his patience at her persistence. Maybe, she didn't fucking understand. "I still shoulda been fuckin' *here*."

"This club needs you right now. Too much shit has gone on in the last four years amongst the members to survive you patching out now. Johnnie doesn't have it in him to pull the MC together if you leave."

"John Boy got more than enough," Christopher snapped.

"You fucking think? That motherfucker almost cried when you quit. He can't fucking do it and he's man enough to admit it."

"He don't want me to leave cuz we fuckin' been in this club together for-fuckin-ever."

"You don't want to leave either."

Not confirming her fucking annoying insistence, he shrugged. Glancing at the clock, he saw the time for the nurses to come in and change Megan's IV drew near.

"Just stay until Sharper is caught. At least see this through. You owe it to the brothers."

Christopher already missed his club and his resignation hadn't even been voted on yet. He'd sacrificed his soul for the MC, only getting a piece back when he met Megan. He was still headed to fucking hell when he bit it and that shit would be for fucking nothing if he just allowed the Dwellers to crash and fucking burn.

"You can get your boy back easier with the resources of the club."

He sure the fuck could. Although he didn't doubt Johnnie's abilities to head the club, *he'd* done a lot on the club's behalf and before he walked away he needed to see to it that it didn't fall the fuck apart. Besides, the club *did* give him valuable resources to aid in finding CJ. If only he could get off his ass to do it.

Clenching his jaw, he snatched his cut and shrugged back into it. "Once this over, I'm walkin' the fuck away," he said quietly. "I ain't riskin' Megan no fuckin' more."

"Okay."

She sounded as if she didn't motherfucking believe him. Words meant fuck-all. He'd just have to fucking show her.

His phone rang. Picking it up from the nightstand, he answered. "Yo, Cash."

"The farmhouse burned to the ground," Cash said in response.

"What the fuck you talkin' 'bout? Logan's place…Fuck, my boy! Was CJ there?"

Because that fucking farmhouse should've burned fucking ages ago. He didn't give one fuck about it. Unless CJ…

"No bodies were found, Outlaw, but I think Digger is the one who set it on fire. He knows of the place, so it seems logical he'd go there to hide out."

"Yeah, but Sharper probably fucking know 'bout it, too."

"I'll look into it."

"Fuckin' do that, then call me the fuck back," Christopher ordered.

"What you need me to do?" Roxy asked when he disconnected the call.

"I need you to rest, babe," he answered. "Mort and Bailey need you."

He'd get his head on straight, for fucking real this time, and make a list of places to fucking look for his boy. In a little while, he'd find Mort. Who the fuck knew? Maybe, Mort wanted to fucking bail as well. He'd tell Val to settle the fuck down and stay in one more day.

He *had* to do this shit. If only Megan opened her eyes first.

A noise caught his attention and he turned as the door closed behind Roxy's wordless departure.

Fuck. He hadn't meant to shut her the fuck out, but at least she understood enough and left without pressing other fucking issues.

He got the fuck up from his seat and walked to the window. He had to fucking leave his girl to be a father to their children and the president of his club. Find Digger and Sharper and make those motherfuckers suffer. With his decision to stay until this ended, he had no choice if he wanted to make effective fucking plans.

Although, if his son's kidnapping wasn't linked to the club, he'd stay right the fuck with his girl.

"Fuck, baby! This shit not fuckin' easy. Leavin' you to take care of other shit, but I ain't gonna be long. Ima be as quick as fuckin' possible. Hear me, Megan?"

"Okay," a weak, little voice said from behind him.

Afraid to fucking believe she'd actually answered a fucking question he'd only spoken the fuck aloud because he felt as if he was losing his motherfucking mind, he turned.

And found his wife's blue gaze focused on him.

Lifting her lashes, Bunny frowned at the dim light, the glare hurting her eyes. From the softness beneath her, she knew she laid in a bed, but she couldn't remember how she'd gotten to it. Concentrating really hard and searching her memory she recalled…Trader. Beating her. Taunting her. Getting shot.

No! My God, this couldn't be real. The horrific memories flooding her made her moan and shiver. She was dreaming. She had to be. To prove it, she pinched herself, hard, and sucked in a breath at the sting.

This was real? No! No! No!

More fog cleared from her head and her heart sank as events returned to her in a slow haze. If not a horrible nightmare, her memories meant Trader *had* beaten her and caused her to miscarry. Outlaw had detected something and shot Trader, point-blank, in the head. Then, the club had been attacked. Meggie had gotten shot. Digger had kidnapped her and Little Man and…Oh my God!

They'd been hiding in a wall and then almost burned to death. What she remembered sounded like scenes from a movie script, instead of her life.

Her last waking thought had been asking Digger not to hurt Meggie's son. "Little Man!" she called, bolting up and wincing at the pain shooting through her body. She felt as if she'd been kicked, thrown, and then stomped.

The realization slumped her shoulders. Her sick weakness meant everything she remembered had actually taken place. But where was Meggie's son? For that matter, where was she?

She swung her legs over the side of the bed, just then realizing an IV had been inserted into her hand. Blinking, she followed the line up to the make-shift pole and saw the half-filled bag of fluid. More memories surfaced, including the one where she'd asked Digger not to hurt Little Man after...after he'd saved her from the fire? Or had it been before?

Her thoughts slammed to a halt as another realization dawned on her.

Digger had saved her when he could've left her to burn to death. Not only that, he'd carried her for a while although, at some point, she'd stood on her own two feet and walked. Beyond that, she couldn't remember anything. She didn't know her location or if she'd been left alone...Where was Meggie's son?

Looking around provided no answers to her questions. The bed took up most of the space in the small room. On the dresser lay all types of medical supplies, including more IV bags.

As more awareness filled her head, the pressure of her bladder hurt and she groaned.

"Digger!" she yelled. "CJ!"

Panic didn't have a chance to set in before noise just outside her door alerted her that she wasn't alone. The door burst open.

"Bun-Bun!" Little Man yelled, his little voice cracking with hoarseness. Barreling toward her at his usual top speed, he looked rested and wore clean clothes, with no visible bruises. His runny nose and flushed cheeks worried Bunny, however.

Although it didn't seem to bother him. He dug in the pocket of his jeans and held a piece of donut up to her, interrupting her intentions to check him for fever. "I save it for you," he announced proudly, his breath rattling from him.

She smiled weakly at the smushed treat. Absolutely no telling what adventure the pastry had taken before Little Man stuffed it in his pocket. Happy to see him, she swallowed back her reservations, opened her mouth and allowed him to stuff the food in. She chewed as quickly as possible. "Ummm, yum! Give me high five, buddy."

Beaming a smile at her, he followed her directions and coughed, sucking in the snot that leaked from his nose.

His cold concerned her and she wondered if Digger was giving him anything to treat it. "Where's Digger?"

Little Man spun around and pointed to the door. "Sleep."

"Asleep?"

"Uh-huh. Him go night-night. Too tired to stay eyes open." He pointed to himself. "Him say kid ass beat bad if fuck up."

She scowled. Asshole. The idiot had left a small, curious child awake while he rested, then had the gall to threaten him. How smart was that? Although Little Man wasn't feeling well, he rarely let anything stop him. He could've gotten into all sorts of trouble. Wandered off. Found Digger's gun. Climbed up somewhere.

Sure, he needed to rest but…shit, Digger was sleeping!

Standing as coughing racked the child, she stepped to the dresser, glad the length of the IV line afforded her the short distance.

"How long has Digger been asleep?"

"Loonnggg time."

Stupid question, Bunny. Little Man had no perception of time so an hour might've passed since Digger nodded off.

She retrieved gauze and medical tape, then stared at her hand, grimacing. She hated needles. The sight of them made her queasy. But she needed mobility and she wouldn't have that if she stayed connected to a stationary IV. Swallowing back her reservations and holding her legs together to keep from peeing on herself, she peeled back the tape that kept the IV in place and licked her lips. She squeezed her eyes shut, then grunted as she pulled the thing out of her vein. Doing her best not to look, she snatched the gauze up and pressed it against the spot.

She didn't look at the catheter as she allowed it to drop from her fingers, grabbed the tape and wrapped it around her hand.

Throughout that entire time, Little Man stood beside her, coughing but also watching her with avid interest, the only reason for his lack of activity.

"Potty, Bun-Bun?"

"Yes," she squeaked, so near to peeing on herself, she didn't think she'd make it to the bathroom.

A metal pan slid onto the dresser and into her line of vision. Frowning, she glanced at the boy's happy little face.

"Uh—"

"Dig got for pee for you on potty." He pointed to the pan.

"Go right outside," she ordered, her bladder too full to concern herself with Digger helping her on and off the big bowl fashioned into a bed pan.

Once she relieved herself, she called Little Man back into the room. She had so many questions, but she only needed the answer to one. Their location. The fire had taken place at Logan Donovan's farm, so they'd been on the outskirts of Hortensia. She had a vague recollection of Digger complaining about the car being stolen, so they couldn't have gotten far. Which meant, if she got her bearings, she'd find a public location and ask to borrow someone's phone to call Outlaw.

"I need to rinse my mouth and throw water on my face," she whispered. "Can you show me the bathroom?"

He nodded, then took her "good" hand, seeming to instinctively know not to touch the bandaged one, though it was closest to him. Tugging her forward, he guided her into a small hallway. It took three steps to cross to the bathroom.

When she finished her attempt to revitalize, Bunny glanced at herself in the dingy mirror. She wore an oversized T-shirt and nothing else. Only Digger could've removed her clothes. The thought of his hands on her body filled her with embarrassment and warmth, affecting her more than she wanted to admit.

Although in the scheme of all that had happened, his actions meant nothing. He needed to keep Meggie's son safe to save his own life and he needed Bunny since Little Man promised to behave if Digger kept Bunny. It was ludicrous to read anything else into the fact that he'd saved her life and taken care of her. She wasn't that much of a dummy. Was she? To allow a handsome face and some selfish motives to make her believe he had another side to him. A kinder side. A real, true altruistic one that had led him to saving Little Man.

Any of those ideas, *all* of them, required compassion and she didn't believe Digger had such care in him. If he hadn't been threatening to kill her, he'd been asking to fuck her. Yet he *had* saved her life and he *had* watched over Meggie's son for however long Bunny had been out.

Maybe, some truth lay in his words. Maybe, his heart had been in the right place, but he just had a strange way of showing it.

No time to consider any of that right now. The longer she lost herself in thoughts, the less of a chance she'd have to escape and get to Outlaw. She could find out about Meggie's condition and that of all the others.

She hurried to Little Man and crouched down. "We have to be super quiet," she whispered. "We don't want to wake Digger. He's really tired. But I want to get you back to your mommie and daddy."

His eyes brightened and he nodded. When she stood, he frowned at her legs. She was tall, but the shirt covered all her good parts. Following his gaze, she saw a small amount of dried blood on her lower thighs.

"I'm fine, sweetheart. I just hurt myself when I fell as we walked from the fire."

Quietly opening the door, she peered toward the room ahead and grabbed Little Man's hand. Finger over her lip, she tipped forward. The combination kitchen and living room was small, with the only other door straight ahead. In between them and freedom, Digger lay on a couch sleeping, his feet propped up on the arm so he could fit his long body comfortably. Just like Little Man, he'd also changed from the last time she'd seen him.

A quick scan of the room to search for a coat for herself or something to cover up revealed plain, plastic shopping bags, with no discernible store name, stacked on the table. She saw nothing to identify their location or anything that would afford her more than only a T-shirt.

She didn't want to risk losing time and searching through the bags. This would be over soon. Once she got her and Little Man away, she could put this nightmare behind her. She'd pick up the pieces of her life and move forward. She'd done it once before with Trader. She could do it again without him.

First, she'd contact her mom and dad and try to mend fences with them. Pangs of hunger crept in and her stomach growled, the sound loud in the still silence. Tipping forward and keeping her eyes on Digger, she almost stepped on the toys scattered on the floor. Little Man stopped at the box of donuts, gaping open amidst the mess of toys, to grab one in his hand and bite into it.

Beside the box, on the floor, four donuts were jammed together, pieces missing and a little toy soldier stuck in the middle. Cringing at the thought that her piece of donut had come from that pile, she urged Little Man on.

At the door, she twisted the knob slowly, gritting her teeth at the creaking hinges. Stepping outside, she halted so fast, Little Man bumped into her leg.

She gasped in shock at the barren landscape. Apparently, they *had* gone far. Her surroundings consisted of snow and trees. No civilization. No recognizable landmarks. Nothing.

"Where you think you going, girl?" Digger's question snapped the bitter reality of how much distance separated her and the club, into her. "Close that fucking door and get back in here."

"Bun-Bun?"

At Little Man's confusion, she sighed and backed away from the door, shutting it. Before she even turned around, she knew Digger stood behind her. The warmth of his body surrounded her. Awareness prickling her, she turned and raised her gaze.

"Thank you for saving me," she whispered, the intensity of his stare throwing her off-balance.

At her words, surprise flickered across his face but he dismissed it with a careless shrug. "Go find my smokes, kid," he ordered Little Man, his tone to the child irritating Bunny.

"Okay, Dig," Little Man coughed out, his little feet scampering toward the bedroom and leaving them alone.

"What you want from me?"

"Excuse me? Why in the world would you expect me to want something from you?" She narrowed her eyes. "Beside my freedom."

"You thanking me and shit. You must want something besides me releasing you. We both know that's not in your cards right now. So what the fuck's your game? You want want dick from me? The only time Peyton ever said please and thank you was when she wanted me to fuck her or she wanted money."

"First off? I'm not Peyton," Bunny snapped, her stomach growling again. It offended her that he compared her to his girlfriend. Especially *that* bitch. "Second, you should think more of yourself than just being dick and dollars. Finally," she rushed out when his face darkened, "I'm thanking you because you could've left me to die. It was admirable and honorable of you to come back for me."

He opened his mouth, then snapped it shut. "Whatever," he grumbled. "You were so fucking thankful, you tried to fucking skip out." He stepped closer and pressed his body against hers, his erection hard between them. "Don't you think you needed fucking pants?"

She shrugged. She hadn't known they were...*wherever.*

"I went through a lot of fucking trouble to save you. Now, you want to piss me off and sneak the fuck away?" he asked, burying his nose against her hair.

Bunny stood perfectly still, not sure if she didn't move because she'd encourage him to continue touching her, or if she didn't want to discourage him. Was she crazy? She definitely didn't want to encourage him! "I don't want to piss you off, but I want to leave. Little Man has an awful cold."

"I have meds here I can give to him."

She breathed in Digger's scent—musk, alcohol, and the faintest traces of cologne. Oh my goodness, she was so *not* being one of those women who fell for their kidnappers. He still might change his mind about keeping her alive. What happened when she wasn't useful to him anymore? Not only was he her kidnapper, he was a biker. If she ever hoped to reconcile with her parents, she needed to keep her distance from Digger. Besides, being with Digger meant standing against the club. Unless he resolved the issues he had with them. Even then he'd already made it clear he didn't want a relationship with her. Neither did she want one with him. She couldn't waste her time considering such an unlikely scenario. She wanted to escape Digger, nothing more. At the moment, she needed to point out..."You can't give CJ random medicine!"

He studied her face, her hair, and lingered on her mouth. Awareness crackled between them and the only thing she remembered was the fact that he'd saved her when he could've left her to die. She'd lived when death had been so close. All around her. Walking amongst her friends and stealing them away.

Digger was *life.* He was the here and now. She didn't have to worry about a future between them, because they had none. If she was healed from the miscarriage, she could give herself to him, just to know she had survived and would survive. She wanted to reach out and touch the dreads framing his face, discover his hair's texture. Feel the hardness of his body. Because maybe she *was* a woman who fell for their kidnapper. It could've been a survival instinct. With her, she just wanted to hang onto the security his illusionary kindness allowed her to feel.

"Like what you see?" he taunted.

Hunger and confusion kept her silent.

"I know you do," he continued. "So?"

"So what?"

"Make me an offer. Tell me what you'll do for me if I do something for you."

He expected her to bargain with her body. He hadn't said it, only implied it. And not because she'd been a stripper. Digger demanded a deal because she sensed that's how he conducted his relationships. By bargaining. Emotion had no place in his life.

"I want to get CJ back to his parents, but I won't offer sexual favors to do it. I'm just asking you to let us leave. I'm asking you not to try and treat him with whatever drugs you have here."

"It worked for you."

"Thank God! However, I'm a grown woman, asshole. He's a small child. You can't play Florence Nightingale with him."

"Florence Nightingale?" he echoed, lifting his brows.

"Yes, she was—"

"I know who the fuck the bitch was, Bunny. She pioneered modern nursing or some shit. I'm not trying to play her. I know the kid been coughing and—"

"And it's bad. He's been out in the cold and exposed to fire. He may have pneumonia..."

He glanced away. "The kid'll be fine."

She understood he had to keep CJ as a bargaining chip, to compel Outlaw to listen to his side. But if he let CJ go, she was willing to stay with him. Outlaw had killed Trader on her behalf. If he knew Digger had her, he might allow Digger to explain himself in exchange for Bunny's life. "Keep me, but let's take him somewhere and—"

"You know where the fuck we at?" he interrupted impatiently.

She shook her head.

His arms encircled her waist and he skimmed his lips along her neck, sending a shiver down her spine.

"I enlisted your brother's help," he whispered, his voice deeper and sexier with his mouth so close to her ear. "He got us here. You was in bad shape, so a friend of his got an IV going with antibiotics and fluids. We've been hiding out here since then. Gabe brought us some food, clothes, and money. Left his car, but we have to get the fuck going. Sooner or later, Outlaw's going to his shop. I think Gabe's a dead man for helping me. I didn't have a fucking choice if I wanted to save you."

His callous disregard of Gabe's life appalled her. Yanking herself out of his grasp, Bunny glared at him, but Little Man reaching Digger his cigarettes interrupted her words. The moment the child went back to his toy soldiers and squeezing sticky donuts in his hands, Bunny shoved Digger.

"You fucking asshole! That's all it ever is with you, isn't it? *I didn't have a fucking choice,*" she imitated. "You didn't have a fucking choice but to leave Meggie to die with your father's men so you could kidnap Bailey and save Mortician. You didn't have a fucking choice over delivering Bailey to your father because you wanted to save your brother. Now, you didn't have a fucking choice but to sign *my* brother's death warrant to save me. But you did have a choice in *every* situation. All you had to do was go to Outlaw!" she screamed, slightly lightheaded. "But you not having a choice is bullshit, asshole. You do! *Two* choices as I see it. Outlaw and your father."

"My father? What the fuck you mean? I don't ever want to see that motherfucker again."

"Liar! If it doesn't work out with Outlaw, you'll get back into your father's good graces by delivering me and Little Man to him."

"You think I'd fucking do that after all the fucking trouble I went through to save you?"

Did she really think so? Or was she so overcome with worry for Gabe's safety, she'd blurted that? But she couldn't back down. From the beginning of their relationship, she'd given Trader all the power and control. "Why else would you keep us? Sending CJ back would get you in Outlaw's good graces quicker than keeping him. You have me and Little Man captive to deliver to your father," she insisted.

"That's not fucking true!" he snapped, backing away from her and lighting a cigarette. "What's the matter with your dumb ass?

I could've given you over to him the night he was at Logan's fucking house."

"Yes," she agreed, concern overriding common sense. "You didn't then."

"Sharper don't give second chances. Even if I wanted one, which I don't. Point is I'm out with him and I'm out with Prez. Unless I can reason with Outlaw."

"Outlaw can be reasonable, so please." She raised her hands, imploring him. "Let's find a phone so I can call Outlaw. Please. You're right. He'll kill Gabe and we really do need to get CJ medical help."

As if to emphasize her point, another coughing fit overtook the child.

Regret blanketed Digger's face and he hesitated, his indecision clear.

"I believe you want to do what's right. You must be tired of risking the lives of innocent people. Hasn't that gotten a little old by now? You know CJ must go back and—"

"Comments like that not getting you your way."

He was right, but she'd thought if the obvious was pointed out, she'd get through to him. A shake of his head smashed her hopes of gaining this small favor from him. "I got a burner now, but I'm not trusting Outlaw not to have a way to track the number if I use it to call him."

"All you have to do is toss it. That's what burners are for. Unless..."

"Unless I'm planning on getting back with Sharper, right? Obviously, your ass not been listening. Maybe, you'll understand my explanation this time. My father the last motherfucker I want to find you or the kid," he whispered, a desperate hurt entering his eyes. "Motherfucker killed Tyler, Bunny. I saw him. He stood over a kid and pumped him with bullets. That's not an image I'll ever forget."

"Oh my God," she gasped, her hands covering her mouth. "I'm sorry. I'm so sorry. I-I didn't know."

"Don't worry about it. It's done." His callous brushoff contrasted his lingering devastation. He pulled at his dreads, then shook his head. "Now, you wanna tell me what the fuck happened to you that had your pussy bleeding and you feverish? Not normal bitch bleeding either."

Suddenly, it was too much. All of it. Even imagining Tyler's violent death. She'd never met him, but she knew all about him. What was Mortician going through? Sharper Banks had caused so much horror. The emotional toll his vileness had taken might be unrecoverable. The things those big, strong men valued the most—family, brotherhood, freedom—had been eroded. She hurt for Digger and wanted to comfort him, but she didn't know how. What could she say? Do? Then there was her brother. Imagining the torture Gabe would go through at the hands of Outlaw made Digger's words fly over her head. She sniffled.

"Fuck in hell, Dig," Little Man yelled, catching both of them off-guard. "Ash fuck, made Bun-Bun cry! I tell 'Law and MegAnn."

His small motorcycle-boot clad feet connected with Digger's shin.

"FUCK!" Digger roared, howling with pain and bending down.

Little Man barreled into Digger and toppled him. "Ash fuck," he yelled again, springing onto his chest and sinking his teeth into Digger's chin before balling a little fist and slamming it into the man's jaw.

Bunny rushed forward as Digger grabbed the child's arms. She attempted to take him, but Digger got to his feet and kept Little Man pinioned to him.

"Fucka mudna!" The little boy struggled in Digger's arms, which in turn made Digger struggle to keep hold of him.

Anger tightened Digger's jaw. "If you don't stop, I'm gonna beat your little ass."

"'Law beat you back!"

"Enough!" Bunny said sternly, hard pressed to stifle her laughter and unsure if Digger would lose his patience and truly hurt Little Man. "Let him go, Digger. He's just a scared little boy. And you, mister, stop hitting and cursing. Meggie doesn't approve and neither do I."

"'Law does," he responded as if that was the end of the story.

Well, that explained why Meggie hadn't been able to curtail Little Man's cursing. Of course, Outlaw appreciated his son's foul language.

Digger snickered and Bunny widened her eyes.

"You find this funny, too?" she asked in outrage.

"Fuck yeah. This is what being a man all about."

"Asshole."

He smirked at her, then addressed Little Man, who'd given up his fighting for coughing. "I didn't mean to make Bunny cry," he said when the child quieted. "Won't ever do it again around you. Behave when I set you down. Deal?"

Little Man considered Digger's statement for a moment, then nodded. Digger sat the child on his feet and the three of them stared at each other, not sure what to do next. Until Bunny's stomach growled again.

"Shit, man." Digger pointed to some bags. "I got you some stuff. If you want, take a shower while I scramble up something for you to eat."

"How long are we staying here?"

"I'm leaving tomorrow for a while. Get some information on where Sharper at now that you're awake."

"Is your burner phone new?"

He nodded. "Gabe asked me to take it in case you got too bad off and I needed to call for help."

Her brother's thoughtfulness renewed her determination. "Outlaw can't track you if he doesn't have any information about your phone. Even if you won't agree to returning Little Man, let me call Gabe. Please. I'll be quick."

"Suppose Outlaw have a way? I don't put nothing past him. If he find me here, I'm cornered. I won't ever have a chance to explain my side."

"That's the entire point of keeping us, right? If Outlaw tracks you, you can bargain our lives for yours and a chance to clear the air."

Not responding, he glanced away.

"Do you even know why you refuse to let us go? You don't, do you? This is just another impulsive decision that has no real rhyme or reason. Isn't it?"

"I don't have to fucking answer you," he yelled. "I'm running this show. Not you. That mean no matter what my fucking reason, I don't owe you nothing."

She drew herself up. He was right. She'd allowed herself to forget—ignore—her precarious position in this situation.

Little Man coughed again. Bunny knew her brother might be a lost cause but if she didn't press on behalf of Meggie's son, his cold would worsen.

Grasping at straws, Bunny thought of her parents. She hadn't spoken to them in almost three years and wasn't sure of her reception. But, maybe, she could convince them to let her visit without letting them know Digger and Little Man would tag along with her. Granted, Digger was a biker just like Trader, the man who'd caused the final rift with her mom and dad. She was desperate, though, and if they allowed her to come, half her battle would be won. Even if Digger didn't win points with them, Little Man would. And for all his assholeness, Digger had more redeeming qualities than Trader ever had. More important, she could get CJ to a hospital.

"If my parents agree to let us stay with them for a couple of days, will you let me call Outlaw? I promise I'll tell him you're protecting us."

Backing away, he didn't answer and Bunny's heart sank. Then, he stopped and heaved in a deep breath.

"Let me cook something for you while I think about your request."

His consideration was all she asked for and, really, more than she'd expected.

"Megan?" Still afraid his eyes fucking deceived him, Christopher rushed to Megan's bedside and blinked, expecting to find her still unconscious. But, nope. His wife's big, blue eyes had remained opened and glued to his every movement. They were hazy and fucked up with the effects of all she'd gone through in the past three days.

They stared at each other and his breath came out in short pants, relief replacing his fear and turmoil, until he saw how fragile she seemed, which brought back his uncertainty.

She studied him a moment longer, then removed the oxygen tubes from her nostrils. He didn't try to stop her. She was fucking *awake.*

She groaned and held out her hand to him, and he finally, *finally* gave in to what he wanted most in the world. Her touch. Grabbing her hand, he bent down and pressed her fingers against his cheek.

"Hey," she whispered groggily, blinking at him.

Not knowing what the fuck else to do, he laughed, then leaned over and kissed her forehead. "Hey, baby."

She attempted a smile but grimaced instead.

"Fuck, Megan," Christopher said gruffly, kissing each of her fingertips. She'd come back to him. The fear of losing her and the agony he'd gone through released him. He could breathe again. Think again.

"What happened?"

Drugs fogged her head so she wouldn't remember right off the fucking fly. Right now, he wouldn't clue her the fuck in on all the details. That might jar her memory too fucking much and she'd start asking about their boy. "I swear, the minute you fuckin' heal up and I kill Sharper by di-fuckin-section, I'm fuckin' turnin' in my patch," he began, not surprised when more confusion clouded the fuck out of her gaze. "I ain't ever fuckin' riskin' you a-fuckin-gain. I'm so fuckin' tired of fuckin' hospitals. I can't even fuckin' tell you. In the past three years, I been in these motherfuckers more than my ass ever been in my entire fuckin' life. My ass fuckin' out."

She frowned at him, as if she didn't understand any of his fucking words. Maybe, she didn't. His fucking mouth was running a mile a fucking minute.

He threaded his fingers through her hair and kissed her lips, finding them dry and warm, but she formed a small pucker and sweetly returned his kiss. Now that he'd touched her, felt her mouth moving against his, he wanted to keep kissing her and not because he wanted pussy from her. He was just so fucking happy she was such a fighter. "I'm leavin' the club, baby." He spoke the words like he would a fucking blood vow. "I ain't ever riskin' you a-fuckin-gain."

If she'd missed the announcement when he'd been fucking running off at the mouth, she understood him now and shook her head. "N-no, you can't leave."

"I fuckin' can and I fuckin' will, Megan. My ass your fuckin' husband. I can't fuckin' be both and do them right, baby. Case fuckin' closed."

Her eyes narrowed and she cocked her head to the side, but when her expression changed from irritation to worry, Christopher tensed. already sensing her thoughts as her gaze searched the room. Their kids. What the fuck had redirected her thoughts, he didn't fucking know.

"CJ, Rule, and Rebel?" she murmured, confirming his suspicions.

All at once, their son's kidnapping crashed into him. What everybody had been trying to get through to him hit him head on. Megan would lose her shit if she knew CJ was missing. He couldn't let that happen.

He forced a smile. "Fine, baby," he swore with a straight face. Rule and Rebel *were* okay. He'd tell Megan the truth about CJ soon, but he didn't want to alarm her right now. Hopefully, by the time she grew stronger, CJ would be back with them safe and sound. "I love you."

She squeezed his hand and attempted a smile of reassurance. "I love you too, Christopher."

"Lemme call the nurse. You in pain?"

She nodded.

It didn't take long for Megan's nurse to come in, identified by her name tag as Lea. If not for it, he'd be fucking clueless from one day to the next. "Welcome back to the world, Mrs. Caldwell," she said with a friendly smile, offering Christopher my-pussy-yours-if-you-want-it looks. In her mid to late twenties, the attractive bitch had smooth olive skin and a ripe body. Since the shooting, she'd been taking care of Megan during the day, but Christopher couldn't fucking remember if she'd offered him pussy before now.

He hadn't noticed and he didn't fucking care what she wanted to give him. As long as she fucking took care of Megan, he was fucking happy.

After checking Megan's vital signs and administering a shot for pain, Lea left to call the doctor.

"You look so tired," Megan observed, squeezing his fingers. "Go and rest."

"I just need to fuckin' shave..." His voice trailed off as her eyes drooped and she nodded off to sleep. He stilled, checking the rise and fall of her chest, her vital signs, her color.

Well, if he judged by her pale fucking skin, he'd be a scared motherfucker all fucking over again. As far as he could tell, she'd just fallen the fuck back to sleep and he wouldn't wake her up like a pussified bitch-ass.

He sat back in the chair and stared at her, afraid if he took his gaze away, he'd discover she still hadn't awakened after her surgery. Maybe, she'd open her eyes again after a few minutes, then Christopher would know she was still with him.

"Dr. Paxton will check on Mrs. Caldwell tomorrow morning, during his regular rounds."

Lea's voice broke into Christopher's concern. As her words sank in, he got to his feet. "No the fuck he ain't," he snapped. "Call him the fuck back and tell him my fuckin' club donate a lot to this motherfucker. If his ass ain't fuckin' here in two hours to check my wife, either that motherfucker ain't gonna be on the payroll after today or my club pullin' fuckin' support."

The nurse's surprise changed to wistfulness. "Where can I find a man as devoted as you are to Mrs. Caldwell?"

Jesus, Mary, and Joseph, when the fuck did he become a fucking magnet for psycho bitches? He scowled at her. "Don't know. Don't fuckin' give a fuck. Don't fuck with me a-fuckin-gain cuz this as un-fuckin-professional as it fuckin' get. My fuckin' priority is my fuckin' girl. She just opened her fuckin' eyes, then she went back to fuckin' sleep a-fuckin-gain. I don't fuckin' know if she sleepin' fuckin normal or—"

"She is," Lea interrupted. "She's in pain, so I gave her something for it."

He clenched his jaw, not wanting to admit to his sudden relief. When she'd closed her eyes, his fucking fear had come back.

"I'll call the doctor again and relay your message, sir."

"Fucking do that."

It didn't take long for her to return and tell him Dr. Paxton would come within the hour to check Megan out. He needed a fucking smoke so fucking bad, but before he went outside to take one, he decided to go to Johnnie's bitch's room.

All along the IC unit brothers stood watch, assisting the hospital security. News had traveled fast through the fucking television, radio, and newspapers. Derby and Boy had also sent brothers from their clubs in support and as a sign of respect and solidarity.

Since Val's door stood open, Christopher peeped in and found his RC scowling at the TV, pressing the nurse's call button.

"Yo, dumb ass, settle the fuck down. You ain't leavin' today."

Val startled as an irritated nurse's voice blared into the room. "Yes, Mr. Taylor?"

"Er, never mind, babe," he muttered, throwing Christopher a guilty look.

The nurse huffed out a breath. "Fine!" she grated out before she disengaged and the room went silent again.

"Zoann left me to see about the kids," Val began before his eyes widened. "Wait...you look human again so that mean Meggie still breathing?"

"I decided you some kinda perverted motherfucker and get the fuck off on me kickin' your dumb fuckin' ass. So I suggest you shut the fuck up. And, yeah, my girl opened her eyes." As the minutes ticked by since Megan opened her fucking eyes, he felt more and more like himself. Needing to see Johnnie, he backed away from the door. "Keep the fuck quiet 'bout leavin' for today. I'll spring you tomorrow."

Not waiting for Val's answer, Christopher headed out, slowing at the room where Bailey lay, before continuing on. He'd sit with Mort after Megan's doctor came and went.

A minute later, Christopher reached Kendall's room, finding her door wide open and hearing the faint sound of opera music drifting out. Fucking opera. What the fuck was wrong with that bitch? Poor fucking Johnnie, but if that's the cunt he wanted, let him fucking have her and her fucking ear-drum-fucking-up music, too.

He'd hated *Madama Butterfly* when Big Joe had dragged his fucking ass to a fucking opera in London and it hadn't fucking changed in all these fucking years. If anything, his ears hurt fucking worse at hearing that shit.

"This is your chance, Johnnie. Let the asshole leave. You'll be the president and *I'll* be the old lady everyone looks up to."

Christopher gritted his teeth. The music had halted him, now what he heard kept him in place.

Johnnie sighed. "I thought we were past this competitiveness, gorgeous."

"We are. But why are you the vice president if you aren't prepared to take over for Outlaw?"

"It doesn't work that way, Kendall."

"Don't hand me that bullshit. It does! That's why there are officers in place."

"I'd become interim president until the brothers could vote on it. There's no guarantee they'd even approve me."

"Same if he resigns?"

Yeah, psycho fucking bitch.

"Yeah, gorgeous."

Christopher liked his response better.

"Suppose he'd been killed?"

That cunt would've danced on his fucking grave.

"Shut up," Johnnie snapped on a growl. "Don't talk about Christopher getting killed. Fuck. I could've just as easily been killed. Or you. Or Megan." Whatever Christopher couldn't see annoyed the fuck out of Johnnie, as indicated by his, "I didn't fucking mean anything by that statement about Megan."

Christopher wouldn't even speculate on the look Kendall gave Johnnie when he'd mentioned Megan. If the bitch had seen the way Johnnie touched Megan earlier, she would really lose her shit.

"I know you're emotional right now, but you need to talk to the doctor."

"I don't want to hurt the baby," she said glumly. "Antidepressants during pregnancy is fine. It's my choice not to take them."

Johnnie drew in a deep breath and so did Christopher. Fuck, she was having another kid for Johnnie. Pregnancy left her more fucking hormonally challenged than usual. Fuck, that must've been what she wanted to talk to Johnnie about the other night.

"Did you tell him I'm pregnant?"

"No. It isn't as if he gives a fuck."

Nope, he sure the fuck didn't.

"As for the other shit, if I have to be president I will, but I'm hoping he'll stay. *Fuck*. I was just fucking venting. He didn't even do anything wrong. I didn't expect him to fucking agree with me."

"In defense of him," Kendall began grouchily, "he's as stressed out as you are. With Meggie still out, you couldn't expect him to respond any other way, Johnnie. In essence, you were making him choose between the club and his wife. Did you really expect him to respond any *other* way?"

Yeah, the motherfucker did.

"Yes, fuck!" Johnnie snapped, confirming what Christopher already knew. "We don't fucking live forever. Sharper wants Megan dead and I'm fucking betting he's not going to stop until he sees that happen. Then what? Christopher just turns his back on his club and his children?"

"You don't have much faith in his abilities if you think he'll so easily let Meggie die."

Motherfucker sure the fuck don't. Who fucking knew?

"That's where you're wrong, but Sharper has stayed one step ahead of us for months. In spite of all the resources Christopher has put into finding him."

For a moment, the music went silent, making Christopher realize that shit had been drumming in his head right along with this fucked-up conversation. Why the fuck was he eavesdropping any fucking way? Because he found it quite fucking interesting to hear the fucking dynamics in their relationship. For all the motherfucker's complaining about Megan bossing Christopher, Johnnie allowed his bitch to do the same fucking thing to him.

"You told him he hadn't been looking for Sharper."

"No, I didn't, Kendall. I said he hadn't been searching for Digger. If you find one, you find the other."

"Think about what you're saying, Johnnie. Digger is Mortician's brother and Outlaw's friend. Yours, too. Don't you think those factors weighed in his decision to back off?"

Johnnie snorted. "Big Joe was like a father to Christopher. That didn't stop him from doing what needed to be done. Digger left Megan to fucking die. That's unforgivable, so she's the *only* fucking person who'd change his mind about how he dealt with Digger."

"I see," she said tightly, then cleared her throat. "What stopped *you* from finding Digger yourself? Remind me because I seemed to have missed that memo. Had you found him for committing the unforgivable sin of leaving Meggie to die, your decisiveness would've ingratiated you to the members. Shown your leadership abilities."

"Mortician's the club enforcer. Christopher gave each of us a folder with our targets. Digger and Sharper were assigned to Mort. I've been taking care of the fuckheads I'm supposed to."

"Yeah, but Digger is the one everyone wants, so you should've gone after him and I never would've gotten shot."

"This is going to be a long pregnancy, huh, gorgeous?"

That's why you shoulda kept your fucking cock locked the fuck up and out of her fucking pussy.

Kendall on her antidepressants was tolerable in Christopher's eyes. She was still a conniving cunt, but he fucking ignored her and she ignored him. Off those motherfuckers and she went back to being a mean fucking bitch.

"That's what you have to think about. I was shot and I could've lost another baby. She's just spoiled."

"Kendall, gorgeous—"

"I don't mean that as a slur against Meggie."

The fuck you don't.

"I know, sweetheart."

What-fucking-ever.

"I only had a few hours to enjoy the knowledge of your new pregnancy before we were hit. But I've been thinking about us going away for a few weeks. Let your body adjust to the pregnancy without the stress of club life."

"Where?" she asked with suspicion, just as *Ava Maria* started playing.

"Wherever you want to go."

How the fuck could that motherfucker bring a vacation up, when he knew Christopher intended to resign?

"There's no way we're leaving now when you have a chance to become president. Absolutely not."

His self-serving bitch knew what needed to happen.

"I don't want to risk you, Rory, and the new baby. We've taken all sorts of measures to protect all of you, but Sharper still found a way inside."

"Yes, because Outlaw's an arrogant asshole."

"We're looking in the wrong places," Johnnie explained with annoyance. "On the outside, instead of within. That doesn't make Christopher arrogant, Kendall."

"Are you suggesting there's an enemy on the inside?"

"Doesn't it seem so?"

"I guess, although Outlaw has all but shut the club down, so unless Meggie is betraying the club, who could it be?"

"Megan?" Johnnie asked in shock. "Are you fucking kidding me?"

Apparently, Kendall was still a death-wishy bitch.

"Always ready to defend her."

"I'm not fucking defending her. I'm telling you the idea that she'd betray the club is fucking stupid. She's never been a threat to any of us."

"I used her as an example," she said briskly.

"Poor fucking choice."

Only *La Boheme* filled the silence that followed Johnnie's words.

"I'm glad you saw her today. I know how worried you've been about her."

This time, expectation filled the silence.

"My main concern has been you, gorgeous," Johnnie said slowly. "And thinking about who has the balls to betray us."

Christopher narrowed his eyes, finished with eavesdropping on Johnnie and his bitch. Johnnie had the fucking right way of thinking. Some motherfucker had to have betrayed them to fucking Sharper. Why the fuck else would he be so fucking willing to reappear after so many fucking months on the run?

Riley had just fucking pinpointed a location for those motherfuckers.

The run they'd intended to fuck Sharper and Osti up would've taken place next week. But the script had been fucking flipped and Sharper had hit first.

That meant one fucking thing. Some-fucking-body on the inside had ratted them the fuck out.

Christopher trusted the brothers closest to him. The other women on the inside who were in their inner circle and had the run of the place because of it were Roxy, Bunny, and Dinah…

Fuck. Him.

Immediately, he scratched Roxy off the list. The woman was too straight-forward to pull such bullshit. Besides, she wouldn't do anything to get her daughter killed.

He was on the fence about Bunny. Maybe, Trader had been the fucking traitor and Christopher had popped him just as he was putting his plan into effect. Bunny was a loyal chick, so she'd stick by her old man's side.

And put Meggie and the kids in danger…? Maybe fucking not. She adored CJ.

Dinah, on the other hand…

Somehow, Dinah had been left unscathed, after the clubhouse had been clearly searched. Yet, she'd survived. True, when Logan had put his boy in a trash can and left him to smother, she'd had the presence of mind to knock it over, but she hadn't been half as fucked up in the head then as she was now.

Besides, Dinah fucking hated Christopher and had never quite been a mother to Megan. She'd disregarded Big Joe and somehow been the catalyst for all types of bullshit, so he wouldn't put betraying the club past that cunt. Craziness and all.

After Dinah moved from Seattle to Hortensia, all types of odd shit started happening. Cee Cee showed up. Motherfucking Logan. K-P was killed after being seen with Dinah that morning.

Charlemagne somehow got Bailey's phone number. Yeah, maybe, fuckhead Digger had also given it to *that* cunt, but they'd all fucking disregard a psycho cunt like Dinah because she seemed fucking harmless.

No, fuck this bullshit. It couldn't be fucking Dinah. She didn't have access to necessary information. She and Megan rarely spoke. But if not her, why had she been left unharmed? Where had she fucking been and why hadn't Ghost run across her during his sweep of the club?

When Christopher had first seen Dinah, he'd been too relieved to be suspicious. Hearing Johnnie voice what lurked in Christopher's mind raised all types of fucking questions. And major fucking concerns if Dinah *was* the traitor. He couldn't imagine the fucking pain Megan would go through. Dinah would have to be put to ground. That meant, either he'd have to kill her and *not* tell Megan the reason why. Or he'd have to kill her and offer a full fucking explanation to his girl.

"Fuck!" he roared, thrusting his fingers through his hair.

"Christopher?" Johnnie called, reminding him he was standing just outside Kendall's room.

Stalking in, he scowled at Kendall, who sat in her hospital bed, her hair pulled up in a ponytail. They exchanged mutual glowers. It didn't even fucking matter that she'd kind of defended him by pointing out that Johnnie had backed Christopher into a corner.

"Christopher," Johnnie began, standing.

"Save it," he bit out. "I ain't leavin' the club 'til this shit fixed, then I'm takin' my girl and my kids and gettin' the fuck. I ain't riskin' her no-fuckin-more."

Johnnie nodded. "Okay."

Another motherfucker who looked like he didn't believe Christopher's words. Oh, fucking well.

"Good riddance," Kendall said with a smirk. "Club needs new leadership anyway. I have ideas that I intend to implement as first lady. It's past due for renovations and we need more types of music. Opera would be a good choice."

"Kendall, gorgeous, no fucking way am I hurting my ears with opera."

"Maybe, we can have a cultural night."

"Listen up, Kendall." Christopher couldn't stand the thought of how Johnnie would let her fuck up the club. "My fuckin' ass ain't gone yet, so keep your fucked up ideas the fuck to yourself." He gazed at Johnnie. "Get your bitch in line. Brothers and their bitches gonna fuck her up if she try that bullshit on them."

"No, they won't. I have a lot of friends. Besides, all Johnnie has to do is demand they give me my way like you demand the same for Meggie."

"Pity that fuckin' bullet ain't fucked up your brain. Might've given you some fuckin' sense." Dismissing her gasp and Johnnie's narrowing eyes, Christopher said, "Megan awake. Well, she sleepin' like a motherfucker now cuz of the drugs they gave her. I need to talk to you before I head to the club and check shit out, Johnnie."

"Outlaw?" Slipper called.

Turning, Christopher saw the brother standing just behind him. As usual, Slipper's grayish-blonde, greasy hair hung limply around his shoulders. Next to Slipper an older motherfucker lagged in the shadows.

Christopher thrust his chin toward the runt of a man. "Who the fuck he is? I told you not a motherfucker come up here—"

"We frisked him. He say he got news about your boy."

Days fucking behind in searching for his son, Slipper's words shut Christopher the fuck up. By now, the trail was one, cold motherfucker. He needed the fucking help. "Fuckin' talk, old man."

Slipper shoved him forward.

Fear crumpling his face, the motherfucker remained speechless, his throat working but no words coming out.

"Talk," Christopher repeated with even less patience. "I ain't gonna fuck you up unless you gimme a fuckin' reason."

"You're scaring him, idiot," Kendall called from behind him.

"The quicker you fuckin' talk, the quicker you fuckin' leave." And the quicker Christopher got the fuck away from Kendall.

"Night before last," he began slowly, gazing from Christopher to Johnnie, who now stood next to him. "I came upon a black man holding an unconscious girl in his arms. I didn't notice the little fella until he started talking and I didn't put it all together until I read the newspaper this morning about a Megan Caldwell. The boy spoke of a Meg Anne, who fell and *'got'* red."

Fuck, Christopher's heart skipped a beat at the old man's explanation as it dawned on him that his boy had seen Megan get shot, and Christopher couldn't imagine CJ's fear. Christopher was a grown motherfucker and the image of that fucking bullet hitting Megan kept replaying in his fucking head.

However, hearing those details left no doubt that the old motherfucker *had* run across Digger, Bunny, and CJ.

"That's my boy," he said gruffly. He missed the way CJ mimicked every move Christopher made. Although Megan hated CJ's cussing, it secretly pleased Christopher. His boy was already a formidable little motherfucker. "He call his ma, my wife, MegAnn."

The cussing annoyed Megan, but hearing CJ address her by her name aggravated the fuck out of Christopher. He saw that as disrespect while it melted Megan's heart.

She was so fucking soft with their boy. She could get as upset as she wanted to with him, he didn't stay in line for long. CJ knew better than to pull that bullshit with Christopher. But it didn't matter. CJ could always rely on his ma to coddle and comfort him.

Boys needed a mother's love, too. While Christopher would discipline him and keep him in line, Megan could spoil him.

"He hurt?" he asked quietly. He missed CJ. Rule was barely walking. Besides, he whined for Rebel whenever Christopher tried to take him along. "Was he bleedin'?"

Uneasily, the old man glanced at them again. "Are you Outlaw?"

"Do it fuckin' matter who the fuck my fuckin' ass be? I already fuckin' told you, the boy my kid."

"Does he call you 'Law?" the old motherfucker persisted.

Christopher nodded, CJ's absence suddenly hitting him hard. Even if he'd been in no shape to look after him these past few days, he would've been safe with Ophelia. "Yep, sure the fuck do," he responded after clearing his throat.

"He had a bowel movement in my backseat and—"

"A bowel movement?" Christopher echoed with a frown. "You mean a fuckin' shit?"

"Yes. I still haven't gotten the stain up."

He'd take care of that for him. "What happened? What road you saw them fuckin' at?"

"Near the private access road that led to that deserted farmhouse."

They *had* gone to Logan's house, so he supposed Cash was right, and Digger started the fire. That motherfucking house should've burned down years ago. Digger had done Christopher a fucking favor.

"I fuckin' know exactly where the fuck that's at. I'm gonna take care of that fuckin' stain my boy did. The girl with them was o-fuckin-kay, huh? Just fuckin' tell me what the fuck I owe you and—"

"I came upon them on the main road that led to that house," the man interrupted. "But the black man asked to be taken to a tattoo shop, even though it looked like the girl needed medical attention." He leaned closer. "I found some blood stains in my car where she'd been laying. I'd intended to alert the police until I read the story today."

The badges would've give him a '*thank you*' and a '*we'll check into your story and be in touch.*' Some shit like that. This old motherfucker must know some fuckhead fucking familiar with the club and had found the fucking reward much greater if he came directly to Christopher.

With all the Harleys in the hospital parking lot and the shootings in the news, Christopher had been relatively easy to find.

"The place I dropped them at is called Gabe's Tattoo Parlor," the old motherfucker continued.

"I'll fuckin' look into it," Christopher promised, pulling out his cellphone. "If your fuckin' story check the fuck out, I'll fuckin' call you."

"Name's Nathan," he said, holding out his hand.

Christopher eyed it and exchanged a glance with Johnnie.

"Er, this is my number." Nathan rattled off the digits.

Christopher saved it in his contacts.

"Follow that motherfucker, Slipper," he ordered when Nathan left. "But watch your fuckin' ass."

"Sure thing, Outlaw."

Once he was alone with Johnnie and Kendall again, he fired off a quick text to Riley, along with the old man's phone number.

> *Track this motherfucker. Get back to me as soon as fucking possible.*

"Get Ghost here, Johnnie," he instructed. "Tell him to meet me in Megan room. I just got a fuckin' plan to smoke out fuckin' Sharper."

"In that case, I'll go with you. I need to check on Roxy."

Not waiting for Johnnie to tell Kendall later, he headed to Bailey's room, skidding to a halt when he saw Mort standing right outside her door, hunched over and leaning against it.

Fearing the worst, he reached Mortician and put his hand on his shoulder. "Bailey—"

"Her eyes open. I thought I lost Bailey, Prez. Fuck. Fucking karma for taking out Char." He heaved in a breath. "No, that karma is Tyler being killed."

Saying fucking sorry didn't fucking cut it, so he just shut the fuck up.

"They don't even know if the baby in Bailey still living."

Another innocent life taken away, a third helpless and unborn baby, if it died. Christopher never really thought of that type of shit before. What it meant when a girl lost a baby not even outside of her yet. If he went by Megan, women got attached to their kids the moment they discovered they were created.

Mortician blinked. "Wait, you out here. Meggie girl…?"

"Opened her fuckin' eyes, Mort," he said then gave the updates on the others, including the conversation he had with Johnnie and Roxy. "I gotta get shit goin'," he said after he finished, appreciating the fact that Mortician wasn't trying to change his mind about patching out.

"What you need from me?"

He cocked his head to the side. "You up to this shit?"

"Yeah, Prez."

"Check in on Megan 'til I get back. I might have a lead on Digger, Bunny, and my boy."

Mort nodded.

"I ain't gonna be long."

"Okay, Prez."

Before he left Christopher peeped in on Megan and found her still asleep, oxygen back in place.

Satisfied, he bent and kissed her lips, breathing easier for the first time in days.

Listening to the running water as Bunny showered, Digger cursed the tiny cabin Gabe dropped them at, located in the middle of nowhere. Beggars couldn't be choosers. He needed to get off the grid for a while and Gabe had fulfilled his request. Hopefully, neither Outlaw nor Sharper got a lead on their location before Digger regrouped. That still left Gabe vulnerable. Neither Outlaw or Sharper would offer the man mercy for assisting Digger.

Bunny had been right about Digger impulsively seeking out Gabe. He hadn't liked hearing those words from her. She'd almost sounded disappointed in him. In. Him. A motherfucker who'd never opened himself up enough to feel as if he owed any bitch one explanation. Including Peyton. She hadn't been interested in shit like that, anyway. On the flip side, she didn't listen when he really needed her to.

The thought slammed through him, the irony not lost. Rashness begot rashness.

He'd always kept a part of himself closed off, but he was clueless to the reasons why. It wasn't as if he'd ever attempted a relationship before Peyton. Even before she'd put him through the goddamn ringer, he'd separated fucking from feelings.

Maybe, because of the women he hung around? In the club, the old ladies were exclusive to the brothers they belonged to. Club Ass fucked whoever wanted them. Kiera, Ellen, and some of the other long-time chicks who'd hung around so long they'd become club property, dick-hopped. Digger had never seen a reason to open up fully to any of them.

Ellen. That fucking bitch. That *lying* fucking bitch. She'd gotten her fucking ass killed after she'd planted all that bullshit in Peyton's head. He'd liked Ellen. They all had and she'd had the fucking audacity to claim Meggie stole Outlaw from her.

Another crime on Digger's conscience. The moment he'd found out Peyton's intentions, he should've shut the shit down and went to Outlaw. Bunny was right. He'd had choices and he'd always made the wrong goddamn one. Adjusting his position on the sofa, he opened his bottle of vodka and tipped it to his mouth.

The water stopped, then started again, and he tightened his hold on the bottle, imagining how her lush body looked all wet and soapy,

Lucky for him, he'd adjusted to small spaces in the past few months. Otherwise, these close confines with Bunny would be unbearable. Being introduced as an old lady of another brother had made her out-of-reach to Digger. They weren't the type of club who shared their women, so she'd become like a piece of furniture to him. A cool chick, always around, and Meggie's friend. Beyond acknowledging her and joking here and there with her, he didn't fuck with her.

Being one-on-one with her and having to take care of her changed his impression. He found her quiet strength refreshing. Her calmness settled him down and removed some of the loneliness that had chased him from the club.

Throwing money at Bunny wouldn't matter. Returning Outlaw's son was her main priority. Not their crappy lodgings or her lack of clothes. Had Peyton been with him, she would've made him miserable, asking for dollars, outfits, and good food and all the things he'd pretended he could afford when they'd met.

Tyler would've been on Digger's ass, too. Not that it had been the boy's fault. He'd grown up in wealth, just like Digger and Mort. Whereas their mother had kept them grounded, Tyler's mom had been out-of-control herself.

Tyler.

Tyler. Tyler. Tyler.

Tylertylertylertylertyler...

Swallowing, Digger ignored the moisture in his eyes and swallowed more vodka. He tried his best not to fucking think of Tyler's death. It kept going to the same thing—Sharper standing over a fucking thirteen-year-old and filling him with bullets.

What kind of a motherfucker did that?

The short amount of time Digger had known Tyler before the boy had changed hadn't been enough. He wanted more. A do-over. A chance to impress upon Tyler that the lifestyle they led always had the chance of ending badly. Tyler, more than Digger or Mort, had everything in the palm of his hands, as Sharper's heir.

He could've been anything. The great holy man Sharper pretended to be. A CEO. A physician. Yet, Tyler had followed in their footsteps, taking the worst of each of them. Sharper's violence. His mother's arrogance. Mort's stubbornness and Digger's recklessness. Given that DNA rundown, Tyler hadn't stood a chance.

He'd killed innocent girls. For all of Digger's protests and demands not to hurt women, Tyler had thrived on killing those weaker than him. If he'd lived, would he have been redeemable? No one would ever know.

Blinking to clear away his tears and his hurt, Digger thought about Switzerland and how Tyler had been a pro at skiing.

Overseas, Digger had seen to it that he, Peyton and Tyler had stayed in the finest places. But, once again, he'd overspent and ended up broke. Same old story of an uncontrollable dumbass who never learned shit. Maybe, if he'd taken better care of his money, Tyler would still be alive. He never would've had to return to Sharper to hide from Outlaw and expose Tyler to their father's evil deeds.

He was one broke motherfucker now, and still he continued in the same manner. He'd borrowed money from Gabe without a way to repay him.

Bunny's low opinion of him was well-deserved. Of course he *had* fucking kidnapped her so that might affect her judgment of him too. Yet...yet, she hadn't pouted. She'd occupied Little Man while Digger got food together. She'd made her request and believed he'd think about it, taking him at his word. The idea uncoiled something inside of him.

They'd eaten sandwiches while Bunny looked through all the toiletries he'd purchased for her. Judging by Peyton and Char, women needed all kinds of stuff. Little sewing kits. Tampons. Lipstick. Mascara. Eyeliner. Perfume. Pens. Notepads. Mints. Gum. Deodorant. Travel sized toothpaste. Kleenex. Business card holders. Mini bibles. Guns. Condoms.

Fuck, shit Digger wouldn't have dreamed of.

So he'd gotten Bunny most of the stuff that had been in Char's and Peyton's purses, like shampoo and conditioner. All except the gun. Couldn't do a fucking background check under the circumstances. Besides, she'd probably use it to fuck him up.

The shower stopped for a few moments, then started again.

Digger imagined how Bunny looked with the water hitting her breasts and sliding down her bald pussy. Remembering her study of his mouth and his hair hardened his cock.

"Dig?" a hoarse little voice called.

Scratching his chest, Digger glanced down at Outlaw's son. Not an hour ago, the little motherfucker had cursed his ass out and beat the fuck out of him. Now, he grinned up at him, his cheeks smeared with drying snot.

"Find something to wipe your nose, kid." He sounded like a mean, grouchy motherfucker, but looking after Little Man for the past hours had worn him the fuck out. He intended to do something with his dick so he wouldn't ever create kids of his own.

"Potty," Little Man whined, after swiping his sleeve across his nose.

"Bunny taking a shower. We can't go in there 'til she done."

"*POTTY!*" he yelled. Digger had stuffed him with candy, donuts, and chocolate milk and he'd been going non-stop ever since. On top of coughing and sneezing, he must be tired.

For the entire time Bunny recovered, Little Man had been an angel. The moment she'd awakened, he'd turned into a fucking brat.

Between thinking of Bunny in a sexual way, remembering Tyler's death, and his own tiredness, Digger reached his limit. Crouching down, he glared at the boy. "Hold your piss, you little fucking brat, and that's that. I'm not going in there and looking at her pussy. I've already seen it and got a hard dick. So sit the fuck down and shut the fuck up. Understand?" he snarled, satisfied at Little Man's widening eyes and a bit of fear creeping onto his face. "Another fucking thing. If you piss on yourself, I'm beating your ass."

Tears filled those green eyes, too much like his father's, and he plopped down to the floor, sniffling, as if he wanted to cry but held back. His chest rattled.

Digger frowned. Bunny was right. Little Man sounded as if he had pneumonia. He needed medication.

"Dig mean ash fuck!" he whimpered, his chin wobbling.

What a fucking nightmare. He was treating Little Man the way Sharper had disciplined him and Mortician when their mother hadn't been around. Once she'd died, Sharper had brought his sons to church or to events with the media, but basically allowed the staff to care for them. Unless discipline was required.

"I want MegAnn," Little Man said in a hurt voice.

"What's going on?" Bunny's breathy voice floated to Digger and he glanced to where she stood in the doorway, holding a fucking towel in front of her, her brown hair plastered to her head. She hadn't even bothered wrapping herself up and he glimpsed the hint of an ass cheek from the angle he sat.

"Potty, Bun-Bun."

"The door was unlocked," she explained as if Digger didn't have a working dick that wouldn't respond to an almost-naked woman. "You should've come."

She crooked her finger at Little Man, but he sniffled and blinked, tears finally rolling down his cheeks.

"Dig say sit fuck down and shut fuck up, fuckin bwat."

"He said what?"

Just to piss Bunny off a little more, the kid's shoulders shook with the force of his big sniffs. She threw him an evil look. The little motherfucker repaid him good by tattling to her.

Huffing, she threw Digger another violent glower and held out her hand to Little Man. He ran to her. She stopped him, bent down and whispered in his ear. Glancing uneasily at Digger, he scampered toward the bathroom.

The moment the kid disappeared, Bunny stomped to him. "You fucking asshole, don't talk to him like that!"

"I don't remember telling you I joined a fucking monastery, Bunny. Get fucking dressed or get on your knees and suck my fucking dick to relieve the tension in my balls caused by you looking so pretty and naked."

Hastily, she wrapped the towel around herself, although her movements revealed some pussy and tits. He liked her height, especially now, seeing her gloriously long legs.

"Happy?"

"Nope, woulda been happier getting a dick suck."

Little Man's return interrupted Bunny's response. Instead of coming closer to them, the child ran behind Bunny and peeked around her.

Digger and Bunny stared at each other as if they were seeing one another for the first time. In a way, they were. This was the first time she'd ever looked at him with desire flickering in her eyes.

"He needs a bath," she said, glancing away, a flush creeping into her face. "Does he have any clean clothes?"

"In the bag," he answered in surprise. What did she think all these fucking bags held? "You do, too." He'd only shown her the toiletries, not the clothes and shoes.

Moving away from her put distance between them. Digger picked up two bags from the floor, one with things for her and the other for Little Man. He nodded to the prescription bottles on the table.

"You have antibiotics. I'm not sure what happened to you. But I figured it was fucked up with how sick you was. The way I saw it, you was suffering from more than the effects of the fire."

Vulnerability entered her brown eyes, the kind that made a man want to protect a woman. She nodded and gave him a small smile before backing away and grabbing Little Man's hand. "Thanks. Let me see to him," she said, nodding to the kid.

Several hours later, Digger sat on the sofa, glad that Bunny had finally gotten Little Man settled. The kid had energy to burn and then some. Seeing him in action wore Digger out but Bunny took it all in stride, leaving him to be the odd man out. Once Little Man finished his bath with Bunny watching over him, Digger took another shower—this time cold—not knowing what else to do.

He shouldn't expect anything else from Bunny or the kid. Of course they'd be on guard with him, and shut him out of their world. They saw him as the enemy, an idea he perpetuated with his grouchiness.

Finishing off the pint of vodka he'd been nursing since they'd eaten, Digger stood and went to the bags on the floor, scrounging through them until he found another bottle of vodka. Snapping the seal and unscrewing the top, he guzzled from it, enjoying the burn down his throat.

He started for the sofa but paused at the sight of Bunny in a T-shirt and sweatpants. Seeing how much healthier she looked, relieved Digger. She shifted from foot-to-foot, assessing him. He wished he knew what she was thinking at this particular moment. Could it be with the same interest and desire he felt for her? It definitely wasn't the annoyance and disgust from earlier. Her gaze flickering to the bottle in his hand ruined the moment. She shrank back.

"I…um…"

An idea of exactly why Outlaw had fucked up Trader formed in Digger's head. After taking care of her, he'd guessed Trader abused her, but based on her reaction, he hit when he drank.

Digger searched for words to put her at ease, but didn't know what to say to her, to put her at ease. Not the kind of words she deserved to hear. Deciding talking was better than looking like a fuckwad, he went with what he knew. "I haven't fucked you up yet. Have I, girl?"

Her eyes flared in surprise as if she didn't know he'd figured Trader out.

She licked her lips and hesitated before her shoulders heaved and she spoke. "That can change with alcohol."

He rolled his eyes, disgusted and out-of-sorts. Caring for her while she'd been sedated had softened him toward her. The way she watched over Outlaw's son and protected him, as if she'd given birth to him herself. Digger appreciated her attitude. Of course, she wanted to escape, so he couldn't hold her two attempts against her. In her position, he would've done the same thing. But he didn't like her fear of him, while he drank. "You saw me drunk as fuck before." She acted like he was a complete stranger. "Did I go off the fucking chain then?"

"At some point you did," she retorted. "Otherwise, you wouldn't be on the run from Outlaw."

"Ouch. You go for the jugular."

"I'm just responding to you."

"Yeah, but you left one part out. I'm on the run from Sharper, too."

"You're the one who got the club in the mess with him. Remember?"

"Wrong." Drinking again, he finally returned to the sofa and sat. "I never once betrayed Outlaw. Even when I brought Bailey to Sharper. I wanted to save my brother."

Anger flashed in her eyes, and she opened her mouth to give him the business.

Raising his hands in surrender, Digger hit her with his defense. "Think about how you want to save Gabe. Your kid brother. Well, Mort's my big brother. If I knew Meggie was there, I *would've* called her and told her to stay the fuck away."

"She would've told."

Probably. Meggie had a fucking head on her shoulders. She figured shit out as much as her husband did. But there were inherent difference between their views on life. Whereas she looked at things with emotion, Outlaw viewed shit with stone cold logic. "Wouldn't have been me."

"Technicality."

"Point being, my old man couldn't make Mort suffer as long as I followed his orders."

She tipped closer, though still out of reach. "Why didn't you do it? You're saying this because…" Her voice trailed off.

He shrugged, tired of offering her the reason. Apparently, she hadn't heard a goddamn word.

"I didn't have time to think shit through. I should've called Meggie, even though Outlaw would've had my ass for involving her. It wouldn't have been me telling him or Mort. I could've called Kendall, even."

The words captured her full attention and she didn't respond, so he continued talking and drinking.

"Know why I took Outlaw's kid?"

"You said to save his life."

Another fact she seemed skeptical of. "That's the truth."

"Something else you didn't think through, since you were going to kill me."

"That's why I don't see shit with any gray in between," he explained. "If I'm loyal and it comes time to choose, I go with the person who I have the most allegiance to. I'm sorry for threatening you. If the kid hadn't wanted you, I probably would've shot you."

Even he winced at how callous he sounded. His confession brought back the fear in her face gradually sliding away and she stepped back.

"Sorry," he said again. "I just…I'm an in-the-moment type of dude. That's why I mostly worked the disposal detail in the club." Although Mort had seen more in him, which was how he'd been elected SAA.

She scrunched her nose up. "Impulsiveness is good sometimes. Other times, thought and planning is required."

"Sharper had supposedly been planning to take Outlaw down for months. Then, suddenly, he'd decided to move in. And look how that had turned out."

"A prime example of why impetuous behavior isn't good."

"Whatever the fuck enters my head is what I do."

She didn't like that. Although she made no response to his comment, her disappointment returned.

"Don't judge."

"As if," she replied with so much sadness Digger knew it ran deep within her. "I'm the last person in the world in a position to judge anyone."

"If you not judging me by that hang-dog disappointment, what you been doing?"

"Analyzing you."

"I'm not fucking hard to figure out, Bunny," he scoffed, polishing off the second pint of vodka.

"You're complicated," she insisted. "The only thing I picked up on that you've planned is your intention to leave me here and search for your father. But have you really thought that out or is this just something to do? Suppose you're killed? What happens to me and CJ then? I don't know where we're at. I have no money. No phone. Nothing." She twisted strands of hair around her fingers. Digger wished he was touching the shiny strands. Any place on her body, actually. "Suppose you do find Sharper? You could very well lead him back to us."

"You overthink situations, Bunny," he accused, unsettled by her very valid questions. "I don't need a fucking moral compass, a living, breathing conscience, planting uncertainty in me. I have enough on my own."

"We all do at some point."

"Bullshit."

She rocked back on her heels. “How were you sergeant-at-arms? You have to be a good strategist to keep the president safe.”

“In spite of your low opinion of me, I never got no complaints. I did my fucking job.” Mort kept him on the straight-and-narrow.

No reaction from her at that announcement. He wasn’t sure what he was expecting and why he wanted her to give a response. Bunny was so unlike Peyton, something he needed to remember.

Peyton had been wild as fuck and always wanted something. Revenge. Money. A fuck. Toward the end, she’d worn him out. She’d been evil rather than vengeful.

“So why did you agree to think about my requests to call Outlaw? Thinking doesn’t seem to be your strong suit.”

Ha ha. Fucking hilarious. “Val’s the dumb one,” he countered with a scowl.

“Yeah, but he can learn. You don’t want to, so that makes you the stupid one.”

Damn, she was brutal. “For a bitch supposedly afraid of me, you sure got a smart fucking mouth.”

Lowering her lashes, she snapped her mouth shut and Digger wanted to take the words back.

“I’m not going to hurt you.” He was enjoying her company and if he frightened her again, she’d shut down and walk away. Despite the circumstances, it felt nice just to speak his mind.

She placed her hand on her belly and he jumped to his feet, remembering her pain pills.

“You ever telling me what happened?”

She searched his face and he knew what she was doing. Weighing if he were worthy to confide in.

“Since you took care of me, I owe you an explanation.”

That wasn’t exactly the reason Digger wanted her to open up, but it had to do.

"I was pregnant. Trader didn't want it," she said quietly, shifting from foot to foot. "So he beat it out of me."

"Fuck, man." It was even worse than he'd imagined. "I'm sorry, Bunny. On the real. That's some cold ass shit he did to you. No woman deserves that and a dude should have more feelings for a kid, whether it's his or not."

She gave him an evil look. "It was his baby!" she snapped with indignation.

"That makes what he did even worse. He killed his flesh and blood. Taking your baby away even if it wasn't his, is fucked up."

A muscle ticked in her jaw and she glanced away, the light reflecting on the tears filling her eyes.

Out of words, Digger went to the table and picked up one bottle and then the other, both with the name of the drug scribbled on paper then taped to the bottle. He opened one and tapped out a pills before walking to her. "Open your hand."

Obediently, she followed his instructions. Tears spiked her lashes and her nose had reddened with her effort to not cry. She stared at the pill until she regained her composure, then she shook her head. "I can't take this. Little Man might wake up."

"Who the fuck you think took care of him while you were sedated?"

"That was before you turned into a meanie-pants."

"Did you really just fucking say *meanie-pants*?"

"Yes," she sniffed, lifting her chin. "That's what you are. Threatening a scared little boy."

He hated to break the news to her but that little motherfucker wasn't afraid of him. He'd been tired and he'd wanted Bunny's attention. However, pointing that out to her would piss her off, so he changed the subject. "You in pain, right?"

"I'm not takin that pill."

"Stop being so fucking stubborn. The kid won't fucking die if you're resting. You need it so you can regain your strength."

At first, her look softened. Then, whatever she thought made her shake her head and straighten.

"I appreciate your concern. If you're sincere, fix whatever you've gotten us into. My brother's still in danger. I'm still kidnapped, and so is that child who's trying to be brave, but he keeps crying for his mother and his father. He adores them. You want to do something? Get him back to his parents. Let me call Outlaw. I'll do whatever you ask if you send CJ back so he can get to a doctor."

Maybe, he *could* get Little Man back to Outlaw and keep Bunny as insurance. Meggie liked her, so if Outlaw thought harming Digger would, in turn, harm Bunny, he might be able to get away and hide out at her parents' house as she'd suggested. If Digger left on a blind manhunt, he could either get killed or lead his father back to the cabin, imperiling Bunny and the kid. Little Man deserved to be with his father, just as Tyler should've been with Mortician, but he never got that opportunity.

"If I do this for you, what I get in return?"

"Nothing. I have nothing to give you but my gratitude."

"You have nothing you *want* to give."

She huffed in exasperation. "Why not do it because it's the right thing? Why do you have to get something in return?"

"That's the way life work. Or are you too naïve to realize that motherfuckers fall into the category of a giver or a taker. The ones who give end up losing their souls."

"And those who take end up losing their humanity," she countered softly. "Their empathy."

There she went again, attempting to work on his conscience. "Shut the fuck up. What do you expect me to fucking do? If Outlaw don't value your life, mine's fucked if I give up the kid."

"Please. He's just a small boy."

"This not only about Outlaw kid. This about Gabe too."

"It is," she admitted, her steady gaze on him. He really didn't like the hurt or the hope in her eyes. "Can you hold that against me after what you did for your brother?"

"Don't flip the fucking script."

Her chin wobbled at his shout and she pursed her lip, perilously close to crying. He didn't need to be a brain surgeon to know she'd shed many tears once she'd taken up with Trader.

"We might not be able to save my brother." Swiping at a tear, she sniffled. "But we can save CJ."

Fuck. Little Man needed medical attention, so they could save him. That thought alone guided his decision to change his mind. No other reason. He definitely didn't do it for Bunny or because of anything she'd said.

Stomping to a bag, he found notepaper and a pen and thrust the items into her hands. "You want him sent back? Sit and write exactly what I say."

Little Man had a fever.

After writing the letter Digger dictated to her, Bunny left him alone and went to the room where she'd awakened. Meggie's son had flushed skin and moved restlessly about. When Bunny crawled next to him, she found him burning up. Using cold towels, she lowered his temperature. She had no children's medication available and she feared giving him any of the bootleg drugs on hand.

She'd gotten little rest, so when Digger came in at the break of dawn and announced they were heading out, Bunny breathed a sigh of relief, grateful that he was actually releasing the toddler. They drove in silence, which she took comfort in. The worry about CJ and the intensity of her conversation with Digger had drained her. Once she'd gotten his agreement to return Little Man, and had started writing the note he dictated, she hadn't interrupted, fearing he'd change his mind. Most of what he told her to write led her to believe he was insane. What person of sound mind believed leaving such written evidence was a good plan? To Bunny, it was just another example of his recklessness.

Digger acted. He didn't think.

An hour after they started off, they came across a Walmart, where Digger allowed her to run in and purchase Children's Tylenol. She also purchased disposable diapers for CJ. Knowing Meggie had him potty-trained, Bunny hated to do something that might make him regress. But it was impossible for Digger to stop every time CJ needed to use it.

Now, as dawn turned into daylight, Digger pulled into a restaurant and Little Man slept in the back seat of the car, Bunny kept her mind focused and positive. If she thought about all that could go wrong with the plan Digger had, she'd never go through with it.

Digger opened the door, but before he stepped out, Bunny laid a hand on his shoulder. "Are you sure this is the only way?" she whispered. "He's just a small child and he's sick."

He stared at her a moment, then took her hand in his and squeezed. "I promise I'm going to find somebody to leave him with, in the restaurant."

"They can kidnap him or leave him or murder him. He might never get back to his mom and dad."

"I'm going to do the best I can to see that he does. Even if that mean sitting here all fucking day,"

"Digger, let's take him back to Hortensia. Please." They'd driven even further away from the town.

"Can't fucking do that. I don't know who to trust there. I might come across a motherfucker who just take the kid and let me go. But it's just as likely I'll run across my father and cousin. I won't be able to save Little Man or you. If you want me to do this, then this is the way. Otherwise, let's get back on the road and we get him to a hospital when we get to your folks in Arizona."

That would be at least another two days and Bunny didn't want to risk that. He'd gone long enough without medical attention.

"Okay, we'll do it this way," she agreed, having no choice. "How will you know who's trustworthy enough to leave him?"

"I haven't been too good at judging a motherfucker's character lately, so I'm not sure."

That made two of them. She'd sorely overestimated Trader, a mistake she wouldn't repeat.

Once Digger took Little Man into his arms, the child whined slightly, then rested his cheek on Digger's shoulder, his lids drooping closed again. They headed into the restaurant, passing a skinny kid who couldn't be older than fifteen. He sat on the small patch of grass near the door, a rolled up sleeping bag and knapsack resting near him. He had shaggy hair and such sad eyes.

For a moment, Digger stared at him, before he continued on without a word. After placing their order, Bunny picked at her food while Digger dug in. Little Man lay next to her on her side of the booth.

Digger poured two sugars into his coffee. "I bet that kid's homeless."

"Probably so."

A shadow fell over his face. "At least he's alive."

Unlike Tyler. He didn't say it, but Bunny knew that's who he thought of.

"Do you want to talk about Tyler? I'm a very good listener."

Pausing, he looked away, then shook his head. "Not much to say."

Every time a child was brought up, Digger talked about Tyler. Perhaps, remembering him would ease some of his pain. "What was he like?" she asked, ignoring his response.

He snorted. "Unlike any motherfucker you knew. Tyler was…" His voice trailed off and he turned thoughtful. "Damaged," he said finally. "My fault, too, and another reason I've decided I don't want kids. I don't know how to be a father."

"You could learn."

"Yeah, if I was interested, but I'm not."

"Fair enough. Trader wasn't interested either. He didn't want my babies."

"Fuck Trader, man. He was a fucking asshole. Don't let what the fuck he said fuck with you. If I wanted kids…a woman of my own…I don't think there'd be a better chick than you. You so fucking pretty and sweet. Caring. More than anything, you loyal."

His voice deepened with each compliment he showered on her, curling around Bunny's insides and making her squirm with embarrassment and desire.

"And that fucking body of yours," he continued. "Make a motherfucker say *Praise, Jesus* and hallelujah."

She giggled. "You're silly."

"But I got you to laugh." He gripped his coffee, then shifted in his seat. "Once we leave the kid, it's just going to be me and you."

"And?"

"Don't play fucking dumb. Will we fuck?"

She'd be the first to admit that Digger intrigued her, but not a week had gone by since her relationship with Trader ended. Er, since Outlaw ended her relationship with Trader. More than that…"I'm your captive. I'm not sleeping with you under these circumstances." And if that wasn't enough of an argument. "Besides, Trader deserves some respect."

"You think? Because the way I see it, you just doing it cuz that's what's fucking expected of you by society. You was with the motherfucker so you required to mourn his dumb ass. Don't get involved with no other motherfucker 'til a certain amount of time passed, otherwise you supposedly an unfeeling bitch. That matter if you live for other motherfuckers and not yourself." He thrust his face closer and lowered his voice. "The motherfucker deserved what he got. You know it and I know it, too. You don't want to fuck me? That's cool, baby. Just use a real fucking excuse."

"That is a real excuse, asshole."

"In your goddamn mind. Not in mine. It's not real and it sure the fuck not valid."

"You don't think I'd be dishonoring his memory?"

Digger's eye-roll annoyed her. "Fuck, Bunny, I didn't peg you as a stupid bitch. Misguided, yeah. But after what Trader did, you have the right to give up your pussy on top his grave." He grinned. "*Graves.*"

"What are you talking about?"

He gave her a long consideration, then shook his head in dismissal. "Don't worry about it. Enough about his dead ass anyway. Let's get back to you giving me some pussy."

When she pursed her mouth, Digger raised his hand.

"Look, girl, I'm not proposing nothing more but giving you a few good orgasms. I'm not trying to marry your ass."

Images of the two of them wrapped around each other displaced speculation on what he meant by Trader having more than one grave. No, not speculation. She knew about the meat shack. What went on inside the place was just too gruesome to contemplate.

"Sleeping with you won't do me any good." She'd open herself up and leave herself even more vulnerable. "No matter what you say, you have the power of choosing if I live or die. Besides, why do you want to sleep with me? Is wanting to have sex with me just another impulsive decision of yours?"

"Nope. From the moment I saw your bald cunt, I wanted to fuck it."

Her mouth fell open at his explanation. He shrugged. "Then I got to know you and it stopped being just a pussy to stick my cock in. I've been wanting to fuck *you*."

She couldn't think of a response, so she only stared.

"It's true. So, no, this not one of my 'impulsive decisions'," he said, using air quotations before grinning at her. "Maybe, you'll give me pussy on the way to your folks. You know I can't wait to meet them?"

Wondering if he knew she hadn't really told her mom that Digger was coming with her, she eyed him suspiciously. The conversation had been short and tense.

"Hi, mom," Bunny had greeted when Virginia answered.

"What do you want?"

"Um, yes, a visit." She'd hoped her answer made it seem as if her mom had suggested the visit.

"When?"

"In two or three days."

"Fine." And Virginia had hung up. Only, Bunny had stayed on the phone, pretending to tell her mother that she was bringing a friend.

Guilt at her manipulation of Digger assailed her. He'd become agreeable to releasing CJ because he'd believed they'd have a place to stay, while he got his defense together to present to Outlaw, once he contacted him with news of her continued captivity. If Digger thought they did have a hideout, he might change his mind about releasing Meggie's son. What she'd done was a gamble. Virginia could turn them away, but, at least, CJ would be back with his parents.

"Let's see who pass through here," Digger said into the silence.

A family of five with three well-mannered children and neatly-dressed parents came first. Digger said they'd call CPS before they did anything else.

"Then the FBI. The DEA. The CIA. And whatever other fucking acronymed-agency you can think of," he grumbled. "Too clean cut."

"What about if you don't leave the incriminating letter?"

He didn't respond.

"And what would the CIA need to be involved for? Aren't they like for spies?"

"Don't matter. I don't want to risk it."

Another two families came in. Bunny didn't bother to ask. A female biker walked in, her helmet clutched under her arm.

"Nope. Not a biker. Chick or not."

A parade of people passed through. An older man who seemed to have forgotten his contacts or eyeglasses. He squinted at everything. A younger guy who wore jeans and a T-shirt displaying his bodybuilder muscles. Two teenage girls who giggled with each step they took. An older woman with a bible in one hand and her purse in the other. A pregnant woman pushing a stroller.

One by one, Digger ruled them out for one reason or another.

"Let's just go," he said, hours later, his frustration clear, as he got to his feet.

"Digger, maybe, if we wait a little longer."

"The fucking shifts changing, Bunny. We're going to start looking mighty fucking suspicious hanging around this motherfucker all day. Let's go. Let's move onto Plan B."

They were wasting time arguing. The longer it took to go through with Digger's plans, the worse it would be for Meggie's son. In silence, she followed Digger outside.

As they walked to the car, Bunny caught sight of the boy they'd seen upon arrival. He'd moved toward the back of the restaurant, to dig in the dumpster.

"Do you have twenty dollars?"

Digger slammed the back door shut where he'd situated Little Man. "For what?"

She pointed to the boy chomping on whatever he'd found. "Him."

Looking over his shoulder, Digger cursed, then headed for the boy. She expected him to hand money over, so it surprised her when the boy hastily gathered his belongings and followed behind Digger.

"Bunny, this is Diesel. Diesel, meet Bunny," he introduced. "I think I found a way to solve our problems."

Dear Outlaw

I got a lot to say but a letter no place to say it. I apologize for, fuck, everything. I know you don't believe me, but I haven't betrayed you. Not intentionally. I can't let Bunny go right now. She asked me to tell you to spare Gabe. I went to him because I was trying to get away from Sharper, and Bunny was bad off. Gabe was helping his sister, not me. I swear that's all he was doing. Bunny would be heartbroken if he was killed for doing what any good brother would do. I don't know how far into Oregon the brothers and Sharper is, so I left Little Man as close as possible. I hope this letter fall into the right hands when your kid is found, but I don't know what the fuck else to do. I'm scared to call in case you can track a burner. Speaking of that, I guess I got to touch on some sensitive subjects. Here goes: I took your son to save him. Sharper thought I aimed and accidentally missed. He would've shot the kid where he stood if I hadn't gotten him away. That's the truth. You got him running scared. He's desperate and shit cuz he know you have a hit out on him because of Meggie. He wants to break you and he knows your weaknesses. I did some real stupid shit, but we family, Outlaw. Always. Never knew it til I got jealous of Meggie, Kendall, and Bailey. I felt fucking left out, so I latched on to

Peyton and got in trouble with Sharper. Last thing: tell Mort...tell Mort I miss him. Ride or die forever.
Digger

That was the best he could do for himself, Gabe, and Outlaw's son. Bunny hadn't agreed with the letter, but she didn't agree with most of what he did. Nor did she understand he had to take this shot in the dark. While they were in Arizona, he'd contact Outlaw, now that he felt confident both Little Man and the letter would reach the man with the discovery of Diesel.

Just when Digger had run out of hope, Bunny had pointed out the kid.

Digger hadn't intended to involve him, but the moment he saw him, he knew he was what his father would deem a throwaway. A lost boy who'd either run away or been kicked out of his house for one reason or another.

Once Diesel agreed to keep watch over Little Man and then call Outlaw, he bought the boy a decent meal, some cheap clothes, and then found a motel to check into so Diesel could clean up and get a good night's rest.

Little Man's fever broke for a few hours and Bunny managed to coax him into eating soup. His cough was still really bad, but the kid had courage and tried to tough it out.

At mid-morning the next day, Digger found another restaurant, closer to the beach, while Bunny still slept. She'd had a rough night herself, but seeing her rest relieved him.

"Outlaw's coming for you, okay, kid?" Digger promised, at the end of their meal, as they stood in the bathroom. If he'd brought Bunny, he doubted she would've stuck to the plan and left the kid. It was best that she was at the motel, asleep. "Just listen to Diesel until your old man arrive."

"Okay, Dig," he said hoarsely, his features tired and pulled down.

Digger handed Diesel the throwaway phone he'd purchased. "You fuck this up and you're in trouble. Understand?"

"Yes, sir," Diesel croaked.

"When I peel out, make the call."

Diesel nodded.

Little Man sneezed. "MegAnn come too?"

"I don't know." He didn't know if she'd made it or not.

"Bun-Bun?"

"Bunny's fine, lil dude."

"Her tired."

Smiling, he ruffled Little Man's hair. "Yeah, she is." Pulling out his wallet, he counted the money he had left from what he'd borrowed from Gabe. Not much. Counting off five twenties and handing them to Diesel, he said, "Outlaw will give you more."

Maybe, he'd even take pity on the kid and take him in, but Digger didn't want to give Diesel false hope and mention that.

He headed to the door, where he paused. Diesel and Little Man stood side-by-side. Digger swore he saw more fear in Diesel's eyes than he did in Outlaw's son's. He was so young, he didn't know all that could go wrong.

"Bye, Dig!" he said, running to him and hugging his legs before stepping back and grinning.

"Bye, kid." He offered Diesel a two-fingered salute. "You got this," he said with reassurance.

He wasn't sure, but he thought Diesel straightened just a little bit.

Sometimes, an encouraging word made all the difference in the world. He hoped that was the case this time around.

Megan's eyes were clear and alert, although her doctor warned she'd remain in the hospital a while longer. Four days after she opened her eyes, Christopher knew the time approached when he had to explain to his girl that their son was missing. He hadn't brought CJ to see her or called him on the phone, despite her repeated requests to talk to him. He'd hoped before he told her the truth, he would've gotten CJ back, but that hadn't fucking happened. Bunny's brother didn't value his life enough to give Christopher CJ's whereabouts.

Gabe lay in the meat shake, beaten and tortured but still alive. Christopher didn't believe him when he said Digger had only come and asked for money and transportation. He felt it in his gut that he knew exactly where they were.

His patience had worn down, so he was grounding the motherfucker tonight.

"I'm feeling much better, Christopher," Megan persisted. "Please bring CJ to see me."

Shoving his hands in his pockets, he turned away from the window, glanced at her, peeped at the floor then up to her again. "Ain't doin' that, baby."

She cocked her head to the side and studied him. His time fucking up, he had to confess to her. If only he know how. Apparently, he didn't need to. Before he said a fucking word, tears rushed to her eyes.

"Where are they?" she whispered. "They're dead?"

"No, fuck, baby! I swear they ain't..." He closed his eyes, not sure about CJ. Drawing a deep breath, he focused on her again. "Rebel and Rule fine. Roxy, Zoann, and Fee watching over them."

"CJ?" she croaked.

She'd fucking hate him once he'd dropped his news. The fucking idea that he'd fucked up one time too many torturing him, he started off with his decision. "Remember, I said I'm leavin' the club. Turnin' in my patch, baby. As soon as this shit behind us."

"Christopher, where's CJ?"

Fuck. She didn't fucking want to hear what the fuck he fucking planned to do.

Yes, Megan pussified him, and right now he wanted to run the fuck away with his tail between his legs rather than tell her their son was... "Gone, Megan. Don't fuckin' know where. Digger fuckin' took him, and Bunny."

Horror twisted her face and she squeaked. Fucking *squeaked* like a frightened little mouse before her tears overflowed from her eyes and she covered her mouth, her blood pressure spiking.

He'd promised her he'd never turn away from her when they went through a crisis, but he almost walked away then, unable to bear watching as Megan went from grief to disgust toward him.

"You have no idea where he is?" she asked around her sniffles.

"After I got some fuckin' order at the club, I came here, baby. Yeah, I'm a shit father, but I fuckin' couldn't fuckin' think past any-fuckin-thing but bein' at your side."

"He could be dead," she cried, and Christopher flinched, hating her sobs.

A nurse walked in. Not Lea today, but an older bitch who looked like she never smiled. "Everything okay in here?"

"What the fuck it look like to your fuckin ass?" Christopher yelled, startling the woman.

"If you're upsetting my patient, and you are, I'm going to have to ask you to leave," she shot back when she recovered.

"The fuck you will—"

"What's going on in here?" Johnnie walked in and paused, followed by Mort, Ghost, and Val. By now, Megan had usually fallen asleep because of pain medicine, so they'd been discussing plans for Sharper in her room. Christopher still couldn't be away from Megan for too long. Just like Mort with Bailey. While Bailey stayed in the hospital and, for now, her kid seemed fine, Mort wanted to be as close to her as possible.

"I'm calling security!" the nurse-bitch blared.

"It's okay, Sally," Megan called pitifully.

"He has to leave."

"Bitch, you fuckin' say that to my ass one more fuckin' time and I'm fuckin' tossin' you the fuck out that fuckin' window."

He didn't need her fucking bullshit with Megan so upset. If she wanted to leave him, he'd live with it. At least she was alive, but this cunt picked the wrong fucking time to push around the fucking authority she thought she had. He and Megan were at a critical point.

"Fine, Mrs. Caldwell," Sally said, although Christopher wasn't sure to what. She turned on her heel and stomped out.

"She know Little Man gone, Prez?" Mort whispered.

Clenching his jaw, Christopher nodded.

"Christopher?" she called in a tired sounding voice.

He turned to her. "Yeah, baby?"

"You've never made it a secret that you put me before anyone."

"Fuck, I know and I fuckin' know my ass supposed to fuckin' prove that shit fuckin' wrong when our kids in danger. But, fuck. Sharper still on the fuckin' loose and he fuckin' want *you* dead before he fuck my ass up. I been doin' my business fuckin' here, instead of tearin' this fuckin' town up, lookin' for CJ." He wasn't about to mention using Gabe to torture information from. Even if the shit had worked and he'd told the fucking truth, she didn't have to know. "I'm gonna find our boy, settle this shit, and then we ridin' out, Megan. I swear."

She swiped at her cheeks. "You can't quit your club," she said softly, shocking the fuck out of him. Blinking back her tears, she gave him a sad smile. "You can be so stupid sometimes and I'm so mad at you for not looking for our son—"

"Megan—"

"But I know *you*, so I don't blame you for *not* looking for him." She frowned. "If that makes sense. I love you. Whether you find him or not, I'll still love you." Her voice cracked through the words and her chin wobbled, but he saw the sincerity in her gaze. "And you love your club. You *are* the club." Biting her lip, she looked guiltily at the others, then lowered her lashes. "I know a lot of damage has been done amongst the brothers."

She didn't know the half of it.

"You ain't gonna love on me if I patch out?"

Rolling her eyes, she sniffed. "I'll love you in any way you are, but what would you do if you leave the club?"

"Fuck, I ain't thought about that. But I got a lotta fuckin' contacts. I'll do something with my fuckin' ass."

Hurt now clouded the lucidity in her eyes.

"I ain't doin' my boys right, Megan. Puttin' you first and shit. Fuck, yeah, I love the club. Life come up with different shit for you to fuckin' do, baby. That's what the fuck this be. Me lookin' out for my fuckin' wife and…and children." He hung his head. He *hadn't* looked out for his children.

"Okay, Christopher," Megan said quietly, sounding as defeated as he felt before she gasped and straightened. Thoughtfulness crossed her face and she did her head-cocking study of him. "That's it right there."

"What the fuck you talkin' 'bout, baby? What the fuck it?"

"Christopher. You're being *Christopher*. My husband and my children's father. Where's Outlaw? Christopher does the mushy. Outlaw does the mayhem."

"You ain't makin' no fuckin' sense," he grumbled, annoyed that she called any part of him mushy.

"Yes, Christopher," Johnnie said slowly, studying her with the admiration that Christopher hated to see in his eyes toward Megan. "I think she is."

Mortician shifted. "Yeah, Meggie girl got a point, Prez. For real."

"I ain't a stupid motherfucker, but what the fuck I'm missin' here?" he asked Megan since *she* came up with her analyzing bullshit.

"The entire point, moron," Megan snapped at him.

Yeah, she was one pissed lil motherfucker, but she didn't hate him.

"It means Christopher the *'family man'* needs to go sit down somewhere. Maybe, next to your wife."

"Them drugs fuckin' with your brain or some shit. You my wife and—"

"No, Outlaw, I'm not your wife," she fired back. "I'm your old lady who needs her man to *find* their son." She closed her eyes and hung her head. "Dead or alive. I just want him back. When his family is threatened, Christopher can't do that. Outlaw can. Outlaw loves his woman and he loves his club. He'd let nothing come between him and either one of them. He'd say, *'ain't nothin' but a thing,'* and find whoever hurt the club and whoever made me cry over CJ and make them pay. If you walk away, you're letting them win. If you'd been talking about leaving *before,* I'd support you. But this is just a knee-jerk reaction to *me.* Life happens, Outlaw. Know why? Because it *ain't nothing but a thing."*

During the course of chewing his ass out, she'd sat up. Now, she'd plopped back down, exhausted, and winced. "It hurts," she said, rubbing near where her bandages were.

"You through reamin' my fuckin' ass out, baby?"

Nodding, she closed her eyes. "I love you," she murmured, wiping away the silent little tears falling again.

"I love the fuck outta you," he responded, impressed by and admiring her strength as well as humbled by her devotion to him.

His phone rang. Digging it out his cut, he glanced at the unfamiliar number. "What the fuck you want?" he greeted.

"Mr. Outlaw?" a boy's trembling voice asked, sounding at the fucked up stage, where the timbre was starting to fucking change.

"I ain't no fuckin' *Mister* Outlaw, motherfucker. Stop playin' on the fuckin' phone. I ain't got time for this shit."

"Wait. No, wait!" he responded, pissing Christopher off.

"Want 'Law, ash fuck," he heard just before he would've hung up.

He dropped into the seat, glad it was near him, otherwise he'd would've fallen the fuck on his ass. Relief and disbelief battled inside of him. From the sound of it, the boy had CJ. "No fuckin' wait," he snarled, impatient to talk to his son. "Put my fuckin' kid on, assfuck."

"Yes, sir."

A moment later, a sneeze and a sniffle greeted him.

"CJ?" Christopher asked on a swallow.

"Ohmigod!" Megan screeched.

"Want MegAnn, 'Law," he cried and he sounded as if he had a very bad cold. "Her falled."

"Your ma right here," he said, reeling in shock, the moment as surreal as the day CJ had been taken.

"Let me talk to him, Christopher," Megan demanded.

"Hold a minute, boy. She wanna talk to you," he said gruffly, turning to Megan and putting on the speakerphone.

"CJ?" Megan asked, hope and fear in her eyes.

"*MEG-ANN!*" CJ yelled.

"Hey, buddy," she answered, laughing through her tears.

"Want home, Mommie," he said, forgetting all about calling Megan by her name. "I got donut for you."

She laughed and then coughed. It was contagious because CJ joined her. "Bet I know where?" she said hoarsely.

"Where?"

"Your pocket."

He screeched with joy.

"Where the fuck you be?" Christopher called.

"At eatin," he responded. "Dig say potty. He took Bun-Bun."

At eatin? Where the fuck was that? He wasn't going to think about Digger leaving his boy at the moment. That shit would come later.

"Put that fuckin' kid on the phone, CJ," Christopher ordered.

"Mister Outlaw?"

"Where the fuck you at?"

"At Port of Call Restaurant in Brookings."

Christopher snapped his brows together, sure he'd misheard. "You in fuckin' Oregon?" he asked with surprise. They weren't far from Oregon. Unfortunately, Brookings happened to be on the other side of the state, right near the California border. About seven hours away.

"Yes, sir, Mister—"

"Boy, you call me that one fuckin' more time and I'm beatin' the fuck outta you."

"So that's where he gets it from," he grumbled and from the muffled sound, he'd moved the phone away.

He glanced at his watch. Just after 11:00 AM. "I need your keys, John Boy," he said, already taking his motorcycle key from his pocket and handing it over to Johnnie. "Yo, kid. Got any fuckin' place you can bring my boy? It's gonna take me a minute to get there."

He didn't need two children hanging the fuck around a restaurant for someone to bring in the badges.

"We can go to the skating park. He's been having fever on and off, so—"

"Shut the fuck up," Christopher ordered, seeing the worry creeping into Megan's eyes. "He fine, baby."

Megan gave him a skeptical look. She had fucking ears. She could hear their boy coughing like a motherfucker. "How far away is the skating park from where you are?" she asked, looking pale.

Christopher would find that nurse-bitch and send her ass in there to see to Megan.

"Don't worry 'bout how the fuck far away it is," Christopher interrupted. "Get my boy there and keep him fuckin' safe for me 'til I arrive."

"Yes, sir."

"Wait, let me tell him goodbye," Megan cried.

"Put him back on. His ma wanna talk to him."

"Mommie?"

"Daddy is coming for you," she swore the moment she heard CJ's voice. "Behave for the boy, okay? As soon as I see you I'm going to hug you so tight."

"You ain't tell me you fuckin' knew my phone number, boy."

"Dig put in pocket."

And then fucking left him.

"Listen up, CJ. How 'bout this? How 'bout you talk to your old man as fuckin' long as our fuckin' battery work?" Once his son hung up, the connection would be severed. Although the kid didn't have to call, he had, but Christopher wouldn't relax until his boy was back with him.

"Hang on," he instructed so he could give out orders. "Ghost, hang with Megan. Mort in between sitting with Bailey, check on Kendall. Johnnie, walk with me and get rid of the shit in the meat shack."

Anyone who'd helped Digger was their enemy, so Johnny nodded, unperturbed.

"Mister…sir, there's a letter," the kid said, sounding as if he'd wised the fuck up and got the speakerphone on.

"What does it say?" Megan asked.

"Um, can I get killed if I read it?" the boy asked.

"Sound like you already fuckin' read it, motherfucker," Christopher growled. "Answer my wife so I can get the fuck."

"Where's Gabe?" Megan asked into the silence after the kid finished the letter.

Christopher's mind spun. On the one hand, he couldn't fucking believe Digger had fucking left such an incriminating fucking letter in his boy's pocket. On the other hand…

"Christopher?"

"Fuck, go get that motherfucker and see to his injuries," he grumbled, under his breath. "Don't fuckin' release him yet. Just take him somewhere until I think 'bout this fuckin' letter." He turned and kissed Megan. "Gabe fine."

"Are you sure? Bunny loves him a lot."

He sighed. And Megan adored Bunny. "Fuck, I know she love the motherfucker. He fine."

"Okay."

Because she believed him, she dropped the subject.

"Rest," Christopher ordered, determined to put Gabe to rights again. Once she was out of the hospital, he'd tell her the truth. "Hear me? I'm gettin' our boy and bringin' him home."

She thumbed his lips and smiled sleepily. "I know."

"Hold on…what the fuck your name, kid?"

"Diesel," he called.

"Listen up, Diesel. If I lose the fuckin' call, dial me right the fuck back. Don't show a motherfucker that letter. Okay?"

"Yes, sir."

He dialed and a moment later Megan's hospital room phone began to ring. He handed her the receiver, after answering. "Diesel? CJ?"

"'Law!" CJ squealed.

"Megan?"

Her shining eyes told him he'd done this shit right. "If my phone die, boy, your ma on a land line. If she fall the fuck to sleep, Ghost in here with her." He kissed her again. "Bye, baby."

She smiled at him. "Bye, Outlaw."

Although he snickered, he shook his head. He'd gotten her point, but he still didn't like her to call him Outlaw.

Walking out into the hallway, Johnnie said in a low voice, "You really want Gabe spared?"

"Yeah," he whispered back, well aware Megan was on the phone.

Within five minutes, he hit the road in Johnnie's Navigator, basking in the sound of his son's little voice.

Christopher broke every fucking traffic law on the fucking books to get to his boy. By some fucking miracle, the badges didn't stop him, and he figured it might be fucking time to sit the fuck down with Father Wilcunt and ask some fucking questions about spirituality. The little fat motherfucker was now the club's chaplain. Megan and Bailey had put it the fuck in his head he should be fucking called Jazzman. He hadn't liked Christopher's suggestion of Priestboy. Mortician had wanted Prelate.

What-the-fuck-ever. The self-righteous assfuck was in and happier than a motherfucker.

Christopher's cell phone had died a couple of hours ago, so he'd lost the connection to his son and Megan had fallen asleep before that. Johnnie had taken her place on the phone, and Christopher wouldn't think about why that motherfucker was in Megan's room and not his fucking bitch's.

The skating park came into view. Patches of frozen grass dotted the areas between large swatches of concrete that dipped into steep valleys and swerved up high. Several parking areas were located amongst the skating rinks, so Christopher pulled Johnnie's Navigator into the closest one and exited. He walked the perimeter, scanning the area, but finding no sign of his son.

Swallowing hard, he headed toward an arched wooden entry to another smaller park.

Before he adjusted his gaze to get a good look, a ball of energy barreled from behind a tree.

"'Law! 'Law!"

Laughing, he bent and opened his arms as CJ reached him. Relief flooded him and he lifted his son into his arms, squeezing tight, tears stinging his eyes.

Fuck, Megan was right. Where the fuck had Outlaw gone? Outlaw wouldn't fucking cry under any fucking circumstances.

CJ coughed and leaned back in Christopher's arms, grinning at him and squeezing his cheeks. "Where MegAnn?" he wheezed.

"Your ma waitin' for you, boy," he said, deciding not to correct him about using Megan's name. There'd be time for that later when he was rested and didn't look so flushed and weak.

Christopher felt CJ's forehead. Hot. His boy was sick and had been left without medical attention. Assfuck, Digger, wouldn't die easy or fucking quick.

"I'm gonna fuckin' bring you to see your ma, but first you gotta see a fuckin' doctor."

"Want Mommie! No hospital. Doc ashfuck. Make me get boo-boo." He pointed to his shoulder.

He couldn't promise he wouldn't get a shot of some type, which was the reason he was complaining because of the vaccinations from the last time. "You need to see the motherfucker cuz you sound real fuckin' sick," he explained as he started toward the Navigator.

"Um…mis…mist…I-I mean…O-Outlaw," a cracky-sounding voice called.

Gasoline! He'd forgotten about the little motherfucker.

"S-sir…um…O-outlaw?"

Fuck, had he fucking sounded so fucked up as a teenager? He turned and found a skinny kid with brownish-blond hair and blue eyes staring in his direction. “Yo, Gasoline. Lemme bring you home.”

“It’s...it’s Diesel,” he corrected in a trembling tone.

He knew his fucking name had had some-fucking-thing to do with fucking fuel.

Christopher stepped in his direction and Diesel backed up. “Listen up, Diesel,” he said on a sigh. He needed to get his boy to the fucking doctor, not pacify some scared little motherfucker. “You ain’t got no fuckin’ reason to be fuckin’ scared of me.”

Diesel looked at his sneakers. “Digger said the same thing.”

At hearing Digger’s name, Christopher tensed. “What the fuck else that motherfucker told you?”

“That he’s sorry and you’d reward me if I took care of CJ, then he left and went back to get Bunny.”

Adjusting CJ in his arms, Christopher studied the kid. Ghost said he’d fucking seen Digger kidnap Bunny and CJ, but was she still with Digger because she wanted to be? Or because she had no choice?

But if Digger’s letter was true, then he was on the run now, because he had no choice himself. He’d fucked up. The fucked up part was all the brothers believed Digger had betrayed the fucking club and any fucking change-of-heart now on Christopher’s part would make him seem like a weak motherfucker.

“CJ called him *Dig*,” Diesel continued. “He didn’t mistreat him or Bunny. He was just really nervous.”

Christopher gave Diesel a small nod. Something about the kid reminded Christopher of himself at that age. He wondered if Diesel had grown up in a houseful of women like Christopher had. Or if he had some-fucking-body close to him who fucking despised him, like Logan had with Christopher.

CJ laid his head on Christopher’s shoulder. “I tired, ‘Law.”

“Okay, boy,” Christopher said gruffly. “Digger—”

"Dig say we gotta a venture."

Christopher frowned. "A fuckin' what?"

"Adventure, I think," Diesel said around a cough.

That made fucking sense. Digger had always been fond of CJ. Maybe, he *had* taken him to get him away from fucking Sharper. Per-fucking-haps, he *should* let assfuck explain before he blew him the fuck away. In spite of leaving his boy with a little unknown motherfucker, he'd tried to fucking ease his boy's fears *and* he'd fucking instructed Diesel to look the fuck after him.

He started for the Navigator again.

"C'mon, Diesel," he called over his shoulder, not talking again until Diesel hurried to his side. "Lemme drop you the fuck off at your fuckin' house and stuff your fuckin' pockets with a few fuckin' bills for lookin' after my boy. Tell your ma you got the fuckin' dollars from workin' or some shit. Or what-the-fuck ever. Tell her what-the-fuck ever you fuckin' want." He reached the SUV, opened the back door and strapped CJ in. He hadn't had time to stop by the club and get the car seat. Once he finished, he straightened and shut the door. "C'mon, hop in," he ordered Diesel.

The boy hesitated. "I don't have a ma, sir. Um, M-mister Outlaw. I-I mean Outlaw." He frowned. "I don't even remember her. All I remember is my dad. I woke up one morning and he was gone." His throat worked but then he shrugged. "He just left me, so you don't have to drop me nowhere because I don't have nowhere to be dropped off."

The last bit he said with an attitude, almost as if he dared Christopher to comment. Instead of getting angry at the kid's disrespect, he rubbed his hands through his hair. "Sound like to me your fuckin' pops was a fuckin' assfuck."

Diesel's lips compressed into a tight line, and his jaw clenched.

"Ain't nothin' but a thing, boy. Cuz I been knowin' a lot of fuckin' assfucks in my fuckin' life. A bunch of them motherfuckers shoulda covered their fuckin' cocks cuz they wasn't fit to have their cum make innocent fuckin' babies. Even better woulda been havin' their fuckin' nuts crushed in a fuckin' vise cuz they coulda covered their dicks a coupla times and dropped their loads in some bitches a few other times."

Diesel's widened eyes made Christopher smile.

"My ass take some gettin' used to," he said. "But I ain't hurtin' no women and I sure the fuck ain't hurtin' no kid. How the fuck old you be?"

"Almost sixteen," Diesel responded quietly.

"When your pops skipped out?"

"Six months ago."

That was a fucking long time for a kid to be looking after himself. Even when he was at his worst, Christopher had always had his mother to go to. And if not Patricia, Big Joe had been right there. Diesel sounded like he had no-fucking-body. "You been livin' on the fuckin' streets ever since?"

Nodding, Diesel bowed his head.

"You go to fuckin' school?"

"Not in the last six months."

Christopher shook his head. "Get the fuck in. From this fuckin' point forward, you ain't alone no-fuckin-more. You took care of my boy so we fuckin' family now."

Diesel didn't move immediately. He just studied Christopher. From the fear, uncertainty, and hope playing on his face, Christopher knew the kid's mind was whirling. Not that he fucking blamed him. He was a strange motherfucker, inviting him to go to some fucking unknown place.

Finally, Diesel nodded and looked toward the windshield, waving at CJ, who'd unstrapped himself and was sitting in the front passenger seat.

"CJ loves you a lot," Diesel said, loping to the passenger side. "I don't ever remember talking about my dad, the way your son talks about you."

"Yeah?" Christopher said, careful to keep his face blank and not puff his chest out with pride.

"Is MegAnn his mom?"

"Yeah. Her name Megan. His mom and my wife."

Diesel gave him a small smile. Christopher didn't need to ask if CJ had talked about her. He already knew.

He looked up at the darkening sky. "Come on. We gotta get the fuck on the road. My boy need a fuckin' doctor."

"Okay."

The moment Christopher and Diesel slid in, CJ squealed and scrambled to the back seat, clicking his seatbelt back into place while Christopher and Diesel did the same.

"Deel come, too?" CJ asked as Christopher pulled out of the parking space.

"Yeah, boy, Deel comin', too."

He'd get his son medical attention and put everything else on the back burner for now. Sometimes, a motherfucker had to do what a motherfucker had to do. His boy needed him, so revenge against Sharper and what-the-fuck ever for Digger would wait.

Once his boy and his wife was straight, Outlaw would return with a vengeance and end this fucking game with motherfucking Sharper once and for fucking all.

Deciding to bring CJ to the emergency room of the same hospital Megan was admitted and Zoann worked at, it relieved Christopher to discover his boy hadn't developed pneumonia, but he did have an infection that needed to be treated. He held CJ while the nurse administered injections.

CJ squirmed in Christopher's arms. "Ashfuck, 'Law!" he yelled around a pitiful wail. "Fucka mudna!"

"Hey, boy, I'm gonna beat your little ass if you fuckin' curse my ass out one fuckin' more time. I know this shit hurt, but I'm still your fuckin' old man. Respect my ass."

"Fuck in hell, 'Law," CJ screamed. "Want MegAnn! I want my mommie."

Growling, Christopher gripped his screaming son closer to his chest, keeping him still until the nurse finished her slow ass up. The moment she did, she gave him a disapproving scowl.

"Did that child say what I think he said?"

Unless the bitch was deaf, she knew exactly what the fuck CJ said. But he'd play her fucking game. "Don't fuckin' know. What the fuck you fuckin' think he said?"

"Never mind," she snapped with indignation. "I know what he said and so do you. My ears didn't deceive me. You should be ashamed of yourself."

"I should be, but I fuckin' ain't. Now if all you got for me is some fuckin' lecturin' bullshit I ain't interested in fuckin' hearin', I'm gettin' the fuck outta here, so I can bring my boy up-fuckin-stairs to see his ma."

Although visiting hours were long over, they made an exception for Christopher.

The nurse shoved some forms at him. "The doctor's instructions and two prescriptions. See that he takes every bit of that medicine, Mr. Caldwell. He's very vulnerable to pneumonia."

"Okay. Can I get the fuck gone now?"

"Sign that paper." She nodded to the form in question, waiting until Christopher set CJ down and signed his name before saying, "You're free to go."

Scooping CJ back into his arms, Christopher gestured to Diesel who'd been sitting in the corner, out of the way. Seen but not heard. "C'mon, I'm gonna introduce you to Megan."

"Yes, sir," Diesel responded, following Christopher through the double doors and toward the elevators.

"Hear that, boy?" he asked his son, who'd quieted to sniffles. "We goin' see your beautiful ma," he said when they stepped onto the elevator.

Instead of answering, CJ glared at him and Christopher scowled, satisfied when his boy dropped his gaze. He didn't want CJ afraid of him, but he sure the fuck wasn't tolerating disrespect. Sick or fucking not. "I under-fuckin-stand you pissed cuz that needle fuckin' hurt, but the shit gonna help you. By now the pain gone, boy, so drop the fuckin' attitude. Hear me?"

"Okay, 'Law," CJ said in a small, pitiful voice.

Christopher sighed but fell silent. A moment later, the elevator arrived on Megan's floor. As he headed to her room, he nodded to the brothers who were assigned night duty.

In her room, he found Megan's eyes closed, while Ophelia and Ghost sat side-by-side on the window seat, whispering to each other. Ghost caught sight of him first and got to his feet, his guilty look almost identical to Ophelia's.

"Hey," Ophelia said, as CJ yelled, "MegAnn!"

Startled, Megan jerked awake and blinked a couple of times before her gaze cleared. "CJ!" she said, sitting up and wincing.

"Hey, bud," Ophelia offered with a smile, ruffling CJ's head and earning a laugh.

"Ant Fee," he responded, coughing.

"Oh my, you have a bad cold," she said.

"Yep, already got him checked out downstairs," Christopher explained, still trying to figure out what the fuck was going on with Ophelia and Ghost. *Why the guilty fucking looks?*

"I sick, Mommie," CJ explained, reaching for Megan.

Before she could move, Christopher sat him next to her, then kissed her lips.

"Hey, you," she said, thumbing his lips.

"Hey, baby."

"I hot, Mommie."

CJ's words pulled Megan's attention away from Christopher and she put her uninjured arm around their son's small shoulders.

"I'm going to get home," Ophelia said, standing on her tiptoes to hug Christopher and kiss his cheek.

Christopher nodded.

"I'll walk you out, Ophelia," Ghost told her before he lifted a brow to Christopher. "That's okay with you, Outlaw?"

Ophelia blushed and Christopher glared at Ghost. "They got some deranged fuckheads on the loose, so, yeah, walk her the fuck out. But from this fuckin' moment forward, keep your fuckin' dick outta her."

Megan groaned, but mortification raced across his little sister's face. She was the youngest. They'd reconciled since the rift caused by their mother's death, but they'd never been as close again. That didn't mean he wouldn't look out for her, and Cash McCall was the last fucking person she needed to involve herself with.

"Hear what the fuck I'm sayin', Cash?"

A smirk on his face, Cash shrugged. "Fine with me. It was nothing serious."

That wasn't fucking true if the hurt in Ophelia's eyes was any fucking indication. But she was gentle and fun-loving and artistic. She didn't have the temperament to deal with any of the motherfuckers in his club, especially a complicated man like Ghost.

Before he could say anything, Ophelia ran out.

"Ant Fee cry, 'Law," CJ said, his voice filled with confusion.

"I know, boy." He studied Ghost. "Ain't know this shit for a while, but Fee's last old man beat her the fuck up a few fuckin' times. The night Ryan was born, Fee called Zoann cuz Mike had beat on her a-fuckin-gain. Ain't fuck all Bitsy could do cuz she'd just had her kid. They just fuckin' decided to tell me a few fuckin' months ago." He dropped into the chair close to Megan's bed, feeling the weight of her gaze. Not looking at her, he met Ghost's eyes. "Ask me where the fuck that motherfucker at now, Cash."

Ghost swallowed. "I have a fucking idea."

"You fuck with her again, I'm fuckin' you up."

"Because of Stretch, I take it," Ghost said coolly, the first time he'd almost admitted to the affair with their treasurer.

"Yeah, but not for the fuckin' reason you thinkin', motherfucker. You could have a bitch that you ain't sure what the fuck to do 'bout and I'd tell you to stay the fuck away from my little sister. You could be fuckin' single and I'd still tell you the same shit. Know fuckin' why? Cuz you interested in gettin' fucked and nothin' else. Stretch gotta figure that fuckin' shit out for himself. But Fee? You fuckin' dead, motherfucker. Now, get the fuck outta my face."

Without another word, Cash stalked off and Christopher faced Megan, his tension deflating at the understanding in her eyes.

CJ tugged on her hair. "I still sick, Mommie."

Megan kissed the top of his head. "Yeah, buddy, but take your medicine when Daddy tells you to, and you'll soon be feeling well again."

"MegAnn stay in bed?"

"Uh-huh," she answered, kissing him again. "Just for a little while, but I promise I'll be home soon."

"Mommie, you falled and get boo-boo?"

"Kind of, sweet potato," Megan answered slowly. "But what do you mean?"

"Mommie get all red and falled and get boo-boo."

She exchanged a glance with Christopher, and he knew she realized their boy had seen her get shot. She squeezed CJ against her and he smiled. "Mommie's boo-boo is almost better now," she said softly.

CJ coughed. "MegAnn?"

"Yes?"

"'Law say you not MegAnn. Him say you Mommie."

He hadn't said that shit once to his son since he'd picked him up. At least his boy remembered.

"Daddy's right. I *am* your mommie."

"Law call you MegAnn." He frowned at Christopher. "'Law fucka mudna. 'Law let meanie lady hurt me. Ashfuck."

"I owe you a ass-whippin'," Christopher snapped and narrowed his eyes at Megan's dirty look. "Calm down, baby," he ordered before she said anything. "You shouldn't be gettin' excited."

"How many times have I told you not to use bad language around him, Christopher?" she chirped, ignoring the fuck out of his words. "He's just a little boy."

"Sooner or fuckin' later he gotta learn how to be a grown fuckin' man."

"Shut up," she yelled, then turned her attention to their boy. "CJ, I don't want you using bad words. Okay?"

"Okay, MegAnn." His little face scrunched up. "Mommie?"

"Yes, darling?"

"What bad words?"

Megan blinked. "Huh?"

"What bad word I say?"

Smirking, Christopher snickered. "Tell him, baby," he challenged. "Then he could fuckin' know what words *not* to say."

"When was the last time I locked you out of *there*?" she sniffed.

Little bitch. That shut him the fuck up. She couldn't fuck right now, any-fucking-way, but once she healed, he couldn't risk her chaining up her fucking Promised Land, when all he wanted to do was sink inside of her and feel her alive and vibrant beneath him. "I'll try to do fuckin' better 'round CJ," he swore. "Just get better, Megan. I want you home."

Her eyes softened toward him and she held out her hand. Christopher took her fingers and kissed each of them.

CJ tugged on Megan's gown. "Mommie?"

Megan grinned, knowing CJ thought of Megan as *his* mommie and not Christopher's wife. "Yes?"

"Deel keep me for Bun-Bun and Dig."

"Who's Deel?" she asked, reminding Christopher of the boy, who'd taken Ophelia's seat.

"Him by window."

"Oh, yeah, baby," Christopher said, waving the boy over, "this Diesel, the kid who took care of CJ. Diesel, this my Megan and CJ's ma."

Megan smiled and a blush crept up Diesel's neck. "Hi," she said, ignoring the way he gaped at her. "Thank you so much for caring for my son."

"Yes, ma'am," he mumbled after a few moments of studying Megan then turning the same attention to Christopher.

"Why would you get my son for Bunny? Isn't she helping with the others?"

"Diesel ain't got no family or nothin' and he saved our boy," Christopher interrupted quickly since he hadn't told her about Bunny. He sure as fuck didn't want her to find out now and hoped like fuck his boy kept the fuck quiet. "I'm gonna give him a room at the club and help him get in a school."

Even if Diesel was interested, he was too young to become a member of the club. Of course, he could always give him odd jobs like Big Joe had done with him. But he didn't fucking know if Diesel would even fit the fuck in. Right now, he seemed like a respectful little motherfucker. However, a motherfucker showed his true fucking colors when they lived under the same fucking roof.

He thought about Dinah and the suspicions he had that she had somehow teamed with Sharper, and amended his previous thought. *Most* fucking times, motherfuckers showed their true colors.

CJ relaxed against Megan. "I want Harway. Where Wule and Webel?" he continued around a yawn as his eyes slipped closed.

In a moment, he'd nodded off and Megan smiled, tears rushing down her cheeks.

"You okay, baby?" he asked.

"I'm fine. I'm just happy. You got our son back." Leaning back, she swiped at her wet cheeks. "I know you have to take him home, but let Momma keep him while you get things together. Time with him might help her a lot." She gave him a sad smile. "Did she ask to see me?"

No, that bitch ain't asked one fucking thing about Megan. "She been helpin' out Roxy and Fee with the kids," he lied.

His answer satisfied her and some of the hurt cleared away. She nodded. "Okay."

Fuck, if it was fucking Dinah who had betrayed them...he couldn't finish the fucking thought. Despite everything, Megan loved her ma. Since he intended to leave the club after this shit was straightened out, he could always spare Dinah's life and exile her fucking ass some-fucking-where. For Megan.

That's what Christopher would do. But Outlaw? Outlaw would put Dinah to ground for compromising club security and jeopardizing the lives of his family and his brothers.

Fuck, *Christopher* wanted to put that bitch to ground. Fuck being Outlaw. Motherfuckers talked about what had started fucking happening after Megan had arrived, but it wasn't until Dinah's fucking ass got there that the fucking bullshit had really started. And once K-P was killed...

Scrubbing a hand over his face, Christopher sighed. Dinah couldn't fake that kind of crazy, but she *had* gotten better in the last few months since Roxy arrived.

"Christopher?" Megan called.

He looked at her. If he killed her mother, he knew she'd never, ever forgive him. *Jesus Christ, please don't let it be her ma.* The quick prayer surprised him, but he didn't know what the fuck else to do. *Someone* had been watching out for him. His girl had lived and his boy was back. The only thing he needed now was for it to be another motherfucker beside Dinah who'd fucked them up the ass.

"Christopher?"

"Yeah, baby?" he responded, needing Herb and Al to sort this shit out in his head.

"Take Diesel home with you and CJ. He doesn't have to stay at the club. We have a zillion rooms at our house, so he should be able to find one to sleep in.

Diesel smiled shyly at her. "Thank you, ma'am."

Leaning down, Christopher kissed Megan before lifting CJ into his arms. He hesitated, hating to leave her and her look of adoration.

"I love you," she whispered.

"I love the fuck outta you, Megan," he told her quietly. "Just remember that. Okay, baby? If shit get too fuckin' rough…" His voice trailed off. It seemed like whatever a motherfucker feared the most, he ended up being fucking faced with. Thinking of Megan leaving him, or dying, terrified him. "I love you, no matter what."

"I know," she said, "and I'll stand by you, no matter what. Whatever you need to do and whatever decision you have to make, I'll always be in your corner."

He nodded and carried his boy from the room, with Diesel close behind.

As Megan's words rang in his head, he hoped like fuck she wouldn't be forced to prove them.

"Albany."

Bunny winced at her mother's tight-lipped greeting and use of Bunny's given name. She was so far removed from the girl who'd been Albany. Albany had enjoyed the attention of her two loving parents, Walt and Virginia. Albany had excelled in school and on the cheerleading team, where she'd first been pinned with the moniker of Bunny.

Still, back then, she'd been more Albany than Bunny, and had been slated for a career in elementary teaching. She'd wanted to exceed her parents' expectations. Before. Before she'd become interested in boys and parties and good times. She'd always been well-liked, but when her body started to develop and she'd gotten on the cheer squad, she'd really come into her own and her popularity had soared.

The refusal of her parents to bend their rigid midnight curfew had been an interfering nuisance. Looking back, she realized her parents hadn't been bad or wrong in their rules or their expectations. They'd been normal. She'd want her child to have a bright future, too. Walt and Virginia had fought Bunny tooth and nail to keep her on the straight and narrow, so the road that led to her current life was solely on her shoulders.

Her fingers touched her belly. Always perceptive, her mother lifted a brow. Bunny dropped her gaze from Virginia's, sadness and grief settling into her. What she wouldn't give to have the comfort her mom had once offered her but she'd so cruelly rejected.

Virginia sighed and cleared her throat. "It's been a long time, Albany."

Her eyes burned and her throat hurt as she fought back her tears at her mother's distant tone. "It has, Mom," she admitted quietly, her voice thick.

Digger bent and his lips skimmed her ear. "Fuck, girl. Your name Albany?" he asked, his breath fanning her skin as he straightened and stared at her with amusement.

Exhaustion rode Bunny while Digger seemed unaffected. He remained handsome and mocking.

Virginia squinted at Digger from head-to-toe. "Who's this person?"

"Mark," Bunny muttered, elbowing Digger at his pleased smirk.

"How the fuck you know my name?" he whispered, his breath fanning her neck.

"Shh," she chastised, her face flaming at her mother's rude glare. She reminded herself that Digger deserved that and more after what he'd put her through. Except for the past two days on the road, he'd been nothing but kind and solicitous.

They hadn't spoke about touchy subjects. Once she'd awakened and found Little Man gone, she'd cried and begged Digger to take her to him. Although he'd declined, he'd hugged her and promised everything would be fine. To prove it, he'd risked a text to Diesel checking to make sure everything had gone smoothly. She'd wondered why he hadn't just called the boy. Then the text had come through.

Outlaw took me and Little Man.

She realized Digger had suspected as much. He knew Outlaw wouldn't abandon a helpless kid who'd cared for his son.

"Albany, who's your friend?"

At her mother's sharp question, Bunny jumped.

If Digger blurted his road name, he'd ruin any chance they had of staying at her parents' house.

He snickered and focused on Virginia. "Marcus Banks, ma'am," he offered with shocking charm and polish. His brilliant smile almost melted Bunny's panties off and instantly thawed her mother. Virginia stepped aside, allowing them to enter.

"After you, Albany," he teased, winking at her.

He placed his hand at the small of Bunny's back and her pulse leapt.

He made her feel safe and protected and cared about. No, she wasn't doing this, she reminded herself.

Trader had made her feel safe, too. Besides, her feelings for Digger were superficial, brought on by a need for normalcy in a world gone mad.

Pausing in the small entryway, Digger waited until Virginia closed and locked the door, then allowed her to take the lead. Bunny followed, Digger's palm still flat against her back, his touch burning through her clothes. She observed the changes in the house she'd grown up in. Updated décor and new furniture took away the well-worn look of a happy family with two kids who entertained loads of friends that she remembered.

Saddened by the change, she bit her lip, but remained silent. When they reached the kitchen, her mother nodded to the table. Bunny sat while Digger lifted a brow and leaned against a counter, folding his arms and glancing between the two of them.

"Were you expecting your daughter or not?"

She laughed nervously. "You were there when I called my mom."

"Her ass don't act like it."

Oh my goodness, he was going to get them kicked out of the house. "Please," she said with a forced smile. Her mom might look cool and reserved in a pair of Bermuda shorts, V-neck T-shirt, slip-on sneakers and crew socks, but Virginia laid down the law and took no prisoners. But that was then. Bunny no longer knew how her mom behaved.

Instead of tossing them out, Virginia bristled.

"Albany called and I told her it would be okay to drop by." Sniffing, she glared at Bunny. "You didn't tell me you were bringing company. You said you were coming to make amends."

"I am," she said honestly, past time she admitted to all her mistakes. Maybe, her parents couldn't forgive her. Or, perhaps, they'd offer her a conditional pardon. If she returned to Phoenix, then they could start over. The idea of such a provision sent unease through her. She wasn't the wild Bunny, who'd left with Trader, but she'd found a place for herself.

Yet…she might not have a place at the club any longer. Her entire life had become one big question mark.

Digger pinned Bunny with an inscrutable look but spoke to her mom. "So she didn't fucking tell you about me?"

"Not one thing."

"Interesting," he remarked with deceptive blandness.

"I can explain, Mark," she said, the use of his given name making her feel closer to him. More intimate.

He clenched his jaw, his rigid pose indicating his anger.

"What are you really doing here, Albany?" Virginia hissed, not caring about his frigid glower.

Bunny gritted her teeth at Virginia tacking on her name with almost every sentence, purposely reminding her how much they detested the name 'Bunny.' "Mark and I are on a road trip and Phoenix was on our route, so I called you."

Sweeping Bunny with a head-to-toe gaze, Virginia pursed her lips. "You and that biker man are no longer together?"

"You can say that," Bunny mumbled.

"Is this a temporary thing or a permanent breakup, Albany?"

Digger snickered. "This breakup as permanent as a motherfucker. Ma'am," he added at Virginia's glower.

"I know my name's Albany, Mom," Bunny inserted quickly, throwing Digger a death glare at his language. "But I really like Bunny. It's less formal and—"

"And nothing," Virginia snapped, her shoulders stiffening. "Your name's Albany. I'll not address you as if you're still a whore on a pole."

A heavy silence descended at Virginia's terse statement. Wrapping her arms around her waist, Bunny stared at the floor. Her mother had a right to her anger, but that didn't mean she had the right to humiliate her in front of Digger.

Despite the battles between her and her mother, Virginia had stuck in Bunny's corner, making sure she graduated from high school and went into college.

Her partying had almost gotten her kicked out of the university. When her parents stopped paying her tuition, she'd had a full blown I'll-show-you meltdown.

As long as she was in school, they hadn't wanted her to work and had supplied all her needs. They weren't a rich family by any means, but whatever Bunny wanted she'd gotten. Until she'd fucked up and gotten royally pissed at their rightful punishment.

It had never dawned on her that what she did on the side would be taken into account when she applied for teaching jobs. The summer she'd graduated and gotten certified to teach first grade, a fellow coed had come into the club where she worked. She hadn't recognized him amongst his group of friends there for a bachelor party. She'd been their entertainment and they'd showered money on her to watch her dance, to touch her pussy, and to have her suck their dicks.

That was the beginning of the end of her teaching career. Still, her parents had stuck by her. Just when it seemed she was getting her life on track, she'd gotten involved with Trader.

He'd frequented the strip club and had befriended her. She'd thought he was her soul mate. He'd always been so understanding. Until he'd alienated her from her family and moved her to Washington State.

Digger stroked her cheek and she looked up, finding him looming over her. He smiled gently, his anger about the lie she'd told evaporating. "You not a whore, so it's cool, girl."

"Her name's Albany."

"No, *Mrs.* Hamilton, Albany a fucking city in New York. *Her* name's Bunny."

"Bunny was the name her cheerleading squad gave her, Mr. Banks," Virginia persisted, hands on her hips. "The name she took on the stripper pole. Which is where she met Trader. She forgot about the local modeling gigs she had. She forgot about her now-useless teaching degree."

Her mother blurting to Digger about her past made Bunny cringe. It wasn't that she wanted to impress him or that she made it a secret from him. She just appreciated her new persona, that of Meggie's assistant and Little Man's Bun-Bun. She appreciated that Digger didn't seem concerned by what she *had* been and only who she was now.

Before Bunny could decide whether or not to leave and never contact her parents again, Virginia spoke again. "Where's Trader?"

Digger smirked, still standing protectively at her side. "Trader never bothering Bunny again. I told your ass that already, so chill with asking dumb ass questions."

Even though Gabe had taken the money they'd given him to open his tattoo shop and followed her to Hortensia, it was Bunny they hadn't forgiven. It was a double insult as a matter of fact.

Falling for a law-breaking biker and stealing their baby boy away, though her parents had always encouraged Bunny and Gabe to be close and watch out for each other.

"You will respect my house and me, Mr. Banks, or you'll get the hell out of here. We have no times for the likes of you and the company Albany prefers. If you want to stay here overnight, you'll keep your filthy comments to yourself."

"The company she prefers, huh? You don't know me. How the hell you know what type of company I am for your daughter? I could've grown up in a fucking California mansion, having motherfuckers wait on me hand and foot."

"Doubtful," Virginia scoffed, although Bunny knew that was exactly how Digger had grown up. But Virginia's response reminded Bunny of her mother's quickness to pass judgment. That was one reason she'd been so determined to make her own mistakes with Trader.

"Why don't you fucking ask me who the fuck I am before you turn into a fucking self-righteous cunt?" Digger growled.

Bunny gasped and got to her feet. It was time for them to go. This had been a bad idea from the start. Getting here by subterfuge had started the trip off on a wrong note.

"How do you know my daughter?" Virginia spat out. "What's your profession? Where are you from? Who are your parents?"

Looking her mother up and down, Digger's eyes twinkled, as if this was some big joke and not a serious situation. "Is this a form of meet the parents or some shit?" he taunted around laughter.

"I'm giving you the chance to explain your background," her mother responded, her eyes sniping at him. "Giving you the benefit of the doubt. If there's any hope of a reconciliation between my daughter and I, I want to make sure she isn't making the same mistakes again."

"In other words, fucking a biker."

"*Dating* a biker," her mother corrected.

"Who she going to fuck," Digger pressed.

"Well, let's hope she no longer has indiscriminate sex."

Desperate for Virginia to drop the conversation, Bunny jumped to her feet. "Luckily, that's not an issue. Mark isn't a biker."

He stiffened as if she'd offended him. Throwing her a disgusted look, he walked to the refrigerator and opened it, pulling out a Dr. Pepper, before straightening and leaning against the counter again. Once he popped the top and took a long swallow, he cocked his head. "They her mistakes to make, right? Unless she going around killing other motherfuckers for no fucking reason. Or hurting people for no reason, but your daughter not like that. She's sweet and loyal and brave. You just need to give her a chance. By the way, I'm not getting in her pussy, so your fucking questions don't apply to me."

A gamut of emotions ran through Bunny at Digger's defense of her, and if she hadn't been so confused over her lack of feelings toward Trader, she might've admitted Digger stole a tiny piece of her heart in that moment.

Outrage pinched her mom's features. "Is this some type of joke, Albany?"

"No, Mom. Mark and I are friends. Besides, I'm almost twenty-eight, way past the age where you have to give him the third degree."

"Yes, well, your previous lack of common sense makes it my duty to ask the questions I'm sure you overlooked."

Bunny growled. "This is the reason I've always hesitated to contact you."

"Yet, here you are, Albany."

"Here I was," she said briskly and stomped to Digger, snatching his can of soda away and setting it behind him on the counter. She grabbed his hand. "Come on, Mark. We can find someplace else to stay while we're here."

"Albany?"

Just as she started to turn and drag Digger with her, her father's incredulous voice boomed through the kitchen. Dropping her hold on Digger, Bunny spun and met her father's incredulous look. They stared at each other and, for the first time since arriving, tears rushed to her eyes. Her ex-cop father and current private investigator stood there with a wide gaze.

"Dad," she said quietly. "I was just leaving."

Irritation settled into Digger's face and he shifted, his hands falling to his sides. She knew he carried a gun and the fact that they wouldn't have anywhere to sleep seemed to agitate him.

"Dad, this is Marcus Banks. Um, Mark, this is my dad, Walt."

Her dad pulled his attention away to focus on Digger. Her dad's narrowing eyes didn't bode well. Neither did the recognition dawning in Digger's face. But how would they know each other? As far as Bunny knew, they'd never met.

"I don't fucking believe this!" Digger snarled, pacing. He banged the microwave oven. Both Bunny and her mother jumped. "Fucking Meggie, man." He scrubbed his hands over his eyes. "Interfering little fucking cunt!"

Digger pulled his gun just as her Dad raised his, interrupting her intentions to defend Meggie. She had no clue why he'd made such an outburst. That, however, didn't seem as important as Digger and Walt on the verge of blowing each other away.

"Lower your weapon," Walt ordered.

"Like fuck," Digger snapped back, then turned the barrel toward her mother and cocked. "You're gonna pretend you never saw us, *Riley*."

Riley? As in the club's private-investigator-Riley? The Riley serving a club filled with bikers? *That* Riley? The same man who'd turned completely away from her the last time he'd seen her because she'd chosen to date a biker?

No fucking way! That Riley couldn't be her dad. Her dad couldn't be Riley. Absolutely not.

No way her clean-cut father was the club's private investigator.

"Walt?" her mother said in a trembly voice, earning a glare from Digger.

Bunny hurried to him and grabbed his hand. "Don't hurt her, please," she cried.

"Why not?" he sneered. "Is it because I'm not a biker, Albany? Or because you can't be involved with a fucking biker and live your own goddamn life? A biker would hurt her, right? A biker is somebody to fuck in the dark and ignore in the light."

She'd hurt him, when she hadn't meant to. She'd just wanted to find a solution.

"Why the fuck should I worry about a manipulating cunt like you?"

His use of the word sent reminders of Trader through her head and the way he'd christened her with a new name, he called her 'cunt' so often.

"I was the stupid motherfucker, thinking you different from Peyton."

"And I was stupid to believe you're different from Trader."

His eyes widened at her comeback and he winced.

"I'm sorry," she continued with as much dignity as possible. "I shouldn't have pretended Mom knew you were with me, but I just wanted CJ safe."

"Save your lies," he snapped, affording her the extra incentive she needed to never involve herself with him. Even temporarily.

During their entire exchange, he hadn't lowered his weapon, holding it steady and ignoring her dad's. If he got jumpy, Digger might pull the trigger and hit her mother, while her dad fired his own weapon and hit Digger.

As an ex-cop, Walt had firing skills. As a member of the Death Dwellers, so did Digger.

"What are you doing here with my daughter?" Walt demanded, urging her over.

"Stay put," Digger ordered, halting Bunny's movement toward her dad.

"Where's CJ?" Walt demanded.

"Don't worry about the kid," Digger ordered coldly, his hand steady. He sidled a glance to Bunny. "You ever tell Meggie about your folks?"

She nodded, still not understanding why Digger seemed to be blaming Meggie for her father's involvement in the club.

Walt's searching gaze roamed from Digger to Virginia and finally to Bunny. "Did you tell her you missed us and how you regretted your behavior?"

"Yes," she whispered.

Digger and Walt shared a look before Walt heaved in a breath. "When the club needed a PI, Outlaw went to the brothers."

"Put it up to vote and asked the members if they could recommend someone," Digger added.

Bunny remembered Trader mentioning this around the same time she'd confided in Meggie.

Walt's weapon wavered. Digger's didn't.

"Meggie discovered my occupation," her dad continued, staring at Digger's trigger finger. "She tried to talk Outlaw into hiring me. When he finally did get a PI, she didn't know my identity, although I'm sure he took what she wanted into consideration."

"That's why she's an interfering little cunt and Outlaw a stupid motherfucker for listening to her," Digger burst out.

"They needed people they could trust," Bunny told him. "Right? Isn't that why he asked you for recommendations? Did anyone come up with anything better?"

"That's not the point. Trader was the motherfucker who suggested this motherfucker," he snapped, indicating her dad with the gun. "He thought he was doing something. I did, too. Fuck, we all did, but it had nothing to do with us. It was Meggie all the time."

"Trader suggested Walt Hamilton. Just as Meggie did," Bunny's father cut in. "Not Riley with no last name."

Digger threw him a dirty look. "We were all supposed to check our contacts, then take a vote. Two weeks later, Outlaw was putting the vote to have Riley…" His voice trailed off and he glared at her father. "*Walt,*" he spat. "Two weeks later, we voted him in. Now, I fucking know why he didn't take nobody else's suggestions."

"How many other suggestions were there?" Walt asked, shoving his weapon back into the holster at his side.

Scowling, Digger did the same. "Fuck all. But that's not the point. The point is Meggie not a fucking club member, yet *she* running that motherfucker."

"You're an asshole," Bunny fired back, tired, fed-up, and wanting a shower, a meal and a place to sleep. "Meggie saved your stupid life. Trader," of all people, "vouched for my dad. Outlaw must've seen him as trustworthy and felt he was within the network to put it up to vote. Besides, he didn't just arbitrarily approve my dad," she yelled. "He had you all vote to approve him."

"What if this motherfucker had talked? Ever thought of that? You defending Meggie girl, but she need to keep her nose out of men's business. You do, too!"

"You're a jackass," she hissed, suddenly so furious she could punch Digger. "You unfairly resent Meggie."

“Because Peyton was right!” he snarled. “Every time I think about the bad shit, it’s Meggie’s fault. Just because she’s fucking alive.”

“Obviously, you’re blaming her for *your* situation. But it isn’t her fault. It’s yours. You were too stupid and arrogant to know better or to do better. You wanted to fuck them over because you were jealous, so, congratulations, not only did you succeed, but you fucked yourself over, too, genius.”

Walt cleared his throat. “Er, kids…?”

“That’s the way you fucking see me?” Digger barked, ignoring her dad’s attempt to interrupt. “As some weak, pathetic motherfucker?”

“If the motorcycle boots fit,” Bunny returned sweetly. “Outlaw’s a grown man and he puts Meggie in her place when he has to. With them, it works both ways. If he didn’t want my father as the PI, he wouldn’t have hired him, no matter who told him to. You and I both know that.”

“Maybe,” he conceded. “Maybe not. What I do fucking know is you bitches stick together, so fuck you.”

“Fuck you right back,” Bunny screeched, ignoring her mom’s indignant gasp. “You’re such a fucking meanie!”

Digger rolled his eyes, then brushed her mother aside to open cabinets. “You got some vodka around this motherfucker?”

“Walt?” Virginia cried, her eyes wide with uncertainty and hurt. “How could you? After all our arguments to Bunny about her motorcycle man. You’re working with them.”

“I’ll explain everything later, honey,” Walt promised, wincing at the tears in Virginia’s eyes. He cleared his throat. “There’s vodka in the den, Digger.”

Abruptly, the noise of slamming doors halted.

“Outlaw threatened harm to you if I decided to quit and then run to the cops. Or just plain run to the cops,” Walt explained in the ensuing silence.

Bunny shook her head. "He doesn't hurt women."

"I didn't know that at the time. But I do know I'm a dead man if I ever betrayed him." He nodded to Digger. "Which means your presence has put me in a helluva situation. I can't very well call Outlaw and alert him that you're here when you've brought my daughter home to me in one piece."

"He still shouldn't have hired you. Trader might've known you, but he didn't."

"I think I might understand, Digger," Bunny answered because her dad seemed at a loss for words.

"I'm not fucking talking to you," Digger fired off.

"That's because you're an overgrown child."

Walt cleared his throat again. "I accepted because I could keep tabs on Albany. At first, I intended to get her away." He shrugged. "Outlaw never held a direct conversation with me about her. He'd tell me Megan and Bunny planning another fucking party..."

Amusement lit Digger's eyes and Bunny giggled at Walt attempting to imitate Outlaw.

He smiled. "You took care of his wife, which meant nothing and no one could touch you. *Ever.* Even if I got on the club's bad side." He dropped his gaze to the floor. "My way of making amends to you, Albany. I've regretted that last argument between us. We made you choose and you did."

"I did, Dad, but I chose wrong."

"We didn't know that. Trader presented himself as a decent man. You could've been right, but we never gave him or you the chance."

"They've separated, Walt," Virginia inserted.

Walt gave a half-smile. "Indeed."

With that one word, Bunny knew Outlaw had told her dad about Trader.

"Get something to eat," Walt said, backing toward the door. "While I excuse myself for a moment."

"No fucking way!" Digger exploded, grabbing his gun again.

Her mother wrapped an arm around Bunny's waist and hugged her close, as if she were trying to protect her. It was the first time since she'd hurt Virginia to the core of her soul that her mom had hugged her.

Bunny squirmed away and faced Digger. "What are you doing? Didn't you hear—"

"The moment he walk away he's ratting me out to Outlaw."

Walt raised his hands. "I won't," he promised.

"Fucking liar," Digger yelled.

"Give him a chance, Digger," Bunny said frantically. "For me."

Where had that come from? It wasn't as if they were lovers.

"First, I let Little Man go *for you.* Now, you're asking me to do something else *for you*. What do I get in return?"

"Whatever you want from me."

That got his immediate interest and he lowered his gun.

"Virginia," Walt began, "show Albany to her room. I'm sure she needs rest. Digger and I need to talk."

"Dad, don't do anything stupid," she warned.

"Hush, Albany!" Virginia ordered, then slinked past Digger toward the door. "Come with me."

Throwing Digger and her dad last pleading looks, Bunny did as her mother instructed, hoping she didn't regret her decision.

Digger looked around the small office with a u-shaped metal desk where a computer and a landline phone sat, along with a banker's lamp. The scent of air freshener didn't mask the odor of cigar smoke. Two chairs sat on the other side of the desk and a bookcase with photos stood right next to the window. Near the copier stood a trashcan and, above it, a shelf with a projector aimed at the bare wall on the other side of the room.

"Have a seat," Riley...Walt invited, after clearing his throat and indicating one of the beat up chairs.

Folding his arms, Digger shook his head. "I'll stand." In case he had to fire and make a quick getaway.

Bunny's lie and her adamancy that he wasn't a biker pissed him the fuck off. If she wanted to hide the real her from her prissy momma, so be it. He didn't appreciate her hiding the real him. Besides, pretending she'd told Virginia that Digger would be with her could've turned out terribly. They might've been turned away after their long-ass journey that had taken all his cash. If Virginia decided to throw them out, they'd end up homeless and hungry, with not even enough money to return to the club if Outlaw allowed it.

At first, Digger hadn't minded introducing himself by his actual name. He'd thought it would put Virginia at ease knowing there was more to him than a road name. But Bunny's clear shame of him and her attraction to him made Digger glad he hadn't touched her. As long as they were on the run together, hitting and quitting wouldn't be possible.

Shacking up with another lying, deceitful bitch like Peyton wouldn't ever happen. He'd thought Bunny different, but she was just like Peyton.

The sooner he departed Bunny's company, the better. Except the thought of going his separate way didn't sit well with him. He really liked Bunny, something he'd never been able to say about Peyton.

Bunny's dad shrugged out of his sports coat and hung it behind his leather chair that had seen better days. Clear tape was peeling away from several areas, revealing slits here and there.

"I wasn't intending to call Outlaw when I excused myself," the man began tiredly and he rubbed his eyes. He had the beginnings of a pot belly and hair that had gone almost completely gray.

The way the motherfucker had tried to escape told Digger something different. "Who then?"

Riley-Walt's eyes flickered away, but then he shrugged. "No one. I needed to get my bearings. Seeing Albany here shocked me."

Albany. Somehow the name fit Bunny. Albany was odd, a strong name that was sweet in a way. Like Bunny. The thought evaporated some of Digger's anger. She'd been through hell these past few days, receiving one shock after the other. He could give her a pass for the lie about her mother expecting him to accompany Bunny. It would be harder for him to overcome her denial of his biker lifestyle, however. He was who he was. If he knew anything about himself, he knew he was a biker at heart.

"Why Albany?" he asked, unable to deny his curiosity. "Schenectady too hard to spell? Not good enough?"

Some of Riley-Walt's tension eased and his lips curled in a vague smile. "It's the usual reason," he said. "That's where she was conceived."

Fuck, for real? "You telling me if you'd dropped your load in her momma in Schenectady that would've been Bunny's name?"

Shoulders straightening, Riley-Walt glared at Digger. "That's a unique way of putting it, but, yes, I suppose we would have."

"Let me guess. This was your old lady's idea." If he'd still wanted kids, he'd also expect to have a say-so in naming them, too. Half of his DNA would've been in his children, so he had half of whatever rights their mother would've had. Luckily for him, that point was moot. Children were fucking work. One thing wrong in their upbringing and their entire existence became fucked up.

Or simply gone.

"While we discussing names," he began, shoving his last thought aside. "Your name's Walt. How the fuck we know you as Riley?"

"When I decided to take Outlaw up on his offer, I didn't want Albany to know of my connection to the club. Outlaw didn't want Megan to know I'd been voted in." He gave Digger a grave look. "Just as I said in the kitchen, she still doesn't know that Outlaw took her suggestion, Digger. I didn't lie about that."

"Did I say you fucking lied?"

"No," he conceded, "but neither did you seem appeased."

"I wasn't." Thanks to Meggie's involvement. "Outlaw give Meggie too much power."

"I wasn't around four years ago when all the bad blood started and Outlaw got rid of Joseph Foy. Nor did I know Outlaw when he met Meggie a year later. But I'm around now and I happen to know her influence over him saved your life."

Scratching his jaw, Digger blew out a noisy breath. "Bunny told me the same thing," he admitted. Another good reason not to touch Bunny. She and Meggie were besties. With Digger's resentment toward Meggie, that might be a problem with Bunny. Same with the club. Now that Little Man was back with Outlaw, Digger recognized the flaws of the idea. Not only would Outlaw not give a fuck about saving Bunny, he might see her as a traitor to the club.

Then, she'd really be fucked.

"We both decided it was in everyone's best interest not to let too many people know of my connection," Riley-Walt continued.

"Trader really didn't know his recommendation had been voted in either?"

"Outlaw can read people pretty well," he said as if Digger didn't already know that. The man was scary in that ability. "If Trader had been aware that his recommendation had gotten voted in, he'd want something in return. Money. More weight in the club. Even if Outlaw ignored whatever Trader might've wanted, Trader was the type of man who'd assume he had more power than he actually had, simply because Outlaw had taken his suggestion." He sighed and scratched his jaw. "He didn't dislike Trader. Per se. He was my daughter's boyfriend and she was his wife's confidante, so he did what he had to do to protect the integrity of the club and the interests of everyone."

Outlaw would find a way to do that and if it wasn't in the club's best interest, he'd move on to another solution. Whether Meggie wanted him to or not. The thought made Digger hang his head. His outburst toward Meggie girl had been out-of-line and uncalled for, but he was tired and frustrated and needed to find someone to blame for all that had befallen the club. The easiest target was the most vulnerable. Outlaw's wife.

"As for as how I took the name Riley, I'm a BB King fan."

Digger frowned. "And? Shouldn't your ass be BB?"

"No," Riley-Walt answered with a slightly wider smile. "His real name was Riley B. King."

"No shit." Digger loved listening to the Blues, but he'd never known that. *The Thrill Is Gone* was one of his favorite songs. "So what do I call you? Riley? Walt? Riley-Walt?"

"Walt will be fine while you're here with Albany, but I'd appreciate it if you'd stick to Riley all other times."

Silence descended and Digger sat, more at ease now. Walt opened a desk drawer and pulled out a glass and a bottle of vodka. After pouring himself a finger, he slid the bottle to Digger.

"How's…" Taking a swig, Digger studied the bottle and changed the question on the tip of his tongue. Rather than ask about Outlaw, he first needed to know… "Meggie survived?"

"Yes."

He swallowed more vodka to fortify himself. "The others? Mortician?"

"Outlaw, Mortician, and Ghost came out unscathed." He offered nothing more.

Walt was being a hard-ass, making Digger drag information out of him. "Did anyone die?"

"Arrow and a probate."

"K-P's brother?"

Walt nodded.

K-P's death had hit Mortician hard. Though they hadn't known Arrow too well and K-P rarely mentioned him, his death must've affected Mort because of how he'd looked up to K-P.

"Aww man, I'm so sorry," he burst out.

"They buried Tyler the day after the shootings." Walt spoke casually, but studied him closely.

Grief rose within Digger and it took him a moment to compose himself. "How Mort holding up?"

"Better. Bailey's conscious and their baby will survive."

The news lifted a weight from Digger's chest, worsened by the memory of Sharper standing over Tyler. "I wanted to warn Outlaw some kind of way. I thought maybe I'd have a chance before they started firing. I even positioned myself as close to the house as I could, once Sharper got onto the grounds."

"How'd he get in?"

The fucking million dollar question that Digger didn't have an answer to. "I don't know."

Clenching his jaw, Walt looked as if he didn't believe Digger. "Bailey remains hospitalized. It was touch-and-go for both her and her baby, at first."

Knowing how Mortician adored Bailey, Digger's gut clenched. When she'd gotten sick and ended up hospitalized in New Orleans and Digger had gone to talk to Mort, he'd seen his brother's devastation at her condition. By then, Digger had found Peyton and hadn't yet discovered the worst of her worst. He'd finally accepted that he'd fucked up and felt a grudging happiness for his brother. If Bailey had been killed… "I'm so sorry," he said again and guzzled the rest of the vodka, unable to take the enormity of what had happened. "So Bailey the only one still not home?"

"Kendall was released earlier today. Megan should go home in a few days as should Bailey."

Walt finished off the last bit of alcohol remaining in his glass and changed the subject. "Why are you here?"

"Bunny suggested we come here to get away from Outlaw and Sharper."

"You sent CJ back to Outlaw. Why not Bunny?"

"Meggie adore her. As long as she with me, Outlaw won't risk her life and try to take me out. I have time to bargain." He refused to mention his misgivings over the plan.

Walt didn't appear to need any. "What are your intentions toward Albany?"

Frowning, Digger lifted his brows. "I'm not going to kill her," he answered, pretending to misunderstand. The question had more to do with fucking Bunny, than killing her.

Walt scowled. "Good to know," he said sarcastically. "You'll just use her as your shield."

"I wouldn't grab a damn girl to cover me from gunfire."

"I meant metaphorically."

"Fuck, metaphorical. I'm speaking literally. If they catch up to my ass and still want to take me out, I'll make sure Bunny's safe."

"Why?"

Why? *Why?* Did the motherfucker really ask that?

"Because you're screwing her or you're that much of a gentleman to do the right thing for once?"

Digger jumped to his feet. "Fuck off, man. I didn't touch Bunny, other than to take care of her fucking ass while she was sick. As for me being a gentleman, I know I'm not. I'd do it because it's the right thing to do. I've made too many fucking mistakes *trying* to do the right thing already. Her death won't be another one."

"Let her go. If Sharper closes in on you, then she's dead anyway."

Let her go. Three little words that hit him like a punch to the gut. His anger deflating, Digger dropped back into his seat and hung his head. He didn't really want to let her go. He actually liked being in her company and he knew it was for her and not because of fucking. Unlike with Peyton. From the get-go, sexual innuendoes and tension filled their relationship. With Bunny, what started as a dire situation turned into something else for Digger. Faced with the prospect of having her walk away, he was able to admit he didn't want that to happen.

She insisted she'd have nothing sexual to do with him as long as he held her hostage. Until then, her stance had been fine with him. He'd been just as adamant that he never wanted another old lady.

Keeping her with him wasn't fair. She had a place at the club, one he shouldn't take away from her on the chance that her presence would save his life. This was his fight, not hers, and it wasn't right to insist she stay involved.

"I'll ask her," he said finally, quietly. If she left, he'd truly be on his own in this situation. The reason he'd joined the Dwellers was to be close to Mort. He'd gone with the flow. Perhaps, though, that had been the problem. His reasons for joining the club hadn't been because the biker lifestyle had called to him. "If she want to go, then I'll let her go."

Walt drummed his fingers on the desk, then rubbed a hand over his eyes. "Let me call Outlaw."

Digger jumped to his feet. "No! Fuck no. He'll blaze here and kill me."

"No, he won't. I won't tell him you're here. I'll just tell him Albany called and I spoke to you."

"Fuck. NO," he said slowly and precisely, his hands balling into fists.

"Stay in the room with me and listen to the conversation. If Albany wasn't involved, I wouldn't bother," he said with disgust. "You're serious about getting back into the good graces of the club? Grow some goddamn balls and start somewhere."

Stiffening at the insult, Digger knew Walt was right. He did have to start somewhere, instead of resisting each time someone brought up the idea of contacting Outlaw. "Fuck!"

Taking that as consent, Walt pressed a button and a dial tone blared in the room. Another button later, a number dialed and Outlaw answered. Obviously, Walt had the club on speed dial.

"Yo, Riley, whatcha got for me?"

Digger's heart beat a little faster at hearing the man's voice. He sounded as cool and collected as usual, and Digger had missed that, just as much as he'd missed Mort's jokes and advice.

"Albany called."

"Fuck, Walt. I could fuckin' kiss you. My girl been askin' like fuck 'bout Bunny. Megan know Bunny woulda visited her al-fuckin-ready. Only so long I can deflect her fuckin' questions. Bunny okay, huh?"

"Yes. She may return to the club soon."

"You spoke to fuckhead?"

Knowing Outlaw referred to him cut through Digger. As highly as Outlaw regarded him at one time, he hated him just as passionately now.

"Yes, I spoke to Digger."

Digger widened his eyes and he gave the phone a horrified look, as if Outlaw had the ability to see through the phone lines.

"What the fuck he say?" Hot anger replaced Outlaw's coolness.

"That he had extenuating circumstances. That he wanted to warn you about the ambush. He'd like to talk to you."

"What the fuck he wanna say? No motherfucker hurtin' my girl and he did it fuckin' *twice*. Bad. You know how the fuck I found her when that motherfucker took Bailey and left Megan in that fuckin' apartment? On her fuckin' knees with a motherfucker dick stuffed in her mouth."

Fuuuccckkk. For that alone, Digger had no chance at redemption.

"Motherfucker wanted to come in *my wife* mouth before he blew her the fuck away," Outlaw snarled. "You know what the fuck that did to me seein' that shit? I'd rather cut my fuckin' heart out than see my girl hurt. And, yet, she still fuckin' talked me into easin' up on my search for him. She said it was for me and Mort, but Megan like Digger her-fuckin-self."

Something else Bunny had told him and he'd ignored until now. Outlaw screaming about Megan's loyalty to Digger made him feel lower than shit.

"I know none of this is easy, Outlaw. But, at least, hear him out," Riley replied, testing the waters.

"Megan got the conscience. I fuckin' don't and this is one time I don't give a fuck how she feel. Digger need to be fucked up for a variety of fuckin' reasons."

"He was doing what he felt necessary," Walt persisted. "Protecting Mortician. He had to choose."

"And he chose his brother over Megan," Outlaw snapped. "I understand the fuckin' position he was in. But if you don't know what the fuck you doin', who the fuck you fuckin' with, then you fuck your own self. Hear what I'm sayin', Riley?"

"Yes."

In the ensuing silence, Digger's skin crawled and he squirmed in his seat. He hadn't known everything that had gone on after he left with Bailey all those months ago. Now that he did and after feeling such bitterness and resentment toward Meggie, he wasn't sure if he didn't deserve whatever fate awaited him.

"Besides, you told me your fuckin' self, that cunt who shot Megan was with him."

Walt gave Digger a guilty look, but he'd merely been doing his job, so Digger shrugged, worn out by it all. Outlaw's disgust. Bunny's possible departure. Even Walt thinking him a goddamn coward.

"She was Ellen's sister," Walt reminded Outlaw, and from his tone, it sounded as if they'd gone over this already.

"Your ass already fuckin' told that," Outlaw barked. "Didn't make one motherfuck of a difference then and it ain't now. Besides what the fuck that got to do with Peyton ass bein' with Digger un-fuckin-less, he was fuckin' tryin' to help her get her fuckin' revenge? What the fuck Peyton and Ellen bein' sisters gotta do with any-fuckin-thing? Whatever made that bitch come after my wife was cuz of Digger."

Digger shook his head frantically, wordlessly denying the accusation.

"Suppose he didn't know her intentions?" Walt asked quietly.

Walt wasn't coming right out and defending Digger, but he wasn't placing all the blame on him either. He knew it was on behalf of Bunny, but Digger still appreciated it.

"If he didn't know what she planned, he isn't responsible."

"Why the fuck you suddenly all up in my ass defendin' that motherfucker and his cunt?" Outlaw asked with suspicion. "You wasn't this fuckin' adamant when you lifted that bitch's fingerprints to identify her."

"I'm not badgering you about him," Walt said quickly, loosening his tie and the top button of his shirt. "All I'm asking—"

"I ain't payin' you to ask *me*. Whatever the fuck I wantcha to fuckin' know, you already fuckin' know it…" His voice trailed off and he paused. "Un-fuckin-less…"

Movement on Outlaw's end led Digger to believe he'd adjusted his phone. The soft thud of a door closing came next. The rattling of glass and the slosh of liquid preceded the flick of a lighter. "Whatever the fuckin' reason Digger joined the fuck up with Sharper ain't matterin' to me. For all my fuckin' ass know, it was outta some fuckin' type of revenge. And the way I'm fuckin' thinkin', maybe he was hatin' on Megan just a lil' bit? Why? I ain't fuckin' figured that shit out. He left her *and* he brought that bitch 'round to fuckin' kill her."

Outlaw was fucking creepy with his ability to figure shit out.

"You fuckin' listenin', Digger?"

Digger stared at the phone and jerked against the chair.

"I'm the only one—"

"Per-fuckin-haps, Riley," Outlaw conceded, "but I ain't believin' that, not with your fuckin' conversation turnin' the way it did. Now, shut the fuck up."

Walt's face reddened. "Yes, of course, Outlaw."

"Digger, speak the fuck up or don't. I don't give a fuck. My ass been thinkin' and thinkin'. Goin' through the facts and the events of the last few months. Honestly, I don't know what the fuck to do with you, motherfucker. Kill you quick or fuckin' slow. Fuck you up and leave a permanent fuckin' reminder some-fuckin-where on you, but let you fuckin' live. You took care of my boy and, apparently, you ain't hurt Bunny."

No one said shit. *What* could be said after that? Since Outlaw hadn't said he'd let him live, Digger threw an imploring look to Walt. If Outlaw knew he was here, more than likely, he'd head this way.

"Neither one of you motherfuckers got shit to fuckin' say, huh?"

"You've said it all," Walt answered calmly, digging in his jacket pocket for a handkerchief and wiping his brow.

"Maybe, I ain't."

Not wanting Outlaw to detect even his smallest movement, Digger held himself still, afraid to blink.

"Megan once told me about these two motherfuckers," he continued after a tense moment. "A servant parable. One of them motherfuckers owed his master money and the boss told the fuckhead don't worry about it. Then the motherfucker went out and saw some sorry fuck who owed him money and had him thrown in jail. He wanted his fuckin' money and decided to get revenge on that poor bastard, forgettin' entirely what a lucky motherfucker he was cuz his debt got forgave. He might've been a lucky motherfucker, but he was a stupid one, too, cuz Bossman found out what he did and not only threw him in jail but had him fuckin' tortured. He wanted revenge and got fucked himself.

That bitch shot Megan. Well, just like that servant motherfucker, she fucked herself, huh? I blew her the fuck away. But for you, Digger? Think of me as the fuckin' Bossman in this motherfucker. At the fuckin' least, I'm torturin' the fuck outta you when I get my fuckin' hands on your ass." With that, Outlaw disconnected.

Hands shaking, Digger squeezed his temples, knowing it would take a miracle to change Outlaw's mind. Knowing, too, the story the man had just related was as close to religious as he'd ever get.

Digger was so fucked.

A tiny breeze floated in the evening air as the sky adapted the pinks, magentas, and oranges of a dawning sunset, the amazing colors so brilliant, they were almost surreal. The house Bunny had grown up in sat amidst desert landscape, surrounded by saguaro cactus, agave, acacia, and creosote. In the distance, Black Mountain stood, a shimmering, majestic mass in the heat.

"The mountain hasn't changed, Albany," Virginia said, not unkindly, "not in the last few million years, so there's no need to stare."

She had been staring for quite a while, ever since Virginia had escorted her outside after she'd shown Bunny to her old room and left so Bunny could shower. Now, she had on another pair of sweatpants that Digger had purchased for her, along with another T-shirt from that same shopping spree. Her hair was clean and freshly washed. Basically, she smelled good again, like a woman should.

"Sit."

Offering her mom a smile, Bunny took a seat on a chaise lounge, still facing the view of the mountain. She used to dream of what it had been like for the first settlers. Certainly, it had been brutal for both the native peoples and the ones who'd come and claimed the land as their own.

She, Gabe, and their parents had visited Massacre Cave once. Even now, chills ran along her spine when she remembered the bullet holes that served as a silent testimony to the bloodshed that had taken place.

Virginia sat at an angle from Bunny, in a chair with a pattern matching the chaise. "You didn't come to make amends, did you? Not suddenly, after three years of not a word from you."

"I'm sorry for not contacting you sooner, Mom," she said quietly. "I didn't know what to say. I regretted leaving as I did."

"No, you regretted that I was right," Virginia retorted. "Which you still haven't admitted to me."

"I didn't know you were right," Bunny snapped. God, her mom made her so angry. She'd push and prod and grate on a situation until everyone lost control. "Not at the time. Trader didn't start changing until about a year ago."

"A year ago or five years ago, I was right to not want you with him."

"Yes, Mom! You were right. Happy, now? I was wrong and *you were right*."

Absolutely no reason for tears to spring to her eyes, but they did. Her temper rising, Bunny swiped them away.

"You turned your back on us, *willingly,* Albany," Virginia continued, ramrod straight in her chair. "To go with that piece of shit. Now, you've brought *another* piece of shit with you. A piece of shit that could get your dad killed. Why did you come? What wrong turn brought you and the hell that's following you to our doorstep? Haven't you caused me enough grief?"

A sob escaped Bunny in an anguished, bitter sound. She'd always known she wouldn't so easily find forgiveness, especially with her mother, but after discovering Bunny's dad was involved with the club, she'd actually hugged Bunny. It was too much to hope that the gesture had meant bygones were bygones.

The glass door slid open and Bunny turned, swiping frantically at her wet cheeks. Digger sauntered forward as the light from the den angled on them. Ignoring his frown, she popped to her feet. When Walt appeared, Virginia stood, too.

Digger studied her in a way that made her feel wanted, and not so lost and alone. He seemed to have gotten over his earlier anger. "Why you crying?"

"Because she wants an easy forgiveness from me and her father, and she'll not get it," Virginia snapped.

When Digger opened his mouth, Bunny raised her hand, placing it on his chest, to forestall whatever he might say. His muscles bunched beneath her fingertips and she knew he'd have his say whether she wanted him to or not.

"Forgiveness?" he gritted. "From you to Bunny?"

"Yes."

"Virginia, discuss this some other time," Walt said on a sigh. "Albany's home, so let's enjoy the evening with her."

"She's here under false pretenses, supposedly wanting forgiveness when she only wanted a place to hide this biker person."

Her father's words didn't move her mother, and Digger stiffened.

"Bitch, it's you who should beg forgiveness from her, for trying to tell her who to love. All she did was leave to be with her man. *You* her momma. That mean you sure the fuck went with *your* man, 'cause you made her with him. So why the fuck you pissed at her for going with Trader? Nothing she did hurt your motherfucking ass. She only hurt herself. Your bitch-ass not much of a momma for disowning Bunny for fucking nothing."

"Stop it, Digger!" Bunny demanded, torn between outrage at the way he'd cussed at her mother, amusement at her father's gaping mouth, and plain despair at how fast the situation had gone downhill. "I don't care what she did, I won't let you talk to my mother like that. Let's just go," she added.

Digger grabbed her hand. "Yeah. Let's," he growled, turning her toward the door and jerking her forward. "'Cause no motherfucker need a momma like you got."

"No, wait!" Virginia called in a thick voice.

Bunny halted so abruptly Digger stumbled and he scowled at her.

"I'm not a bitch, Albany," Virginia said tightly, sailing forward and stopping in front of Bunny. "But he's mostly right about what he said. I only wanted the best for you and Trader clearly wasn't that."

"Next," Digger bit out in exasperation, "'Cause I do believe Bunny figured that shit out, so you don't have to keep fucking rubbing it in her face."

"You're a grown woman," Virginia continued, only acknowledging Digger's words with a filthy stare. "Being grown doesn't mean we always make the right choices. I don't think you did." Almost defiant, she raised her chin and folded her arms. When Digger remained quiet, she said, "I certainly didn't make the right decision where you're concerned."

"Momma—"

Virginia raised her hand to silence Bunny. "I'm not a bad mother, just an angry one. And so disappointed that you threw your bright future away. But it's time to let go of that. Look forward instead of backward." She narrowed her eyes at Walt. "I must if I'm to overlook your father's deceptions."

Releasing Digger's hand and ignoring the flush creeping over Walt's face, Bunny hugged her mother, breathing a sigh of relief when Virginia returned it.

"Why don't we go inside, Albany?" she said. "Get you and Mark something to drink."

"And eat," Digger inserted. "I'm fucking starving."

"Dad, can you make us some cocoa?" Bunny asked, remembering the Dr. Pepper Digger had pulled out. Her mom must've relented slightly on the health food and allowed Walt a few gastronomical pleasures.

Walt smiled but nodded. "That all right with you, Digger?"

"Cocoa?" Digger glared at Bunny. "Don't ever answer for me, Bunny. The only non-alcoholic shit I drink is water. I'm not drinking cocoa. I'll take more vodka."

"Please leave your Neanderthal-ish attitude out here," Bunny implored, rolling her eyes and following her parents inside. She didn't tell Digger that it was better to have her dad prepare anything for them. If Virginia did it, they were likely to end up with a blue algae shake.

"You know you could've been named Punxsutawney or Schenectady?" he asked as they walked into the house and headed back toward the kitchen.

"What are you talking about?" Noticing the smirk on Digger's face, Bunny lifted her eyebrows, surprised at his sense of humor. "My name has a Latin origin, from Albanus, meaning *of Alba*. St. Alban was Britain's first martyr, you know? But Mom told me people with this name tend to be creative and stubborn and proud, so that's why she chose it."

Digger laughed at her explanation and Bunny punched his shoulder, playfully. "I won't say anything about the name 'Digger', given the reason for it," she retorted, shoving at him when he continued to laugh.

Catching her hand, he kissed the back of it, and gave her a smoldering look. "Yeah, Digger is my MC name, but I like when you call me Mark. You say it like nobody else." His husky tone caressed the words and he slid his tongue over his lips, securing some loose strands of her hair behind her ear.

Her nipples hardened at his brief touch and the wicked promise heating his eyes. Swallowing, she backed away and scooted around him, needing space.

"May I help you with anything, Dad?" she asked, distracted by Digger catching up to her and heading for the refrigerator to swipe another Dr. Pepper. "You don't only drink water."

Pausing, Digger lifted a brow.

"I-I mean, as your non-alcoholic drink. You said only water."

"I was joking with you, girl," he said, his amused tone telling her that should've been obvious.

"Bunny, see to the salad," Walt instructed.

"Okay," she mumbled, squirming past Digger when the rat wouldn't give her sufficient room to get by.

Once again, her body reacted to him. His nearness. His smile. She insisted they had zero chemistry between them. Until times like this. When she felt an urge to be in his arms and enjoyed the attention he showered upon her.

Never mind that he was as drop-dead gorgeous as his strikingly handsome older brother.

God, she wasn't *that* shallow. What was on the inside of Digger counted, too. Maybe, not that shallow, but that doubtful of her ability to choose someone to be in her life, even as a friend. Digger was a biker. Like Trader. He'd held a gun to her head and forced her to come with him. He'd threatened to kill her, basically knowing his words would terrify her. Suppose what was inside of Digger was more rotten than Trader ever was?

"I think that cucumber and tomato washed enough, Bunny," he said, once more laughing at her.

"Pesticides, you know?" she shot back, her cheeks burning at being caught daydreaming. She hadn't realized she'd even moved to the sink. "Can't wash our produce long enough to remove all of them."

His smirk called bullshit on her explanation.

"That's why organic is best," Virginia said, and Bunny inwardly groaned, knowing what was coming. An hour long conversation about the benefits of a vegan diet, sustainable living, and her zero-growth belief.

"Wait a minute," Digger said when the conversation followed exactly the way Bunny thought it would. "Your ass had two children. Didn't that contribute to the planet's overcrowding?"

"I had them before I realized what was happening to the earth by our selfishness," she said, then patted Bunny's hand as she passed by her to get to the cupboard containing the dinner plates. "My life wouldn't be the same without them. Don't get me wrong."

Dumping the quartered tomato and sliced cucumber into a bowl, Bunny went to work on the lettuce, tuning her mother out. She'd heard it all before, so had her dad, which was more than likely the reason for his silence.

"Does your mother hate me?" he whispered to her, just as she finished tearing the lettuce into little pieces.

"Why would she hate you, Dad?" As far as she knew, her mom loved her dad.

"Why?" Walt asked in an incredulous voice. "Because of my involvement with that club."

"You have to talk to her about that. She hasn't brought it up to me."

His face crumpled. "She's angry."

Knowing her mom? "Probably," Bunny agreed. "She'll get over it."

"And you? Are you angry?"

"No, especially considering why you did it. To keep tabs on me."

"So just like that, I'm forgiven? You're not holding that against me?"

Bunny set the bowl aside, grabbed a dish towel, and then slung it over her shoulder. "I hold absolutely nothing against you. I swear. I'm happy to be here. Happy to have us begin to heal and be a family again."

"See, Albany?" Her mom's voice interrupted any response her father might've had. "Mark doesn't want children, either."

"What?" she responded, going still, the news so disappointing her breath caught. Why that bothered her so much, she wasn't sure. She'd just have to get a grip on her emotions. And, maybe, will Marcus Banks to stop being so charming and flirty. "Kids are great," she said, her limbs finally unfreezing and allowing her to move.

"You're a chick. Most chicks think kids are great," he grumbled.

"I want a baby," she said quietly.

"A ring comes first," Virginia chastised, ignoring the sweeping look Digger gave her, his gaze meeting hers before drifting to her mouth down to her breasts and, finally, studying her belly.

"I been thinking about everything, Bunny." Digger shifted his weight. "You want to go back to the MC? If you do, I'll send you back."

"Yes," she said without hesitation. "If I'm still allowed since I'm no longer tied to Trader." And she needed to proceed with caution where Digger was concerned. Even if she jumped head-first into bed with him, he was out bad. Being with him would do more harm than good where the club was concerned.

Disappointment slid across his face before he masked it with a careless smile. "You tied to Meggie. That shit better than ever being tied to another swinging dick at the club."

Virginia clucked in disapproval, but Bunny ignored her. She should've been happy that he was finally allowing her the chance to return, but she wished he'd come with her, although she knew why he couldn't. He still hadn't gotten through to Outlaw, not that he'd tried. So far, he'd been running with no clear timeframe for that to change. She suspected when he finally did, it would be in typical style. On the spur of the moment.

"What's going to happen to you?"

"I'm leaving in the morning," he said, glancing away. "I need to find my old man before he cause more trouble. Since you don't want to be Bonnie to my Clyde, I'll leave you here with your folks. Walt and Outlaw will set everything up and get you back to Hortensia."

Woodenly, she walked to the seat and dropped into it, staring at Digger. She'd be safe with her parents until travel arrangements were made, but what about Digger? He'd seen to her safety and he'd gotten Little Man back to his parents. Most important, he wasn't going to use her as insurance against Outlaw, despite his claim otherwise.

That, along with the fact that Digger had looked after CJ should account for something with Outlaw. Digger didn't need to search for Sharper alone. He needed the weight of the club behind him. He stood a much better chance of survival by siding with the Death Dwellers in his stand against his father. Maybe, she could talk to Outlaw on Digger's behalf. He'd listen to her. Wouldn't he?

He stepped forward and urged her to reseat herself with a firm hand on her shoulder. "You made the right decision since you not well yet. You might need a doctor or somebody who know fucking medicine."

"What do you mean, she isn't well yet?" Virginia asked, hands on hips, before Bunny could backtrack and tell Digger she wanted to accompany him back to the club. "Are you sick, Albany?"

She struggled to find the words to answer her mother and to tell Digger she'd stay with him. She wanted to *stay* with Digger. Somewhere along the way from Oregon to Arizona, she'd lost her mind. Otherwise, she'd been jumping for joy that he was releasing her instead of worrying about not being his buffer when he confronted Outlaw.

"Are you sick?" her mother repeated sharply.

"Um, I-I..."

"Tell her, girl," Digger encouraged, unperturbed by her irritated look. "Everything."

"Do I need a drink to hear this?" Walt set a mug of steaming cocoa in front of Bunny and handed the other one to Digger. "This doesn't sound good."

Nervous, Bunny spooned some of the hot drink and blew on it to cool it down before slurping it into her mouth. And promptly spitting it back out just as Digger yelled, "What the fuck is this?"

"Sunflower milk with vegan dark chocolate cocoa," Virginia answered. "Why?"

Bunny gagged again. "Oh my God, that cocoa is awful. How could you ruin your delicious recipe with sunflower milk, Dad?"

"Fuck his recipe!" Digger snarled, rubbing his hands across his mouth. "How the fuck could you ruin my fucking taste buds? The least you could do was warn a motherfucker that you had concocted liquid shit."

"It isn't *that* bad," Virginia said with a sniff.

Bunny got a cup of water for herself and then refilled it and handed it to Digger before throwing her father an accusatory look. "She's pulled you to the other side."

"I prefer hemp milk," he admitted sheepishly, "but none of it is bad. It's an acquired taste."

Digger picked up a tomato, cucumber, and piece of lettuce and sniffed. "Smell like regular shit," he said, then threw it aside, "but I can't be too sure cuz I sure the fuck didn't smell whatever the fuck was in that fucking cocoa."

"It's organic."

"What the fuck's for dinner?" Digger demanded, ignoring her mother. "You might want fucking organic. I don't, so I'll bring my ass somewhere and find a big ass greasy burger to fill me up."

"We're having sloppy joes," Virginia told him, giving him a look that dared him to challenge her.

"What the fuck will be *on* the sloppy joes?" Digger persisted.

"Black beans."

"Eww," Bunny said before she could stop herself at her mother's response. "On a vegan bun, right?"

"Settle down, kids." Walt pulled out his cell phone and sighed. "How about we order in—"

"Absolutely not," Virginia began.

"It's fine," Bunny said quickly. She didn't want to upset the happy balance her parents seemed to have achieved over her mom's disgusting recipes. "We'll grab something to eat."

"Oh, fine," Virginia relented, stomping to the table and snatching both mugs up. "Be responsible for the death of an innocent animal to feed your barbaric need. See if I care."

"I don't give a fuck if you care or not," Digger said grouchily. "The good thing is I don't give a fuck whether *you* give a fuck. It's my motherfucking ass that got to eat the shit."

Virginia rounded on him. "Do you know what red meat does to your colon?"

"Oh my God, Mom," Bunny cried. "Please stop!"

Walt cleared his throat. "Er, honey, Albany was about to explain her illness, if you recall."

At least the sunflower milk cocoa worked to settle her nerves at having to tell her parents what Trader had done to her. "The reason Digger said I'm not well is because I miscarried Trader's baby."

Bunny pretended not to notice her dad drawing his brows together or hearing her mom's gasp. As she began explaining everything, Digger stood next to her and rubbed her back. She was happy he was there with her.

Virginia pursed her lips. She'd taken a seat during Bunny's narrative and now she rubbed her brow.

Anger flared in Walt's eyes. "Outlaw shot him because of what he did to you?"

"Yes. He didn't know what he'd done," she explained. "Just that he had done something to me. Something bad."

"Well, then, maybe your association with this club is forgivable, Walter," Virginia said tightly. "I insist you two stay here for a few days. At least until you regain your strength, Albany."

"Fuck no. Not if I have to eat whatever the fuck you want to feed me."

"Digger!" Bunny said sharply.

"Buy whatever you'd like. Just as long as my daughter rests and she won't be able to do that if she's concerned about you," Virginia pointed out.

Digger studied her the way he liked to do when he wanted an answer. "Is that true, girl?"

"Yes," she said softly.

He looked at her for another long moment, and the intensity of his gaze threatened to burn her from the inside out. With Trader, her attraction had been immediate. She could count on one finger the number of customers she'd been as taken with as she was when he'd first walked into the strip club. She'd been willing to do anything he'd wanted, skim the outer edges of the sun if that had been possible.

For her, with him, it *had* been as if she'd touched the sun and found utopia. But he'd burned her and she'd tumbled from her perch, hurt, disappointed, and confused.

Now, the tiny spark she felt for Digger was growing. He was a quiet storm, with a price on his head. Steady in many ways, she was realizing, but no less intense.

Sometimes, the quiet storms proved the most dangerous.

Puffing on his blunt, Christopher studied his office. The old sofa where he'd fucked Megan on a regular basis. It should've been replaced when he'd decided to marry her, because he'd fucked so many bitches there he'd lost count. If she realized that, she never mentioned it, so he hadn't either.

It had been Big Joe's first and should've long ago been tossed the fuck out.

And, yet, he'd never been able to bring himself to fucking do it. Same with the set of keys taken from Big Joe's body. He'd identified every key except one and he'd decided it would forever remain a mystery to him.

After pinching on his smoke to douse it, he swigged from his tequila, then rolled his chair to the file cabinet. He found the right key on his ring and then unlocked it, picking up a thick ledger and rubbing his hand over it. The first account book he'd been responsible for.

"You're going to rule this place one day, Christopher. Know it inside and out. Keep your own fucking books, so you don't kill a stupid motherfucker for cheating you. You have heart and soul. Whether Logan likes it or not, you're *the future of this club. The lifeblood."*

He couldn't have been any more than fifteen or sixteen at the time, when Boss gave him that speech and handed him the brand-fucking-new record book.

At first, Big Joe had made him copy everything he'd recorded in another book, then he'd had Christopher to do the accounting *first*. If he fucked up, then Big Joe fucked him up. His fuckup had been so big one time, Big Joe had knocked him unconscious.

Christopher smiled at the memory. It was no more than he'd do. He hadn't even been a member yet. He'd been under-fucking-aged to boot, so Big Joe could've gotten into problems with the brothers for doing what he did with Christopher. He'd believed in him and his abilities. Believed that Christopher had the calculating control to run their club under any circumstances.

Believed that he'd never walk away, no matter what.

Live free. Ride or die forever.

"What the fuck I'm supposed to fuckin' do, Boss?" he asked softly. "This your baby girl I'm tryin' to protect."

Without her here, the fucking club was so quiet. His house was as silent as a tomb, even with the noise of the kids.

"What the fuck that mean, motherfucker? Shit can't be fuckin' quiet and noisy at the same fuckin' time."

But it was. Because he knew she wasn't there. He'd walk into their huge bedroom and find it empty. The sheets still held her scent, the smell of the cherry blossom hair stuff she washed her hair with, the sweetness of her body wash.

But not her.

He still didn't feel like Outlaw. His head hadn't been screwed back on right, despite her waking up and their son being home for five full days now.

Outlaw would've sent some motherfucker to Arizona to drag Digger the fuck back to face his punishment. Christopher *knew* he was at Riley's place. But all he could think of was the silence and the fucking loneliness because of Megan's absence.

He was off his fucking game, still too out of his fucking mind with worry to drum up his killer instincts. Simply because these motherfuckers *kept fucking coming*. Cee Cee. Logan. Sharper. Ellen's sister. He couldn't figure out what purpose she'd had to hate Megan so much. Unless Ellen had fucking lied to Peyton about Megan in some kind of way. He'd figure it out another time.

Right now he wanted to know how fucking many more motherfuckers would fucking rise from the fucking depths of hell before...before they killed his Megan? As long as he was *Outlaw*, they'd come. Every-fucking-body knew, to kill him they simply had to kill his wife. Then, they could walk away, leave him gasping for air, as if they'd fucked him up physically, too.

The other girls would be caught in the fucking crossfire, extra bonuses. Maybe, not so much Bailey, because Sharper wanted Mortician to hurt. But Kendall and Zoann? Sharper couldn't give less of a fuck.

What else *could* Christopher do but leave when they got Sharper? Who the fuck else would come at them next and go for Megan to bring Christopher to his knees?

He didn't even have the fucking energy to resist feeling the way he did about her. He'd tried that after the bullshit Kendall had gotten Megan into with the Torps MC. All he'd done was hurt her and made her believe he was fucking another bitch.

Maybe, it wasn't a matter of having the energy. Maybe, he'd just plain fucking accepted how he felt about her. The shit wouldn't fucking change in this lifetime or the next, so why fucking sweat over it.

He gazed at the ledger again and shook his head. "I wish you was here, motherfucker. Protectin' a girl and runnin' the club out of my fuckin' league apparently. Your fuckin' ass would set me fuckin' straight. Tell me what the fuck to do."

"Christopher?" Johnnie barged into the room before Christopher responded. He halted and lifted a brow. "You okay?"

Setting the ledger back in the drawer and slamming it shut before locking it, Christopher got to his feet. "Whatcha got, John Boy?"

"I need you to see something."

"What?"

"Fuck, just come with me. It's on TV."

Not questioning Johnnie any further, Christopher followed Johnnie to the main room where the words, *Breaking News Alert,* flashed on the screen. Behind the reporter, white smoke plumed into the air from…he narrowed his eyes and saw, *Atlanta hotel fire that is believed to have claimed the life of the Reverend Sharper Banks.*

"You fuckin' kiddin' me?" he exploded.

The club door opened and Mortician walked in, his cell phone raised to his ear. "You fucking one hundred thousand percent sure it's that motherfucker's charred remains?" he asked, normal again with the news Bailey would be released from the hospital in three days. "Uh-huh. Yeah. Do that. Make fucking sure before I start fucking celebrating."

"So you know?" Christopher asked when Mortician hung up.

"He's the one who called me," Johnnie said, looking disappointed. Probably because he wouldn't get Sharper in the meat shack.

"I know," Mortician confirmed, his face blank.

Christopher listened to the broadcaster for a few minutes. He should feel relieved, and not the fucking suspicion prickling through him. But, fuck, with DNA and identification and all types of high-tech shit, how could they make a fucking mistake about a motherfucker's remains?

"You sure it's him?"

"Not yet, Prez. They still doing tests, but a body was found in a room registered in his name."

"Digger know?" he asked, surprising himself and the other two.

"I haven't talked to that motherfucker in a minute," Mort bit out.

"He hidin' out in Phoenix with Bunny and her fuckin' folks," he said, still not willing to betray Riley's true identity.

Johnnie stared at him as if his nose had turned into an elephant's cock. "He's what?"

"Ain't talked to the motherfucker, but I know he fuckin' there."

"How you know that, Prez?"

"Don't worry about that, Mort," Christopher answered. "I just fuckin' do, so..."

A sound drew his attention to the hallway, and Christopher pulled his nine. Only whiny ass Dinah was supposed to be on the premises, but, nowadays, one never fucking knew.

But that's who he found when he turned the corner. Her wide gaze met his, then looked over his shoulder and he knew Johnnie and Mort had followed him.

Christopher stared at the cell phone in her hand, trying to remember when she'd gotten it.

"Arrow bought it for me," she mumbled.

He looked at her, the phone, his bedroom door that she stood too fucking close to. "You been in my fuckin' room?"

Tears filled her eyes. "I want Meggie. I'm looking for her. No one will let me see her and she won't come to visit me."

Johnnie sighed and lowered his gun. "It's okay," he began, starting around Christopher to head for her.

Christopher placed a hand on his shoulder, halting him. Shit wasn't fucking adding up with this bitch. No matter how much he wanted to fucking ignore his gut, he fucking couldn't. "Why the fuck Megan seein' you matter so fuckin' much? You been a fuckin' hateful bitch to her for months."

She shifted her weight and shivered at the sight of his gun. The one he still trained on her.

"C-can I s-see her and my grandbabies?"

"My kids at the fuckin' house." He put away his nine, deciding to test a theory. "Megan got shot. Remember?"

Hatred flickered in her eyes before she swallowed and formed a perfect-assed, lying-fucking 'o' with her mouth. He rushed to her and snatched the phone out of her hand, growling when he saw it needed a password to open the screen up.

"Open this motherfucker," he demanded. "*Now.*"

"Yo, Prez, Meggie not gonna like you talking to this bitch like this."

"Yeah, Christopher…"

The stubborn look Dinah gave Christopher made him drown out Johnnie's words.

"You can't make me," she said, low.

"You fuckin' right," he snapped. "Cuz chokin' the fuck outta your ass won't do me no fuckin' good." He raised the phone up. "But I know a motherfucker who can get into it with or without your fuckin' cooperation."

Before he did something he fucking regretted, he turned away. He needed a new guard for her, but not because she was the original psycho bitch that lived here. No, because she'd become a fuckin' traitorous psycho bitch.

"No matter what I've done, you can't do me anything. Meggie would hate you."

"Megan not fuckin' here, Dinah. She fuckin' shot. *Remember?* That mean, if your fuckin' ass any way partly fuckin' responsible for that fuckin' massacre, she ain't savin' you."

Unease registered in her eyes and she looked at Johnnie and Mortician. "I haven't done anything," she said finally.

He turned back to her and held up the phone. "Then unlock this motherfucker and let me see who the fuck you been contactin'."

"I hate you," she said with quiet vehemence, marching up to him and doing as he asked.

When she held it out to him, Christopher scrolled through her messages and telephone calls. Most of her messages were from Roxy, encouraging her to be a better mother and grandmother. Bullshit he had no interest in. One that came from Roxy and mentioned Bailey's shower. Another one that said, *Bailey's shower is Saturday.*

And on it went. The few he actually opened was just a waste of fucking time, so he moved onto the call log. A lot of calls still registered from Arrow. There were three phone numbers without names attached, so Christopher intended to check those out.

But she seemed completely innocent of what he suspected.

"Get the fuck outta my face," he ordered, pocketing the phone in case he overlooked something. She turned on her heel, scampering down the hallway and around the corner toward where her room was located.

"Prez, what was that about?" Mort stepped aside to allow Christopher to pass. "You can't think Dinah had something to do with what happened two weeks ago?"

"Yeah, Christopher. *Dinah*. She's crazier than a fucking loon."

Fucking truth. But shit just didn't fucking sit right with him, despite finding no incriminating evidence to prove he was right. He had no choice but to drop his theory for now. Obviously, he was the only motherfucker who felt Dinah capable of betraying them.

Once again, the door burst open. Instead of Val, as he'd expected, it was Bitsy, her lip and nose bloody and tears slipping down her eyes.

Bad fucking enough. The gun pointed to her head, however, made the situation fucking dire.

"Hands up," Osti ordered, "or she's fucking as dead as the rest of your sisters."

Christopher wouldn't fall for motherfucking taunts thrown out to fuck with him. If he'd killed them, Osti would've brought proof. Photos of their bodies. Pieces of them. He'd want to gloat with hard evidence.

"Osti!" Mortician snarled, as enraged now as he was calm a moment before. "I'm cutting your fucking dick off and stuffing it down your throat."

"*Hands the fuck up,*" he demanded again, cocking the trigger and ignoring Mort.

Christopher nodded to Mort and Johnnie to follow suit. "Fine."

"I'm sorry, Christy," Zoann cried. "I opened the gate to go to the store, and he got in before I could close it."

Well, that explained it because the codes had been changed.

"What the fuck I have to lose?" Osti managed in a strained voice. "Uncle Sharper's dead!"

"He not identified yet," Mort said with disgust. "It could be anybody they found in that room."

"No! It's him and I can't let him Unk for nothing. I'm fucking finishing it." His shoulders heaved. "I should've been in that fucking room with him. Instead, I was off on an errand.

No, no, fuck no. Shit wasn't fucking right. Timing was off. When he got this motherfucker in the meat shack, Christopher would ask fucking questions later. No fucking way could Osti have fucking been with Sharper in fucking *Atlanta* and already be on the other side of the fucking country, a couple fucking hours later, with such adamancy about his death. If he'd really been burned so fucking bad, he wouldn't be identified so soon.

No. Fucking. Way.

"Bitsy," Christopher said, drawing his little sister's attention, hating the fear on her face. "Stay fuckin' calm."

It was times like this he fucking thrived on, when stupid motherfuckers wanted to fucking draw out his goddamn torture. All it fucking did was allow him to re-fucking-group and fuck them up.

"Think 'bout that fuckin' game we used to play," he told her, making this shit up as he went along. But, fuck, he needed that fucking gun away from her head. "You used to…" What? Fuck. He calculated the risk. If Zoann followed along and dropped to the ground, would Osti automatically fire? Or would she shock the fuck out of him? Fuck it. He couldn't do it this way, so he rolled his shoulders. "My arms gettin' fuckin' tired, Osti, so would your bitch-fuckin-ass shoot the fuck outta me to put me outta my fuckin' misery?"

Grinning, Osti fell right into Christopher's trap. He turned the gun to Christopher, who had just a split fucking second to dodge the fuck out the way before the bullet whizzed by, crossing John Boy's fucking blade. As the bullet shattered the mirror behind the bar, the blade landed in the side of Osti's neck.

Ignoring the gurgling, Christopher rushed to his sister's side and hugged her, whispering reassurances to her. "Call Val," he instructed. "Check on our other sisters."

"Okay," she croaked, breaking away and stumbling toward the hallway.

He turned to Johnnie. "Leave that fuckin' knife right the fuck where it's at so this motherfucker won't bleed out before we get him to the fuckin' meatshack."

"Don't die, motherfucker," Christopher growled, clipping Osti's jaw in an attempt to keep him alive just a little longer. They'd just gotten him strapped the fuck down onto Mort's table in the meat shack. Between the club and the shack, motherfucker had nearly bled the fuck out, and hung on by a bare thread. He glared at Johnnie. "Why the fuck you gotta fuck him up with your goddamn blade, assfuck?"

"Excuse me for trying to save your fucking life!"

Mort splashed a bucket of cold water over Osti, catching Christopher and Johnnie.

Johnnie swiped at his face. "Watch where the fuck the water's going, Mortician."

"Then move the fuck out the way," Mort returned, then focused on his cousin. "Stop playing possum, motherfucker. You not all the way dead yet."

"You got fuckin' jokes, huh, Mort?" Christopher said, snickering.

Osti moaned just as the door roared opened, and Val stormed in. "Where the fuck is he?" he roared, pausing at the foot of the autopsy table and gaping at Osti. "What the fuck? A fucking blade to the neck and that's it? He fucking terrorized my woman. He at least deserve an hour of torture."

"Blame John Boy," Mort said with a shrug, lighting a cigarette. "You could've aimed for his fucking stomach or shoulder or something. But, no. Had to fuck him up in the neck. I hope this calm your ass down now. You fucked him up. Killing urge satisfied."

Christopher opened his mouth to respond, but Osti expelled a short burst of breath and grunted. He frowned and stepped closer, glad they hadn't pulled the knife out in their frustration. "Yo, motherfucker, you hangin' the fuck on. You 'bout to wish you had stayed fuckin' dead."

Catching and holding Christopher's gaze, Osti moved his lips, attempting to speak, but gurgling instead.

"Why don't you tell us now what the fuck you supposedly did," Johnnie taunted. "We're listening."

"I gotta get to Megan," Christopher announced with impatience, "so we gotta hurry this the fuck up." He pulled out his nine, aimed it at Osti's chest and pulled the trigger. He didn't have his silencer with him today and the report momentarily defeaned him. Osti's body jerked at the impact. "For Megan. She got popped in her chest and almost fuckin' died."

Val stepped up, switchblade in hand, and swiped it across Osti's neck. "That's for Zoann."

A cabinet door slammed and Christopher turned as Mort plugged in a circular saw and a reciprocating saw. Cigarette hanging from mouth, he tied his black rubber apron on and stuffed his hands into matching gloves. As they all watched, he lined the floor with plastic, found a pair of goggles, then raised one of the counters used to store shit—or hide shit—and lifted his chainsaw.

Finished preparing, he took his cigarette between his gloved fingers and released the smoke. "Don't mean no disrespect, Prez, but I need some time alone with Osti. For forcing Bailey to suck his cock, motherfucker arriving in hell in pieces."

Christopher nodded. "Get the fuck out, motherfuckers," he ordered Val and Johnnie. At the door, Mort's quiet voice stopped him.

"I'm glad you fucked up, Osti, but I would've let you go just to get my hands on fucking Sharper. He the motherfucker who deserve to be here a little more than you do."

Sharing Mort's sentiment, Christopher walked away. Intending to get his keys to head to the hospital when he reached the clubhouse, Zoann rushing to Val and sobbing against him changed everything.

No, not that. But her fucking words.

"They're dead!" she sobbed. "I-I-I called '911' when you left so they could check on Avery and the others. They're dead, Val. Osti killed my sisters and nieces."

Christopher stumbled back as if he'd been shot, Val's words of comfort to Bitsy and Johnnie's outraged cussing flying the fuck over his head. He dropped into a chair, fucking speechless and heartbroken and furious.

"Christy!" Zoann called, tripping her way to him and launching herself into his arms. "They're gone!"

Hearing his little sister's grief, he knew this wasn't ajoke and their other sisters were gone. "All of them?" he asked in a voice hardly recognizable as his own.

Heaving in a breath, Zoann hiccuped an explanation. "All except Fee since she was on the grounds with us."

"For fuck sake!" Johnnie snarled. "Come on, Christopher. Mort's going to have to move the fuck over. We're due a fucking piece of Osti now."

Instead of complying, Christopher blinked and took Zoann back into his arms, whispering words of comfort to her. He'd always believed only Megan had the power to bring tears to his eyes.

He was wrong. He cried then.

Wrapping his hand around his cock, Digger thumbed the moist tip and grunted, caught between sleep and wakefulness. He stroked up and down in a lazy rhythm, not ready to let go of the fantasy that Bunny lay in bed with him, jerking him off. Or, even better, spreading her gorgeous long legs, and welcoming him into her pussy.

He'd seen her looks all through dinner last night. The heat in her eyes sent signals to his brain and his dick. She wanted him, but she didn't *want* to want him. Quite a new experience for him, although he understood why, given all that he'd put her through and all but told her he hated her best friend.

Fuck, what a dickhead he'd been. Not only to Bunny but in his thoughts about Meggie...

No, wasn't going there while his hand stroked his cock. He'd seen Meggie naked so the fantasy would be easy enough to go to. Here and there, he'd even jerked off to thoughts of Johnnie's woman, whom *all* of them had seen without clothes at Outlaw's bachelor party.

He stopped his hand and slowly lifted his eyelids. Odd but his thoughts made him feel as if he were betraying Bunny by thinking of other women while he got himself off. How many times had he fucked Peyton and pretended she was someone else? *Anyone* else but the bitch she'd been.

How many times had he thought about walking away from her? What were his reasons for not doing so again? At the moment, he couldn't fucking remember. Maybe, if he had Tyler would still be alive.

Maybe, if Peyton hadn't been there, Tyler would've taken Mort up on his offer and returned to the MC with him, instead of going on the run with Digger.

His erection deflating, Digger sat up and hung his head, so very sorry for all the heartache and trauma he'd caused. Now, he was exactly where he'd been before.

Alone.

This loneliness was different than the one that had driven him off. This loneliness was deep, not that superficial shit that made him a stupid motherfucker. Anger didn't feed *this* loneliness, but regret.

If only he'd accepted, *truly accepted*, Meggie and Bailey. Johnnie and Val were his partners, as well, but not like Mort and Outlaw. He hadn't even known he had such fucking resentment until Mortician hooked up with Bailey, and left him the odd man out.

All he'd had to do was wait. His father would spout words about faith and patience.

But faith required patience, and Digger lacked both, even though he was a preacher's son. Fucking boo-hooey sad, considering the great Reverend Sharper Banks was his father. He had vague recollections of his mother, but knew nothing about her spirituality. She might've possessed real, true faith and patience. Not the phony kind his false prophet father had. If Digger needed photos of his mother, he could always search the internet. Sharper had destroyed every memory of her the week after she'd been killed in that car accident.

Shoving the covers aside, he got out of bed and decided to piss, in no mood to come. After he finished, he searched through one of the bags he'd brought in from the car last night and found a fresh pack of cigarettes and a lighter.

He needed a fucking blunt. Grumbling under his breath at the unlikeliness of having one in this goddamn house—fucking *sunflower milk*...

Jesus, who fucked up food like that?

At least, Walt had had a pizza delivered for them. Virginia had kept a close eye on her man, who'd only stared at the pizza with longing. A call had come through and the moment Virginia stepped out of the room, Bunny had darted to her dad and shoved a small piece of pepperoni, gooey mozzarella still stuck to it, into Walt's mouth.

She'd pealed in laughter when Virginia returned during Walt's mid-chew. The look she'd given him meant one thing—pussy lockout. After showing Bunny to her brother's old room, Virginia had led Digger here, to the guest room, formerly known as Bunny's bedroom.

He wondered how it had looked when she'd lived here. The yellow walls and brown décor was gender-neutral. He couldn't imagine Bunny being in such a bland room. She'd probably enjoy soft pastels.

Puffing on his cigarette, dick swinging, he strolled to the single window and opened the blinds. Not much of a view. Mainly, the neighbor's house and the rest of the Hamilton's driveway leading to the small, detached garage.

"Mark?" Bunny's teary voice floated through the door and he frowned at the sound.

What had her bitch of a mother said this time to make her cry?

Tempted as a motherfucker to open the door with his dick out, he decided she deserved more respect from him.

She sniffled.

"Hold up, girl," he called, stuffing the cigarette into the corner of his mouth and then pulling on his jeans.

The moment he opened the door, she barreled into him, her arms circling his waist. At first, he stood frozen, not sure what to do since he hadn't expected this. She trembled and sobbed, compelling him to return her hug.

"What's wrong?"

"Oh my God, it's horrible!" she cried, jerking out of his arms and palming her eyes. "Outlaw called my dad and..." Covering her face, she dissolved into more tears.

"Baby, c'mon," he soothed, grabbing her arms and guiding her to the edge of the bed. "Sit."

Once she complied, he went to the bathroom and flushed his cigarette down the toilet, before grabbing a washcloth to wipe her face off. He couldn't imagine what had her so upset.

Fuck!

Returning to her, he sat next to her and dabbed at the side of her face. "Meggie girl...?" He couldn't even finish it.

"No," she said, glancing at him with pitiful eyes.

"Fuck! The kid? Outlaw's son?"

"No!" She jumped to her feet and scrubbed the towel over her face. "His sisters and his nieces. They're *dead*! Avery, Nia, Bev...murdered," she sobbed. "Do you know Sasha? His youngest niece. She was turning eight in a few months!"

She covered her mouth and doubled over, and Digger knew, without being told, his father was responsible for the deaths.

Bunny continued in near hysterics, but Digger only stared, numb inside. One way or the other, they wanted to destroy Outlaw and...

"And he's so upset, but he still doesn't believe Sharper's dead..."

Those words broke through to Digger and he jerked. "*What?*"

At Digger's sharp word, Bunny stilled, her chin and lips trembling. "I thought you knew about the explosion."

"What fucking explosion?"

"At the hotel," she said hoarsely, tears slipping down her cheeks. "In Atlanta. Yesterday."

No fucking way would his dad die so easily. After months of living with him and watching him in action, Digger couldn't believe his death would be so fucking anticlimactic.

"Digger, Albany," Walt trumpeted, storming into the room, a panicked look on his face. "Get dressed," he said, nodding at his daughter. "It's time for you to go."

"Wh-what?" Shock etched into Bunny's face, the emotion coming through in her gasp. "We weren't doing anything, Dad."

Yeah, because they had some type of fucked-up rule where Bunny couldn't fuck under her parents' roof.

"Look, Walt," Digger retorted, "have more faith in your daughter. *I* might've tried to get pussy from her, despite your stupid rule, but she wouldn't disrespect you, so—"

"Shut up," Walt snapped. "I just came home from my morning jog." He indicated his running attire with a sweep of his hand, although the towel around his sweaty neck might've given him away if Digger had been paying attention. "A vehicle with very distinct license plate has made several circuits through the neighborhood. The personalized California plate has a cross and the letters *REVSB.*"

His father had had that plate for as long as Digger remembered. The motherfucker wasn't dead and he wasn't in Atlanta. Not if his car was rolling around this neighborhood.

Last time Digger had seen the Benz was in the church parking lot two nights before Outlaw had blown up the Banks mansion. Unless his father *was* dead and Osti was using it. That was the logical explanation. But, fuck, they'd been hot on Digger's and

Bunny's trail to have so quickly tracked them to her parents' house.

"Fuck! Bunny, I have to leave," he said, turning and blindly grabbing his belongings. "I'm not bringing her with me, Walt. It's safer for her here with you."

"Digger—" she began, but her father interrupted her.

"I'm begging you," he said, desperation threaded into his tone. "They've killed three of Outlaw's sisters and his three nieces. Someone gave away your location and now none of us are safe. Take her with you."

"No. It won't be safe with me." No matter how much he wanted to use this as an excuse to keep her.

She glanced at him and the panic in her eyes gave him pause. "I'd like you to take me back to the club," she said. "You need them to face your father."

"Bunny, you was happy enough yesterday to be seeing the back of me. This is just stress talking, so—"

"Please, let me come with you," she begged, laying her palms against his chest. "I didn't want you to go alone then. I just didn't know how to ask you."

"You don't want to leave me?" he asked curiously, cocking his head to the side.

"What's going on in here?" Virginia called from the doorway.

"No, I don't," Bunny answered him, ignoring her mother.

"For real?" he persisted, to be absolutely certain.

"I want to come with you."

"Absolutely not," Virginia hissed, sailing into the room and offering Digger and Walt an evil-bitch face. "If you wish for a real reconciliation between us, you'll not go anywhere with this person."

"Hush, Virginia. There's extenuating circumstances."

"Don't you hush me, Walter. Not after all your lies."

"Lady, please shut the fuck up," Digger growled, not wanting to lose this crucial moment between him and Bunny because of her mother's demands.

Virginia drew herself up and folded her arms. "Us or him, another biker," she spat.

Fuck. Now, he got why Bunny had tried so hard to convince her mom he *wasn't* a biker. She couldn't see beyond that one detail. Danger didn't matter. Friendship. Feelings. Nothing but that he was a biker.

"Mark isn't like Trader, Momma," Bunny said softly.

"That's your vagina talking. You're not happy unless it, and you, is being used."

Bunny sucked in a breath, mortification blending with her grief.

"You're angry with me, Virginia," Walt began, red-faced and unable to meet Bunny's eyes. "I know my words will only make you angrier, but you're not running Albany away again. If she wants Digger, that's up to her. It's her life, not yours. Right now, she has to go with him so she'll have a life to live."

"Come with us, Dad," Bunny said frantically, her eyes wide with all kinds of things Digger wished he could take away from her. "You and Mom and—"

"No. We're staying here."

"Dad, but—"

Walt pulled Bunny into his arms and kissed the top of her head. "They need a diversion so you can escape."

She opened her mouth to speak again, but Digger interrupted her.

"Bunny, girl, get your stuff, so we can get on the road. I'm going to do whatever I can to protect your folks, but we have to go and we don't have time to argue about this."

She gave her dad another tight hug but stumbled away.

"Albany!" Virginia called, stalking behind her daughter.

"I have a thousand dollars in my safe and a loaded .38." Walt's frantic look halted Digger from following Bunny and her mom. "Get my daughter to safety."

Walt believed that Digger could look after Bunny. *Bunny* believed in his abilities. Their faith in him boosted his confidence and he nodded. "I will. Now, do me a favor? Find me the telephone number to the rectory for Epiphany, then get dressed. I have an idea."

Walt opened his mouth to argue and Digger glared at him.

"Just fucking do it."

"That's her," Christopher said in a toneless voice, identifying the final body. The last of six. Three women and three little girls, all related to him.

The motherfucker behind the glass in the morgue allowed the curtains to close. Not caring if they were done with him or not, Christopher somehow made it outside. In the bright sunshine when he felt so hollow and dark inside. When his nieces and sisters would never see light again or feel the breeze against their faces. They'd never walk again or talk again. *Live*. Because they were dead.

Toeing the kickstand and mounting his Harley, he pulled on his fingerless, leather gloves, then gripped the handlebars. Not seeing. Not thinking. Just there.

Megan's gorgeous face popped into his head and spurred him to move. If no one else did, she needed him, so he had to pull himself together. He had to figure out how and when he'd lost control of everything.

The realization reinforced his decision to leave the club. He was no good at the shit anymore. He'd allowed personal feelings to interfere with club business.

No, he'd allowed *Megan* to interfere. Not only with her words but because of his own fears. *Fears.* He was scared! Him. For Megan and their children. He'd known Sharper would wage a vicious campaign, annihilating anybody he could in an effort to get to Christopher. Even innocent women and children. But, most especially, *his* woman and children.

So he'd hidden behind the excuse of Digger being Mort's brother. Of Megan liking him and wanting Christopher to give him a chance to explain. Of anything except the real reason that he hadn't had the fucking balls to admit until now.

When it was almost too late. When he'd lost almost his entire fucking family.

When he'd almost lost his girl.

The thought drove him a little insane. But loving laid your heart on the line, left you vulnerable in all kinds of ways. Yet, if it meant the difference between never having Megan in his life and *this,* he wouldn't have it any other way.

Jumpstarting his bike with that thought pounding in his head, he returned to the club, greeting motherfuckers here and there, before going to his house.

CJ barreled to him as Christopher walked into the mud room. "'Law!"

Crouching down, he opened his arms and hugged his son close to him, lifting him off his feet as he stood. "Hey, boy."

"Deel show games on Mommie iPad."

"You been in your ma's stuff again, huh?" He didn't have it in him to discipline his boy. At the moment, he had nothing but the images of his sisters and nieces with bullets in their heads.

"Uh-huh."

"Don't be mad." Diesel's voice carried to Christopher from the doorway between the mud room and the kitchen. "CJ said she lets him play with it."

"I ain't mad," Christopher said on a sigh, brushing past Diesel and into the kitchen, where Roxy leaned against the counter, Ophelia stood at the stove, Kendall sat on a stool, and Zoann emptied the dishwasher. They all turned to him.

"Christy?" Zoann whispered, her hands going to her mouth, tears forming in her eyes. Something in his expression tipped her off, confirmed the deaths before Christopher said a word.

He nodded. "I fuckin' identified them."

Zoann turned and ran toward the den, where Val probably sat. Her sob floated to him. Ophelia said nothing. She just followed in Zoann's wake.

"Outlaw, sit," Roxy instructed.

"No, I…my ass need to be alone." And what better place than his bedroom, where Megan should be but wasn't because he'd been a pussy.

"Are you sure?" Kendall asked with a frown. "This doesn't seem to be the night to try and make it without seeing your wife."

Roxy grimaced. "Don't take it the wrong way. Kendall's concerned about you."

Christopher snorted and handed CJ to Diesel.

"When's Meggie coming home?"

"In two or three days, Kendall," he answered, wishing he didn't have to talk to her, not sure why he did now.

"She's not going to end up pregnant, is she? I'll only have to share the baby spotlight with Bailey, right?"

"Kendall, sugar, shut the fuck up. Please. Now's not the time for this."

Kendall ignored Roxy. "You did get your dick snipped, right?"

"Keep my dick outta your mouth, bitch."

"You wish your dick had been in my mouth," she retorted.

Growling, Christopher stepped toward her.

Roxy caught his hand. "Just ignore her. Her hormones are all over the place."

"Her fuckin' hormones gonna get *her* brain all over the fuckin' place if she don't shut the fuck up."

Kendall threw him a dirty look.

He lifted a brow and snatched away from Roxy's grip. "You need a fuckin' refresher on what fuckin' with me get you?"

"You never answered me. Will Meggie turn up pregnant while I'm carrying this baby? Zoann says she doesn't want any more kids right now, so it'll only be me and Bailey."

Christopher was even less inclined for Kendall's bullshit today. She had a lot of fucking nerve, once again placing herself above Megan when she had the worst reputation of all their women. "Kendall, lemme clue you the fuck in on something. Out of all these girls, you the *only* one who was the fucking whore."

She and Roxy gasped.

"Megan and Bailey ain't ever had dick before their husbands. By choice, the only motherfucker Zoann got dick from was Val. But you? You fucked every-fuckin-thing you could. To get shit. The fuckin' definition of a slut, so before you fuckin' keep up with this bullshit cuz of your hormones and you ain't takin' your medicine and just because you a fuckin' psycho cunt, think about that shit."

Tears slid down her cheeks. "You're cruel."

"No!" Roxy interrupted with exasperation, glowering between the two of them. "He's right, sugar."

Kendall's face crumpled. Roxy had always championed and protected the bitch, serving as the mother she'd never had. But even mamas grew frustrated and practiced tough love.

"How could you, Roxy?" Kendall sobbed. "You're *my* friend. I thought you were on my side."

"Shut up with that bullshit. You know I *am* your friend. Possibly the only one in this motherfucker and that includes Meggie since you're always up in that little girl's ass when you get in a fucked up mood."

"No!"

"Yes! I hate to tell this shit to you, but you *are* the only woman here who fucked other men besides your husband and the only one around here *still* trying to fuck Outlaw."

She glared through her tears. "That's not true! I love Johnnie."

"Love don't have shit to do with how your pussy feel and *your* pussy pissed it never got Outlaw's dick in it. You can't take that. Just like your goddamn husband can't take the fact that Meggie wouldn't fuck him. That's some fucked-up bullshit. You two love each other, but both of you are spoiled, sadity motherfuckers. Johnnie thinks every fucking girl have to fall the fuck all over him because he turns his pearly whites on them in a charming smile. *You* think because you're a tad better educated than the rest of the girls, you're better than they are—"

"Well, you ain't, cunt," Christopher cut in, too frustrated and upset over today's fucked-up events to hold his tongue any longer. "That just make you a snobbish, educated whore."

Roxy rounded on him. "Back off, Outlaw."

"Fuck you," he fumed, only taking so much. "This my fuckin' house, Roxanne. Where this bitch happen to be at. I appreciate your words but I say what the fuck I wanna, *where* the fuck I wanna, but especially in my fuckin' crib." He ignored the hurt creeping into Roxy's eyes. "Kendall ain't learned shit from all the fuckin' bullshit we *all* went through cuz of her fuckin' miserable ass. She might be fuckin' educated but she the stupidest fuckin' bitch I ever met."

"She'll learn," Roxy said in a quiet voice, still hurt by his words. Women and their soft, fucking feelings. Even Roxanne, one of the toughest bitches he knew.

He sighed. "Look, babe. Although I meant what the fuck I said 'bout my ass sayin' what the fuckin' I wanna, I ain't mean to hurt your feelins."

She sniffed and pretended his words didn't matter but he saw her shoulders relax slightly. Not commenting to Christopher, she turned back to Kendall. "Kendall, baby, unless you change your attitude about a lot of shit, a lot of people will see you just like Outlaw do. No matter what the fuck my ass say to defend you, *your* words and actions fuck it up. You're not better than anybody, sugar. Just different. I get that you're pregnant and I understand the side effects of the medicine, but right now, I think you need to stay on them with your OB's approval, which you have. After you deliver, than talk to your psychiatrist about modifying your medicine or trying another one."

The bitch cried harder.

Not wanting to hear more, Christopher stomped out, leaving Roxy to chew her ass out however much she wanted to. Bitch deserved it. His cell phone rang. Expecting it to be Megan since she used the hospital phone sometimes and her special ringtone didn't come through, it disappointed him to see the name *Wilcunt* flashing on the screen. "Yeah?"

"Outlaw?"

"You know this my ass, so what the fuck you want?"

"It's Jazzman."

Christopher scowled at the priest's furtive tone and use of his unearned road name.

"A situation has come up."

"Just fuckin' tell me. I ain't got time to fuck with you today."

Wilcunt cleared his throat. "Digger called me."

That stopped Christopher in his tracks. Of all the news he'd expected to hear, Digger calling the priest wasn't it.

"For what fuckin' reason? To pray for his fuckin' soul when I fuck him up?" If Sharper was really dead and Osti was gone,

Digger was the last one remaining that Christopher could use for revenge. "I ain't understandin' why else he'd fuckin' call you, other-fuckin-wise."

Could this day get any fucking worse? All the fuck he needed was more deaths of innocent people. Riley working for the club didn't make him completely innocent, but his wife was. "He say how he was fuckin' tracked so quick?"

"He doesn't know. According to Digger, the only time his location was discussed was when Bunny's father called you."

Fuck, but he hoped Digger hadn't given Riley away. Christopher didn't doubt Bunny and Digger knew Riley's identity, but he'd prefer not many other people know. That wasn't the biggest fucking problem at the moment. "His fuckin' phone might be tapped." How the fuck else could their location be sniffed out so quickly? Cell phones were harder to listen in on, but with the right technology and enough money, nothing was impossible.

"He needs refuge for Bunny's parents. He believes his father sent men to kill all of them."

"Fuck."

"What do you want me to do?"

"What the fuck you did?"

"If you're going to kill him, I'd prefer not to say. He sounded frantic and not like a man against the club."

Christopher didn't want to fucking hear this right now. Digger was the only one he could make suffer. He wanted revenge for his sisters. His family.

Megan.

"We're all redeemable," the priest began. "He is. You are, too. Helping him in his time of need would help in your salvation."

"I ain't interested in no fuckin' salvation," he yelled. "I want fuckin' revenge."

"On a man who risked his life by calling me to help a woman and her parents? A woman your wife thinks highly of, might I remind you."

"You know what the fuck I just got through doin'?"

"Being mean to me," Kendall sniped in the background.

Glaring at her, he turned his back as the priest answered.

"I know, Outlaw. John Boy called me."

"Then you know how the fuck my ass feelin'."

"Completely," he lied.

No fucking way could he understand Christopher's pain and guilt.

"At least give him a chance to explain. Without your backing he's on his own, attempting to save Bunny's life and get back to the club."

"The motherfucker comin' here?"

"After he deposits Bunny's parents in a safe place."

"That you fuckin' provided for them."

Silence.

"I'll fuckin' think on this shit," Christopher said and disconnected the call before the motherfucker said another word.

"You were harsh."

Christopher frowned at Roxy's stiff words.

"To who?"

"Kendall, of course."

Oh, yeah. A quick glance and he saw that the bitch was gone.

He shrugged. "She need to keep her fuckin' mouth shut."

"Somebody got to be the adult and back the fuck away."

"Maybe, but this my fuckin' house. She can get the fuck out and stay the fuck out."

"She's pregnant."

"Don't give a fuck. I was tellin' the fuckin' truth."

"Didn't you say the club would go to shit if you and Johnnie were always at odds over Kendall and Megan?"

"We ain't been at odds in over a year. Kendall been halfway fuckin' normal."

Roxy harrumphed.

"If you don't need me for nothin' else, I'm goin' up-fuckin-stairs."

She straightened. "You not going to see Meggie today?"

Glancing away, he bowed his head. "No. She ain't needin' to be worried 'bout me and if she see me, she gonna know shit ain't right."

"But—"

"But nothin', Roxanne. I just wanna be left the fuck alone so I can think."

"Thinking fucked up your head."

Not responding, Christopher bypassed the den and went straight to the staircase. He heaved in a breath, knowing what awaited him. A bedroom without his wife, images of his dead family, and the dilemma he faced over Digger.

Should he kill him? Help him? Or just fucking tell Wilcunt to inform Digger to keep riding because he had no place at the club any longer.

Christopher suspected neither did he.

Detached garages were *not* cool when deranged motherfuckers were hunting you. Even worse than detached garages were long fucking driveways, where Dodge Chargers had been parked right outside of said fucking garage.

After talking to Father Wilkins and begging the priest to call anyone he might know in the Phoenix area, Digger decided to monitor the street. It wasn't easy. With his dreads, he could be spotted immediately, so he stood sentinel by loitering behind the neighbor's palm tree, weapon in hand, while Virginia packed whatever bullshit was more important than their fucking lives.

He wanted to leave that bitch behind so fucking bad, but he couldn't add to Bunny's distress. She was really torn up over Outlaw's sisters and nieces.

Digger kept his outrage at bay. To him, fury was quite fucking different from outrage. Outrage might be soothed away, since it came about for a fucking lot of reasons. A jacked up utility bill, for instance. Fucked up restaurant service. Rude motherfuckers.

But *fury...*? Fury grew from an epic catastrophe that could've been avoided if not for the existence of colossal assholes. Only one thing soothed fucking fury. The shedding of blood.

A Mercedes crept in front of Walt's house and paused. Digger didn't need to see the license plate to know his father's car. The black luxury sedan with tinted windows and custom rims was easily recognizable. Waiting for someone to burst out, or for gunfire to begin, his breath caught. The dark windows made it impossible to know how many motherfuckers were in the vehicle.

Sharper rarely traveled alone. He'd fucked over too many people not to have bodyguards. The public assumed he needed protection because of his popularity.

At the least, Osti was there...Or, maybe, not. Osti was probably the motherfucker who'd shot up Outlaw's family.

After several heart-stopping moments, the car drove away. If he didn't know how his father operated, he would've taken the departure as a good sign. But he *did* know the machinations of Sharper, and the car leaving was a bad omen.

Digger counted to thirty before he sprinted from behind the neighbor's tree and across Walt's driveway. He burst into the house at breakneck speed.

"We have to go now!" he yelled, running toward the bedrooms.

Virginia peeped into the hallway. "I'm almost done."

"Like hell, lady," Digger barked, happy to see Bunny no longer crying. Her eyes were red-rimmed and swollen, and her hair was pulled up into a messy knot, as if she couldn't bother to style it any other way. "We getting the fuck *now* or we're leaving you the fuck behind. Your goddamn choice."

Walt stepped around her and into the hallway. "Come on, Virginia. He's right. We'll replace whatever is destroyed."

Outside, a car door slammed. Then another. And another.

"Move!" Digger said in an exaggerated whisper, spinning around and drawing the gun. "I'll cover you."

"Mom, Dad, come on." Bunny shoved her dad while simultaneously yanking her mom into the hallway. Instead of going toward the back door that led to the garage, she headed to the guestroom, turning the lock on the knob.

A loud noise indicated the front door had just been kicked in.

"Cover me," she unnecessarily ordered Digger. He already had her back. Running to the window, she lifted it, then urged her mom through. "Hurry, hurry, hurry."

Glass broke and orders to *find the motherfucker* peppered the air. Once her dad climbed out the window, Bunny slipped through and Digger quickly followed suit.

By the time Digger reached the car, Walt and Virginia were scrambling into the back seat.

Bunny slid into the driver's seat. Not having time to argue, he ran to the passenger side, barely closing the door before she rocketed the car backward, smoke rising from the concrete she went so fast. Pausing, she shifted the car into drive as a motherfucker exited the Mercedes and aimed his gun.

"Get down!" Digger yelled. The window on his side exploded from the impact of the bullet and glass flew in all directions.

Tires squealing, Bunny sped off, while Digger leaned halfway out and aimed at the driver's side tire on the Benz.

"Booyah!" he crowed when he hit his mark. He settled back into his seat, and brushed off the glass shards, noticing the cuts on his hands and the blood blooming on his sleeve.

He'd been fucking shot.

"Where to?" Bunny asked in a high-pitched voice, still speeding like an Indy 500 racer. Her white-knuckled grip on the steering wheel twitched. She hadn't even asked about her mom and dad, so Digger lowered the visor and opened the mirror.

Virginia had her face buried against Walt, who kept his arm protectively around her, but they were unscathed.

Bunny peeled left onto the main road, toward the interstate.

"Bunny?"

"I'm okay." She clutched the steering wheel like a lifeline and tore down the road, straight past a stop light. A series of horns blew. "I'm fine. We survived, so I'm okay."

"Bunny, listen to me," Digger said firmly. "You're going to get us fucking stopped by a cop, so pull over. Let me drive."

In response, she swerved onto a side street without warning and slammed to a stop, breathing hard.

"Keep your foot on the brake. If you move from the pedal, we'll strip the gears while I'm shifting," he said as calmly as possible, sliding the gear into park as he spoke. "Let's switch seats."

She didn't move.

"You've been doing so good," he crooned. "Don't fall apart on me now. It won't take them long to get a roadside service and have their shot-out tire changed. We have to go."

"Albany!" Walt called, and Bunny flinched.

Talking to her wasn't working, so Digger got out of the car. Ignoring the ache in his arm and the glass falling to the ground, he stalked to the driver's door and opened it. "Get the fuck out of the fucking car, Bunny. Get in the fucking back seat. We have to fucking *go*."

"Where'd the bullet go?" she asked, dazed. "It could've hit you or Mom or Dad and then you'd be dead just like Outlaw's sisters and nieces."

He crouched down and touched her thigh since she refused to look at him. "You could've gotten shot too, girl. But that didn't happen. We made it through. You drove your ass off and got us the fuck out of there. I'm so fucking glad you did. If I would've been driving, it would've been hard to fucking shoot that fucking tire out." It would've been fucking impossible, actually. His fingers skimmed up, along the curve of her waist. "We have to get your folks to this old colleague of Father Wilkins, then get the fuck out of town."

"In-in this car?"

He nodded and her face fell. "You don't like cars?"

"Bikes are faster."

"Fuck, yeah, and I wish I had a bike, but I don't, so we have to take what we can get. But we need to fucking get, so I can take."

She frowned at him. "You're weird."

"And you're pretty."

"I'm scared."

He caressed her cheek, then settled his hand behind her neck and pulled her forward to kiss her forehead. "You got a right to be, but you brave, too."

She turned her body to him, settling her feet on the ground. Instead of moving, she touched his lips, his jaw and, finally, his hair.

Walt cleared his throat and Bunny flushed, pulling her hand away.

Digger didn't appreciate the man's interruption. Her fingers had been so soft, almost unsure, as if she'd tired of fighting their attraction but still hadn't convinced herself completely.

Adjusting his hard cock, he got to his feet, careful to keep his back to her mom and dad. "Passenger side is full of glass. Sit in the back with your parents."

Once the switch occurred and Bunny sat next to Virginia, Digger started off again, the bullet wound more of a nuisance than actual pain. Odd. He sure the fuck didn't see a bullet anywhere, which meant the shit must still be lodged in his body.

Keeping his right arm at his side, he used his left hand to maneuver the car in the direction Walt instructed.

The drive to the priest's house took almost six fucking hours, heading in the opposite direction from the way Digger needed to go and into New Mexico. Albuquerque to be exact.

Father Struthers was waiting for their arrival. Before Digger had a chance to exit the car, the man had opened the door to his house, located directly across the street from a huge cathedral. He didn't appear as old or as uptight as Wilkins, a plus in Digger's eyes.

"I've been expecting you," he greeted, walking down the three steps to meet them at the driveway. "Marion gave a very good description of you," he added, nodding to Digger, who stood near the bumper now.

"Who the fuck's Marion?"

Struthers lifted a brow. "Father Wilkins," he clarified in surprise as if Digger should know. He turned to Walt and held out his hand. "And you must be Marion's brother."

Virginia straightened. "Walt doesn't—"

"I am," Walt interrupted, offering a shit-eating grin to Struthers and then to Digger. So that was the line Wilkins had used to gain them a temporary sanctuary with Father Struthers. He'd claimed to be Walt's brother.

"You've been shot!" Bunny screeched, grabbing Digger's arm. Pain shot through him. "You drove all this way with a bullet wound?"

"Chill, baby," he said, pretending Bunny touching the wound didn't hurt like fuck. "It's cool. I'm going to look at it soon, then clean out the car, so we can get back on the road."

"Young lady, why don't you go inside and find some medical supplies. I'd like a word with Mr. Banks. I have money for you," he said, the moment they were alone, "and orders to ditch the car. A bike was delivered earlier. If you're up to it, we'll take care of your arm, then get you on the road. Marion requested that you consider leaving Bunny with me and her parents."

"It has to be her choice. If she wants to come with me, I'm not forcing her to stay." He wouldn't even bring it up. He'd already asked her and she'd made the decision. If he kept going at her with the same shit, she might change her mind.

Struthers left it at that. Efficient and connected, the priest called someone in to see to Digger's wound. Within an hour, the bullet was dug out and he was stitched up. They'd been fed and Walt and Virginia had been shown to their bedroom.

While Bunny showered, Digger brought Walt's car to a chop shop. Not that the motherfucker knew, but it couldn't be helped. Whoever had been in that Mercedes had probably gotten the license plate from Walt's vehicle and identified Walt's address.

Not shocking his father would think to do that. What *was* shocking to Digger was the shit Father Wilkins had thought of. More money, a map of a route back to Hortensia on lesser known roads, and, most importantly, one of the most beautiful Harleys Digger had ever seen, all royal blue enamel and gleaming chrome.

Looking at it reminded him how much he missed his bike. Digger had patched in a few weeks after his twentieth birthday, and a fucking Harley had been his gift, supposedly from Mort, Outlaw, K-P, and Big Joe, but since Mort and Outlaw didn't have a lot at that time, Digger knew it had been from the two older bikers.

He'd fucking loved it. He'd already learned to ride, so once he had his own hog, he'd hit the fucking road as often as possible, loving the freedom of the open spaces.

"I don't know how I'll get this back," he said.

"You don't have to," the priest returned with a shrug.

"Father Wilkins *bought* this for me?"

Struthers widened his eyes. "No. Outlaw did."

He was crying. No, he was motherfucking screaming because he'd lost his fucking mind. Identifying child murder victims did that to a fuckhead.

All the things he should've and could've done were useless, because it was too late. The only reason Zoann and Ophelia hadn't been killed was because they'd been on-premises, as he'd asked. The others had refused his request.

Christopher should've insisted, but he hadn't been in any condition to do so. Just like he was in no condition to do any-fucking-thing right now, except drink and sob and destroy his fucking bedroom.

And destroyed it he had.

Bleary-eyed, he staggered through the broken glass of the flower vases Megan kept on each bedside table, and sat on the edge of the bed. He'd never, for as long as he lived, forget the fucking medical examiner opening that curtain and asking if the small body belonged to Sasha, followed by Tammy, and then Michelle.

All before, he'd never kept their names straight. Sasha had been friendly, always calling him *Uncle Chris,* so he never forgot her name. He hadn't paid much attention to his other two nieces.

In death, he'd remember all of them, as he never had during their lives. As for his sisters, Avery, Bev, and Nia, they'd stopped giving a shit about him years ago, so he'd returned the favor.

But he'd never wanted them dead. Murdered.

He'd beefed up security on Megan's hospital floor, the best he could do until her doctor released her. Osti was fucking dead. Supposedly, Sharper was, too, but Christopher couldn't be certain about the last, so he wouldn't take any chances until he somehow verified that motherfucker's death. Preliminary reports aside, firm DNA still hadn't been obtained.

Despite what every-fucking-body told him, shit just didn't fucking add up right. Just like with whiny-ass Dinah. He squinted. Where the fuck had he put her fucking phone? He needed to check it, see if she'd somehow contacted Sharper or Osti and gave away Digger and Bunny's location. Who else would know except a bitch who blended into the shadows and heard everything? No, what the fuck was he thinking? The fucking phone wasn't fucking important. He was probably barking up the wrong fucking alley, thinking Dinah had some-fucking-how connected with Sharper.

Sharper…

Assfuck was smarter than Christopher after all. The motherfucker knew exactly what the fuck to do to bring him to his fucking knees. Shoot Megan to fuck with his head, so Christopher couldn't focus on fuck all, and then fucking *kill* children related to him to finish the head-fucking job.

On top of every-fucking-thing, he had the Digger situation to contend with. The brothers still wanted Digger's ass. Fine with Christopher since he still intended to fuck Digger up. But the motherfucker reaching out to Wilcunt coupled with the deaths of his sisters and nieces changed his mind about killing him. Besides, Digger had Bunny.

Christopher suspected she stayed so CJ could be returned, although he wasn't sure. He wasn't fucking sure of anything nowadays. Except he didn't want any more civilians killed. While Digger wasn't innocent, Bunny was. Once he'd thought about it, he'd called Wilcunt back and found out where the little motherfucker had sent them, then he'd contacted the president of a Dweller chapter in Albuquerque and set shit in motion.

The door knob jiggled and Christopher scowled. All those motherfuckers had already paraded in front of him, begging him to come down, swearing the deaths of his sisters and nieces wasn't *his* fault.

"Get the fuck away from my fuckin' door," he roared.

Instead, it swung open and he shot to his feet, intending to blast whoever used a goddamn key to invade his space.

"Megan?" he whispered, wondering if Herb and Al fucked with him a little more. He hadn't seen her in two and a half days, too ashamed to face her. He swayed, hurrying to her when she started tipping through the mess he'd made. "Why the fuck you home, baby?"

"I checked myself out, Christopher," she said quietly.

"You shouldna fuckin—"

She lifted herself up to kiss him. Automatically, he bent to make his mouth accessible. "It's done. You need me here with you."

He swayed again and she circled her arms around his waist, attempting to move him.

"No, don't fuckin' strain yourself," he said, allowing her to guide him back to the bed and sitting when she pushed on his chest.

She stepped between the 'v' of his thighs and thumbed at his wet jaw, rough with stubble. But he was so full of alcohol and marijuana, he couldn't remember. She had no place in his head right now, not while so much blood and death filled it.

"They were lil' fuckin' kids," he whispered, needing her comfort. With Megan, he didn't have to say anything at all. She'd know what bothered him. "Sasha ain't got to her eighth fuckin' birthday. Tammy just turned eleven. I never knew that. Did you?"

"No," she whispered, gliding her fingers through his hair and cradling his head against her.

"Michelle was gonna be twelve. They ain't ever goin' on a fuckin' date. They ain't never gettin' married or graduatin'…I don't fuckin' hurt kids. They were fuckin' kids!" he repeated.

"I know," she said, stroking his nape but not commenting on his yelling at her.

"We fucked up that motherfucker. We got him in the fuckin' meat shack."

She cleared her throat. "He's still there?"

Christopher shrugged, unsure of what Mort had done to Osti's body. He hoped like fuck he hadn't gotten rid of that motherfucker yet.

"You need to clean-up," Megan told him, her voice still soft and soothing.

"You need to lay the fuck down, baby," he countered. "I ain't able to watch over you like I should right now, so get in fuckin' bed and rest."

She glanced behind him and scrunched her nose. "The bed is strewn with glass, flowers, and water. I have nowhere to lay. I'm in pain and I'm tired, but I promise I'll keep. Let me take care of you. You're hurting."

Standing up forced her backward, but he caught her arm so she wouldn't fall. He stared at her, attempting to count how many days had gone by since she'd been shot.

She knew him, knew what kind of comfort he needed right now, and through his jeans, gripped his suddenly hard dick, squeezing. "I don't want to end up back in the hospital with too much vigorous exertion, so I think it'll work better in a bath. Okay?"

"Yeah, baby," he said tiredly.

She pointed behind her. "Now, sit. I have to call Roxy and ask her to help me." She moved away and walked around the room. "How much did you drink?"

A quart. A fifth. Who the fuck knew? Enough to give him alcoholic poisoning.

"You don't get wasted so easily," she said, "so I know it was a lot. You need food to soak up some of that."

A series of beeps drummed through his head as she dialed and asked Roxy to come upstairs to help clean up the room, requesting a plate of food, as well.

"Will you eat what I give you?" she asked, once she'd disconnected the call.

"I'll eat your pussy. I ain't fuckin' hungry for food."

Megan smiled, removed the hairband she had around her wrist and twisted her hair up, securing it with the purple-colored elasticized material. Fatigue ringed her eyes.

He swayed again and crooked his finger at her.

"What?" she asked, even as she walked to him.

"Get the fuck in bed."

"No."

Before he could respond the door opened and Zoann walked in, gasping as she took in the fucked-up room. He hadn't even thought of how Zoann must feel about him now that he'd gotten their entire family wiped out and after they'd come so fucking far and made up.

As if protecting him, Megan stepped in front of him, although he could clearly see over her head. The side of Bitsy's face and her mouth was bruised and her eyes were swollen from all the crying she'd been doing.

Staring at him, Zoann bit on her lip, before offering him an encouraging smile. “I came to check on you, Christy.”

“Zoann,” he began. “I fuckin’ ain’t ever meant…”

She held up her hand. “It isn’t your fault. You offered them your protection. They declined,” she finished on a sob.

“I shoulda made them.”

Megan snorted.

“You *couldn’t* make them,” Zoann insisted. “The whole fucking MC had been shot up. You couldn’t worry about them because they wouldn’t listen to you.”

“We was still fuckin’ family.”

“Yes, Christopher,” Megan inserted, “but they chose not to act like it, so you can’t blame their deaths on you.”

“Meggie’s right.”

“Them bitches probably blamin’ my fuckin’ ass and campaignin’ to fuckin’ Satan to fuck me up.”

“Only a psycho say shit like that.” Walking into the room, Val glanced around and whistled. “Can I fuck up our shit like this without you getting mad, Zoann?”

“Omigod, get out,” Megan ordered. “This isn’t a joke.”

“Asshole,” Zoann said, pinching Val and making him yelp. She started toward Christopher, but paused and looked at Megan. His wife shifted slightly, allowing his sister to reach him and wrap her arms around him. “I love you, Christy,” she whispered on a sniffle. “We’ll get through this like we have everything else. You’ll get us through. Just rest now.”

Roxy carried in a tray as Zoann and Val left. “Lawd, Jesus Christ, what the fuck you did, Outlaw?”

Sitting down again, he scrubbed at his face. “Fell the fuck apart, like the pussified bitch my ass be.”

Roxy sat the tray on the sofa since the table lay on its side. “More like fell the fuck apart like the drunk motherfucker you are.”

He scowled at her while she closed the distance and bent to observe his eyes.

"Like the drunken, *high* motherfucker you are."

"Christopher, I think we need to go to a guestroom," Megan said. "It's going to take a while to clean everything up and you really need some peace and quiet."

"You fuckin' think? What the fuck I need is pussy from you. I need to know you fuckin' here with me."

"Just come with me," she said. "I swear I'll take care of you."

"Fuck, baby, you need some-fuckin' body takin' care of you."

"She's looking at him, Outlaw," Roxy said, righting the table.

"Christopher," Megan whispered. "I'll try to have enough energy to...um...you know...suck you," she mumbled, slanting an embarrassed glance to Roxy. "You know why?"

Fuck, his head was starting to fucking hurt. "Cuz you love my fuckin' ass?"

"Well, that's it, but remember what you once said to me?"

He'd said so much to her, he couldn't fucking remember most of the shit, at the moment. "No," he murmured, laying back and wincing at the combination of water, flower stems, and pieces of glass under his head.

"Sit up," she demanded, "before you get a piece of glass in your skull."

"What the fuck my ass said to you that you want me to fuckin' remember?" He sat up, so she wouldn't worry herself, but he really wanted to sleep, so fucking much that he couldn't hold his head up. He laid back again.

"You're the strength I need to carry me."

He remembered telling her that. He also remembered when.

"You are, Christopher, but right now, *I'm* your strength to carry you. It doesn't mean you're weak or you've failed us. It just means you're human, so grieve for your sisters and rage at the deaths of your nieces however you must. I won't let anyone blame you or say mean things to you. But no one blames you. You have to know that. And, if someone does, well, *fuck them*."

Her lovely face blurred in front of him as she cussed. Although laughter rumbled from him, his eyes slipped closed and he fell asleep, finally succumbing to the rum, tequila, and weed.

Like its sister city of Alburquerque, Spain, Albuquerque, New Mexico sat in the shadows of a mountain range. And similar to his current trip where the Sandia Mountains served as a beautiful backdrop, his stop in the city located in the Badajoz province in the valley of the San Pedro Mountains, had been just as unplanned. Then, he'd been on a road trip to Portugal and had gotten lost.

At first, Digger thought maybe some bumbling official had accidentally misspelled the city's name. But, no. Somewhere, he'd been told Alburquerque, Spain had been dubbed the city with the extra 'r'.

Then, he'd convinced himself he was running for his life, when actually he'd been enjoying the sights, the food, and the people. Outlaw had allowed him to *live*. That had been child's play, where he and Peyton had engaged in a fuck fest across Europe. Now, however, he was truly on the run, and he couldn't pause to enjoy any of the wonders of *Albuquerque.*

He focused on navigating the roads that would bring him and Bunny to safety, and away from Sharper or the men who'd come after him on Sharper's behalf. Besides keeping him and Bunny alive, Digger's main objective was trekking the twenty plus hours back to the club.

As they neared the city of Farmington, and he pulled into a rest stop for Bunny to stretch her legs, a sign reminded Digger of the Four Corners, the point where Arizona, Colorado, Utah, and New Mexico met, was nearby.

When he walked out of the public bathroom, he found Bunny standing in the breezeway, staring at the contents of a vending machine. It occurred to him that she didn't have money. She didn't even have ID.

"Hey," he greeted, walking next to her.

Her smile didn't hide her exhaustion. "Hey."

"We been on the move for hours, huh?"

She nodded. "Since about eight this morning."

In between that, they'd been almost killed, took a six-hour trip, before hitting the road again almost five hours ago.

"How's your arm?"

"A pain in the fucking ass, more than anything."

"You've been shot before?"

"No. Gunshot virgin."

"Oh my goodness, you did not just say that!"

A wink and a grin accompanied his careless shrug. "Badge of honor."

"You're an asshole." The words carried no heat and judging by the amusement in her eyes, she was teasing him. "I'd think having a bullet lodged in you and then dug out so primitively would hurt like hell."

"It doesn't," he said honestly. "At least not right now. Maybe, it's the adrenaline."

Refocusing on the vending machine, she asked, "Do you have a couple of dollars?"

"I have more than a couple, girl. Unfortunately, I have no ones, fives, or coins of any type."

"I'm hungry."

Understandable. He didn't remember her eating much at Father Struthers's place.

"Let me find an area map. Maybe, we can find a nice place to eat."

All area maps were gone from the clear plastic rack hanging near the front of the building, but he noticed what looked like a map, crumpled nearby in the grass. When he picked it up, he discovered he was right, and quickly honed in on a nearby shopping mall. Unfortunately, the place had been closed for an hour. Reading further, he found an alternative and headed to Bunny to offer his idea.

"How about we check into a hotel for the night?"

"Won't you lose time?" she asked around a yawn.

"We will, but I'm fucking tired and so are you."

"I'm more hungry than tired."

If she wanted to believe that, Digger wouldn't fucking argue. She looked ready to drop. "A hotel will have room service. You can eat and I can rest."

"Well, I won't argue with that."

When they arrived at the hotel, displays of brochures for the various landmarks caught his attention. He intended to scoop a few up and bring to his room, so he'd pass the time. Resting wouldn't happen, not with his mind so filled with *everything*.

Most importantly, he was debating on calling Outlaw now or waiting until he got to the club to face the man.

"We don't have two adjoining rooms," the clerk announced as Bunny joined him, a small stack of brochures in her hands.

"Why do we need adjoining rooms?" Bunny asked with a frown.

Was she fucking serious? He scowled at her. "Only so much torture my dick can take, girl."

The chubby clerk with a cherub face smiled.

"I'm with you," Bunny said in a soft voice, a blush coloring her features.

"Don't," he growled, low.

Her eyes narrowed. "Don't what?"

"You know what the fuck you doing, Bunny," he snapped. "Teasing my dick. Stop it before I take you up on your offer, park this motherfucker inside you, and fuck your brains out."

"Excuse me, sir?" the clerk said. "Will it be one or two rooms?"

"One," Bunny answered, at the same time Digger yelled, "Two!"

"Please, Mark."

He gritted his teeth, unable to decline her, despite how much common sense told him to. "One room."

"Double or king?" Cherub face said. "Never mind, my guess is double."

"Oh, so you got fucking jokes, huh, clerk woman?" Digger grumbled, glaring between Bunny and the hotel clerk.

"I'm a reservation agent, sir," she corrected.

"Whoever the fuck you are, give me what the fuck you have available and closest to the restaurant that offer room service."

"You got it." She keyed in some shit, her fingers fucking moving faster than the speed of lightning, her eyes going between her screen and Digger's ID. Finally, she held up two key cards. "You're in room two-oh-seven, sir. It's a—"

"I don't want to know," he interrupted. All it would do is add shit to his already crowded brain. If it was a double, he'd be disappointed. If it was a king, he'd begin to devise ways to get into Bunny's pussy.

Opening the door and flipping on the light, he allowed Bunny to enter first. Her snorted laughter clued him in on what he'd find. Sure enough, in all its glory, stood a nicely made up king-sized bed.

Bunny quickly chose a side and lay on her stomach, groaning. "We can't do anything right now. I need a few more days to heal from the miscarriage, I think."

Her words halted his advance to the heating unit. "You mean you'd let me in that sweet pussy?"

Seeing the very pretty shade of deep pink her cheeks turned intrigued him. She'd been around crude motherfuckers for years so he couldn't believe she actually blushed.

"Trader didn't call your cunt a pussy?"

She sat up with a huff, releasing her mass of hair from its elastic band. "Yes," she hissed.

He grinned. "So it's me figuring out you'd give me pussy that's making you blush, huh?"

"Just stop it, Mark. There's more important things at hand."

The words sobered him somewhat and he nodded. "Fuck, yeah."

Instead of continuing to the heating unit, he detoured and sat on the bed. She scooted next to him and laid her head on his shoulder. He wrapped his arms around her, as if it was the most automatic gesture in the world.

"So many lives lost in such a short period of time," she said in a voice tinged with despair. "When will it stop? Who's next?"

He had no answers to either. At this point, he wasn't even sure Outlaw *would* do anything else. He'd never been close to his sisters, but they were still his family, and he took protecting his family seriously. Their deaths had probably crippled him. He'd see it as a monumental failure on his part. There was one small difference in the psychological warfare Sharper engaged that gave him the edge. Outlaw truly cared about his family, his club, and his brothers. Sharper cared only for himself, so every life except his own was expendable.

"What are we going to do?" she asked. "Do you think we've lost your father's men? Are you sure my parents are safe? We can't keep running."

"No, we can't. That's why we're heading back to the club. Outlaw had the bike delivered for us to get away."

"Yes," she agreed slowly, "but he might still hurt you bad."

Fucking right, he was due some serious injuries, but he wouldn't tell her that. "Live or die, I'm going back."

"Are you sure? I-I mean…you know…you betrayed…" She scrunched her nose. "Outlaw might…he might—"

"Fuck me up?" he finished for her.

"Yes."

Digger leaned away from her, to better study her face. "Would you care?"

"Yes."

He needed more than yesses and noes from her. "Why?" he asked, hoping that solved the problem of her monosyllabic answers.

She slid to the head of the bed, and stretched her legs out, avoiding his gaze. "I don't really know."

Instinct told him she couldn't bring herself to say what was really on her mind. Every time she seemed to let her guard down and show her attraction, she pulled back.

"Trader hasn't been dead very long."

Trader had also been a fucking assfuck, but he refrained from pointing that out and patted her foot. "S'alright, Bun-Bun."

"It isn't. It *so* isn't. I really don't know you. Until a few days ago, I mostly associated you with betrayal, bitterness, and violence."

That about summed him up. "You do know me. You met me before I left," he quickly added when disappointment flashed in her eyes at his corroboration of her assessment.

"You were always smiling, so very easy-going. Just like Mortician."

Why did everybody compare him to Mort? That galled the fuck out of him, especially having *her* do it. "I'm not my brother. We two different motherfuckers. Okay? I'm out of his shadow now and I'm me. Not *him*."

"But who are you?" she pressed on a whisper. "The real you? Do you know?"

He made a mirthless sound, unwilling to tell her most of what he'd found out about himself wasn't worth shit. "You don't know me," he conceded, relenting at her softening look. "*I* don't really know me. I want to be the man I've tried to be since I let Outlaw's son go home. But I'm not that guy, Bunny."

"Who are you?" she repeated, searching for an answer to some unspoken question.

"A motherfucker who would take your pussy and not look back. That what you want to hear?"

She shook her head. "I don't believe you," she came back, shocking him. "You're not Trader. If I got pregnant with your baby, you'd never kill it by beating it out of me. Even if your intentions were to take my pussy and not look back. You wouldn't abandon your own flesh and blood."

What the holy fuck was *wrong* with this bitch? Either she didn't fucking know how sensitive his dick was, or she was purposely teasing him. He couldn't even summon fear or outrage at the thought of getting her pregnant. Hearing the word *pussy* in her breathy voice heralded a fucking dick suck, at the least, to relieve the pressure in his balls.

Resting his elbows on his knees, he sidled a glare at her. "You want to fucking know all about me? My name is Marcus "Digger" Banks. I've watched people die. I've killed motherfuckers. I've dug fucking graves for dead motherfuckers. I got rid of girls that Big Joe fucked up because he forgot his own rule that we don't hurt women. My father is sewer scum. But I don't have to tell you that. *That*, you already know."

"Mark!" she cried. "Stop feeling sorry for yourself."

"I'm not." A little voice said maybe he was. "I'm just telling you about me. We've been fucking dancing around each other for days. You want to fuck me, but you don't like that you do. I'm helping you to decide, to put both of us out of our fucking misery. You need to know the man you're thinking about letting in your cunt."

Digger didn't know why he felt the need to tell her his life's story. Maybe, to cleanse his mind of all the fucking dirt clogging it. He wanted to unburden himself to her. She'd listen. She had strength and courage. *Compassion*.

Lying side-by-side on the bed, he told her most of what he'd already said to her, describing his time with Peyton and his ambiguity toward her.

"Do you miss her?"

After a few moments to consider the question, he turned on his side, happy when she did the same, allowing them to face each other. "No." Before she could ask anything else, his stomach growled and he remembered they hadn't eaten yet, so he called down for room service and went to the bathroom to check on his injury while they waited.

It had bled somewhat, but he'd survive.

He returned to the room just as Bunny opened the door for the room service delivery.

As she stabbed pieces of spinach, orange, and chicken with her fork, Digger swallowed his bit of roast beef sandwich and resumed his story, explaining how he felt both envy and love for Mortician.

"That's fucked up," he conceded when she didn't comment, grabbing the beer he'd also ordered.

"A lot of siblings feel that way about each other. It doesn't mean you wouldn't do anything in the world for each other."

Having no response, he chewed more of his sandwich and chased it with beer before talking about Tyler and Sharper. She didn't comment, so he broached the final topic.

His feelings for her.

"I like you. You're different." He settled back in his seat, sudden tension rising between them. Before, things had been easy, but now she shuttered her expression and waited for him to continue. "You make me want to be different, too. For you. For my brother and my *brothers*." Mostly for her.

She studied him through her lashes. "The only time you want to change for someone is when you care deeply for them."

"Asking me shit again without really asking me, huh, girl?"

"Sometimes, it's best that way. It won't set anyone off and I could test the waters."

"You talking about Trader's dead ass, right?"

She gave a hesitant nod, setting her fork aside carefully and pushing her salad away.

"Bunny, girl, you been keeping my ass in line from the moment I forced you in the car. You have to know I'd never hurt you, no matter what you said to me or asked me. Or did to me. So keep doing what you've been doing with me. That's why I like you so much. That's why I want to fucking live and prove to you I can be whatever the fuck you want me to be."

Intrigue lit her eyes and she chewed her bottom lip.

"Are you sure? Or is this another rash decision?"

"I have the ability to think through shit too."

"Do you? Just a few days ago…no, half an hour ago, you said you'd take my pussy and not look back."

He grunted in frustration. "Do you have to overthink every goddamn thing you do?"

"I'd prefer to overthink than underthink."

"Neither way good."

"Maybe not," she conceded. "My way at least allows a little caution."

"And my way provide excitement."

"But that's the part of you that makes me hesitate to involve myself with you in any way."

Score for her. He'd walked right into that one. As much as he wanted to, he couldn't deny her logic. "I told you I'd change. Be whatever you want me to be."

"It still wouldn't work. You can't change for me. You have to change because you want to."

"The thought of you leaving didn't sit well with me. Then, I thought it was for the best. We thought Sharper was still on the loose."

"Someone is."

"Yeah," he agreed bleakly. "I didn't want to see you hurt no matter who I faced. Even Outlaw. If I don't fix shit at the club and you with me, you out too. I don't want to lose your friendship or your company. The type of loyalty you offering to a motherfucker like me is rare. Something I want to hold on to."

For long moments she didn't speak, then she nodded. "It doesn't matter *what* I do to you?"

Out of everything he'd said that was all she'd picked up on? Unease swept into him at her curious study of him and he swallowed the last of his beer. "Almost anything."

"Lie down on the bed for me."

The bed? She couldn't fuck, so he didn't know what the fuck she wanted him on the bed for. He had to have misunderstood. That was it. Now sure he'd misheard, he stared at her stupidly for several seconds.

"Please get on the bed."

Loud and fucking clear this time. "Why?" he got out, once his brain started functioning properly again.

"Just do it. Why do you question everything?"

"Says the chick who does the same," he retorted, standing and going to the bed to do as she asked. "My questions keep my ass alive."

A moment later, she crawled next to him, leaned over and placed her mouth on his. Her slow, thoughtful kiss sent desire straight to his already aching dick. For most of the night, since they'd arrived, the motherfucker had been half hard. Now, it stood at attention.

Bunny's lips were so soft and the hesitant warmth of her tongue as she changed their kiss from chaste to passionate made Digger thread his fingers through her hair and take over the kiss. Unlike her sweetness, he ravaged her mouth, his need to possess her overwhelming.

Thrusting his hard cock against her belly, he groaned and flipped her onto her back, sliding his tongue along her throat, frustrated by the sweatshirt she wore.

Instead of allowing him to lift the material, she turned her head away. "Wait, stop."

Fuck him, those were the last fucking words he wanted to hear, but he pulled away instantly and flopped onto his back. "This motherfucker didn't just stop me now," he mumbled, jerking when he felt her fingers at his fly.

She took his dick into her hand. Stared at it. Then at him, before studying it again, offering distracted strokes and fingering the pre-cum leaking from him.

Without warning, she dipped her head and took him into her mouth. He shuddered at the feel of her lips wrapped around his cock. Somewhere, he swore she'd fucking told him she didn't like sucking dick. Whatever in fuck made her blow him, he thanked.

Moaning, he fisted her hair into his hands and watched her. She was so fucking skilled, he couldn't imagine why she didn't like to give head. When she lapped at his cock head and tongued the underside, he decided he'd walk across fucking water to get his dick in her mouth.

His body stiffened and his back arched as his release flooded from him. She immediately pulled away, ran to the table where napkins were located and covered her mouth to spit.

He collapsed against the bed. "You could make a fucking living sucking dick."

"I did."

Fuck, he'd forgotten her days as a stripper-slash-whore. Judging from the tone of her voice, it was a sore spot with her. Bunny had been mostly a mystery to him. He suspected to most of the brothers. Now, Digger knew her. Knew what she'd faced. Her mother enjoyed throwing her past in her face and he bet Trader had held it over her head and threatened her with exposure. Presenting her to the brothers as a whore would've made her little better than club ass. She wasn't an attorney like Kendall nor did she have a crazy fucking killer as her old man.

Only a woman beater.

Whether they were good or bad, thoughts of Trader made Bunny think of her youthful indiscretions and fucked with her head.

Digger vowed to protect Bunny from any-and-everybody, and he'd start right after he met his fate head-on in the form Outlaw. The man who'd assisted his escape.

At the thought, his heart beat a little faster and his hope soared a little higher.

"I didn't mean nothing by my comment about you making a living giving head." He sat up, the relaxation he'd felt from coming slipping away at her sadness. "You did what you felt like you had to do. Even if I'd met you while you danced. I'll bet you were still the cool chick you are now."

"If you say so."

She crawled into bed next to him and slid under the covers, her back to him.

Digger sighed. Sweet chicks were on the sensitive side and he really didn't want her feelings to be hurt. He needed to understand why she'd sucked his dick, if she intended to withdraw from him.

"I can't give you pussy right now and my kissing you made you a little frantic," she answered after he questioned her. "I thought I'd help you along, since I started it to begin with."

"Why'd you even kiss me?"

"Because I like kissing and I've been wanting to kiss you for a couple of days now."

"Is it the dick sucking you don't like? 'Cause let me tell you, girl, you sure the fuck acted like you enjoyed it. Or is it the taste of cum that turns you off?"

Looking over her shoulder, she frowned. "I hate the taste of semen."

"So if I'd pulled my cock out of your mouth and came on your cheek, maybe that would've been better?"

"Why my cheek?"

"Your fucking tits are covered. The only skin available is from your fucking neck up."

"I've never tried it like that."

"So motherfuckers always came in your mouth when you sucked dick?"

Too late, he realized his tone was sharper than necessary. It didn't surprise him when she turned her head away again.

"Yes."

Fuck, but he didn't like that thought. Not because he saw her as a lesser person. It was knowing she hadn't enjoyed doing it, which made it seem wrong. The problem was no one had *forced* her to do it, so he didn't know what to say to her without it sounding as if he was condemning the choices she'd made when she'd been younger.

"If you ever take my dick in your mouth again, I promise I won't come until I pull out." Just, please, dear Jesus in heaven, let her do it again.

"I'll think about it," she mumbled, curling herself into a ball.

"Do that. Please?"

Silence and then, "So what are we? Lovers? Friends with benefits? Fuck buddies on the road?"

"Do you need a label on us right now?"

"I just want to know so I don't expect too much."

He winced at her answer. Where relationships and men were concerned, she was quite vulnerable.

"Are you in love with me?" he asked.

"No. No one falls in love after a few days."

"It's happened."

She snorted. "Whatever. Are you in love with me?"

"No, but I told you I care about you and I want to be your man."

"Why? Because I'm convenient and us being together will mean you're not alone?"

"It's because I like you." Much easier to understand, since she'd seemed to have disregarded his more in-depth one.

Nodding, she didn't answer and slowly drifted off to sleep.

Digger kissed the back of her head, impatient to get into her cunt. As soon as she was well enough, they'd have a fuck marathon. He was determined to erase Trader from Bunny's memory.

He didn't know his fate, only knew that Outlaw had taken care of him so he'd get to safety. He wanted to believe it had to do with him, instead of only Bunny. His bike was a beauty, an unnecessary gift on Outlaw's part. But it made Digger believe he had a chance at a fresh start, not only at the club but in finding the love of a good woman.

It all clicked in his head. He'd had fucked-up ideas when he'd met Peyton, so it was fitting that she'd been a fucked-up bitch.

"Church adjoined," Christopher declared, tired to his fucking bones as he banged the gavel and scowled when CJ yelled, "Ashfuck, Wye!" in reference to Zoann and Val's son, Ryan.

The brothers laughed. On the other hand, Christopher didn't find his son's outburst so amusing right now. Megan would have his fucking ass. She hadn't even wanted CJ to attend, but the brothers wanted to see his boy, in the wake of recent events. And it wasn't as if he'd never brought his son to church.

He headed to where the little boys were wrestling on the floor.

"Remember, what I told you, Ryan?" Val called, laughing like a fucking lunatic. "Call him an assfuck back."

As he reached Val, Christopher thumped him on the side of the head. "Shut the fuck up, motherfucker," he growled.

"Ow," Val whined, rubbing his head.

"Yo, CJ!" Christopher called even as he broke the wrestling match up and scooped his son into his arms. "I'm sendin' you fuckin' home to your ma. I fuckin' told you to be-fuckin-have."

His son's green eyes widened and his face crumpled. His boy's fucking chin wobbling reminded Christopher of how Megan looked when she cried. A tug at his T-shirt made him look down.

"CJ mean," Ryan said hoarsely and sniffled, as silent tears ran down CJ's cheeks.

"Do you need anything, Outlaw?" a female voice asked before Christopher formulated a response to his nephew's words.

He glanced at the girl with a shock of white-blonde hair and a lewd smile on her wide mouth. More bitches were parading from the kitchen, all in their normal keyhole thongs and high heels. The Bobs and their fucking friends were on hand to serve the club members who'd come in from near and far in the wake of all that had happened.

"Can I have a plate of food, sweetheart?" Johnnie asked, standing on the other side of Val, next to Mort.

"Make that two plates," Val added, bringing Ryan over to him.

"Hungry, 'Law," CJ said, staring at the whore's exposed tits. His boy talked like a motherfucker. That meant Megan would hear all about this nearly naked bitch right near their son.

Fuck it. If he'd get a fucking earful from her, he might as well do it on a full fucking stomach. "Bring six fuckin' plates to that table, babe," he said, pointing to his normal table in the corner, a prime location to monitor everything.

He headed to the table, still carrying his son. Before he dropped into his seat, he sat CJ on the chair nearest him and then waited until the others had sat as well.

"Listen up, you two," he started, glancing between CJ and Ryan. "Wrestlin' okay if it's a fuckin' game, but it *ain't* okay as a fuckin-fight-in-fuckin-disguise. You two the fuckin' oldest outta all the kids and I fuckin' expect better fights. That shit set a bad fuckin' example for them other ones."

Although if he wanted to be honest, he knew CJ took no fucking prisoners. Either the other children kept the fuck up or suffered the fucking consequences. That was one reason his boy adored Harley so much. She was fucking hell on wheels already.

However, he couldn't fucking single either CJ or Ryan out in front of each other. He didn't want either of them to feel fucking bad or develop some type of complex.

"Good fuckin' leaders don't pick fuckin' fights just fuckin' because." Words for CJ's benefit. "But they don't cower to no motherfuckers either." For Ryan. "Either way can get you fuckin' killed. More fuckin' important? You two fuckin' family. You look out for each other, *especially* around other motherfuckers. You stand together through thick and fuckin' thin. Hear me?"

Ryan nodded his head vigorously, while CJ said, "Yes, 'Law."

"You do realize these boys aren't yet three?"

Ignoring John Boy, Christopher ruffled his son's curls, as four girls swarmed their table. The white-haired chick thrust her tits into his face as she sat his plate down and glided her fingers through his hair.

He frowned at her, intending to tell her to move the fuck away.

"Tell MegAnn!" CJ yelled, glaring at the bitch before Christopher said a word.

Her brows snapped together and she opened her mouth to speak.

"I fuckin' suggest before I toss you the fuck out for openin' your fuckin' mouth to *my* kid, you walk the fuck away. You come back to this fuckin' table for any fuckin' reason, you keep your motherfuckin' hands to your fuckin' self."

She glanced at him through her lashes. "I didn't mean any harm," she said sweetly. "I'm a new Bob and—"

"New, huh?" he grunted, biting into his slice of brisket before setting the meat down and sliding CJ's plate to him, so he could cut the beef into small pieces. "Well, let me clue your new fuckin' ass in, babe." He finished with his boy's food first before staring into her gray eyes. "Don't fuckin' put your goddamn hands on me." He raised up his wedding ring. "You fuck with me, that mean you fuckin' with this, and that shit ain't happenin'. *Ever.* I don't know why the fuck Arrow..."

It hit him. Arrow hadn't had a chance to tell any new bitches much before he'd been killed. They'd acquired six new girls to replace the half-dozen who no longer wanted to associate with them because of the threat posed by Sharper.

"Forget 'bout it, babe," he said quietly. Him and Arrow had never particularly gotten along, but the man had been K-P's kid brother and loyal to the club. He was just a shit-stirrer who could be a pain in the ass sometimes. He was a lifer gone nomad. Now, a Freebird. "You fuckin' know now. Okay?"

Dismissing her, he begin to eat, not paying much attention to Val, Johnnie, and Mort's conversation.

Six days had passed since his sisters and nieces were killed, and four days since he'd lost his fucking mind and went on a fucking crying-bitch party that appalled him to his fucking soul.

Despite the faith Megan had in him and his abilities to run his club, he no longer had the faith in himself. As dis-fucking-gusted as he was over that realization, it was the truth. Whatever else he'd gone through in his life, he'd fucking never once questioned his leadership capabilities.

Okay, so that was a motherfucking lie, but he'd never questioned it to the fucking extent he did now.

Church had lasted most of the fucking day. There'd been so fucking much on the agenda. The hydro-grow distribution. Financial reports from the legitimate businesses. Monetary disbursement. Sharper's attack on the club. Fuck, the motherfucker's "death" that Christopher still didn't fucking believe, despite every-fucking-body else believing it. Digger, and Christopher's decision to hear the stupid assfuck out *before* deciding whether or not to blow him the fuck away.

Despite those topics, his boy had been the star of the meeting. CJ wasn't shy by any means, so he'd eaten the fucking attention up.

What Christopher hadn't brought up was his resignation. Megan insisted he needed shit to settle down before he made the announcement and threatened to punch him in the nose if he acted now.

After he'd promised not to be an assfuck to her, they'd gotten into a huge fucking argument early this morning.

"Deel!" CJ squealed around a mouthful of food, his lips and chin greasy from the brisket and barbeque sauce.

Diesel approached the table, his wide eyes roaming from naked-tittied bitch to naked-tittied bitch. After receiving greetings from everyone, he focused on Christopher. "Meggie was wondering if the meeting was over."

Belching, Christopher wiped his mouth with a paper napkin. "Why the fuck she ain't called and asked me her-fuckin-self?"

The kid shrugged. "I volunteered."

She was pouting. That's what the fuck that meant. "The meetin' over," he said flatly, unable to believe Megan wasn't supporting his decision to leave his club.

"She wants me to bring CJ to her. She said he's probably tired after not having his afternoon nap."

"CJ, your ma wantcha home." He stood and lifted his boy out of the chair. "Be-fuckin-have, cuz she still not all well."

"Ryan, go with CJ and Diesel," Val instructed. The little boy yanked out the napkin he'd stuffed in front of his shirt, threw it aside, then hopped to his feet.

"Fuck, Prez, but Arrow got some pretty ass bitches again," Mort grumbled, his head craning in all directions to look at the women. Now that the food was served, some of the girls were settling in at various brothers' tables.

Arms folded, Johnnie glanced over his shoulder. "Motherfucker had a sense of humor," he said, nodding to a tall, busty redhead.

"Could be just a fuckin' coincidence," Christopher offered, pulling out his smokes. He lit one up, then handed the pack to Val. "But you fuckin' right. He found some fucked-up shit funny."

He wouldn't put it past Arrow to have gotten the redhead to fuck with Johnnie. Not to make him cheat on Kendall, but rather to taunt him with the knowledge of what his life had been like pre-Kendall.

"You think Little Man telling on you?" Val asked with a smirk.

"Fuck, yeah," Christopher said with a sigh. Megan trusted him, but it stil aggravated the fuck out of her when bitches offered pussy to him.

Val puffed on his cigarette. "Then why didn't you tell him that was a secret between men?"

"Cuz, number fuckin' one, fuckhead, my boy ain't no goddamn man. Number fuckin' two, that mean lyin' to his ma and that shit ain't ever happenin'. My kids respectin' their mama or I'm kickin' their fuckin' asses and if they lyin' to Megan, they ain't fuckin' respectin' her."

"Me and my boys keep secrets from Zoann all the time, Outlaw."

"Cuz you a stupid motherfucker. That shit on you. As long as it ain't hurtin' Bitsy, I ain't got fuck-all to say."

"Hurtin' her? Like fuckin' other bitches?"

He nodded.

"Outlaw, fuck, you know I'm not doing anything to fuck up with Zoann. I'm just talking about shit like Ryan getting my tablet to play a fucking game and pulling up a porn site. Or a few weeks ago when a girl offered to suck my cock. Me, Ryan, and Devon was at the fucking park and she was with two of her friends. They kept looking at me and my cut and my boys.

Finally, the one who'd been staring the most came and offered to let her girlfriends look after the boys while she took me to her car and sucked me off because doing a biker was on her bucket list."

Snickering, Christopher shook his head. Some shit never changed.

"Zoann would've fucking flipped," Val went on. "I made the mistake of telling her about a similar event and she didn't fucking talk to me for an entire fucking day. Like it's my fault a bitch offer me pussy or want to give me head. So, yeah, I told Ryan there was some shit that was better if their mommie didn't know."

"Bitch-ass," Mort said with a short chuckle. "Chester would kick you in the fucking dick. That's why you told Ryan and Devon to keep your secret."

"I agree," Johnnie said. "It wasn't to spare her hurt feelings, but your whipped ass."

"Fuck off, cunt licker," Val growled, his frown darkening when they all laughed.

A shadow bounced over the table, then quickly disappeared. Christopher jumped to his feet and headed for the hallway. Flipping on the light illuminated the area, and he found Dinah lurking in the shadows.

"What the fuck you doin', Dinah?"

She shifted from foot to foot. "I want Meggie," she said, not meeting his gaze. "How is she?"

"You already fuckin' know how the fuck she doin' cuz Megan told me she saw you two days ago."

"Then she's still the same? She's still alive?"

Christopher narrowed his eyes, trying not to read too much shit into that fucked-up statement. She was a fucking psycho like Kendall. They were psycho bitches on different ends of the grid, but still fucking looped out their fucking heads. He folded his arms, determined to draw this bitch out one way or the other. He couldn't quite shake the fucking feeling that she'd betrayed them. Psychoness and all.

"My Megan not fuckin' dead like Arrow."

She bristled, but whispered, "I'm going to miss Arrow. He was my only friend here. Because of you, not even my own daughter thinks much of me."

"The fuckin' door that way," he snapped, pointing over his shoulder. "The motherfucker open in and out. Leave any-fuckin-time your ass want. 'Til you do, stay the fuck away from me and get the fuck back to your goddamn room."

Without waiting for a reply, he stalked back to the table, finding Val, Mort, and Johnnie all with bottles of rum, vodka, and scotch, respectively. An unopened bottle of tequila awaited him. He opened it and took a long swig.

"Prez, I never got the chance after church to say thanks."

He drank more tequila. "What the fuck for?"

"For making a case for Digger. I…fuck…"

"We'll see what the fuck the motherfucker gotta say for himself, Mort." Beyond that, he couldn't make any promises. For now, it was best to change the fucking subject. "Whiny-fuckin' Dinah lurkin' in the fuckin' hall. Something ain't fuckin' right about that bitch."

Johnnie lifted his brow. "In what way?"

"C'mon, Outlaw," Val said. "She crazier than a bag of fucking bunnies. That's what the fuck not right about her."

"What you getting at, Prez?" Mortician scratched at his jaw. "You still think…what exactly…?"

"She ain't seemin' all that concerned 'bout Megan and she barely blinked a fuckin' eye when I told her 'bout Arrow."

"Kendall always got the impression Dinah didn't like Arrow," Johnnie said with a shrug. "She's probably dancing for fucking joy that the poor bastard got fucked up."

Thoughtful, Val drank some rum. “She was fucking Arrow and his death don’t seem to matter.”

“She fucking brother-hopped?” Mort added with disgust.

“With both the motherfuckers ending up dead,” Johnnie concluded aloud.

Until Roxy had put the bitch in her place, Christopher bet Dinah hadn’t remembered she had a pussy to be fucked. “She ain’t shed one fuckin’ tear over Arrow, the way a bitch getting dick from a motherfucker usually do when their man get his ass shot off.”

“Not even a mumbling fucking moan?” Val asked for clarification.

“Not a motherfuckin’ mumblin’ peep,” Christopher responded.

“What are you getting at, Christopher?” Johnnie asked.

Rolling his eyes at Johnnie not putting two and fucking two together, Christopher sighed. “I’m thinkin’, John Boy, Dinah the fuckin’ traitor. She fuckin’ betrayed us.”

Silence descended over the table for a moment before the other three bombarded him with denials.

“No fucking way, Christopher. Dinah isn’t capable of that.”

“Outlaw, you know what you saying?” Val’s concern came through in his fucked-up look and his gaspy tone. “That mean Dinah have to be grounded and that would…Meggie love that bitch.”

“Prez,” Mortician began, staring at Christopher with an unreadable expression, “say that shit true? Then what? You think she found a way to contact Sharper? Or Digger, maybe?”

Christopher drained the bottle and nodded, addressing each of them one-by-one. “John Boy, bitches fuckin’ surprise motherfuckers all the time. Her fuckin’ ass wouldn’t be the first fuckin’ bitch to pretend looniness for some type of fuckin’ gain.”

He nodded to Val. "Yeah, I know what the fuck I'm saying, Val. That means I'd lose my girl cuz of fuckin' Dinah."

"Holy fuck, Outlaw," Val said with another fucking gasp, his eyes widening. "You'd fucking kill Dinah?"

"When you didn't kill Digger?" Johnnie added in outrage.

"Shut the fuck up, John Boy," Mortician warned.

"Why? You know I'm fucking telling the truth, Mortician. He'd spare Digger, but kill Dinah?" Nostrils flaring, Johnnie gritted his teeth. "Yes. I forgot. Megan will forgive you anything."

"Fuck you, John Peter." Nerves already on edge and blood roaring in his ears, Christopher got to his feet as the other three jumped to theirs. "Don't worry 'bout what the fuck Megan fuckin' do in this situation. Just fuckin' worry 'bout the fuckin' effect this bullshit had on the fuckin' club."

Brothers and Bobs were turning their way, watching another of Christopher's and Johnnie's face-offs. A tense moment slid by before Johnnie clenched his jaw and focused on his drink. "All I want to know is why you're so willing to take her out?" he asked, low. "You could exile her somewhere."

Yeah, he could. Except…he couldn't. If Dinah was the one betraying them, she was more dangerous than Digger ever had been.

"Fuck, man, we don't need this shit today."

At first, Christopher thought Mort was talking about him and Johnnie at each other's throats, until he noticed the man staring at the monitors. Particularly, the one with the camera monitoring the entrance gate, where Digger and Bunny had just been allowed in.

Swallowing back her nerves and clutching the saddlebags, Bunny opened the door to the clubhouse and paused at the huge crowd of people. The sea of bikes and overflow of men in the parking lot had been a giveaway. Still, she hadn't seen the main room so crowded in months.

This wasn't how she'd imagined approaching Outlaw, in front of most of the brothers, not only in the chapter, but the entire club. Or so it seemed. When she'd spoken to her dad right after she and Digger hit the state line a while ago and pulled over for a rest, Walt had assured Bunny Outlaw would be receptive to listen. Her parents intended to fly to New York and stay with family for a few weeks. She wasn't sure if she should be happy or concerned that they'd leave the protection of Father Struthers. Her dad was adamant it was safe to travel. The priest had only agreed to shelter them for a couple of days, which meant they needed to find other living arrangements until they could return to their house. And they couldn't do that until Sharper's men were taken care of.

Bunny had to abide by her parents' decision.

Walking through the main room and ignoring the whistles and leers coming her way, she threaded through the crowd, relieved to find Outlaw and the guys at the table. They were already standing. Now, though, instead of glaring at each other, they were focusing on her.

Outlaw's careful consideration of her made her believe he was checking her for wounds or injuries. Other than that, she couldn't detect his frame of mind. She couldn't tell if he'd deem her a traitor if he labeled Digger as one.

She'd stayed with Digger of her own accord. Not only that, but she'd instigated quite an intimate act with him. Because she liked him. Because he'd been so sweet to her, more so than any man had ever been.

In her head, she thought maybe her dislike of giving head might be linked to the men she'd performed on. That hadn't been it at all. It was the taste, even though, for the first time ever, she'd felt the true power of the act, and it hadn't been borne from monetary incentive.

"Bunny, babe, you okay?"

Her face flamed. She was thinking about sucking Digger's dick, instead of focusing on speaking to Outlaw on his behalf. "H-hi, Outlaw," she squeaked. "Mort, John Boy, Val," she added.

"Bunny," Mort said on a nod. "You looking pale as a motherfucker."

She rocked on her heels. "I'm okay. Um…Outlaw, can I talk to you?"

"Say whatever the fuck you gotta say. I'm all fuckin' ears."

Hesitating a moment, she set the saddlebags on the table and nodded to the blade peeping out. "Digger's gun is also in there." Actually, it was her father's gun. Or had been. She suspected Digger now claimed ownership. "Stretch asked me to bring the bags to you, while he and Cash searched Digger."

Although Digger hadn't been worried that Cash was dragging him toward the metal shed rumored to be named the meat shack, Bunny was terrified. "He's innocent, Outlaw," she burst out, just as Outlaw started searching one of the saddle bags, while Mort took charge of the other one. "I was there when he stole Little Man. He took me so I could take care of your son. He took care of me...he saved me from the fire when he could've left me to burn."

"He started the motherfucker," Mortician snapped. "He better have saved you, girl."

"No," she denied, shaking her head frantically. "We…there was a hidden passageway in a bedroom wall. Really, little more than a space about four feet deep…and we hid there. I fell asleep or fainted. When I came to…he said someone named Osti set the fire to smoke us out. He almost burned the three of us alive."

CJ, too. Although those words went without saying since Little Man had been with them, the implication still hung in the air. Pain and fury slashed Outlaw's features.

"Digger got us out," she said again, desperation blurring the words she spoke.

"How'd he leave you behind, sweetheart?" John Boy asked, as if the answer were important.

"I couldn't go anymore. I-I don't remember much. All I remember is the heat. I think he wanted to get CJ to safety."

"Suppose he couldn't get back out?" Val called into the silence. "Little Man would've been alone and might've wandered back into the house."

And burned to death. Bunny wished Val hadn't asked the question here. They had an audience. Of course they did. Everyone knew the bad things Digger had done. Now, they were trying to turn his heroism into something that had had little thought involved.

"That was a possibility," she conceded. "One I never looked at because the gamble paid off and we both survived. If he hadn't chanced it, I'd be dead."

Outlaw's inscrutable gaze worried Bunny. Instead of answering, he glanced at the monitors. Turning, Bunny saw Digger come into one of the frames, hands raised. Cash had a gun pointed to his head, although he was marching him toward the clubhouse.

"Fuck," Mortician managed, worry clouding his face.

The pin-drop silence seemed an ominous portent for Digger's chances of surviving. For every action Outlaw took, he expected certain reactions. By helping Digger, he'd expected, and gotten, Digger to breathe a little easier and led him to believe his life would be spared.

"Look who the Harley rode in," Cash chortled, not even an inch between the back of Digger's head and the barrel of Cash's gun.

"Shoot the fucking traitor," someone yelled.

"Let us have a piece of him, Outlaw," another voice hollered.

Digger smiled at her, his eyes encouraging her to stay strong even as calls for his death boomed all around.

Silent, Outlaw walked up to Digger and slammed his fist into his jaw in greeting.

"No, please, stop!" she begged as Digger fell to the ground and Outlaw kicked him. She started forward but Mortician grabbed her around the waist. "Stop!" she said again. "You can't kill him."

Forcing her around, Mortician grabbed her shoulders and shook her. "Outlaw doing what he have to, to save his life," he whispered.

It didn't seem that way, not what she swore she heard a bone break, but prayed it was just her overactive imagination. Digger groaned and she covered her ears, but still saw Mortician wince with each blow.

"Now, motherfucker," Outlaw snarled, around the force of his exertions, "When you fuckin' heal up, I'm fuckin' ready to fuckin' listen. You fuckin' convince me wasn't no way else to go with the shit you fuckin' done, you fuckin' live. Otherwise, I'm puttin' you to fuckin' ground."

Digger lay on the ground, coughing and bleeding from his nose and mouth. Besides Outlaw's heaving breaths, the only other sound was Digger's moans. The brothers had long since stopped their calls for his blood, since Outlaw had spilled a lot of it.

"He didn't do anything," Bunny insisted. "You can't kill him!"

"Shut the fuck up, Bunny. I know you gettin' dick from this motherfucker, so now you beggin' for his fuckin' life." Outlaw fell silent and stared at her as if he was trying to impart something to her. She couldn't understand the look he gave to Johnnie, the small nod. "Motherfucker left Megan to die. If nothin' else, he should be put the fuck to ground for that."

"We all know not to mess with Outlaw's woman," Cash said, then took in a few of the members. "Don't we?"

"What about *my* woman?" John Boy snapped, his voice so cold it almost sounded exaggerated.

Outlaw shrugged. "What the fuck 'bout that cunt?"

"Just that. You're fucking ignoring all the shit Digger risked his life for that *helped* us in the last few days."

Johnnie's words confused her. Until then, everyone had blamed Digger for all the ills befalling the club. With Kendall shot on the attack, Bunny couldn't understand Johnnie's reasoning.

"He wanted to warn us. If he'd gotten to you in time, my wife wouldn't have been shot, Christopher. Though he couldn't prevent Kendall's injuries, he saved your son. Saved Bunny."

Again, Outlaw gave her a look, one that she couldn't understand but she knew he expected her to. Then, he spoke.

"CJ *or* Bunny *or* Kendall not Megan."

She opened her mouth to scream at Outlaw. For all his good qualities, especially his blind devotion to Meggie, in this instance, it was one of the worse.

"Play along, girl," Mortician whispered, close to her ear.

She stiffened. This wasn't a game. This was life-and-death. "Outlaw, please. He saved your son. Have a heart."

"He doesn't have a heart," Dinah inserted.

As Johnnie backed up and Outlaw turned, Bunny blinked, not believing that Dinah aimed Digger's gun at Outlaw. Her hand shook and her eyes were wild and wide. "Anyone move and they get a bullet before Outlaw does."

"Put that fuckin' gun the fuck away, before you get fuckin' killed, Dinah," Outlaw growled.

Everyone else was staring at her in stunned silence. Digger, now completely unconscious, lay forgotten.

"You think you have all the power, huh, *Christopher*?" Dinah taunted, waving the gun frantically. "The power to decide whether a man lives or dies. Well, you don't. Not anymore! Arrow stole it from you and Meggie," she spat. "You turned my baby against me. You caused all my woes. You and…and…and Thomas and…and…and…"

Outlaw took a step toward her, but Dinah backed to the hallway entrance.

"You loony, fuckin', whiny bitch," he began.

"Shut the fuck up, prick," she screamed.

And, yes, Bunny could say with certainty that Dinah was insane. The desperate light in her teary eyes lacked lucidity.

"You deserve to die! You k-killed Big Joe," she sobbed. "Arrow told me."

Outraged grumbles arose amongst the men and Bunny cringed.

"Fuuuuccccckkkk, this bitch going to get us fucking killed in this motherfucker," Mortician grumbled under his breath.

"Dinah, I ain't fuckin' sure what the fuck Arrow was fuckin' smokin', but I ain't fucked up Boss."

"Arrow was just filling your head with lies," John Boy added.

Uncertainty slid into her face, but then she shook her head. "No…no! That isn't true. It can't be! That's why I helped him," she cried, her body trembling.

Outlaw held up his hands. "Dinah, put the fuckin' gun down," he repeated, softer this time. Or hand the motherfucker to me. You sick. Ain't nobody hurtin' you. We don't fuck up crazy bitches. Just gimme the fuckin' gun."

Outlaw was at a disadvantage, right in Dinah's line of fire. That didn't stop him from inching closer to her. "Dinah, you hate

Megan e-fuckin-nough to shoot me down and have her grieve for me?"

"I don't hate my daughter," she swore, slob dripping down her chin. "She hates me. She didn't do anything when that deputy put his fingers inside of me. Her main concern was protecting you and this stupid club."

"Dinah," Outlaw gritted, above another round of outraged murmurs. "Keep fuckin' talkin' and a motherfucker gonna take it on themselves to fuck you up for disrespectin' the fuckin' club. Shut the fuck up. Whatever the fuck you gotta say, take it the fuck up with me. We gotta move Digger to his old room and—"

"No! That deputy humiliated me and she…she didn't care. She interrupted me when I would've told everything. You and your stinking club would've been in jail and Meggie would be mine again. She didn't make a sound when he searched her, too, and twisted his fingers inside of her."

Rage darkened Outlaw's face and a muscle ticked in his jaw.

"He hurt her and nothing. She pretended to care about Zoann and me, and talked to us, but she hates me. Then Arrow told me I could have her back, if I helped him. He'd always said that, but…but I…I didn't want to do it, until that search. And then…then Bailey was kidnapped. Because of *letters*. K-Kaleb told me Logan was a bad man." She swiped at her cheek with the hand holding the gun. "K-P was going to give you the letters, but he wouldn't tell me where they were. When Logan got to us, I begged Kaleb to give him the letters. He wouldn't listen. He kept telling me to shut up and…and…and…Logan killed him. He just killed him! Right there. In front of me."

Not responding, Outlaw rushed toward Dinah, overpowering her and yanking the gun away, then shoving it into his waistband. He subdued Dinah against him, ignoring her struggles.

"I gave them the codes! I told them Meggie had the letters," she ranted, clawing at him. "That's why Sharper sent Cee Cee Caldwell to my old house to search. I didn't know that until later when Arrow explained. Sharper thought Big Joe had hidden the letters with Meggie. All this time, they'd been right here in the club! They kept insisting she carried the key to everything."

"Where the fuck they at now?" Outlaw grunted, pinning her to him. "Cuz them motherfuckers gone."

She laughed wildly. "They're with Meggie now and she doesn't even know it."

"Dinah, fuck, listen to me!" Outlaw demanded. "Mort gonna make you up a drink to calm you the fuck down. We gonna get you help. You really is fucked up if you saw K-P get offed by Logan, so we ain't holdin' shit against you too much. You just gotta co-op-afuckin-rate."

"No, fuck you! Fuck you. All of you killed K-P and all of you killed Big Joe. And now you're killing my baby. That's why I fed Arrow whatever information I could and what I couldn't feed to him, I gave to Peyton. Me! I did. I let them in that morning. They were supposed to ambush you in your house. In your fuckin' bed and give me back my Meggie once I led them to the letters. Me and Meggie and Arrow were all going to live happily ever after, but you shot Arrow and you shot my baby."

Outlaw loosened his hold on Dinah. "I didn't shoot Arrow and I'd never kill your baby," he said in a soothing voice. "No matter what else you think of me, you know I love her."

"You don't! Everyone knows that. And Peyton hated you like I did. You threw her sister over after you promised to marry Ellen."

"*What?*" he bellowed, shock etching into his face. "I ain't ever fuckin' intended to marry no bitch. Not even Megan—"

"Liar! Ellen told Peyton how Meggie took you away from her. She wanted revenge."

Nostrils flaring, Outlaw swallowed. Bunny couldn't remember ever seeing him so upset. It wasn't only anger in his eyes, but regret and sadness.

"Dinah—"

"No! Peyton wanted revenge."

Outlaw shook Dinah. "Against Megan," he snarled. "Not me. Fuck, Dinah, that's why that cunt shot Megan. Now the shit make sense to me. But *you* let her on the premises to hurt your own girl."

She pounded against his chest. "I didn't," she yelled. "They were giving Meggie to me."

Johnnie stepped closer when Outlaw released her completely. "Where did Megan's kids fit into this?"

Mortician nodded to his unconscious brother. "And Digger?"

At the mention of Digger, Bunny worried her bottom lip and glanced at where he lay prone between two tables, before gazing at the clock. Only twenty minutes between the time Outlaw had begun beating Digger to *now.*

"What about Digger?" Dinah wept. "Sharper thought he was nothing but a fucking idiot. He was going to shoot him down but he got away. Always loyal to you and you and you and you," she repeated over and over again, pointing to Outlaw. Mortician. Johnnie. Val. Cash. And brothers whom Bunny had never seen. Dinah was just randomly selecting men to point to and pin the word *you* on. "Arrow and Sharper wanted to reach their goals and they were going to help me and Peyton reach ours."

Sagging into a seat near Digger's saddlebags, Dinah buried her face into her hands and cried so hard Bunny couldn't help but to pity her. The woman had been through a lot and thought she had been doing the right thing. Most other outfits would've put Dinah down for such a betrayal, but Outlaw meant they didn't hurt women if it could be helped.

"Mort, get Digger to his room," Outlaw began hoarsely, and Bunny had never seen him look so haggard, sound so exhausted. "John Boy, escort Bunny to my house. Cash, find a place for Dinah where I can send her to. She'll need twenty-four hour guard. Val, mean-fuckin-time, get Dinah to her room for now and keep watch on her, 'til I talk to..." He glanced away, but then cleared his throat and stiffened his shoulders. "I gotta let Megan know her ma not doin' well."

"No!" Dinah's shout sounded inhumane as she flew behind Outlaw.

His eyes widening, he staggered back and fell hard into a chair.

"You fuckin' stabbed me," he pushed out, then slumped over, revealing a knife in his upper back.

Dinah gasped, shock traveling over her face, her mouth open in a silent scream.

Everyone stilled for a split second. Then, suddenly, gunfire burst from various directions, bullets hitting Dinah in the head, neck, and upper body. The blasts drowned out Bunny's horrified shrieks at the sight of all the blood flying from the woman as she fell, dead before she hit the floor.

The near-inconsolable sobs breached Christopher's fog and he lifted his eyelids, his upper shoulder burning like a motherfucker. Weakness threatened to topple him right the fuck over, so he knew he hadn't been stitched yet. Blood still oozed out of him.

But he felt her weight, too. His Megan, clinging to him, her fingers pressing against his wound. To keep pressure on it, he knew. The scent of cherry blossoms filled his nostrils and he drew in deep, fortifying his strength by the smell and feel of her.

"Megan, sweetheart, we've got to move Christopher," Johnnie crooned softly, and Christopher felt the tug, knew his brother was attempting to pull his wife away.

Instead, she held tighter, cried harder. "I'm so sorry. I'm so sorry. I'm so sorry," she chanted. "I can't believe Momma stabbed him. Where is she? I swear, Johnnie, when I get my hands on her, I'll escort her myself to wherever Christopher wants to send her."

"Oh, please," Kendall said around a snort.

Christopher tensed and a little more blood seeped out.

"You're all full of blood, Meggie," Kendall got out.

"Meggie girl, c'mon, make sure everything ready in Prez's room," Mortician cut in. "We have to move him."

"He needs a hospital," she countered.

"No," Johnnie came back harshly. "He doesn't fucking need a hospital. This is club business. We'll handle it here."

"He needs a hospital," she insisted stubbornly. "I was sent to a hospital and that was club business."

"You were dying," Johnnie snapped. "He isn't. We'll stitch him back up just fine, but you've got to move…fuck it," he growled.

All of a sudden, Christopher lost the feel of Megan completely.

"What are you doing, Johnnie?" Kendall gasped in outrage.

"Put me down!" Megan shouted.

Christopher slid his eyelids up a little more, just in time to see Johnnie set Megan on her feet and shove her toward the hallway.

He grunted, too low for anyone to fucking hear him, because the fucking anarchy continued.

"There I put you fucking down, Megan," Johnnie yelled. "But if you don't fucking *move,* so we can get Christopher to his room, I'll fucking pick you up again and *carry* you myself."

She must've listened because Christopher no longer felt her presence. If he wasn't so fucking weak, he'd get the fuck up and slam his fist down Johnnie's throat, then cut off his fucking hands for shoving her.

"You think that shit was wise?" Mortician gritted. "Meggie girl going through enough without *you* getting your full asshole on."

"It got her moving," Johnnie retorted. "She can cry on him once he's stitched up."

A shadow loomed over Christopher and he grunted a-fucking-gain. Still not a motherfucker heard him.

"Meggie needs to know *everything* about Dinah's betrayal," Kendall said briskly. "She thinks the woman escaped. She doesn't know she's laid out riddled with bullets or that *she* was the one who betrayed the club."

"Red, c'mon, girl, what'll that do to Meggie girl but break her heart knowing her mama was such a traitor. Don't you think she's been through enough?"

"I'm not blaming *you*, Mortician. I blame *him*."

Christopher shifted slightly, amping up the fucking grunt to a fucking groan.

Nothing. Motherfuckers were letting him fucking bleed to death. That's fucking why he was too fucking weak to move.

"Blame me, gorgeous," Johnnie said with an irritated sigh. "It was my call."

"The asshole won't agree with it," Kendall pointed out. "He thinks Meggie should know everything. It's *Johnnie* who wants to protect her from the truth. Well, protecting me never helped. You can't take it upon yourself to protect another man's wife, especially if your wife doesn't agree."

"Kendall, fuck," Johnnie said in exasperation. "It'll be Christopher's final decision, but none of us want Megan to suffer that type of heartache. Please, take a few deep breaths and be reasonable about this."

Better yet, go sit the fuck down somewhere and be as fucking unreasonable as you fuckin' wanna. Just get the fuck away from my fuckin' stabbed ass.

"Megan's finally a full-grown woman. Twenty-one. As an adult, she has no choice but to handle this."

"Jesus fucking Christ, Kendall. Go and fucking tell her," Johnnie bellowed. "If it makes you happier and this time on you easier, go tell her all the fuck about Dinah."

"You called me to help!"

Yep, cuz he was a stupid motherfucker like that.

"My opinion is that withholding information from her isn't in her best interests."

"No, it's not in *your* best interest," Johnnie snapped, cheering up Christopher until Kendall started to cry.

"Great going, motherfucker," Mortician said sarcastically.

Christopher squinted, trying to bring the scene into sharper focus. He thought he saw Mort hug Kendall.

"Red, what the fuck's got into you since you got shot? I mean, we going through enough bullshit."

"She's pregnant," Johnnie mumbled.

Yeah, Christopher would mumble that shit, too, cuz that meant the return of super psycho bitch.

"Well, fuck. Now, I know what the fuck got into her."

Christopher grunted a laugh. Leave it Mort to make a joke.

"Prez?"

Squinting, he opened his eyes further. A blurry image of Mort loomed in front of him. "Yo."

"Christopher?" Johnnie called, sounding relieved.

"You fuckin' shoved Megan, motherfucker," Christopher got out weakly. "I'm beatin' your fuckin' ass for that."

Mort snickered. "Meggie girl don't have to worry. You going to be just fucking fine."

Instead of responding to Christopher, Johnnie pulled Kendall into his arms. "I'm sorry, sweetheart. Okay? Let me escort you to our old room, so you can rest."

"Okay," she said miserably. "You think I should get back on my medicine?"

"Uh..." Johnnie's voice trailed off. "Whatever you want to do, I'm behind you one hundred percent."

"That's the fucking problem," Mort said under his breath.

"Mortician's right," she said tearfully. "I don't want to start...I'm way past that. Meggie and me have made up and everything."

"Shhh, it's okay," Johnnie swore. "Kendall, listen to me. I'd prefer if you were on your medicines. The OB has assured you it's safe for the baby."

"None of those drugs are safe!"

Johnnie sighed. "Sit, gorgeous. Let me help Mort get Christopher to his room and then we'll talk."

"Okay."

"You up for walking, Prez?" Mort asked, already positioning himself on one side of Christopher, while Johnnie got on the other side.

The clubhouse was quiet, as if the massive crowd from earlier had all been an illusion, although Christopher knew better. He knew the scene with him and Dinah had played out in front of officers and members from this chapter and others.

Fucking Dinah…whiny, *loony* motherfucking Dinah had fucking *stabbed* him and…*fuck*.

He halted halfway to his room. "Dinah dead?"

"As a motherfucker," Mort confirmed. "*We* didn't pull on her, but brothers take it as a personal fucking insult when she try to fuck up our Prez. Not only do you run the mother chapter, but you the prez over the entire organization. That's serious shit, Outlaw."

"Fuck, I know, Mort," Christopher growled, starting forward again, his shoulder hurting with each move he took. "After she fuckin' bragged about bein' a fuckin' traitor, she fuckin' stabbed me." None of his brothers knew if she would've turned a weapon on them. He *understood*. That didn't fucking mean he had to like it.

Johnnie pushed his bedroom door fully opened and Christopher swayed between them. Megan sat on the edge of the bed, her eyes and nose red from her silent weeping. How many fucking tears had been shed over the past month?

How much *blood*?

He'd known the cost of getting to Sharper would be extraordinarily high, so he'd dragged his ass about bringing shit to a head.

"Christopher!" Megan cried, running to him, but just catching herself before she launched into his arms. She smiled through her tears. "You're on your feet."

He nodded. "Take more than…" He trailed his voice off, not sure what to say.

"More than my mother," Megan whispered, an endless amount of hurt in her eyes. "I'm so sorry."

Grabbing her hand, he started forward again before he fell on his fucking ass. Together, the four of them got to the bed, where Christopher fell onto his stomach.

"Call Bitsy. Tell her to come stitch me up."

"I'll do it," Johnnie volunteered. "She's helping Roxy with the kids."

"Is anyone looking for momma?" Megan asked quietly.

"We will, Meggie girl," Mort promised. "We just had to get shit under control here first. Don't worry about nothing."

Silence, and then, "I need to talk to Christopher alone."

Out of the corner of his eye, Christopher saw her draw her knees up and lean against her favorite brick wall. When they were alone, he waited for her to speak.

"The wound has to be superficial," she said finally. "Otherwise, you'd been dead by now."

He tried to smile at her soft words. Mostly, he just wanted her pain to go away. He'd give up his fucking life if it meant she didn't look so devastated. Despite her rapid blinks, tears streamed down her face and he reached out his hand.

She stared at it, instead of automatically taking it as usual. Closing her eyes, she shuddered and Christopher removed his hand. Even as he understood, her withdrawal stung. He wanted to believe their earlier argument contributed to her action.

"Megan—"

"She's dead, isn't she?" she interrupted.

"I didn't kill her," he blurted before he considered the words confirmed Megan's fear. "Megan, baby…"

"There's nothing you can say that'll take this away," she said quietly. "She was my mother and I loved her."

He swallowed. "I know."

"You've got to let me grieve for her."

"Whatcha tellin' me?" Or trying to tell him, because she was getting at something, that was for fucking certain.

"That I loved my mother." Her face crumpled and she licked her lips, trying and failing to control her tears. "But she tried to hurt you. Take you away from me. I don't…" She cried harder. "Had she lived, how could I have had anything to do with her *ever again*?"

Instead of holding out his hand, he fucked with his stab wound by lifting up and dragging himself closer to her. This time, she curled next to him and allowed him to thread his fingers through her hair. Pain and confusion darkened her blue eyes.

"Where is she?"

"I don't fuckin' know, baby."

"Please don't let them…the meat shack…"

"Fuck, no, baby, I swear, I ain't gonna let that happen to her. We'll give her a proper fuckin' burial."

"Put her in Daddy's grave."

"Let's talk 'bout it later, Megan." When she wasn't so upset and he could remind her that the grave had just been opened for Arrow. It was still sealed. Dinah would have to go in the grave with Patricia. "Tomorrow or the next day."

She nodded. "Do you think she's finally at peace? Her and Daddy are together again?"

"I don't fuckin' know. I ain't ever thought 'bout questions like that too fuckin' deep. Me and God ain't got the best relationship."

Her fingertips skated along his jawline and he leaned into her touch.

"We're going to survive this," she whispered. "And we're going to come out stronger for it. We've both lost so much and…and I still don't really know why. Because of your grandfather's sex trafficking? Sharper's involvement? Both? Does it have something to do with Big Joe? Or Sharper's mega-church? What's so important that so many people have had to die? Our son, Patrick. Kendall's unborn baby. Her sister and mother. Bev. Avery. Nia. Sasha and your other two nieces. Tyler. K-P and Arrow and Momma and…" Voice trailing off, she swallowed a sob, but Christopher knew what she'd been about to say.

"And Big Joe, huh, baby?"

Her chin wobbled, but she nodded once more. He palmed away her tears.

"I know you…don't see it that way. That he was just an evil man who deserved to die."

"Megan, baby, if I once fuckin' did, I don't now. Not all the fuckin' way. In that fuckin' moment, I had to fuckin' choose. Him or me. I fuckin' chose me and I hated him for makin' me have to make that fuckin' choice. But Big Joe ain't even had a fuckin' choice. He was as much a casualty as Arrow and K-P, and don't let no motherfucker ever fuckin' tell you other-fuckin-wise."

"If Daddy hadn't been killed the year before we met, I'd think this had something to do with me."

It did, thanks to fucking Dinah, but he'd never tell Megan that. Some shit she never needed to fucking know, and he'd fucking kill whoever he had to, to keep her in the dark.

"We gonna get through this," he swore, echoing her words. "We gonna bury our family members and we gonna stand fuckin' strong. You and me. Just like we always fuckin' do. Just trust me to get motherfuckin' Sharper and make this shit right."

She lifted up on an elbow and touched her lips to his before asking, "Isn't he dead?"

"That's what the fuck motherfuckers reportin'. I just don't fuckin' believe it. I ain't *ever* fuckin' believin' it."

Sharper's death in a hotel accident was just too fucking anticlimactic to stomach.

"Christy, I'm sorry I took so long," Zoann cried, rushing into the room without warning.

"Fuck it, Bitsy," Christopher responded, turning his head toward her. "I got fucked up more than a fuckin' hour ago. This shit hurt like a motherfucker, but it's fuckin' superficial."

Megan helped Zoann to get him out of his cut and rubbing each little spot she touched. "He lost consciousness."

Like a pussy. "Initial fuckin' shock, baby. Motherfuckers ain't expectin' to get stabbed in the fuckin' back."

Her hand hesitated before continuing her touches. "I understand," she said in a small voice.

Before Christopher pulled his foot the fuck out of his mouth, Roxy rushed in with Mort and Johnnie right behind her.

"Meggie, sugar, we think we know where Dinah—"

"I already know she's dead," Megan said in a trembly voice.

Johnnie choked and Christopher glared at him.

Mortician coughed. "You do?"

"You're okay, Megan?" Johnnie asked.

She didn't answer and Christopher wished he could turn to see her death stare. As long as he wasn't the fucking recipient, he thought her looks fucking hilarious.

"Look, fuck, I'm sorry. We needed to get Christopher to his room and I had to get you moving."

"Yeah, and your ass was about to be incinerated into dust with the way Red was looking at you when you picked up Meggie girl."

"Kendall has been irritated," Zoann said in distracted tones, pressing against Christopher's wound. "Why? Something going on at the office? Or is this because of the shootings here?"

Christopher waited for Johnnie to speak into the silence, clouded with anticipation.

"She's decided to stop all meds until she delivers the baby."

"Well, fuck," Roxy said as Meggie groaned.

"Congratulations, Johnnie," Zoann chortled. "You've just re-entered fucking hell."

"Megan, the point is—"

"The point is nothing, Johnnie," Megan huffed. "Okay? Nothing at all. I'm not your whipping girl to take out all your frustrations on. Every time you're stressed, I take the brunt of your anger. I have a remedy for that."

"What?" he asked carefully.

"Not talking to you. *Ever* again."

"I don't want—"

"This is..." Her voice broke and Christopher reached out blindly to her. He couldn't turn because Zoann had begun to prep his shoulder for the stitching. He didn't even know exactly where she sat. "The body count is so high," she continued, grabbing Christopher's hand and holding tightly. "We need to stick together. We all know how Kendall gets when..."

When psycho bitch wasn't fucking doing what the fuck she was supposed to do.

Instead of saying that, Megan cleared her throat. "We can overlook that because we know it'll pass once she delivers your baby. But us? She's going to need our support and this club definitely needs our support. We need to stand together."

"Sugar, you right," Roxy agreed. "But what you need right now is a good cry. All this has been so fucking stressful and you need a moment to process it."

No the fuck she didn't. At least, not with Roxy, until Christopher clued her the fuck in on *what* Megan knew.

"Meggie?" Bunny called.

"Bunny!" Meggie gasped, bouncing the mattress as she scrambled off. "Oh my God! You're here. You're safe. And…Where's Digger? Is he okay? He saved my son. You, too. I have to thank him. Thank *you*," she rambled. "Momma's dead. She…she attacked Christopher for no reason at all and…and…"

She didn't pick up on this round of silence, but her tearful babbling had just saved motherfuckers from opening their fucking mouths and letting Dinah's betrayal slip.

"Where's Digger?" she finished.

Bunny cleared her throat. "Resting."

"Resting?" Megan echoed suspiciously. "But…but you stopped in to say hello."

Gritting his teeth at the alcohol Zoann kept fucking pouring on his open fucking skin, Christopher decided to come clean. "Cuz the motherfucker was here already, baby. I stomped the motherfucker for what the fuck he did. When he heal the fuck up, I'm gonna thank the fuck outta him for what he fuckin' did for our boy."

Bunny watched Meggie's surprise morph into acceptance. She looked completely wrecked, so Bunny hugged her again. She'd left Digger's room to search for food, but, as she passed Outlaw's old bedroom, she saw the door opened.

"Would it be okay if I went to the house and saw Little Man, Rule, and Rebel?" she asked, still unsure about where she fit in here.

"Of course!" Megan said automatically. "Why would you even ask such a question?"

Outlaw sighed. "Oh, yeah, probably cuz I fucked up Trader, the mornin' of the fuckin' attack."

Even injured, the man made no apologies.

"Omigod, you did what?" Meggie whirled to her husband, then back to Bunny, as if she didn't know who to look at.

"Ain't had a choice, baby. The motherfucker was fuckin' up Bunny some kinda way just like you said. I ain't got fuckin' time to try to make that bullshit right. Motherfuckers know I ain't toleratin' that bullshit, but half the members think how another motherfucker handle their old lady *that* motherfucker business, so they wouldna fuckin' taken no sanctions against Trader. Blowin' him the fuck away was the only fuckin' option."

"Umkay," Meggie responded after a few moments of working her throat to form a reply.

"Outlaw, I need to show you something," Cash announced, breezing into the room, holding up a flip phone.

"You 'bout finished, Bitsy?"

"Almost."

"We have to leave, right?" Meggie asked, sounding as if that was the last thing she wanted to do.

"Yeah, baby. Just for a few minutes."

"I'll check on Digger," she said, backing toward the door.

Bunny followed her friend back to the room she'd been in, tending to his injuries.

"Christopher did that?" Meggie asked on a gasp, staring at Digger's swollen and bruised face.

Bunny pursed her lips and nodded slowly.

"He went a little overboard," she grumbled.

"I think so, too," Bunny agreed. "I thought he was going to kill him."

"All right, you two, don't go blaming Outlaw for what the fuck he had to do as the club's president," Roxy chided, gliding into the room and hugging Bunny. "I missed you, sugar. I was so worried about you."

"I'm fine," Bunny reassured her, warmed by Roxy's genuine tone. "And I'm not really blaming Outlaw. I know Digger had it coming to him."

Roxy went to the side of Digger's bed and adjusted the covers, patting him when he grunted. "Digger had death coming to him. We all know that. Right, Meggie?"

"Yes."

"You angry at him for what he did?" Roxy asked.

"Not really. It's just all the death…"

"Sharper's gone," Roxy soothed. "So things should get back to normal."

Megan swiped at her tears. "Christopher doesn't believe Sharper's dead. And even if he is, what about the girls? The church needs to go. I'll bet that's where the ring is operated from."

"Listen to me, sugar. Don't worry about the girls. If there are any left. Sharper was on the run for months. I doubt the operation could continue with Logan dead and Sharper gone."

"I'm going…there are probably brothers here and…they need to eat," Meggie said as if she were in a trance.

"Fuck them," Roxy commanded. "You been through too much shit today, so let Digger rest."

"Do you know where momma is? I want to see her."

No. Meggie really didn't want to see Dinah filled with holes, her eyes and mouth wide open.

"Why don't we go to her room?" Bunny suggested instead.

"Christopher said I could bury her."

"Then that's what's going to happen," Roxy promised. "Go with Bunny and I'll see who to call to get her."

"She was shot?" Megan asked.

Bunny drew her brows together. "You don't know?"

"No. I just knew…she tried to stab *Outlaw* in front of a roomful of his brothers." Meggie snorted. "There was no way she'd survive that."

It was that as much as her actions before the stabbing, Bunny knew, although she remained silent. It seemed as if Meggie knew nothing about the rest of it.

"You right, sugar," Roxy said.

"What happened exactly? Why in the world would my mother try to kill my husband? Whatever he might've said, or did, nothing was bad enough to do what she did."

"Dinah grabbed the knife from Digger's bag and stabbed Outlaw when he turned his back. I don't think she intended to do it," Bunny explained because Meggie needed to know some of the facts. "She just wanted to have you to herself again and saw him as the obstacle. Only a moment went by before guns were blazing."

Meggie covered her mouth to hold back a sob. "I'm so angry with her for hurting Christopher and getting herself killed."

Roxy hugged Meggie, who laid her head against Roxy's shoulder and cried. "It's okay, sugar. I'm mad as hell at her, too. However you need to get through this, do it. Now, let's go sit in the main room and wait for the boys to finish whatever the fuck was so important."

Moses: *Do you have the key?*

Dinah: *Yes.*

Moses: *Meet me at the park entrance.*

Dinah: *Will it end now?*

Moses: *As soon as I kill Outlaw, Johnnie, Val, Digger, and Mortician.*
Dinah: *But Meggie will be spared? You promised.*
Moses: *She will. Her kids won't be.*
Dinah: *I don't care as long as she loves me again.*
Moses: *I'll take care of it all. I promise.*
Dinah: *Sharper, K-P wouldn't have wanted all this death.*
Moses: *Sharper burned to death in a hotel explosion, cunt. Remember?*
Dinah: *Now I do.*
Moses: *K-P? He was with them, so of course he wouldn't want them dead. You're on Arrow's side. Again…remember?*
Dinah: *I think.*
Moses: *Just bring me the fucking key. Now that they think I'm dead, I'm sure security will be relaxed. It'll be easier to hit the club this last time. I've recruited more men. All the girls are sold and I have your share to make a new life for you and your daughter. Just trust me.*
Dinah: *That's what Arrow told me.*
Moses: *You've done excellent.*
Dinah: *What about the letters?*
Moses: *I want to take them into possession myself in victory. I will have breached Outlaw's fortress. I just need the key so I can get back to LA for my, er, funeral in three days. I want to personally see my send-off.*
Dinah: *But I thought you were alive.*
Moses: *Forget it.*
Dinah: *Meggie loves him. Will she hate me?*
Moses: *Only if you tell her your role.*

Unlike the first three times he read the messages aloud, this time around, Christopher recited each line under his breath, finding no satisfaction in being proven right about Sharper.

A few facts stood out to Christopher as he leaned against the headboard, still weak and in pain. The most noticeable detail was Dinah hadn't been completely present for her role. She'd had one goal, but both Sharper and Arrow had used her fragile mind for their gain.

That made her death all the more fucked-up, but Christopher tucked that away for when he got his hands on motherfucking Sharper.

The next item he finally figured out was there was an actual fucking key. What the fuck it led to was a fucking mystery and what the fuck it was...

"You find any other fuckin' phones in her fuckin' room, Cash?" Christopher asked, not looking up and scrolling through the messages again. Apparently, Johnnie had sent Cash in to search Dinah's room, once she'd been killed. So the phone he'd confiscated had been legit while the fucking burner had been stashed.

"Nothing but that, Outlaw."

"I need to get in that fuckin' church for Sharper's send-off," Christopher announced, another idea forming in his head.

"You got a fucking death wish, Prez? You'd look like you killed an innocent motherfucker if you go and blast Sharper."

"True, Mort. Unless we got my fuckin' ass in there without that motherfucker seein' me and then gave all those motherfuckers a reason to fuckin' run."

"We don't kill innocent people," Johnnie reminded him.

Christopher scowled. "I ain't talkin' 'bout killin' no-fuckin-body but fuckin' Sharper and whoever the fuck else on his fuckin' side."

"Prez, we don't—"

"This simple shit, Mort. Put me in a fuckin' casket, roll my motherfuckin' ass to the front of the fuckin' church. When I can't take the fuckin' bullshit 'bout Sharper bein' such a wonderful motherfucker, I raise the fuckin' lid. You think motherfuckers ain't gonna scatter?"

"Where do you come up with this shit, Christopher?" Johnnie asked, and Christopher didn't know if he was awed or fucking outraged.

"The fucking logistics of that might not make this possible," Cash pointed out.

"The plannin' and shit gonna be a fuckin' nightmare," Christopher agreed, "but this shit gone on long e-fuckin-nough. We blowin' that motherfucker to hell."

"Fuck, Christopher," Johnnie groaned. "Somehow I knew you'd say that."

"Prez, you trying to get us caught. Blowing up Sharper's church is going to make international news."

"We either fuckin' doin' this now or we sittin' round this motherfucker waitin' for Sharper to fuckin' move."

"So if we do Sharper in LA, we won't get him in the meat shack?" Johnnie asked with a disappointed sigh.

"Fuck, you right. Tell you what. Let's try to fuckin' take him a-fuckin-live. That's one motherfucker who need to be awake when we start."

Cash headed for the door. "I guess I better start planning everything."

"You're sure about this?"

"John Boy, I know your woman got your kid in her again, so you ain't gotta come. And, Mort, Bailey carryin' your kid, too, and still recoverin'. I understand if it gotta be just me and Cash."

"Prez, you know we not letting you do your kamikaze shit alone. I'm in. If you got the fucking balls to get in a fucking casket and roll in that motherfucker, I got the fucking nuts to back your ass up."

"I'm in," Johnnie said without hesitation. "It would just be easier if we got him on *our* turf."

It sure the fuck would be, but it was what it was. “Defense ain’t never been something I cared for,” Christopher explained, although he was sure they fucking knew his style. “This shit require goin’ on the offense and wipin’ that entire fuckin’ organization out. Sharper started this fuckin’ war. My ass endin’ it within three days, any fuckin’ way I gotta.”

Moaning, Digger stirred on his cot, drawing in a long breath. It didn't hurt to breathe, but pain exploded everywhere else on him. Jaws. Head. Stomach. Back. Legs. Ass.

He blinked the eye that wasn't swollen to a mere slit, narrowing his view of his surroundings. Fuck. He'd survived. Outlaw had beat the fuck out of him, but he hadn't taken his life. What that meant, he wasn't sure. One thing he *did* know was other brothers might sneak and put a bullet in his head. The calls for his death underscored the many enemies he'd made with his actions.

Even if that didn't happen, Digger wasn't so sure he'd ever be welcomed back into the club. Drawing in another breath at his stupidity destroyed everybody's trust in him, Digger glanced around, taking in the familiar comfort of his old room.

It surprised him to find not much had changed. Posters of Rick James, Wiz Khalifa, muscle cars, and naked girls still plastered his walls. A framed music sheet with the lyrics to *Mary Jane* and *So High*—Digger swore they were the best songs ever made—hung beside the picture of Rick and Wiz, respectively.

Mort had gotten one of the bitches he'd fucked pre-Bailey to write the words in calligraphy. Even the copyright information at the bottom was in a pretty scroll.

"No, I didn't tear that shit off the fucking wall and throw it the fuck away after your dumb ass deserted me."

Mortician's growl forced more awareness into Digger and he glanced around, clutching the covers tighter as Mort stepped out of the shadows, dragging a chair he must've been sitting on, with him.

"Mort?"

Dropping into the seat, Mort's jaw clenched. Only the bedside lamp lit the room, but his brother sat close enough for Digger to see every emotion on his face. "It's me, Mark."

Mark. Not Digger. He hadn't been Mark to Mortician in years. His heart sank at the strongest indicator yet that he no longer had a place in the club. Struggling to sit up, he grunted at his efforts, too stubborn to ask for assistance when it had to be clear to Mort that Digger needed help.

"I guess you here to blast my ass," he said, once he managed to lean halfway against the headboard. When Mort stayed silent, a horrifying thought occurred to Digger. Outlaw had once charged Mort with the task of killing him. Not only because Mort was the enforcer but because Outlaw wanted to test Mort's loyalty. Maybe, that's why his brother had been lurking in the shadows, awaiting Digger's return to consciousness. Irony was a fucking bitch. He'd always laughed at Mort's tales of motherfuckers pissing themselves when they discovered Mort waiting for them. This shit was *not* funny. At all.

Digger measured his brother's size against his own. He was taller than Mortician, but so much leaner. Mort's massive hands alone could cause serious damage to Digger with one or two blows. He didn't even want to think about his brother's arm strength that would allow the man to snap him in half.

His locks framed his face, so Digger didn't know if he wore his diamond studs or not, but the skull ring on his right hand was as prominently displayed as his wedding band on the left.

Tension hung in the air, perspiration beading Digger's brow, despite the comfortable room temperature.

"I don't blame you for hating me," he began, understanding why motherfuckers just started blurting pleas and excuses to Mort when he hunted them down. "The shit I did unforgivable."

Narrowing his eyes, Mort glared at him.

"With the exception of trying to warn Outlaw about what was coming with Sharper's attack, I'd do it all over again to save you." Would any words make a difference in this situation?

Digger squirmed under Mort's darkening stare, the same he'd directed at motherfuckers set to die at his hands.

"You want to beat my ass, too?" In serious fucking pain, he croaked out his challenge.

"Don't tempt me, fuckhead," Mort gritted.

Digger heeded the advice, in no position to defend himself. At one time, he'd been ranked third in the organization. If Mort hit him, he had the authority to retaliate. That never stopped Mort from fucking Digger up on several occasions. Caught between being a traitor and a civilian again, his brother would be brutal. Therefore, he'd let Mort have his say, so he could leave.

"I know you're angry, Mortician. Just get whatever the fuck you have to say out and get the fuck going."

His burst of bravery faltered when Mort leaned forward, elbows on knees, and cowered Digger with his unconcealed fury.

"You know how much I fucking vouched for you? Not only to Prez but the entire fucking club."

"I know," he confessed, hanging his head.

Outlaw had wanted Mortician as Sergeant-at-Arms and Digger as the enforcer, but Mort had declined and asked for the ballot to be switched. "You been elected in my spot yet?"

"Fuck you," Mort spat.

Digger started to bolt to an upright position until he moved and bumped against the headboard as he plopped back.

"I never understood why you passed up the position in the first place," he groaned. "Some bullshit about my rash decisions. I was still the same motherfucker, only in a higher position in the club. You could've become SAA and said I just wasn't fucking qualified to be the enforcer."

"I swear to Jesus Christ, you one ungrateful motherfucker, son. You want to know why I asked Prez to choose your dumb ass?"

"Because you felt sorry for your kid brother. He didn't have it in him to become an officer without *you*."

"You sure the fuck didn't," Mort returned without remorse.

Digger flinched at the brutal honesty, the first time this was out in the open between them. Before it had been a dirty little tidbit that no one talked about.

"You think I didn't fucking know how much you hated living in my shadow?"

The question shocked him into silence. It was something else he hadn't considered. He'd just accepted it as his life as Mortician's brother.

"Stupid motherfucker," Mort said with disgust. "I wouldn't have been qualified to be your goddamn brother if I didn't know what the fuck yanked your chains. Even though your dumb ass responsible *for* putting yourself in my shadow. It wasn't something I ever wanted. You fucking helped it along."

By imitating Mort in almost everything. Hair. Attitude. Clothes. But the truth couldn't be hidden forever if the reality he'd chosen for himself had been a lie.

"Can't live in my fucking shadow ranked third in the fucking club," Mort grumbled into the silence.

Digger stared at the ceiling, during the one-eye blinking again. "I don't understand how I envy you so much but love you as much."

"You don't envy me, Digger. You jealous, straight-the-fuck-up, so don't try to call it nothing fucking else. Give me that much respect and credit to tell me the goddamn truth."

"Mort—"

"Shut the fuck up, you stupid motherfucker."

"Second time in thirty seconds you fucking called me that. Don't fucking do it again."

"Or what? You getting up to beat my ass? *Stupid motherfucker*."

Growling, Digger squinted his good eye at Mort.

"I have a right to be pissed *and* to call you a stupid motherfucker every hour on the fucking hour for the rest of your fucking life. You know what the fuck you put me through these past months? No, fuck that. Your dumb ass know what the fuck you put me through *today*? I had to watch you get your brainless fucking ass beat to a fucking pulp this evening. I had to listen to Prez and John Boy pretend to pit Meggie and Kendall and who was more important. But it wasn't far from fucking pretense. One of them motherfuckers said something *too* real and shit would've got ugly real fucking fast and you would've ended up with a fucking bullet in your brain."

"As if that made a difference. Outlaw and John Boy always pitted against each other because of Meggie and Kendall."

"Shit's gotten better in the past year. It's a little fucked up again with Red pregnant right now."

"I don't understand how Outlaw and Johnnie's words about their women made a difference."

"No?" Mort bared his teeth in a semblance of a bitter smile. "You beaten half to death and Prez say he finishing you off because of Meggie girl and how you left her. John Boy mention you being involved in the attack that got Red shot. Prez saying he didn't give a fuck. It didn't even matter that you came to warn us or that you saved Little Man or that you took care of Bunny. None of the shit you did for the club mattered because of your actions against Meggie. He knew what the fuck he was doing. Did he mean that shit? I know he fucking meant every word, but if he took it upon himself to stop after he'd been accused of going easy on me for not finding you, who the fuck know what would've fucking happened."

"Mortician—"

"Don't *Mortician* me, motherfucker. You turned your fucking back on me, Prez, and the entire club. For what? You and me the only motherfuckers left in our family."

"No. Maybe, you are for me, but you have Bailey and your daughter."

Eyes widening, Mort stared at Digger, before he began to laugh. But it wasn't a happy laugh. It was more of a so-pissed-it's-too-fucking-funny-to-describe sound.

"I finally fucking get it," Mort said, shaking his head, still chuckling without humor. "Although I haven't until right now. Fucking sad, too, because maybe some of this would've been avoided."

"What do you get, Mortician?" Digger snapped, this conversation wearing on him. He needed something for the pain. He needed to think.

He needed Bunny.

Bunny. "Where the fuck Bunny at?"

"With Meggie."

"Can you call her and ask her to come in here to keep me company?" he asked, unsure where his burner was.

"I might," Mort agreed, not in the least curious about Digger's request. "Once I finish with you."

"Will there be anything left for her to entertain?"

Mort threaded his fingers through his locks. “Prez knew about all the times I crossed fucking paths with you and let you live. He knew he was risking my life and his own. But he fucking did it anyway. For months, he let me half-ass on the search…He…” Blowing out a frustrated breath, he shook his head. “Don’t you think I have a fucking right to be pissed?”

“Yeah, Mort,” Digger agreed gravely, swallowing hard. “I don’t know how, but I’ll make it up to you. I promise. I-I don’t know what else to say. I guess the only thing left *to* say is I love you.”

“I know,” Mort said, nodding. “That’s why you did a lot of what you did.”

The grin Digger gave his brother hurt his face. “Sound like you suffering from the same brotherly love sickness that I am.”

“Fucking dumb ass,” Mort grumbled, flipping Digger off and straightening in the chair.

“I’m sorry for what I did. For everything.”

Sliding his chair as close as he could, Mort raised his fist and Digger did the same. His hand trembled through the fist bump, but the sudden reconnection he felt to Mort lifted his spirits.

“Tell me something.”

“Something.”

“I still owe you a fucking ass whipping,” Mort said with impatience. “I haven’t decided if I’ll exonerate you from it because that would be cruel and unusual punishment to an already fucked-up motherfucker, so don’t fucking tempt me.”

“What do you want to know?” Digger asked. Mort was right. He’d committed a grave infraction against Bailey and Mort had every right to re-pulverize him.

“Bunny give you her pussy yet?”

“That’s—”

“Because, let me tell you,” Mort interrupted without giving Digger the chance to say that wasn’t his fucking business. “You giving her dick and you fuck over her, Meggie going to have a shit fit. Which mean Prez will too. Bunny not the type of girl for you to fuck over."

"You was sniffing behind Bailey so much, how the fuck you know what type of girl Bunny is?"

"I'm going to fuck you up yet, son. Keep talking about my woman."

"Fuck. You morphing into a mini-Outlaw? A possessive maniac about Bailey like he is with Meggie?"

"Nope."

"Thank fuck."

"Morph already fucking completed, for your information. I've accepted my pussified award with honors."

Digger frowned.

"As for Bunny…" He gave him a sly smile. "*Albany*, I mean."

"What?"

"I fucking know. Prez still have Meggie watched." He shrugged. "I just happened to be in the next room when Meggie, Bunny, and Roxy was talking one day. About two months ago."

"You heard that her real name is Albany?" Digger asked for clarification. No one needed to know about her past that shamed her so much. Not if she didn't want them to.

"I heard *everything*. That she was a stripper. That she lost her teaching position and the reason for it. Sounded like Meggie already knew and they were just telling Roxy."

"It doesn't make Bunny any different than the other girls," Digger started heatedly, unable to pick up on how his brother felt about her past as a bout of sharp pain overrode the lingering dull aches.

"What the fuck you on? I just warned you *not* to fuck over Bunny. You think I'd tell you that if I gave a fuck about who she threw pussy at in the past? Or the reasons she did? It could've been just because she liked dick and it wouldn't have mattered, so drop the fucking attitude, fuckhead. Your woman a cool chick."

"How did we go from me only getting pussy from her to her being my woman?"

"Your reaction. You gave it the fuck away."

"I really care about her," Digger confessed and then cleared his throat. "But she's been hurt and she can't seem to forgive herself for what the fuck she did."

"You been hurt, too. By that bitch Peyton."

"It's funny. The way I feel about her. After one or two times of her bullshit, I stopped giving a fuck. When Outlaw blasted her away, all I felt was fucking relief. That's some cold ass shit."

Mort steepled his hands, rested his chin on them, and studied Digger. "Peyton was to you what Charlemagne was to me. A fucking parasite. An evil fucking bitch. I fell hard for Bailey the minute I laid eyes on her. My dumb ass almost ruined it. I almost lost her because I didn't want to see she was nothing like Char. She never wavered in fighting for me. For us. Until one day she did after I went overboard in my fuckedupness. Don't let that happen with Bunny. You don't need to know a bitch forever to know you love her."

"You not listening, Mort. I told Bunny I want us to see where we can go. She's the one who's hesitating." Although she'd sucked his cock and sent him fucking flying when he came. That had to account for something. She didn't like dick sucking and yet she'd done it to him. "I mean she giving me signs that she might be willing."

Standing, Mortician went to Digger's desk that had two drawers and a door built into it. He opened the door and pulled a throwaway tumbler and a nearly empty bottle of gin. Because Mort drank vodka, Digger had stopped buying the liquor when he'd been on his quest to change.

When Mort poured the liquor into the tumbler and handed it to him, Digger accepted it. "Don't happen to have vodka, huh?"

"Behind the bar, but since I didn't tell you to stop buying it in the first fucking place, deal with what the fuck you got." He pulled out three little green pills that were oval in shape. "160. Take one."

"As if I don't know. I'm not fucking around with overusing Oxy." He snatched one of the pills and washed it down with the gin. "I have to pay you your two hundred forty back?"

"Nope, I bought a few from the club myself. They come in handy sometimes."

"For?"

"Enforcing," he answered with nonchalance, sitting the two remaining pills on the bedside table and then returning to his seat.

"You really care about Bunny? Then pursue her until she sees you for real," he said without allowing Digger to respond. "As long as she look interested, keep at it until you wear her down."

"She is. I know it. Some of her actions prove it."

"So you have gotten in her pussy?"

"No. I just know it."

"You want to tell me what she did that convinced you?"

"That's between me and her."

"That's cool. I hope you and Bunny work it out."

"So you're closing your advice line now?"

Mort grinned. "Take it or leave it, assfuck, but, yeah, I'm shutting the fuck up."

"What's next, Mort?" Digger asked quietly, some of the pain beginning to float away as the pill got into his system.

"You have to fucking heal. That's going to take a few days, considering…"

How fucked up he was, Digger silently finished on Mort's behalf.

"We going on a run, so you'll probably be at my house or Prez's while we gone."

Fog clouded his brain, stole away a little more of his aches. "Where you going?"

"To fuck up Sharper."

"I should be with you," he slurred, not able to tolerate strong opioids worth a fuck.

"You should, but you can't be this time, so just hold down shit here."

"Yeah." That didn't seem the correct response, but fuck it. His pain was gone.

"Mark?"

"That's my name."

"Give your woman some major attention time. Remember, it's not always about *the dick*. Let the heart get involved too."

"The heart's already involved," he mumbled.

"You kind of fucked up, so maybe I should leave the instructions in writing."

"Ha ha ha," he mumbled. "You such a funny motherfucker."

Mort snickered. "You can start living again. All this shit, including the ass whipping, is fucking history."

A chair scraped against the concrete and footsteps pounded away from him. The hinges on the door creaked open, and Digger slid his eyelid closed. Still, Mort's quiet voice floated to him.

"I missed you, bro. I'm so fucking glad to have you back."

A moment later, the door closed and Digger sank into sleep with the knowledge that he was finally back where he belonged.

"How are you feeling, Bunny?" Meggie asked as they sat at the table in the breakfast room, the next morning. They'd both picked over breakfast and now pretended to drink their coffee.

Sunlight gleamed through the bank of windows. Winter was finally releasing the area from its hold as the month of April crept closer. Although Bunny had missed sleeping next to Digger as she had during their return trip, it felt so good to be in her old room at Meggie's house.

"If you need anything, let me know."

"I should be offering that to you, Meggie. How are you? You're the one who was shot."

"Yes. And Christopher was stabbed and my mom is dead as are men I've known for a very long time. When will it end?"

"Soon, baby," Outlaw replied, sauntering into the room, heading to Meggie, as if he owned the world, and kissing her. His luck amazed her. Any other man would've succumbed to one of the various injuries he'd received over the years.

Somehow, Outlaw managed to survive it all.

"Hey, you," Meggie breathed, once her husband pulled his mouth away. Her cheeks flushed, she forced a smile. "How's your back?"

"Zoann stitched me up good, so don't sweat it."

"You've got yourself a super man, Meggie," Bunny said with laughter.

"Fuckin' right," Outlaw responded, kissing Meggie again before backing away to lean against the wood and glass buffet. "Listen up, Bunny. Since your man wasn't so fuckin' super, motherfucker wasn't even qualified to be a fuckin' man, and the assfuck ain't here no more, we have to talk 'bout your fuckin' plans."

Squirming in her seat, Bunny looked at the floor, then the table. The subject, while expected, took her by surprise, considering everything else going on. She'd also hoped to stay long enough for Digger to heal. "I…well…I thought I'd…I-I mean…you know…"

"No, the fuck I don't fuckin' know cuz you ain't makin' fuckin' sense."

Meggie frowned at Outlaw.

"Well, she ain't, baby."

In turns, he intimidated Bunny and made her feel accepted. She knew his bark was greater than his bite in household matters, so she squared her shoulders. "If Meggie still needs help with the kids, then I'd like to stay on as her assistant."

"So you choosin' to stay here?"

"Yes."

Outlaw folded his arms and cocked his head. "Ain't like you got other places to go."

"Um, Trader's apartment. I mean…it was my apartment too, but the lease was in his name, so I'll have it transferred to me."

"If you had other fuckin' options, would you still wantcha job here?"

"I want you to stay, Bunny," Meggie said hurriedly, throwing Outlaw a dirty look. "We're friends. However, if you have other plans, I understand."

"Fuck, I ain't puttin' you out. I'm just askin' if this what you *want* to do or if this something you ain't got a choice in doin'. You ain't gotta leave cuz you ain't givin' your pussy to no club brother."

"Oh my God, Christopher!"

"What, baby?"

Meggie rolled her eyes in exasperation.

"Oh, yeah, my motherfuckin' language, right? CJ upstairs with Diesel but because you been through so much fuckin' shit, I'll change up my words for you, Megan." He smiled at Bunny. "You ain't gotta leave cuz you no longer fuckin' one of the brothers."

Meggie and Bunny looked at each and laughed before Bunny answered Outlaw. "I *want* to stay here. I enjoy what I do. I also want to look after Marcus. He's, um…" Her voice trailed off. How could she phrase what she needed to say when Outlaw was the reason he was so messed up.

"He fucked up," Outlaw finished. "Cuz I fucked him up."

"Yes, you did." She couldn't quite hide her edginess. "You went overboard in my opinion," she mumbled.

Apparently, not quietly enough because Outlaw lifted his brows. "It's fuckin' like that between you and that motherfucker, huh? Lemme clue you in, babe. You could do worse than fuckin' Digger. The last motherfucker fucked over you been put to ground. Digger? Your *current* motherfucker in danger of the same fuckin' thing happenin' to him if he ever cross that fuckin' line with me. He on fuckin' probation, so until we see which way the wind blowin', don't get too fuckin' attached."

Too late. Bunny already felt an attachment to him. Even after she'd rested and found herself safe under the roof of this house, her thoughts were with him and his desire for them to be together.

"How's Digger doing?" Meggie asked.

"I haven't seen him since last night. He was still unconscious when I left, but Mort sent me a text and said Digger was resting in oxyland." She sighed. "That means he was given some type of drug, right?"

"Oxy," Outlaw responded.

"I called him....Mortician, I mean," Bunny clarified. "I wanted to know if I could talk to Digger, but he said not to worry because Digger had opened his eyes and they'd talked."

Outlaw's brows snapped together. "Yeah? Already? I must be losin' my fuckin' touch."

"Be quiet, Christopher."

"I'll do fuckin' better than that, baby." He came to her again and massaged her shoulders. Leaning against him, Meggie looked up and he smiled at her. "My ass fuckin' leavin'. Got fuckin' business to take care of." He bent and planted a slow, upside-down kiss on her lips. "Get well, Megan," he said with a groan. "My dick so hard I could use it as a fuckin' bat in a ball-fuckin-game."

Meggie giggled at her outrageous husband.

"One more bit of business with you two," he said, straightening again, but still touching Meggie. "I talked to Riley and Brooks." Rolling his shoulders, Outlaw winced and swore under his breath. "And they workin' with some fuckheads to tweak your records."

"What does that mean?" Meggie asked.

"It mean if she wanna go for a license to fuckin' teach in this state, if shit go down like I want, then your ass can fuckin' teach again. You wanna live here or the fuckin' apartment you lived in with Trader, that shit between you and Megan. I'm just givin' you fuckin' options. Or *tryna* give them motherfuckers to you."

"Are you serious?" Bunny asked, almost afraid to hope this was real.

Not because she intended to leave Meggie. She did enjoy working for her. But if she had her teaching license, then she'd always have options. Few teaching positions included a morality clause in their contracts, but it was an unspoken expectation. The reason she'd been fired could follow her forever.

But she'd never even tried for another position. She'd been too humiliated and so angry with herself that she'd just accepted what happened to her as a form of deserved punishment.

"I ain't promisin' fuck all. Just wanted to let you know what the fuck I'm tryna do. By the way, your folks safe. We set 'em up where they ain't gonna be found 'til after Sharper get fucked up."

"Thank you," she said, unable to think of another response.

He spoke of 'Riley' as casually as he always had, giving no indication he knew that was Bunny's father. "Go see 'bout the man you wanna give pussy to. Roxy and Zoann arrivin' soon like they been doin'. Megan got help with the kids. As a matter of fact, walk the fuck over with me."

Bunny thought Outlaw might discuss in greater detail what they'd talked about in the breakfast room, but he didn't speak to her at all. In a strange way, it comforted her. He was always nice, but he rarely held in-depth conversations with her if it didn't pertain to Meggie and his children.

At the clubhouse door, five minutes later, he paused long enough to open it, but didn't follow her in. Greetings were thrown her way, refrains of *glad you're safe* and *welcome back* coming at her.

She didn't know how many of the brothers were aware of Trader's death. Right now, though, they were treating her with the same respect they had as his old lady. It took her a good ten minutes before she reached Digger's room and found him still asleep, once she flipped on the ceiling light.

Closing the door quietly, she looked around, taking in everything she'd missed last night in her panic to clean up his wounds. The place wasn't the cheeriest with the small, naked window higher up than most windows were. Perhaps, it served to keep assholes from easily climbing through. Still, a small valence would add some color to the overall grayness. The posters *did* add color and Bunny admired the ones with the cars. She recognized Rick James because of Roxy. The naked women could definitely come down as well, but she'd never push the subject.

Trader had been a porn fanatic and had dared Bunny to complain. She scowled at the memory. He'd always said that men were men no matter what pussy they fucked and liked looking at other bitches' cunts. But she'd felt so strongly in her belief that his excessive interest disrespected her.

She glanced at Digger again, startled to find his gaze fixed on her.

"Hi," she said softly, annoyed that she paralleled every thought connected to the man in front of her with Trader. Moving forward, she seated herself in the chair close to his bed. "I thought you were still asleep."

"I don't have clothes on," he said with amusement, sounding awful, hoarse and groggy.

She folded her hands together in her lap. "Yeah. Val helped me with you."

He scowled. "I don't want no motherfucker around my cock."

"I did cock duty," she said primly.

He snickered, and Bunny couldn't stop her grin. The swelling was still prevalent, but it had gone down by a small degree. She hated the black bruising marring his handsome face.

He shifted and began to lift himself up.

"Keep still!" she ordered, flying to him and halting him with her hands on his shoulders. The covers had fallen away and she frowned at the wrapping around his chest. That wasn't her handiwork. "What happened? Did someone else hurt you and they had to bandage you up a little more?"

"Nah, baby. Outlaw just sent a doctor in early this morning. Doc determined I got some cracked ribs."

"He can't do that without an x-ray," she flared.

"*He* can't do fuckall cuz *he* was a *she*."

"Oh. Right," Bunny responded in a small voice. But what did she expect? Although the club had its fair share of male civilians on their payroll, women were easier for them. All a woman had to do was become enamored of one of the bikers and she would be loyal.

That's why they'd searched for a female attorney and Kendall had come for the job.

"What's going through that overthinking brain of yours?" Digger asked with resignation.

"Uh…" She huffed in agitation. "Just the female doctor seeing you." At a loss for words for her unaccountable jealousy, she gestured from his head to his toe. He opened his mouth, but Bunny raised her hand before he could berate her. "You don't have to say it, Mark. I'm stupid for feeling that way. I have no claim on you and no right to feel that way."

He patted the empty space on the other side of him. Embarrassed and confused, Bunny still scooted where he wanted her to and laid her head on the pillow.

"We got some fine bitches in and out the club, Bunny. I'm not even going to lie to you."

"You don't have to. I've seen them."

"I'm not going to lie about that doctor chick neither. Bitch was rocking. But I wasn't even tempted to show her my cock or flirt with her. If she'd looked at it, it would've been professional on her part and my part."

His words comforted her and eased her stupid jealousy. She should know better. Yet, Digger's response also validated her feelings. Made her feel important.

"Are you feeling better?"

To her ears, she sounded sad, so she could only imagine how it went over with him. But she *was* sad. She didn't want to fear rejection or punches. She didn't want to see rejection on Mark's face because she couldn't get her head together.

"What up, girl? You upset about something."

"I'm…yes, I am," she admitted. "It's me, not you."

"Fuck, how the fuck you kicking my ass to the curb and we not even together yet?"

"No, I'm not kicking you to the curb," Bunny rushed out. "It's just…"

"We better than this, right? We should be able to talk to each other. Tell each other anything and everything."

"We should."

"I don't ever want to be the cause you sad. I'll walk away from our pre-relationship before I bring you pain."

"Wh-what's a pre-relationship?"

"My term for chasing you 'til I get you in a real relationship. Since you seemed interested in me. I'm not a stalker, so the moment you got uncomfortable I'd stop my pursuit." He reached out a hand to her, groaning in pain. "Like now."

Alarm raced through Bunny and she grabbed his hand, kissing the back of it. "I don't want you to leave me, Mark. I just…we've known each other for such a short time, but I care about you a lot."

He snorted and withdrew his hand.

"What?"

"Girls, that's what. Y'all a bunch of confused, confusing bitches. How the fuck a motherfucker know what to do, when one day you want me and the next day you don't, but you still do?"

"Huh?"

"Welcome to the confused club. Not too much of a good feeling, is it?"

"No," she agreed. "It isn't."

"Tell me what you want me to do so you'll be happy."

So *she'd* be happy? Just the sound of that warmed her heart. She hadn't been *un*happy, but she hadn't been particularly happy, either. She'd just...*been.*

"I'd like us to move forward. Together."

His grin lit up his face. "Damn, Bunny...*Albany,*" he teased. "You just made me a happy motherfucker. On second thought, my dick might be happier knowing what he getting from you."

Laughing, Bunny rolled her eyes. "You can't do anything until you're healed."

"You want to fucking bet? I can't do anything *today*. Even having you bouncing up and down on my cock would probably have me vibrating with pain."

"You're insane," she giggled, the image of riding Digger making her pussy throb.

"I don't know what love supposed to feel like," he confessed when their moment passed. "I never experienced love before, not on the giving end or the receiving end. Sounds like you might be that way as well. Let's give each other a chance and find out about love together. Can we do that?"

"Yes," she agreed without hesitation.

"Give my ass three or four days to heal, then prepare to fuck both of us into oblivion. I'll do some thrusts here and there, but probably not too many."

"I'll take care of you," she promised, her entire body anticipating sex with Digger.

Silence and then, "When was the last time you came?"

She frowned, attempting to remember if it had been two or three months since she'd came while having sex. "On my own about three and a half weeks ago."

"How strong are your leg and thigh muscles? Could you hold a squat, for instance?"

"I'll be able to ride your cock a very long time," she swore. "Don't worry."

"Fuck, girl. Saying shit like that make me want to say *fuck it* and bear the fucking pain."

"What about your ribs?"

"I'd say fuck them too. Crack them motherfuckers to pieces."

Scooting closer to him, she placed a soft kiss on his split lip and he grunted.

"Fuck."

She pulled away. "I didn't mean to aggravate the pain."

"Don't worry about it, baby. It's cool. My lips going to be involved in eating your pussy. That is *if* you think you can hover close to my mouth without touching me anywhere."

Between her legs grew wetter and the tips of her nipples beaded. She absolutely loved having her pussy eaten, almost more than she enjoyed sex itself, but what he was proposing sounded impossible. "Would your tongue be able to reach?"

"Depends on how close you could squat over me. I can't suck your cunt but I can lick it."

Her breaths came in short, little pants and she squeezed her legs together.

"You can always balance yourself with the headboard, but I need you to hold your pussy lips open."

She moaned, willing to try any of his suggestions at this point to ease the pulsing ache in her core.

"Take your clothes off," he instructed her.

Too lost in lust, she got entirely naked, when really only her bared pussy was required.

He crooked a finger at her. "Guide one of your delicious looking tits to my mouth."

She leaned over him, the thought to tease him with her breasts hitting her. Keeping them just out of his reach, she jiggled them, pulling away whenever he brought his mouth close.

"Fuck it," he growled in frustration, catching a nipple between his fingers. A look of agony slid across his face and he gritted his teeth, halfway lifting to tug her nipple into his mouth.

Not wanting him to feel any discomfort because of her, Bunny relaxed and guided him back, holding her breast up for his benefit. He alternated between tugging her nipple between his teeth and dragging his tongue across the peak.

Throwing her head back, she moaned at the pleasure bursting through her. She could've allowed him to suck her tit for hours, it felt so good. The tips of her breasts had always been one of her pleasure points.

He moved his mouth away. The intensity of his stare made her feel open and vulnerable, but she refused to look away from the hot promise in his eyes.

"You ready to feed me your pussy? I'm sure the fuck ready to eat it."

Groaning, she carefully lifted herself over his face, holding onto the headboard to balance herself.

"Fuck, but you got a pretty cunt."

Each word he spoke made her wetter until her cream was sliding down her thighs. Her clit actually hurt. Her legs and thighs had once been pretty strong. First from cheerleading and then from her moves on the pole. Hesitantly, she released her hold on the wood and lowered herself to within an inch of his mouth, then used her fingers to open her soaked pussy lips.

"Jesus, look at the clit on you," he growled, a moment before he slid his tongue from the top of her mound right to her ass. She was already so close to orgasming after he'd finished with her nipples and having her pussy licked always made her come quick. But she wanted to savor this moment with him. When it was over, he'd expect another dick suck. Want to come in her mouth again since she'd release in his.

Maybe, if she didn't orgasm on his tongue?

He blew on her clit, his hot breath sending shivers through her.

"Kiss me. Or you don't like the taste of your pussy juice?"

"Not really," she managed, throbbing in anticipation of more of his tonguing.

"Stop thinking. Just feel my tongue sliding up and down your cunt, stopping to dip inside your opening then teasing your asshole."

She grabbed onto the headboard again, her heart pounding, unable to bear his words with much restraint.

He taunted her with a quick lick and then snickered. "Bet you want to plaster your cunt to my lips and grind your pussy until you come."

She whimpered.

Another mocking tongue stroke. "You want that?"

"Yes," she whispered.

He kissed the opening to her vagina and she trembled.

"If you stop thinking for a minute, I might let you come. But whatever the fuck in that gorgeous head of yours keeping you from enjoying this. Why should I give you a tongue bath if you holding back on me?"

"Please, I swear I won't think about anything," she gasped out, twisting her hips slightly. "I…I don't want to have your cum in my mouth, so I'll use my fingers to finish myself off. Just please, lick me a little more."

In response, he caressed her wet, swollen clit with the tip of his nose, sniffing as he went along and making her toes curl.

"Get over me again like you were before."

Releasing the headboard, she balanced herself as she'd been before he'd stopped. Before she had a chance to open her lips, his tongue danced across her flesh. Instead of teasing her as he had, his ruthless licks pushed every thought right out of her head and she rolled against his mouth, the lapping sound combining with her moans and turning her on a little more.

Vaguely, awareness of his mouth covering her pussy and sucking seeped into her. Her hands slid into his locks and she gripped them, bouncing against his lips in a fast motion.

Her orgasm hit her hard, starting from the tips of breasts and spreading to her pussy. Her body jerked and her thighs trembled, her cries of pleasure ringing in her head. She felt as if she floated in a haze of pleasure, and she rode the wave until her nerve endings overloaded and she collapsed at Digger's side, panting.

"I've eaten a lot of pussy in my life, but I think caring about you make yours taste sweeter."

His wondrous words stole some of her ardor. They were sweet in their own way, but she really didn't need to hear about all the pussy-eating he'd done in his life. "Mr. Romantic," she said hoarsely. "Thanks for the compliment. Such as it was."

Licking his glistening lips, he grinned at her. His cheeks and chin were soaked from her orgasm and a hot blush spread over her at the evidence of her powerful orgasm.

"What got you turning so fucking red?"

"My cream is all over your face."

"It shouldn't be?"

"I was sitting on your face so it was unavoidable…" Her voice trailed off and she bolted upright. "Oh my goodness! I *sat* on your face. I didn't stay hovering like you told me."

"Do I look upset? It let me know you finally stopped *thinking* and just felt your pussy being licked."

"Stop saying that, please."

"Making your pussy hot again? Wanting more tongue from me? Or some dick?"

"Dick," she said as if she hadn't come a few minutes ago. "Both."

"Baby, I'm in bad fucking pain from the way your thighs hugged by fucking battered face. Otherwise, I'd tell you to sink your cunt on my cock right fucking now."

Her eyes slid to the rise in the sheet. Pushing the cover aside, his cock sprung free, thick and hard. She scooted down, knowing what she had to do. Before she changed her mind, she slurped him into her mouth, rewarded with his groan.

Fondling his balls, she sucked him in hard, fast draws, just wanting it over with. He was close, worked up by eating her. Wrapping her hands around his cock base, she pulled on him, even as she continued to blow him.

He fisted her hair and tugged, but she ignored him.

"Bunny, move, if you don't want me to come in your mouth."

The words surprised her and she relaxed her grip on him, allowing him to pull her mouth away from his cock just as cum shot from him and landed on her cheek. At the last minute, she took him in her hand again, and the final bit of cum bubbled from his dick tip.

"Lay next to me," he puffed out.

She easily complied, sated and languid.

"Whatever mistakes you made," he began, "not as bad as you think. You was a young bitch and we learn from what the fuck we do during that time in our lives. It's our learning period. So forgive yourself. Stop punishing yourself, doing shit you don't really want to do because you think you deserve whatever you're getting."

"I hurt my mom and dad so much, and if Trader hadn't taken me away I might be dead now."

"Why even wonder what you *might* be, girl, when you know what you are? Alive. Strong. Loyal."

"I'm fine, Mark. I promise. I don't know why we're talking about this now?"

"Because I couldn't say it before you attacked my cock. And considering you almost gnawed it the fuck off in your desperation to make me come, I wish the fuck I would've spoke up."

"Gnawed?" she echoed. "Why didn't you tell me?"

"Your teeth hurt slightly but nothing I couldn't take. But I couldn't tell you. I had to fucking show you. My telling you I didn't eat your pussy to have my dick sucked is one thing. I should've stopped you to show you that part. Since I didn't, I wanted you to see I won't come in your mouth if you suck my cock."

"Okay," she said.

"Forgive yourself. Your folks have forgiven you. It's time for you to do the same."

She smiled hesitantly.

His stomach growled.

"Are you hungry?"

"Starving," he answered. "I haven't eaten since way before I got my ass kicked. Your man need something more to eat than just pussy."

She shook her head. "What did you do? Graduate from the School of Rude and Crude with top honors?"

"No. That distinction go to Outlaw."

Bunny reached for her panties, where they lay at the edge of the bed.

Digger's stomach growled again, so she hurried to redress.

"I won't be long," she promised, skipping to the door as she put one flat on and then the other.

"Wait, before you leave, can you hand me one of the pills Mort left on my nightstand?"

"Um…can't you get addicted?"

"I'm not going to," he promised. "I just need something for the pain. Mort only gave me three. My broke ass couldn't afford one."

Reluctantly, she did as he asked, and watched as he washed the pill down with tap water she'd gotten from the bathroom faucet.

"I'll be right back."

"I'm not going nowhere, baby."

Bunny wasn't gone any longer than ten minutes, the amount of time it took her to scrounge up chips, sandwiches, and sodas. Yet, by the time she returned to the room, Digger was asleep.

Kissing the air since her hands were occupied with the tray and she couldn't blow the kiss to him, she backed out of the room, bumping into a hard body.

"He sleeping?" Mort asked, gripping her arms to steady her.

Once she wasn't in danger of falling, she turned, holding the tray up when his gaze dropped to the sandwiches. "Want one?"

"Thought you'd never ask," he chortled, grabbing one. "You his old lady now or what?" he asked casually, as he chomped away.

She hadn't acknowledged her relationship with Digger, even when Outlaw had suggested what was happening between them. But she was involved with him and she didn't want to pretend otherwise. She nodded.

"Welcome to the family, girl. If he get out of line with you, tell me so I can kick his ass. He better not fuck up a good thing."

"O-okay." An idea occurred to her at Mort's easy acceptance. "You don't use your room here anymore. Do you?" She didn't think he did, but she wasn't one hundred percent certain.

"No."

"Can…can Digger have it? It's bigger." A little brighter, as well.

"Without all the naked bitch photos hanging on his walls, I bet?" he asked with a knowing grin, taking the tray from her.

"Yes," she said, unable to stop her smile.

"He can have it."

"Don't let him know yet. I want to surprise him." Her head was already running through what she needed to turn the room into a cozy little nest for the day she rode him into oblivion.

"Thank you for coming, Georgie. You don't know what it means to have you here right now."

"You're my friend, Meggie. I couldn't…I wanted to be here. I know what it's like to lose your mother unexpectedly."

Georgie Mason embraced Megan and whispered words Christopher couldn't hear. They'd just arrived at the church and as they passed a black limousine parked near the entrance, the door to the vehicle had opened and the pregnant, dark-haired girl had emerged, her husband, superstar, Sloane Mason, following behind her. Their eight and a half-month-old daughter and the other kids were at the house, with Bunny and Roxy watching over them while some of the old ladies of the club members took care of the food.

Christopher stood next to Sloane, watching Megan and Georgie's exchange. He had to say Georgie almost came close to being as gorgeous as Megan. *Almost.* With her purple eyes and black hair, she looked exotic. Her and Megan were roughly the same size, except, for Georgie's full belly. She was also only eighteen and had almost been responsible for sending her husband to jail for a very long time.

Christopher understood. It had been his luck that Megan turned eighteen the day they fucking met or else he might've been in the same situation.

Megan started toward the door again, tears slipping from her eyes. Instead of going to her, he allowed Georgie to put her arm around Megan's shoulder and guide her into the sanctuary, where she crashed to a halt.

It was already crowded, but he couldn't miss the front of the church, where seven caskets stood. He knew Dinah's was in the middle, right in front of the altar.

Watching his wife closely, Sloane moved when she did, protective of her, a man after Christopher's own heart.

"I'm so sorry for your loss, Outlaw," Sloane told him.

"Yeah," he responded with a sigh, as Megan headed toward the first casket. "It is what the fuck it is."

Down the line she went, placing her hand on each of his sisters' caskets. She skipped her mother's and repeated the process with his nieces. Christopher placed a hand on her shoulder, her body tense beneath his fingertips. Megan was hurting. He was, too. He thought, maybe, his pain went as deep as hers. But he didn't fucking know. All he *did* know was they'd been his family. He hadn't had a relationship with them as he did with Zoann and Ophelia. Yet, he felt their losses keenly.

Finally, Megan moved again, this time to Dinah. Her shoulders shook and he knew she wept. Resting her head on the lid for a moment, she slid her hand over the top.

"I love you, Momma," she whispered. "I always will. I promise I'll tell your grandchildren about the love you had in you. You were just too sick to give it." She swiped at her cheeks.

Christopher wanted to pull her away and into his arms, as Sloane had with Georgie, but he'd learned the hard way not to interfere with her grieving after their son's death.

"I hope you're at peace." She planted a kiss on the coffin before lifting her head and facing him.

"I'm so fuckin' sorry, baby," he told her, not knowing what else to say. He wrapped her in his arms and held her tight, threading his fingers through her hair and closing his eyes when she returned his hug and clung to him.

A throat cleared behind him and Christopher turned, to find Father Wilcunt frowning in Sloane's direction. The little fuckhead was an honorary member of the club, but he was still a self-righteous motherfucker.

"Well, well, if it isn't the cradle robber," he said dryly. "In my very own sanctuary."

Georgie gasped. Sloane lifted a brow.

"Father Wilkins, please," Megan implored. "Not today."

"Madam…"

"Wilcunt, you kinda a member of my fuckin' club, which mean I kinda get to fuck you up quicker if you fuck up, so before you fuckin' continue, I'd fuckin' think about that shit," Christopher warned.

Amusement danced across Sloane's face, but his girl rounded her eyes.

"Shocking, isn't he, Mrs. Mason?" Father Wilcunt said, indicating the church. "With absolutely no respect for his holy surroundings."

"You ain't gonna feel like a real fuckin' member 'til I fuck you up, yeah? Other-fuckin-wise, I can't fuckin' understand why the fuck you insist on jerkin' my cock the way you do."

Sloane laughed while Wilcunt scowled and stomped off.

Kendall inserted herself between Georgie and Megan, ruining Christopher's day a little more. "Meggie, how are you?"

"I-m—"

"How the fuck you think she is?" Christopher snapped.

Kendall had already pitched a fucking fit when she was told to leave Rory with the rest of the kids. Roxy convinced her it would be easier at the church and the graveyard if young children weren't there.

Fuck, if the thought of her psycho ass in one of those coffins didn't bring a small smile to his face.

Sloane and Georgie stepped back to allow Johnnie to greet Megan.

"Protocol is for the family to stand at the back of the church to receive condolences," Kendall said crisply.

"I don't feel up to it," Megan answered. "But why don't you do it, Christopher? You, Johnnie, Kendall, Zoann, Val, and Ophelia."

"No, baby. If you ain't standin' up, I ain't," Christopher said, noticing Wilcunt taking his place and guiding Megan to her seat without another word.

Several hours later, Christopher observed the people who'd been invited to their home, still keeping a close watch on his wife as she guided CJ to Sloane and Georgie's daughter, Bryn, her dark hair falling all around her.

"Do you remember Bryn, buddy?" Megan's voice floated to him, from where she sat on a sofa, close to where he stood.

"Yes, MegAnn! Bwyn!" CJ squealed, his trademark wide grin in place. He studied the little girl, much closer than he ever did with his own little sister, then looked at Megan. "Mommie?"

"What is it, son?" She sounded calm, happy even, in spite of what she'd been through.

Christopher suspected she willed happiness into her for the sake of him and their children and he vowed he'd make things right for her even if he had to fuck-up every crooked motherfucker who ever knew fucking Sharper, to get to that motherfucker. The last minute plane tickets had been fucking expensive, but this shit would end tomorrow, at Sharper's farce of a funeral.

"Who Bwyn, Mommie?"

Georgie laughed. "Your brand new cousin."

"And the one you said you knew," Megan added with a smile.

"John-John," CJ called, when Johnnie walked in from the kitchen, going to where Kendall sat with the rest of the women and kissing her.

"Outlaw!" Val called from across the room, holding up a glass in salute and downing it.

"Yo, assfuck," Christopher responded, folding his arms and leaning against the wall, aware that CJ had paused to listen to the interaction. He had to fucking remember his boy picked up on this shit. When he least expected it, CJ would call someone an assfuck and then Megan would be pissed.

Sloane approached Christopher and held out at plastic cup to him. "This has to be hard on you."

Nodding, Christopher accepted the drink and glanced at it, before sniffing and discovering he held rum. "It is."

"Georgie has been really concerned about Meggie."

"This can't be fuckin' easy for her, considerin' she ain't long lost her own ma."

"No. She still grieves for Cassandra. Though I think she got what she deserved. She'd never win Mother of the Year."

"Neither did fuckin' whiny-ass Dinah."

Tasting his own drink, Sloane nodded. "Cash called me," he said finally. "Told me what went down. Dinah's betrayal and to whom."

"Motherfucker ain't supposed to share fuckin' club business. Megan don't even fuckin' know everything."

"Understood. But since he did and you offered me help with my father, I'd like to return the favor."

"Club fuckin' business, Sloane. I ain't discussin' this shit with you." Too many lives had already been lost. He had civilians on the payroll. Sloane wasn't one of those people.

"You're flying to LA later," he persisted.

Christopher would pull Cash aside and remind that motherfucker to keep his fucking mouth shut. What the fuck was wrong with him?

"I'm offering the use of my plane. Manifest will be easier to alter than if you took commercial flights. If you're identified as a passenger on a regular flight, your steps will be traced and lead back to you if something happens that isn't supposed to. "

The words whirled through Christopher's head. Going commercial was risky and expensive as a motherfucker, but they'd had no other option. If not for the funerals, they would've rode to LA. They couldn't do that now, with time so limited. Christopher liked Sloane's alternative.

"Lemme round up my boys, so we can talk in private in my office."

Megan's image firmly in his head, Christopher stepped off Sloane's plane and onto a private tarmac, not moving until Johnnie, Mortician, Val, and Cash had deplaned, too. Everybody except Cash carried small bags, containing black clothing and earpieces. Cash's big duffel bag had wires, explosive, and weapons.

Their plane ride had been subdued and relatively quiet. No one had shit to say because this was it.

One motherfucker would win while the other motherfucker lost, and the loser and his crew would be fucked up. Christopher not only had his own life in his hands but those of his brothers, too. Fucking ironic the shit hadn't crossed his mind until Megan was shot, then every-fucking-body, in Christopher's eyes became more than bikers and brothers, his officers, and members.

They became human. Husbands. Fathers.

Family.

"What the fuck ever you motherfuckers thinkin' leave on the goddamn plane," he ordered as he started walking toward the black SUV Sloane had promised to have for them. "Fuckin' focus on the hours ahead." Words as much for his benefit as theirs.

"We focused, Prez," Mortician reassured him. "We ready for any motherfucker thinking they ready for us.

"You assfucks know what the fuck we doin'?"

"Besides you being in a casket to get into the church and Cash blowing it up, not really," Johnnie admitted.

"That's because you missing the fucking planning again," Val complained.

"Kendall needed me."

"Yeah, well, Zoann needs me, but I sure the fuck get my ass to the club when Outlaw calls."

"Enough!" Christopher bellowed. "Shut the fuck up. The two of you motherfuckers sound like arguin' bitches."

Nobody spoke again until they were on the road in the SUV, heading toward the mortuary in charge of Sharper's funeral after dropping Cash and Val off at the church to begin wiring it to blow it the fuck up.

Christopher really couldn't wait for that to happen. After all the misery Sharper had caused, all the girls he'd hurt, and the sons he'd abused, he needed more than a big pow to take him out. Christopher intended to try his absolute fucking best to keep Sharper alive until they got him in the meatshack, which would be a challenge with two states between it and them.

"Stop here," Cash instructed, right near the old diner where Christopher had first met Val so many years before. It was closed down and boarded, a for sale sign hanging in one of the windows.

"How long this shit takin' you, Cash?" Christopher asked, briefly reflecting on how different his life was compared to then.

"Fuck, a few hours. At least. We'll still be there when the casket is brought in."

The one containing his fucking ass. Well, the shit had been his idea, so he'd see it through.

"Osti gone and most of Sharper's loyal bodyguards," Mortician said, "but the motherfucker got hired fucking guns. Keep your fucking eyes and ears open."

"That's what the earpieces are for," Johnnie said, then studied Christopher. "You're sure about this? Coffins have tight confines."

"I know that, John Boy," Christopher growled, annoyed the motherfucker reminded him of that. "I ain't fond of closed-in shit and there ain't no fuckin' air in a fuckin' closed casket. A real dead motherfucker don't need no air. Only, my ass ain't dead."

"Right," Cash agreed, settling his duffel bag on the seat he'd just vacated and unzipping it. He handed Christopher a small oxygen tank. "After three hours, you're fucked."

"Well, make sure my ass out of the motherfucker before three fuckin' hours passed."

"Prez, you ever been to a Baptist Going Home Celebration?" Mortician asked with a knowing grin. "You need two fuckin' tanks just to get through all the praises and speeches."

"Fuck me. That shit ain't happenin'. Say something in my ear-fuckin-piece at the ninety-minute mark, then I'm comin' out."

"Fuck, I wish I could capture that moment," Johnnie said wistfully. "You're going to give some fuckers nightmares for years to come."

"We through chit-chattin'?"

"Yeah, Prez," Mort answered as Val hopped out of the driver's side and Johnnie slid in.

"How fuckin' far away we gotta fuckin' be when the shit blows?"

Cash turned and grinned, walking backward. "About four blocks should do it."

"Val?" Christopher called. "Come back in one fuckin' piece. Bitsy love you and it would fuck her up if you got fucked up."

Val gave Christopher a two-fingered salute. "Not planning on going back any other way but in one piece."

"We're ready?" Johnnie asked, once Cash and Val turned the corner, which put them out of sight.

"Yeah, John Boy. As ready as my ass'll ever be."

Fuck, but the noise was driving Christopher fucking insane. Music and weeping and accolades for Sharper. Disbelief that he was *Gone onto Glory*.

Motherfucker wasn't there yet, but for Christopher having to lay perfectly still, laid out like a real corpse, his piece resting on his chest, Sharper needed an extra fucking up.

It had been relatively easy to get the funeral director to agree to the proposition. Along with the money—double what Sharper offered him to wheel in an empty casket—Christopher explained what would happen if he didn't cooperate or if he betrayed them. As extra insurance, he had two members from the LA chapter escort Nate Jenkins's terrified wife and three children into his office, where they would stay until the plans had been carried out.

Christopher hated using an innocent woman and her children so he tried to make amends by allowing them to be with Nate, whom he still might fuckup because he didn't quite believe that he hadn't known all the shit Sharper intended.

Nate knew everything, right down to where Sharper said he'd be sitting with his men. Three on each side of the reverend's long lost sister. Or a fuckhead in drag who was *supposed* to be his fucking relative. Apparently, somebody had told Sharper he was pretty somewhere along the way. Christopher couldn't understand why else assfuck would believe he could get away dressed as a woman.

None of them had barely slept, working out the fine details, so nothing would go wrong. When it came time for him to actually lay his ass out, the other motherfuckers had all stared down at him.

"You motherfuckers make one fuckin' joke and Ima fuck you up when this over."

That felt like fucking hours ago. But Christopher knew only about an hour had passed. Maybe, a little longer. Entombed as he was, he'd lost all sense of fucking time and he knew he'd have a split fucking second to adjust to the lights after being in darkness for a long while.

"We're just about ready, Christopher." Johnnie's voice came through Christopher's earpiece. "We're in the back, able to see everything."

"Outlaw, you got thirty minutes to make all these motherfuckers scatter and get the fuck out yourself," Cash warned. "This baby is set to blow."

In thirty fucking minutes?

"In thirty minutes, son?" Mort asked with as much fucking shock as Christopher felt.

"No, fucker. I'll set it once Outlaw's out of the fucking coffin."

"You should've explained yourself better," Val complained.

"You fucks didn't give me a chance."

Christopher decided to tune those motherfuckers out. Listening to them bickering wasn't helping his goddamn headache.

"They're about to eulogize him," Johnnie said a moment later. "It's show time, brother."

Fucking finally.

Jenkins hadn't closed the lid as tightly as it should've been so Christopher thunked his head against the inside to pop the top, then used his head to push the rest of the way out.

The first scream blared over the microphone and Christopher realized it was the motherfucker who'd been about to do the eulogy. The second scream was high-pitched and created a chain effect, with motherfuckers running and tripping the fuck over each other to get the fuck away from a dead man coming to life.

Jumping to his feet, Sharper froze in shock, not bothering to smooth out the hem of his black dress, and allowing a muscled thigh to show. The lacy veil Sharper wore hid his expression from Christopher, but he still pinned a glare on Sharper. A shudder rippled through Sharper's body. He began to push through the chaos, not caring about the panic-stricken mourners running in every direction.

Before Sharper melted into the crowd, Christopher fired his nine, determined to stop the motherfucker. The shot hit him in the shoulder, propelling him forward and into a man in front of him. The suited dude spun, gazed at Sharper and the veil hanging half off his face.

"A ghost!" Suit screamed at the top of his lungs. He elbowed Sharper away from him and plunged over two other people.

The bodyguards Sharper hired were finally getting a fucking clue as to what was happening and turning toward him. Bullets flew in all directions.

Laying back in the coffin, Christopher raised his hand and fired blindly. Innocent motherfuckers might get hurt, but the bodyguards didn't care, so Christopher couldn't either.

Not if he wanted to survive.

If he wanted to live, he needed to get the fuck out the casket.

"It's fucking hilarious how quick motherfuckers have cleared out."

Christopher barely heard Johnnie's voice through the gunfire.

"Get the fuck up here," he ordered. "I'm outta fuckin' ammo."

One of the bodyguards loomed above him and pointed the gun at Christopher's head. He knocked the gun away and the shit landed in the raised lid. Undeterred, the bodyguard re-aimed. Christopher grabbed the motherfucker hand, attempting to dislodge his fingers. Their struggle put Christopher at another disadvantage. If only he could leverage himself and get the fuck out of the casket before his ass really needed one.

The fuckhead punched the side of Christopher's head, momentarily stunning him. He wasn't going to survive this. After all the gunshots, knife wounds, and injuries from fistfights, this would be his end. Meeting the eyes of the motherfucker who'd gotten the drop on him, Christopher prepared himself for the impact of the bullet to his head, thinking of Megan. The image of her in his mind's eyes brought him comfort, even as he knew his death would destroy her.

Gunfire exploded and Christopher waited for the sudden burn before he drifted into nothingness. It never came. Instead of having a bullet in his brain, a dead motherfucker suddenly slumped over him.

"Prez!" Mort called, clearing the dead ass and holding out his hand to assist Christopher out of the coffin.

"Go! Go! Go!" Johnnie roared through the earpiece. "Badges are turning the fuck in."

"We have Sharper secured in the back of the vehicle, Outlaw," Val reassured him before Christopher could even form the thought.

"We need a diversion," Cash said with amusement. "Lucky you, I have just the thing."

Near the altar—the one Christopher had just ran from—an explosion blasted around them, sending pieces of wood and upholstery, plaster, and paper, in all directions.

"Fuck you, Cash," Christopher snarled, as another explosion rocked the side of the building.

"It's either this or get fucking caught, Outlaw," Cash snapped. "Take your fucking pick."

They finally reached outside, where police officers were ushering a sea of people back.

"This way," Mortician said, cutting between the church and the Life Center that stood next to it.

"Tell me when you're fucking clear," Cash demanded.

"You'll see our fucking asses, son," Mort said, as they came to a side street, where the black SUV awaited them.

After Mort and Christopher jumped in, Johnnie swerved away while Cash reset the timer on the explosives.

With a few adjustments, glass, metal, wood and plaster flew high into the sky, disappearing in a cloud of dust. Just like that, the church belonging to the Reverend Sharper Banks was no more.

Tomorrow was the day Bunny would ride his dick. If not for that, Digger would've been more upset than he was because he'd been left behind, while Outlaw and the others headed to LA.

"You weren't strong enough to go," Bunny pointed out for the tenth time since she'd arrived in his room with breakfast a little while ago. Yesterday evening, she'd just let him rage, although he suspected she'd tuned him out after an hour. She hadn't even raised her head from the game she'd been playing on her phone whenever she muttered 'uh-huh' or 'I understand, Marcus'.

"I'm not too fucking weak to hold a fucking gun, Bunny," he said, now that he had her full attention. She sat at the foot of the bed, looking so pretty in a long-sleeved, ankle-length dress. This morning, she wore no makeup and she allowed her hair to hang free. He liked the look. Eight times out of ten, she had her hair in a ponytail.

If he asked her to wear her hair unencumbered more often, would she agree?

"You aren't weak at all," she said finally, as the silence stretched.

Yes, he really did have her attention. He preferred this comment much more than he had the distracted one from yesterday.

"I don't believe they trusted me to cover them."

"Give it a chance. You've just gotten back. It's going to take time for everyone to get comfortable again."

Snatching his pack of cigarettes from the nightstand and shoving one between his lips, he shook his head. "Time, huh? Time is fine if I knew where I stood with them." He grabbed the lighter and lit the cigarette.

Bunny leaned forward and snatched the cigarette away, tapping it out in the ashtray that also sat on his nightstand.

"What the fuck, girl?"

"Smoke enough of those and you don't have to worry about getting shot. Cancer will do a better job than any bullet ever could."

"Everybody around this motherfucker smoke."

"I'm not concerned with everyone. Only you. I want you to stay healthy."

Although he'd continue to smoke in the future, her sweetness melted his irritation away. He grinned. "Yeah?"

She nodded.

"You mean that?"

"With all my heart."

Her simple words didn't declare everlasting love, but, still they affected him. He heard her sincerity, saw how much she cared about him by the tender look in her eyes.

"Want to fuck?"

She rolled her eyes. "So romantic."

He snickered. "I am. I'm willing to risk pain to fuck you a day earlier."

"No."

"We don't have to fuck, then, baby. Let me just eat your pussy again. Maybe, for an hour or two. See how many times I can make you come on my tongue."

Her cheeks flushed and her breath caught. Desire heated her eyes as she squirmed on the bed.

"Meggie is coming over to see how you're doing."

Digger snapped his brows together, his irritation firmly back in place. "What the fuck I'm going to say to her?"

"Why don't you start with the truth," Bunny retorted as Meggie's voice came through the door.

"Knock, knock," she said, opening it. Holding CJ's hand, she guided him in.

"Bun-Bun!" the kid chirped, rushing to her outstretched arms. After he hugged her, he leaned back. "Webel and Wule home with Ant Woxy. MegAnn say come see Ant Bun-Bun."

"Why didn't you bring Rebel and Rule?" Bunny asked him.

He squirmed out of her arms. "*My* Bun-Bun," he said, as if that explained everything, catching sight of Digger. "Yo, ashfuck!"

Digger hooted with laughter. The kid greeted him like a long, lost friend.

"Christopher Joseph," Meggie said sternly. "Time out for two minutes! I told you not to say those words. That was really naughty. Do you understand me?"

"Yes, Mommie."

"Tell Uncle Digger you're sorry."

"Sowwy, Dig. Mommie?"

"Yes?"

"Why I sowwy?"

"Oh," Meggie groaned. "Never mind."

"Let Outlaw explain," Digger suggested, still chuckling.

Bunny poked him, then stood. "Why don't CJ and I take a little walk? Maybe, we'll find cookies in the kitchen."

"Cookie! Cookie! I want cookie!" Little Man chanted.

Holding out her hand, Bunny looked at Meggie. "I know it's early, but can he have one?"

Meggie nodded. "Just one."

Digger watched the sway of Bunny's hips as she led the kid out of the room and left him alone with Meggie. He couldn't imagine what she wanted to say to him. He, himself, didn't know where to start talking to her. Sighing, he bowed his head, deciding to begin with the basics.

"I'm sorry about what happened to you. Leaving you in Bailey's apartment..." His voice trailed off and he finally met her regard. "Peyton shooting you."

"Did you tell her to shoot me?" she asked, cocking her head to the side.

"What? Fuck no, Meggie. I'd never do that."

"Then I don't blame you for her actions. She chose to shoot me."

"I'm still sorry. For everything."

"I believe you," she said, after a moment of consideration. She sat on the edge of the bed, almost in the exact same spot that Bunny had been in. "Your actions caused a lot of mistrust and damage."

"I know and I truly regret what I did. Outlaw was more than fair in my punishment."

"You think?" she asked with a giggle. "Have you seen yourself lately?"

He smiled. "No, but I can feel how I must look. Fucked up." He regarded her. She was still gorgeous, but there was a maturity about her that hadn't been present when she'd first arrived. She looked sad. Considering all she'd been through, however, Digger understood. "I'm glad...I'm glad things didn't go too bad for you."

"I know. I feel the same about you," she admitted. "We're friends. You and me. As long as I'm not in the way of saving Mortician, I can trust you as such. I understand your actions. I'd do the same for my husband and my children. There are degrees of loyalty. When it comes to your brother, everyone takes a backseat. Just like with me and my family."

Did everyone take a backseat? A few days ago, he would've wholeheartedly agreed that he'd put no one's safety before Mortician's. Now, he wasn't so sure. He couldn't imagine turning his back if Bunny was in danger. Even for his brother.

Meggie scooted closer to him. Before he realized what she was doing, she hugged him. Knowing how Outlaw felt about anyone touching her, he patted her back and pulled away.

"What was that for?"

"To welcome you back."

"Outlaw would beat my ass all over again."

"He wouldn't," she said with vehemence. "I've hugged Mortician before."

He nodded, not knowing how to answer that. A lot of shit had changed in his absence.

She started for the door, then turned. "Bunny's my friend and my children adore her."

"Meaning you'll have Outlaw kick my ass if I hurt her."

"No, I wouldn't want him to beat you up, but she's been through a lot and so have you. Especially these past weeks. I don't want you to get back into the club life and then decide Bunny is in your way of being with other girls."

"My dick ready to settle down, Meggie."

She pursed her lips. "So you've, um, come to grips with seeing one, er, vagina, for the rest of your life?"

"I did say that shit to you about Outlaw, huh?"

She nodded. "Yes, when Christopher was in the hospital after Snake shot him."

And she'd wanted to leave. He'd told her to stay and give Outlaw a chance to realize what she meant to him. "I'm glad you didn't leave."

"I'm glad you came back," she returned, once again starting out of the room.

"Meggie?"

Halting, she turned, but didn't say anything.

"Bunny my girl. All I want to do is protect her and make her happy."

She smiled at him, as bright as the sun. "As soon as I find her and my son, I'll send her back to you," she promised, then exited the room.

Not sure why Outlaw summoned him to the meatshack the next day, Digger limped along the trail. Straight ahead, the woods loomed before him, the pathway to the tin outbuilding where the most gruesome of their tasks were performed veered off to the right. If he went left, he'd reach the two outbuildings, one containing their drug distribution center and the other strictly for Outlaw's hydro-grows.

At just after noon, the sun beamed around him, highlighting the new green of spring. The scent of dirt and foliage assailed his nostrils and he breathed in deeply, praying he'd get to enjoy these smells again. Logically, he knew the summons more than likely pertained to his father. Or one of his father's men. Or *anybody* other than him. But some moments in life required irrationality, especially if it involved Outlaw.

Digger thought about Bunny and what she'd come to mean to him. Their friendship. He'd found in Bunny what he never had before—a woman in his corner. All he'd needed to do was fucking wait until it was his time to find a girl. But, no. He'd been a miserable motherfucker and he'd forced a situation with a bitch who only thought of herself. Peyton could've been an angel, but if they weren't into each other, neither of them would've been happy in the long run.

Bunny, though, was vulnerable and allowed Digger to see that side of her. Despite the hurt she'd gone through—the hang-ups she had—she'd retained a small bit of innocence that allowed her to trust him, even if just a little bit.

Until Outlaw stepped out of the meatshack, puffing on a joint, Digger didn't realize he'd stopped. At first he didn't notice Digger, but the moment he caught sight of him, he lasered him with a cold, green stare.

Uneasy, Digger glanced over his shoulder, knowing if he bitched out he'd have no escape. First of all, he was a crippled motherfucker so he wouldn't get far. Second, Outlaw would pull his piece and shoot the fuck out of him. Only so much leniency the man handed out.

"You plannin' on gettin' the fuck in this motherfucker today?" Outlaw called, pinching the weed to extinguish it and then shoving it in the pocket of his jeans.

Instead of answering, Digger hobbled the rest of the way, his heart pounding at Outlaw's unyielding study of him. Right outside the door, Digger averted his gaze, not wanting to set Outlaw off.

"Get the fuck inside," he ordered, turning around and disappearing through the door, leaving Digger no choice but to follow.

Arms folded, dressed in his meatshack uniform, Mortician lounged against the wall, looking bored. Johnnie paced, the light in his eyes making his current sanity questionable. Val leaned on a counter, cleaning his fingernails with his blade. On the table? Sharper, strapped, already exposed and bloodied, his mouth taped.

"You can stay or you can go," Mortician said, lifting his brow. "I asked Prez to let you come and decide for yourself."

Closing his eyes, Digger hung his head. Any remorse stinging him melted away at the memory of his father standing over Tyler's body and pumping him with bullets. He remembered how his father had allowed Char to terrorize Bailey, pregnant with Harley at the time. Indeed, Sharper had tried to fuck Bailey himself. But she'd been so fucking drugged, Digger doubted she actually recalled all that had happened to her. As he pushed thoughts of his sister-in-law out of his head, all those dead girls marched through his mind, especially the last two. The one Tyler had raped and killed and left with a knife protruding from her eye.

The girl barely alive who Digger had killed.

He stared at his father, so helpless now, naked and stripped of his dignity. Poetic justice. How many innocent women had he terrorized? Allowed Char to use for her amusement before disposing them, if Sharper deemed them a *true throwaway*, unable to follow the rules of society and not good enough to sell in his sex ring.

Everything his father represented disgusted Digger.

He walked the short distance to the top of the table and studied Sharper. They'd never been particularly close, not even when Digger had run to him, but they shared blood. He swallowed. "Why?"

When the question fell from his lips, it surprised him. He didn't need to ask that because he already knew his father was one of the most evil motherfuckers around. Years ago, something had tainted his stability and he'd taken out most of his anger on women.

"Misogynistic motherfucker. How the fuck it feel having the roles reversed? How it feel knowing you about to fucking die?" He narrowed his eyes. "I want you to fucking scream like you made all those girls scream."

Sharper grunted, his eyes traveling between Digger and Outlaw, who stood at the foot of the table trembling with rage.

Mort ripped the tape from Sharper's mouth. "You said something?"

"The key," he managed with a small laugh.

Johnnie stopped next to Outlaw. "What fucking key?"

"You keep talking about a key," Digger announced, shaking his head in confusion. "I always thought Meggie was that, but I'm thinking there's an *actual* key. What does it all mean?"

Through his haze of pain, Sharper smiled. The curve of his mouth and his bloodshot eyes gave him the appearance of a demon. "B-both. She's the key to the key."

Before Digger thought of a response, Sharper howled.

Digger jerked, his gaze traveling from his father's face and the sudden tears leaking from the corner of his eyes down his body, honing in on the ice pick protruding from one of his knees. Outlaw went to the counter and grabbed another ice pick, stabbing Sharper's other knee. His pitiful wails only enraged Outlaw further. He aimed his gun at Sharper's cock.

"Prez! You promised," Mort said quickly. "The motherfucker mine."

Outlaw's trigger finger twitched.

"Six-three-four-two-six." Sharper's voice was shaky.

Val squeezed next to Johnnie. "What the fuck does that mean?"

"Never know if you kill me."

They all looked to Outlaw. With a growl, he re-aimed before firing his nine into Sharper's arm. "Now, motherfucker, Ima put fuckin' holes all fuckin' over you, until you talk, but Ima leave your fuckin' ass alive so Mort can finish you off. I fuckin' owe him that after what the fuck you did to his boy."

"Take my secrets to my grave." Even now, Sharper was arrogantly defiant.

"You fuckin' think?" Outlaw roared. "How 'bout I fuckin' keep you the fuck alive for six, seven months and torture you every fuckin' day?"

Uncertainty and fear slid across Sharper's features before his face cleared, leaving behind only pain. "You wouldn't."

"Oh, I fuckin' would. We already fuckin' saw to the gunshot from the church."

"And ripped the bandages away when you strapped me on your inhumane table."

"None of your fuckin' injuries life-threatenin'," Outlaw said coldly. "At least, not fuckin' yet. I can keep you fuckin' alive however the fuck long I want to."

They all knew Outlaw backed up his words with actions. Perhaps, that was the reason Sharper blurted directions and said, "You have a key somewhere? One that you may or may not know the origins of?"

Outlaw's brows lifted in surprise. "Yeah."

"Follow the directions I gave you and that key will work."

"That was Big Joe's key, assfuck."

"It's still good," Sharper insisted.

"What the fuck the key go to?"

Instead of answering Outlaw, Sharper clamped his mouth shut.

Outlaw fired into Sharper's other arm.

"Christopher, if you fill him full of fucking holes, he's going to die before any of us get a chance at him," Johnnie protested.

Shoving his nine away, Outlaw scowled. "Ain't no fuckin' *us*. It's Mort and this motherfucker if he wanna stay," he said, pointing to Digger.

"The fuck you say!" Johnnie yelled. "This motherfucker raided our club and shot my fucking wife."

"Wasn't me," Sharper protested weakly.

Johnnie cursed, dug into his cut, and grabbed his blade, jabbing Sharper's thigh and slicing downward, unconcerned at the screams. "Now, he's fucking yours, Mortician," he fumed and stormed out of the building.

Slob sliding down his chin, Sharper sobbed, twisting against the restraints. "Please!" he hollered. "HELP! Someone, please help me! They're going to kill me. I don't deserve to die like this. My only crime is loving Logan! And hating him." He struggled on the table, although the restraints didn't allow much movement. "Help me!"

"Lemme get the fuck outta here before I fuck this pussy up," Outlaw snarled in disgust and stomped away.

Val shrugged and followed behind Outlaw.

"You staying?" Mort asked, studying Digger.

"Yeah," he answered without hesitation, drowning out Sharper's wails.

After grabbing a toolbox and setting it on one of the stools near Sharper's head, Mort snapped on a pair of plastic gloves, doubling them before sliding on longer rubber gloves. He sat in the second stool, opened his toolbox and retrieved a pair of tooth extraction forceps.

Mort smiled nastily. "I think it's time you really screamed, old man."

Following the directions yanked from Sharper and with the numbers six-three-four-two-six in his head, Christopher coasted to a stop as Mortician, Johnnie, and Val did the same. The key so long amongst the others on his ring now had a place to go with it. A house from the looks of it.

"What kind of a fucking game is this?" Johnnie bit out, staring at the neat, two-story house with the red shutters. "This house? This is where Caroline killed herself. Where Logan stayed while he was here."

"Somebody been keeping it up," Val said, pointing to the manicured lawn.

Mortician rocked on his heels. "Think this a fucking set up?"

"Fuck, it made fuckin' sense Sharper would fuckin' provide Logan a place to stay," Christopher said aloud, drawing his nine and moving forward.

"You're going in?" Johnnie asked in outrage.

"Yeah, motherfucker. Whatever the fuck in that fuckin' house caused a lot of fuckin' mayhem."

The key opened the door without any glitches. Before they did any-fucking-thing else, they each went in different directions, doing a sweep of the house to make sure no motherfucker lay in wait.

Everything was clear, except for dust and bloodstains and an eerie feeling, not one fucking thing looked out of order.

"This motherfucker got a basement?" Christopher asked as Val walked through the house opening and closing doors.

"This might be something," he called down the stairs.

As they walked up, Johnnie explained how he'd killed a motherfucker from a rival gang in that very place.

Reaching the second floor, Christopher looked up and down the hallway, brightly lit by the sun glimmering through the windows. "Where you at, Val?"

"This way. Last room, left side."

In the room, they all halted and stared at the door Val had found. What made this one different was it sat behind a wall that Val had somehow opened and had a combination lock clamped onto it.

"How you found this, Val?"

"I was just pressing on the wall and it clicked open, Outlaw."

Fuck. What the fuck was beyond that door? With Sharper and Logan, anything was possible.

"What do you think is through that door?" Val whispered, sweat beading his brow as he echoed Christopher's thought.

"The fuckin' bogie man," Christopher snapped. "How the fuck I know? My ass seein' this for the first fuckin' time just like you."

Val frowned at the dirty door. "How are we supposed to get in there?"

"I…" Christopher's voice trailed off, the numbers Sharper had taunted him with rising in his head. "Hold my nine," he instructed Mortician. Once Mort complied, Christopher dialed the numbers on the lock, rewarded when it clicked open.

"Fuck, that was a combination he gave you?" Mort asked, caught between outrage and fear as a staircase came into view, seemingly leading into nothing but a black void. The pitch darkness didn't offer a clue about what the fuck lay down those stairs.

Johnnie shoved a flashlight in Christopher's hand. He hadn't realized the motherfucker wasn't with them until just then. "Use this."

"Wait, Prez." Mortician halted him when he would've gone forward. "What was those numbers again?"

"Six-three-four-two-six," he answered, wondering why Mort found his phone so fascinating.

"Look at your phone. The letters that go with those numbers," Mort said.

It took a moment, but the word M-e-g-a-n finally clicked.

Val gave him a wide-eyed look. "Holy shit, that spells Meggie's name."

She's the key to the key. Sharper's words rose in Christopher's head.

Not wasting any more time, he stepped onto the rickety landing, shining the flashlight down the steps. At first, he saw nothing but two file boxes, until he scanned the far side of the room.

"Ain't this a motherfucker," he said.

Johnnie peeped in. "What?"

"There." Christopher pointed to what he'd seen and raised his flashlight higher. "That."

"What the fuck that be?" Mort called.

"*Fuck*," Johnnie whispered.

"Is that a good fuck or a bad fuck?" Val asked.

Lined along the walls were two pallets, one stacked with bricks of cocaine, Christopher assumed, since it looked similar to how they packaged their merchandise. The other pallet contained bricks of money. To make sure the shit was real, Christopher walked down the steps and got a closer look, ignoring the closed-in, musty smell.

"This a lot of fuckin' money." More than he'd ever seen in his life.

"All real?" Val asked.

"Fuck if I know. The shit might be counterfeit." That was the only explanation for all this money forgotten in a fucking basement in a house best forgotten.

Before he decided what to do, Christopher carried the two file boxes upstairs and headed to the kitchen, where the only table in the house sat.

The first box contained letters, some of them the originals of the copies Bailey had found in KP's closet. Along with the letters were photos of Sharper and Logan in every imaginable sexual position.

"Fucking hypocrites," Christopher growled, disgusted by the hell Logan had put him through when he himself lived a double life. He shoved the box away and focused on the second box.

Inside it were more photos, but these were of Megan as a three-year-old, almost a carbon copy of Rebel. As he flipped through the photos, he saw a beautiful little girl had turned into a gorgeous woman. One whom her daddy had loved, if all the photos were any indication.

And Christopher had no doubt these pictures had been Big Joe's. One giveaway was his presence in the photos, especially between the years Megan had been born and had grown into a toddler. After that, it was mainly Dinah and Megan, the exception being photo of the three of them at Disneyland, where Megan looked to be nine or ten.

"Prez?"

"Yo, Mort?" he answered, distracted. Big Joe had seemed so happy in the photos when Megan had been a baby. He'd looked like a family man, but he had to have missed the club, which was the reason he returned.

Would Christopher miss it, too?

"I think I know why Sharper decided to get to Meggie."

Frowning, Christopher looked at Mort, grabbing the piece of paper he held.

It was the deed to the house. In Megan's name.

"That means all the contents in it belongs to Megan," Johnnie said, his eyes wide.

Including drugs and money that Sharper had known about, but Logan hadn't. Or, maybe, he had.

"Might be what kept Big Joe alive." Christopher spoke the thought aloud. "If only he knew where this shit was and only he knew the combination and it was making that type of bank, they wouldna wanted him fuckin' dead."

"At some point, Sharper found what the combination was," Johnnie pointed out.

Christopher thought for a moment. "Probably durin' one of Big Joe's drug-induced hazes he blurted the shit out. But even then the motherfucker had a sense of survival. He wasn't givin' up the fuckin' key."

"Maybe, not even the location," Val offered. "Some fucker took great pains to hide that."

Val was probably right.

"Where you think all that cash came from?" he asked. "If it's real?"

"The drugs," Christopher answered, trying to put two and two together, but it was hard when all he had to go on was what he knew about a bunch of dead motherfuckers. "And I think Big Joe bought his fuckin' life by supplyin' the fuckin' money to bank roll the sex ring. They musta fuckin' known this house in Megan name. Once Big Joe was gone, only she stood in the way of Sharper gettin' to that fuckin' stash."

That's why she'd been the key and motherfuckers had come from all directions once Christopher married her.

"Are you telling Megan?" Johnnie asked.

"I'm bringin' her the photos. The rest of this shit? No. I ain't gonna have her lookin' over her fuckin' shoulder the rest of her fuckin' life wonderin' if another motherfucker out to take her out."

"The drugs?" Mort said.

"We gotta get some light in this motherfucker and we'll check the shit. It looked pretty fuckin' airtight."

"The money?" Val asked.

Christopher shrugged. "We split it equal."

"You know by right that belongs to your wife," Johnnie said tightly.

"That mean the drugs do too, motherfucker, and I ain't gettin' her involved in this shit. If you don't want the fuckin' money, more for fuckin' us."

They fell silent and Christopher carried both boxes to his Harley, stuffing his saddlebags to the brim with photos and documents, and making the others do the same until he'd taken everything. Before he left, he secured the door, breathing in the fresh air. Inside had been oppressive, surrounded by the presence of Logan.

Motherfucker tainted wherever he touched.

At least, he knew what the fuck the key represented.

He only wished Megan wasn't involved.

Nervous, Bunny surveyed Digger's new room one last time. It was bigger, with a wider, longer window, more closet space, and a bigger bathroom. As much as she wanted to make it female-friendly, she knew better than to add plants or frills. Instead, she spruced it up by splurging on a new comforter and curtains. As a room-warming gift, she also purchased a skull grinder and a tobacco pipe of a big-breasted girl. She found marijuana-themed wrapping paper with her friend, Gypsy's, help. The gifts sat on the desk, right in front of the entertainment system.

She'd left his walls bare, except for the sign that read *Welcome to your new room*. If she'd taken the posters off the walls in his current room, it would've raised his suspicions.

Chewing on her lip, she glanced around again, hoping she hadn't forgotten anything before she called him to come in. With that in mind, she studied herself in the mirror she'd hung on the front of the bathroom door. Her green cutout chemise with black garters and stockings and black stilettos pleased her.

Wearing the outfit to seduce Mark because of the mutual attraction left her feeling empowered. She couldn't remember the last time she'd seen herself as a sexual being. She'd been *goods* and she'd had to market herself as such to make money.

Tossing her hair, she puckered her lips, giggling at her silliness.

She wasn't sure if Digger wanted her to jump on his cock immediately or if she was supposed to entertain him first and then they ease into it.

Deciding to play it by ear, she went to the desk and opened the door, pulling out a bottle of red wine, a pint of vodka, a flute glass, and a highball tumbler. After preparing her wine and his vodka and checking one last time to make sure everything was in place, Bunny texted Digger.

Come to Mort's old room

Nerves set in as she awaited his response and she shifted from foot-to-foot, then checked the song on the MP3 player connected to the stereo. Still nothing from Digger.

Had he changed his mind?

Chewing on her lower lip, she turned toward the closet, intending to find a shirt to cover her near nakedness. The opening door interrupted her intentions and she halted.

"Didn't mean to keep you waiting," Digger began, limping into the room and stopping when he saw her. He placed the brown bag he carried near her wrapped gift, not commenting one way or the other. Instead, he studied her from head-to-toe and a slow smile curved his mouth. "Fuck, I *really* didn't mean to keep you waiting."

She giggled like a virginal school girl, her face heating up, her brilliant idea suddenly not as appealing now that he faced her, his smoldering gaze promising her all types of wickedness. He closed the door, unconcerned at her bout of uncertainty. Not taking his eyes off her, he hobbled to the bed and sat on the edge.

Bunny grabbed their glasses and brought him the vodka. "This is for you." Their fingers brushed as he accepted the drink from her and desire shot raced through her like an electric current.

He sipped his drink, then patted the bed. "Sit next to me."

"I had a surprise for you." She tasted her wine. "I-I m-mean another surprise."

"What's the first one?" He winked at her. "You in here looking so gorgeous and sexy and good enough to eat?"

Licking her lips, Bunny relaxed by a margin. "You're a smooth talker."

"I'm a *truthful* talker."

She nodded, determined to push all her hang-ups aside, some borne of her own doing and others because of Trader. Digger wasn't Trader, not by a long shot. She wanted to prove to him—and herself—that she trusted him with her body and her emotions. And, yes, she wanted to see his reaction to her dancing. Would that change his opinion of her? Could she even tell immediately, if it did?

But dancing had been a part of her life, good or bad, and the more she hid from it, the more it tortured her.

"You think too fucking much."

She frowned. "We all think."

"You overthink, Bunny." He finished his vodka and sat the glass down, leaned forward and took her glass, finished the contents, then sat it aside too. "Come here."

As if she had a choice, with the way he pulled her between his thighs and settled his hands at her back. He skimmed his lips along her breasts, the material of her chemise serving as no barrier against the heat of his tongue.

Bending her head and thrusting her fingers through his hair, she kissed him, groaning into his mouth at the feel of his tongue against her own.

"Slow down," he whispered, when she would've forged ahead. "Not a fuckin' place I gotta be, baby. My ass still hurtin' too much."

"Okay."

He touched the corner of her mouth, his brown eyes soft with patience and understanding. "If you not ready to give me my surprise, I got something for you."

"What is it?"

"Go look in that bag for your first present."

The prospect of a gift exciting her, Bunny turned on her heel and rushed to the plain brown bag, almost ripping it apart in her haste to open it. In her wildest dreams, she hadn't expected to find a cut with her name stitched on the front and the words *Property of Digger Banks* embroidered on the back.

She turned to face him, clutching the leather to her breast. "For me?"

He rolled his eyes. "You know another bitch named Bunny?"

"Actually, several," she admitted with a small laugh. "It's an excellent name for the pole." She scrunched her nose. "And college cheerleaders."

Digger snickered. "I bet it fucking is. So let me ask you this. Any other chick around here that *I* know named Bunny but you?"

"No."

"So then the fucking cut must be for you." He cocked his head to the side. "Do you want it?"

In response, she shrugged into it, covering most of her chemise.

"Fuck, girl, it's harder to disregard your pussy when the edge of that cut stop right over it."

"Why would you want to ignore my pussy? I thought the point was to get in it."

"Stop with the dirty talk. I'm trying to put you at ease. The only way to do that is to overlook the pussy."

"I'm sorry," she blurted. "It isn't you, I swear. It's me."

"Don't do that shit," he snapped. "A motherfucker don't like to hear the *it's not you, it's me* speech. I don't know what the fuck got you so up in arms, but if you not ready to fuck me then we wait 'til you are."

He sounded neither angry nor disappointed, although some impatience laced his words. "I'm nervous because I want to dance for you and I'm scared of what you'll think of me. With my past—"

His raised hand interrupted her. "The only person your past fucks with is you. Well, maybe, your mom, but that's your mom and all mommas want the fucking best for their children. Even before I got back, you was amongst friends. People who don't give a fuck if you danced naked from the moon and let the world see it. Those who do, not your fucking friends. You send any motherfucker *my* way if they hurt you, although I don't think that'll happen. Not many motherfuckers know about the old you. Just the new you. One other thing. Whoever the fuck got a problem with what you did? That shit on them, not you, and you not accountable to a motherfucker or his momma for what you did then or fucking now."

The more Digger spoke, the better she felt. Stiffening her spine, she gave him a level look. "I was fine before I sent the text. I felt like…I felt feminine and sexy, but nerves set in when you took so long."

"I'm not exactly in a position to run around this motherfucker. It would've been much simpler if you would've come to my room, then having my stiff, cripple ass staggering to this one."

"About that." She cleared her throat. "This is another surprise."

"What? This room?"

"Yeah. Mort doesn't use it anymore, so I asked if he'd give it to you. I spruced it up a little and everything."

Genuine shock lit his face and he glanced around, touching on the window with the new dressing and the updated comforter. He grinned at her. "Where my pictures of my naked girls?"

"On your walls," she answered with a sniff and folded her arms. "If I would've taken them down, you would've known something was up."

Drumming his fingers on his thigh, he cocked his head to the side. "Suppose I leave them right the fuck where they at? I don't need to look at those bitches when I got a beautiful woman of my own. Would you like that?"

She nodded, surprised at how well attuned to her he was. Even more shocking was his attentiveness, different from what he'd shown her in the past. He was going out of his way to show her she meant something to him.

He leaned back and dug into his pocket, producing a platinum ring with a small diamond in the center.

"Oh my god!" she breathed.

"This not an engagement ring," he said, catching her gaze and holding it. "Not yet. We still getting to know each other and I don't have my cut back." He snorted. "That's some shit, huh? You got a fucking cut and I don't."

He fisted the ring in his hand and she sat next to him, leaning her chin on his shoulder. "If you don't get your cut back, I won't need mine."

"You got a place here, Bunny. Without the support of the club, I don't know what the fuck I'll do. I grew up a fucking rich boy and became a biker. Wealth and mayhem the only shit I know."

She did have a place there. That was one of the reasons she'd stuck with Trader for so long. And, yet, if she walked away tomorrow, she knew she'd always have a place to return. Outlaw and Meggie had become her family, and they—*everyone*—accepted her for who she was.

It was time she did the same. Time to look toward the future, instead of allowing her past to hamper her and block the happiness she knew she could find with Digger.

She hugged him. "Wherever you go, I'm coming, if you'll have me."

Taking her into his arms, he settled her onto his lap and groaned. She squirmed in an attempt to move, but he tightened his hold on her, his erection throbbing against her ass.

"As long as you want to be at my side, I'm not fucking stopping you, Albany." He grinded his hips against her, laughing at her small moan. "As for the ring, it's a promise. I promise you that I'll always protect you and do right by you. I like when you smile. It lights up your entire face and thanks to that motherfucker Prez popped, you not been smiling too much lately. I promise that as soon as we ready, I'll marry you and give you whatever I can. Whatever you want. To the best of my abilities cuz, I can't have a repeat of the last two years. The ass-beating Prez put on me opened my fucking eyes more than Mort bailing me out or Sharper blackmailing me ever could. I don't *ever* want to hear the words Outlaw looking for you. That motherfucker don't play."

She laughed at his stagy sing-song voice. "You're so silly."

"Silly, I might fucking be, but I'm fucking truthful."

"In other words, if Outlaw had beat your ass at the beginning of all this, a lot of crap would've been prevented?"

"Fuck, yeah. It's going to take me fucking weeks to recover."

"Poor baby," she murmured, nipping his ear.

"So what do you say to everything I told you?"

What should she say? That she felt her feelings for him deepening? After the past half hour, she'd fallen just a little in love with him. But was she ready to tell *him*? She suspected he wasn't ready for those words from her and even if he was, she wasn't ready to put herself out there.

"You give motherfuckers a complex. If you have to think that long on a simple fucking question, that don't seem good for me."

"It is," she said quickly. "I was just thinking how lucky I am to have found you and what a wonderful man I think you are."

To her, he didn't have as hard of an edge as the rest of them. She knew he was still lethal, still a killer, but so much less intense than Outlaw, Mort, Val, and Johnnie.

Taking her hand into his own, he slid the ring onto her finger and grinned at her. "Now, can I have some pussy?"

"In a minute."

His brows snapped together, but she placed her finger over his lips and got to her feet, hurrying to the entertainment center and pressing 'play.' The moment *You Can Leave Your Hat On* blasted through, Bunny put her body into motion. Realizing her intention, Digger straightened, and followed her every move, her every grind. When she removed her cut, in time with the music, she dangled her breasts in front of him, teasing him as she laid the leather next to him. He reached for her but she twirled out of the way, just out of arm's reach.

She knew the song so well. It had always been one of her favorites. The sultry tone energized her. Counting down in her head, she noted the thirty-seconds left until it ended and grabbed the halter of her chemise and yanked. The snaps keeping it closed, popped open. She let the chemise slide to the ground, her breath catching when Digger managed to grab her hand.

Plastering his mouth over hers, he settled her onto the bed and rolled onto her. With a few, quick maneuvers, he sank into her and they both groaned.

"I'm going to make it up to you for just sticking my cock in you without no foreplay," he said huskily.

She lifted her hips, her body stretched with the thick length of him inside of her. "No complaints from me," she promised on his gasp, pleasure streaking through her at a particularly deep thrust.

Whatever else her future held, she knew Digger would be right at her side and she couldn't have been happier.

Six weeks later, Christopher sat at his table in the corner, keeping a watch on Megan as she spoke to a few of the brothers she hadn't seen in months. The clubhouse was filled to capacity and not because of church or lockdown. It was crowded *just because*. Just the way his clubhouse was supposed to be.

His. He couldn't deny that this place was his. It was him. Except it wasn't only him, any longer. Walking away because his family was endangered was for the best. Although his heart hurt that he would resign before he was ready, he'd have no fucking regrets. He'd always carry the memories, good and fucking horrendous, inside of him.

Mort, Bailey, and Roxy came into his line of vision, stopping where Megan was. He thought they'd just arrived, but he wasn't sure. He'd been lost in thought for a minute and had only paid attention to what went on with his wife. Digger rounded the corner from the hallway, dragging Bunny along with him, just as Zoann and Kendall walked from the kitchen.

As if that bitch felt his eyes on her, Kendall turned and frowned at him, settling her hands on her belly, like he was supposed to give a fuck.

Sunlight angled in, indicating the entrance door opening. Diesel walked in, carrying CJ.

Scowling, Christopher beckoned them over, hoping Megan didn't intercept. This was supposed to be a kid-free day. No such fucking luck. Just like he kept a fucking eagle-eye on her, she had radar where their kids were concerned.

She reached the table just as Diesel and CJ halted and his boy wiggled to get down.

"Hey, buddy," Megan greeted, running her fingers through CJ's hair when he barreled into her and hugged her legs. "You're giving Diesel and Aunt Ophelia a rough time, aren't you?"

"Wule wants me play with him and I tired, Mommie. I want Harway, but Wule not let me."

"It's hard being the big brother, sweet potato." She raised her gaze to Diesel. "Get Harley and take her and CJ outside."

"What you doing, Meggie girl?" Mortician asked, overhearing the last comment. He dropped into one of the chairs at the table. "Getting Little Man to corrupt my daughter?"

"No. Just trying to reward my son for being a good brother."

He smirked at her. "Well, when Bailey deliver my son, CJ can teach Harley how to be a good sister."

"Omigod!" Megan screeched, clapping her hands. "You're having a boy?"

"I'm not, but Bailey is," Mort quipped.

She hugged Mort. "Congratulations. How long have you known? Bailey didn't tell me."

"We wasn't going to find out, but then she just changed her fucking mind today at her appointment."

"'Law?" CJ said, and Mort and Megan's conversation grew into white noise for a moment.

"Yeah, boy?"

Without invitation, CJ climbed into Christopher's lap and laid his head against him.

"I tired, 'Law."

So he wasn't only tired of fucking around with Rule, but he was sleepy.

Shifting his weight, Christopher readjusted CJ on his lap. "Close your eyes, then."

Unnecessary words since CJ relaxed against him and nodded off within moments.

Megan held her phone up. To take a photo, Christopher knew. She loved snapshots of him and their children. "Diesel, take him to the nursery," she instructed. "I'll be home in a little while, to put Rebel and Rule down for the afternoon naps."

Not protesting, Christopher allowed Diesel to carry CJ away. He and Mort exchanged glances, before he sighed and looked at Megan. She didn't mention Dinah much and neither did he. The less that whiny bitch was discussed, the better. He never wanted Megan to find out about Dinah's betrayal and if they talked about her, chances were high Christopher would let it slip.

He'd learned his lesson when he'd withheld the fact that Big Joe's grave was empty.

"It's been a long month," she said softly.

"Yeah, baby," he agreed. "And it was all cuz of me."

Frowning, Megan narrowed her eyes. "You? Please explain to me how that's possible. You didn't cause all the chaos of the past few days. It was outside forces."

"Yeah, Prez. Namely Sharper fucking Banks."

"Yeah, Mort, assfuck wanted my ass dead, but he wanted Megan…" His voice trailed off and he shook his head. "You got no fuckin' idea what it'd do to me if I lost you. So, yeah, Ima fuckin' resign come church in two days."

"Prez—"

Megan silenced Mort with a look. "You should, Christopher," she said, walking to him and kissing his lips.

Of all the responses, he'd never expected her agreement. Until then, she'd been on his ass to remain in the club. "You fuckin' *want* me to quit?"

She sat in the chair closest to him as Johnnie and Val came to the table. Digger lagged back, although he looked as if he'd love to join them. One fucking thing at a time.

"Meggie girl, you know what you saying, right?" Mortician asked, sadness in his voice.

"Yeeppp," she drawled out. "I want whatever Christopher wants. Although Outlaw might be a little unhappy if Christopher resigns."

"What the fuck, baby? You make my ass sound like a fucking split-personality, deranged motherfucker."

"You are," Mort, Johnnie, and Val chorused.

Megan giggled. "We've had this conversation before. Remember?"

How could he fucking forget the day she'd ripped him a new one for wanting to resign?

"I still think even Christopher would be bored out of his mind with nothing to do."

"Fuck you all day."

"Um, no," she answered, throwing the other three filthy looks at their snickering. "I like walking. Twice a day is enough, thank you very much."

He smirked at her, accepting her roundabout big dick compliment.

"When you leave, what'll happen to Outlaw?" she asked, and, suddenly the men at his table stilled. They wanted to know the answer.

Fuck, *Christopher* wanted to know the answer.

"Oh, well," Megan continued cheerfully, "I guess you'll keep up with the home repairs and help out with the kids."

"Little bitch," he growled.

"Who? Me?" she asked innocently.

"Yeah, you, baby, cuz you know exactly what the fuck you doin' to my ass."

"Nooooo, I don't. What am I doing to you except supporting your decision to leave your club?"

"You want me to fuckin' leave or not?" he snapped, losing patience because he *had* accepted his decision, but her words were putting all types of doubts about his future in his head.

"What does it matter what I want?" she fired back, glaring at him. "*You* decided to leave without discussing it with me, so *you* make that decision."

Were they really about to descend into an argument? Why? Because he was being a stupid motherfucker? Insisting on resigning when every-fucking-body knew that was the last thing he wanted to do?

She stood and removed her cut, handing it to Mortician, who wore a shit-eating grin that Christopher wanted to punch the fuck off his face.

"Put that fuckin' cut back on, Megan."

"No."

"Look, baby—"

"No, you look, *Christopher*. If Outlaw isn't in the club, I'm no longer his property. Therefore, I can't wear my cut."

He got to his feet and she placed her hands on her hips, drawing attention. Not that Christopher gave a fuck.

"I ain't tellin' you a-fuckin-gain, Megan." He pointed to the cut that let the world know Megan was his. "Put that motherfucker back on."

"I'm not repeating myself again, Christopher," she challenged, then changed tactics on him. "Who am I? Outlaw's property? Or Christopher's wife?"

"You fuckin' both," he snarled, the answer so automatic he didn't have to think. "Right now, though, you a lil' pain in the ass motherfucker."

"And you're a moron, so we're even." Tossing her hair over her shoulder, she gave him an I-wish-I-could-fuck-you-up look. "The only way I'm Outlaw's property is if *he's* in the club," she said, and stomped away.

"Fuck, Meggie girl brutal," Mortician said proudly.

"You taught her how the fuck to play me, motherfucker."

"I advised her one time, Prez. The rest she figured out on her own."

Not responding, Christopher walked behind the bar and nodded to Bunny as he whistled for silence. He didn't start talking until she returned with the box he'd asked her to keep.

"Lemme start by sayin' we been through fuckin' hell and back, but we fuckin' survived."

No one spoke, and he got the impression his argument with Megan had been overheard, so he supposed he needed to address that.

"Wasn't so long ago I ain't had nothin' but my club. Yeah, I always fuckin' knew all you motherfuckers had my back just like I had yours. But I ain't know no different but stickin' my cock in every cunt I chose, the open road, or *this*." He indicated the clubhouse with a sweep of his hand. "Not knowin' no better, I couldn't do no fuckin' better. Then I met a girl." He looked at Megan now, his words wiping the scowl off her face that descended when he mentioned other bitches. "And, suddenly, my life didn't just fuckin' have meanin' *here*, but everywhere. Suddenly, every-fuckin-thing was better. When you know better, you do better. Megan drive my ass, but I don't think I ever fuckin' loved her as much as I do right the fuck now."

That shit said a lot because he'd been fucking crazy in love with her before.

"Then, my two worlds collided, and fuckin' blindsided me. So I made a fuckin' decision without discussin' it with my girl. But see, I ain't ever fuckin' realize what the fuck it meant if I fuckin' left my club to protect my family. Not 'til Megan took off her cut cuz Outlaw wasn't gonna be in the club no more. Her sayin' that shit and demonstratin' it two different motherfuckers altogether."

"Do you want to leave?" one of the brothers asked.

Christopher had everybody's attention. They were all staring at him, in shock. In sadness. In disbelief. "No. Biker or husband, I'm still fuckin' me. That shit worked before and it's gonna work a-fuckin-gain."

There, he'd said it. He'd spoken the truth, from his heart. He'd make the shit work, even if he had to blow every motherfucker away who reached for any-fucking-thing around Megan.

"To Prez," Mort called, raising his pint of vodka. "Ride or die forever."

Shouts, yells, and whistles was the response. Even Digger smiled a little, although he still looked like a lost puppy.

"Come here, motherfucker," Christopher called when the noise died down. He waved Digger over and grabbed the box he'd had Bunny get. "Listen up, Digger. You ever fuckin' pull the stunt you fuckin' did, you fuckin' dead. Understand?"

Digger swallowed but nodded.

He held out the box. Although Digger hesitated, he finally took it and opened it, his breath suddenly sawing in and out as he raised his cut.

"You lettin' me back in?"

"You wanna come back in?" Christopher countered, not looking at anyone. The only one who'd known what was in the box was Megan. Allowing Digger to patch back in was supposed to be Christopher's last act as president.

Instead, it seemed as if a new era was being ushered in.

"Yeah, Prez. Besides my girl, not much else I want."

Christopher held out his hand, clutching Digger's when he mimicked him. "Welcome back, motherfucker."

At ease for the first time in weeks, Digger smiled. "You, too, Outlaw."

"As soon as everyone is up to it again, we'll proceed with the shower," Megan said a couple of hours later as he stepped out of the shower, grabbed a towel, and secured it around his hips.

She, on the other hand, stood freshly washed and naked, revealing all her pretty skin and golden pussy.

"Roxy said we'll add in Kendall, too."

He grunted and lifted her into his arms, carrying her to their bedroom. Her hair was still damp, but he didn't care. He guided her down onto their bed anyway, ravishing her mouth before drawing back and caressing her cheek.

"You happy, baby?"

"Yes. Your alter-ego is happy, too."

"Fuck, Megan, don't fuckin' start with your Clark Kent bullshit."

"Are you comparing yourself to Superman?" she asked with a laugh.

"Bruce Wayne then. All them motherfuckers have alter-fuckin-egos. That's how the fuck you makin' me sound."

She lifted up and gave him a quick kiss. "We'll all die someday. In spite of what's happened at the club, I could slip and fall, and break my neck. Or I could live to be ninety. Don't let circumstances you have no control over dictate how you live, Christopher. That isn't you."

"That ain't Outlaw," he grouched. "Apparently, fuckin' Christopher fine with that shit."

"Your members and officers admire and respect you. You're their fearless leader. *My* everything. But we only have one life to live. In the end, *how* we've lived is all that matters."

"You right, baby."

She thumbed his lips, one of her favorite things to do. "You taught me that."

"I ain't ever said that to you, Megan."

"No, but I learned by watching you. Since the day we met, you've lived your life the way you've loved me. Hard, fast, and without regret."

"Fuck, here I fuckin' thought you was with me cuz I licked and fucked you so fuckin' good."

"Omigod, you're sooooo bad, Christopher!" she complained. "I'm being serious and you're thinking of *down there*."

Shaking his head, he nosed her hair. She spread her thighs and lifted her hips in invitation to get into *down there*.

"You want some dick?"

"Yeah," she said, inserting her hand between them and opening his towel. She fisted his cock and kissed his chest.

He sank into her and closed his eyes at the sound of her soft sigh of pleasure.

"Christopher?"

Placing his elbows on each side of her head, he halted his thrusts. "Yeah, baby?"

"You, um, never got your vasectomy."

"Fuck, I know. Lemme fuck you then we'll talk 'bout it."

"Oh, well, I might be having another baby. I-I mean I *am* having another baby."

Fucking... *"What?"* Withdrawing from her, he got to his feet. "How the fuck this happen a-fuckin-gain?"

She shrugged. "I didn't really start taking my pills again after the shooting."

Fuck. Him. He stared at his cock accusingly, outraged as his erection deflated.

"I have a solution, though."

"Helpin' me hack my cock off or what?"

"No, silly. Getting my tubes tied after I deliver."

He wouldn't even bring up abortion because he knew she wouldn't agree. He started to turn away from her until he looked into her eyes and saw her uncertainty, but also the hope and the happiness. Instead of walking away to sulk like an assfuck, he climbed back in bed and drew her into his arms, kissing the top of her head.

"You're happy?" she whispered.

"The same shit apply. I ain't gonna like the lil' motherfucker 'til it's outta you. But we in this shit together. Ride or die."

"Forever," she added.

Depression is a serious disease, one that has many facets. I've suffered from clinical depression since my teenage years. By no means am I downplaying the disease by portraying it through Kendall's eyes.

Unfortunately, I know all too well what happens with the wrong medications. Sometimes, even the *'right'* ones affect not only the areas in your life it is meant to help but also the parts of your life you'd prefer to stay as is. Such is the case with Kendall and her courtroom abilities. I, too, was faced with antidepressants during pregnancy. It isn't an easy choice.

I've chosen to treat my depression with medication and have finally found a combination that works for me. However, what works for my fictional characters by no means reflect my views on real people facing real depression.

Medication, a healthy diet, and exercise all play a factor in the battle. There are also underlying causes, other illnesses you may or may not be aware of, that affects your mood.

Just know whatever battle you may be facing, there's help.

Stay strong. Keep fighting and always look ahead.

Love, Kat

If you are in emotional distress or struggling to cope, and are affected by any of the issues covered in this book, please contact:

The Samaritans USA 1(800) 273-TALK

The Samaritans UK 08457 90 90 90

Lifeline AUSTRALIA 13 11 14

Mistake Number 3 by Culture Club
This Life by Curtis Stiger
GDFR (feat. Sage The Gemini & Lookaas) by Flo Rida
The Prayer by Andrea Bocelli
Madama Butterfly: One Fine Day by Giacomo Puccini
Ave Maria, "Ellens Gesang III", D839 by Franz Schubert
The Thrill Is Gone by B.B. King
Cross Road Blues by John Lee Hooker
Champagne & Reefer by Muddy Waters
Gin Bottle Blues by Lightnin' Hopkins
A Good Man Is Hard to Find by Bessie Smith
Lick It Before Stick It by Denise LaSalle
Better Than Me by Hinder
Chains by Nick Jonas
Candy Shop by 50 Cent, Olivia
Free Fallin' by Tom Petty
Mary Jane by Rick James
Son Of A Preacher Man by Dusty Springfield
Gangsta's Paradise by Coolio
Had Enough by Breaking Benjamin
Locked Away by R. City, Adam Levine
Watch Me (Whip/Nae Nae) by Silento

No Apologies (feat. Jussie Smollet, Yazz) by Empire Cast
Earned It (Fifty Shades of Grey) by The Weeknd
Because Of Who You Are by Bishop Paul S. Morton, Sr.
Praise Is What I Do by Shekinah Ministries
So High (feat. Ghost Loft) by Wiz Khalifa
Brick House by the Commodores
Something's Come Over Me by Ernie Halter
Stuck On You by Lionel Ritchie
Not Strong Enough by Apocalyptica, Brent Smith
Time of Our Lives by Pitbull, Ne-Yo
Say You Love Me by Jessie Ware
You Can Leave Your Hat On by Joe Cocker
Shake Your Bon-Bon by Ricky Martin
Boom Boom by John Lee Hooker
Voodoo Child (Slight Return) by Jimi Hendrix
Honey, I'm Home by Shania Twain
You're Still The One by Shania Twain
Gone Too Soon by Michael Jackson

Thank you for reading Misconduct.
If you enjoyed it, please consider leaving a review at your point of purchase and on Goodreads. It means a lot to me to hear what you think.

Check out these other books from Author Kathryn Kelly.

Death Dwellers MC Series

Misled
Misappropriate
Misunderstood
Misdeeds
Misbehavior
Misjudged
Misguided
Misalliance
Misconduct

Coming Soon – Misfit

The conclusion of the series tells the story of Cash "Ghost" McCall, Louis "Stretch" King, and the woman they will bring into their turbulent relationship, Ophelia Donovan.
Release date to be announced.

Kathryn Kelly

Phoenix Rising Rock Band Series

Inferno
Incendiary

Other titles

All My Tomorrows
Dangerous
Pink: Hot 'N Sexy for a cure: The Books for Boobies 2015 Anthology

Twitter

Twitter @katkelwriter

Email

katkelwriter@outlook.com

Facebook

https://www.facebook.com/AuthorKathrynKelly?fref=ts

Goodreads

https://www.goodreads.com/author/show/7422779.Kathryn_Kelly

In Kat's head, she's the ultimate biker babe. In reality, she's an everyday, ordinary girl who loves scotch, reading, writing, and football.

Made in the USA
Lexington, KY
01 October 2018